# OLYMPIAN
# BLOOD

# CRYSTAL RENEAU

This novel is intended for mature readers,
and is not suitable for children.

Copyright © 2016 Crystal Reneau
All rights reserved.
ISBN-13: 978-0986096228
ISBN-10: 0986096229

Library of Congress Control Number: 2016907508

OLD CASTLE PRESS, LLC
http://oldcastlepress.com

Cover Design by The Killion Group
http://thekilliongroupinc.com

# DEDICATION

This book is dedicated to the amazing people who fight every day
to eradicate human trafficking from the world,
and to the many dear souls who have triumphed over it.

# ACKNOWLEDGMENTS

An endearing thank you to my husband and daughters who are always there for me, and believe in me;

To God for being my light;

To Wendy for your helpful ideas, attention to detail, and for trekking through Asheville;

To Patty and Kathy for your edits, ideas, and for cheering me on;

To Melanie and Latashia for your counsel and ideas;

To Jackie, Barbara, Beth, Denise, and Lori for taking the time to help a fellow author with your invaluable critiques;

To Terri for being a lifesaver, and having such a good eye;

To Alesia for your priceless reviews and guidance;

To Colleen for your unending support, and advice on recovery;

To Angela Knight for lending excellent advice and encouragement;

And a special thanks to Neli S. for your wonderful wisdom about Romania.

# CHAPTER 1

Waves of power brushed over Aislinn like fine sand on an ocean breeze stinging her delicate skin. She looked up from her electronic tablet to examine the room of diners between her and the front door. Two men in long coats and sunglasses had entered the quaint Romanian café. They removed their sunglasses in sync, and perused the room as they stepped toward the empty counter. Conversations in several languages softened to a whisper.

Aislinn snatched one of the fifty travel brochures she had collected in the ten hours since her plane landed in Bucharest. She shielded her face with a blue pamphlet entitled *Bran Castle and Rasnov Fortress in One Day*. She lowered it in increments to accommodate her line of sight.

The first man was tall, tanned and handsome, with thick, wavy black hair, a strong jaw, straight nose, and piercing dark eyes. His floor-length, charcoal coat sported gray and white fur on the collar and hung unbuttoned, revealing an expensive-looking black suit underneath. There was a regal air about him in the controlled way he moved and the authority in his gaze, as if he was used to being in command.

The second man was several inches taller and looked like a golden, fair-skinned version of the first. Sandy-blond locks hung almost to his shoulders and haloed a stern, brooding face. His eyes glistened a ghostly silver-gray like pearls of frozen water. Like his companion, he was dressed for cold weather in a floor-length brown coat over a white dress shirt and gray trousers.

Aislinn's jaw slackened and her brochure slipped from languid fingers. She regained control of the paper before it could escape to the floor, and glanced at nearby tables to see if anyone had noticed her. Fortunately, all eyes were on the new visitors.

She repositioned the trifold to allow further scrutiny of the two men, then realized the blue light reflecting off the inside of the brochure was the glow of her electronic tablet. She clicked the Sleep button to smolder its radiance and conceal her covert observation.

The dark-haired man stepped toward a table and greeted several older patrons. They pushed back from their seats to shake his hand and offer wrinkled smiles. The fair-haired man nodded to them as if remembering it was the polite thing to do, though his alert, frosty eyes followed every hand that reached toward the black-haired man.

Aislinn slowed her breathing and aimed all her senses toward the tall blond. Coldness, danger, and an indefinable gloom answered her, sending a chill deep into her bones. It was as if the man had not experienced joy or love in decades.

The dark-haired man progressed to another table to greet patrons. Aislinn remained focused on the tall blond, unable to curb her curiosity. There was a feral wildness about him, as though someone had rescued him from the jungle and dressed him up to look civilized.

She soon regretted her lock on his energy, as savageness seeped into her awareness. Unfettered power radiated from him with the ruthlessness of an assassin, someone who could kill a man and smile afterward. She shuddered. Hints of such dark vibrations had wafted from people before, but never so overwhelming that it caused her to physically shiver.

The inn and café owner, Mrs. Tănase, came out of the kitchen and broke into a smile. Her plump face flushed as she scampered toward the dark-haired man.

"*Bună seara*, Mr. Brancusi. So nice of you to visit us, sir. I've some tripe on the stove, and it turned out delicious. May I serve you both a dish?"

"*Bună seara*, Mrs. Tănase, and thank you for indulging my English," Mr. Brancusi replied with a kind smile. "My Romanian is still a little rusty. It's been some time since I visited. And, do call me Marius. I insist. While I am tempted by your offer—my wife says your tripe is the best for a hundred miles—I must politely decline. We stopped by to make sure there have been no further wolf attacks on your cows. All is well, I trust?"

Mrs. Tănase's cheeks grew redder and she clapped her hands together. "Thank you, sir. Yes, my herd is well and safe, thanks to you. How did you…?" She stepped away from the nearest diners and her voice grew to a whisper. Marius leaned his head closer to reply.

Unable to pick up the whispers, Aislinn ignored them and fixated on the deceptively stoic blond listening to Mrs. Tănase's conversation. The man furrowed his sandy brows and lifted his chin, his attention no longer on Mrs. Tănase. With a slow turn of his head, he scanned the room and focused silver-gray eyes on Aislinn.

A sizzling shock, like an electric current, traveled through Aislinn's chest and arms.

*He knows.*

No one ever felt her. Well, there *was* the time she went to a mall in Virginia with psychics in booths. When she had tried to read one of them, the woman turned away from her customer to gaze at her in surprise. Sometimes people sensed something from her and would appear uncomfortable, as if she had taken an invisible blanket off them, yet they never appeared to *know* she was reading them.

Painful prickles rained over Aislinn's body. With piercing aim, the man was reading *her*. Suspicion and malevolence colored his ghostly gaze. She decided he was too gifted, not someone she wanted curious about her abilities. If she ignored him, perhaps he would lose interest. She returned the brochure to her growing stack and opened another, reading several lines of text but not absorbing the contents.

"May I introduce my cousin, Mr. Bastian Radescu," Marius Brancusi was saying to Mrs. Tănase. Since he was no longer whispering, Aislinn picked up the conversation over the soft murmur of the diners. Risking a lightning-fast glance, she saw Marius touch his fair-haired cousin's arm to reclaim his attention. She sighed with relief at the respite from the knife-like tingles.

Bastian Radescu nodded to the innkeeper and presented his hand, palm up. When Mrs. Tănase placed her chubby hand in his, he bowed and kissed it, though still with his dour expression.

"A pleasure to meet you." His deep voice reverberated in an accent Aislinn could not place.

Mrs. Tănase chuckled but her smile was hesitant.

The café door banged against the wall as three men sauntered into the dining room talking in loud, bawdy voices.

"Just great," Aislinn hissed, recognizing Razvan Dragomir, an arrogant, overbearing man she had met the night before. He and his two devoted wingmen had driven past the inn while her baggage was being unloaded. She had been polite when they stopped to introduce themselves, but became firm in her rejections as Razvan pressed her to join him at Mrs. Tănase's café across the street. Thankfully, Mrs. Tănase's brother, Mr. Miclos, had rescued her by leading the way to a room on the topmost floor of the inn. She groaned at the memory of three flights of stairs.

Stumbling over several chairs and bumping a table, the hefty, unshaven Razvan mumbled a sarcastic apology to an old couple as if it were somehow their fault. When the elderly man moved as though to stand and reprimand Razvan, his wife laid a cautious hand on his. The couple reached for their coats as if deciding a premature exit was the better option.

"Oh, don't leave on account of me!" Razvan guffawed. All patrons in the room glared with severe disapproval.

Having found Romanian people to be extraordinarily polite and respectful, Razvan's drunken swagger was doubly repulsive to Aislinn. She hated emotions that blasted from intoxicated men, often lust, arrogance, and disjointed fantasies. Fortunately, some became harmless, rambling teddy bears. Razvan projected all of the displeasing attributes. He and his companions were in a mood to bully.

Of the ten wooden tables, seven were occupied, with Aislinn in the farthest, dimly lit corner. She had chosen the most inconspicuous area of the café out of habit. With her empathic abilities growing, distance from people was the only weapon she possessed against the onslaught of their emotions.

Mrs. Tănase hurried over to the three men, wringing her hands. "Mr. Dragomir, what may I serve you this evening?"

Puzzled that Mrs. Tănase did not throw him out, Aislinn wondered what hold Razvan had over these people whom she had grown to love in just one day. She stole a glance at Marius and Bastian to see if they reacted the same. Like hawks observing mice, the two watched the three rowdy men, Marius with a fierce look of displeasure, Bastian with the cold stare of a predator anxious to take the first lunge.

"You got anything better than that *sarmale* you had last week? Stuff gave me a stomach ache."

"Sorry to hear that, Mr. Dragomir." Mrs. Tănase grimaced as if it pained her to say the words. "My tripe is delicious, I assure you. Everyone here has enjoyed it."

Razvan scanned the room as if hoping to find someone not in good health. He froze when he spotted Aislinn.

*Don't come over here. Don't come over here,* Aislinn chanted in her mind, pushing the energy toward him. Making the suggestion work in a crowd would be difficult. She needed precise focus, but did not want to stare at him.

Razvan pushed his way past chairs and tables like a bull. "Looks like Mizz Goldilocks is come for supper. You waiting for me, pretty face?"

*Go away. You don't want me. Go away,* Aislinn repeated, this time directing the command at Razvan's brown eyes. *You don't see me. You want another table.*

Razvan paused mid-step and shook his head. One of his companions shoved a hand into his shoulder and encouraged him to approach Aislinn. Razvan looked puzzled, but when his companion chided him again and pointed, Razvan's confusion left and a haughty smile returned to his red face.

"Have not seen anyone as pretty as you in a long time, Mizz Goldi. Let's not waste all the room at this big table. It's made for a party."

As the men began scraping chairs along the floor and seating themselves, Aislinn stood and shoved her brochures and electronic tablet into a satchel, which took some doing considering all the brochures.

"Have a good evening, gentlemen."

Razvan's arm shot out as she tried to scoot past him. "What's the rush, Mizz Goldi? Have some dessert with us, or, *be* dessert." Though his words were slurred, the last two he said low enough that the other patrons would not hear. But his companions could. They burst out laughing like school boys.

Aislinn felt a powerful cloud of energy hit the side of her body. Before she could turn to investigate, Razvan's face registered shock. A pale hand had encircled his plump wrist and twisted, forcing him to dislodge his grip on Aislinn's arm. Razvan garbled a small yelp of pain.

Though grateful, Aislinn shuddered as she watched Bastian lean menacingly toward Razvan.

"You do not vant her," Bastian whispered in a voice as deep and smooth as a cello.

"I... do not want her?" Razvan managed to ask, entranced.

"Your only concern is the delicious tripe that Mrs. Tănase is serving. You are going to enjoy it."

Aislinn was as mesmerized by Bastian's velvety words as Razvan was. His accent was similar to the German woman she had sat next to on the plane. She could feel the magic surrounding his words and knew with a shudder that he was using persuasion. She did not want to fall prey to it.

Razvan nodded compliance. "I am going to enjoy it."

"And tell everyone how good it is."

"Yes, how good it is."

"Tell your friends all about it. Now."

Razvan turned away with unfocused eyes and began to mumble something to his confused friends.

The vice-like grip was suddenly on Aislinn's arm. "Come," Bastian ordered.

With a sharp intake of breath, Aislinn opened her mouth to protest, but decided to do as he asked rather than risk Razvan remembering his previous intentions. She had used persuasion countless times in high school when she realized the thoughts chanting in her mind had an effect on people. When necessary, she used it on teachers, and sometimes on classmates, though it made her feel guilty. She had never met anyone else that could do it until now, and with such instant results.

Bastian released her arm but motioned a hand toward the door, urging her to walk in front of him. Feeling heat rush to her face and self-conscious of her body's movements, she skirted between tables and hurried to leave money for Mrs. Tănase on the counter. Marius was saying farewell to

Mrs. Tănase, but the plump woman averted her eyes to Aislinn and nodded at the waitress, Nadia, who hurried to collect Aislinn's money.

Aislinn exited the café and gulped deep breaths of cold, mountain air.

"Who *are* you?" came a deep voice beside her.

Aislinn flinched. Bastian was standing beside her on the wooden porch, soundlessly closing the door behind him and glowering. She had hoped he would stay inside to ensure Razvan did not follow. She had not heard his steps, which was unusual for her. Her hearing was another ability that had heightened along with her empathic and psychic awareness over the past tumultuous year.

"Miss Aislinn Thomas," Aislinn answered. She remembered to be formal, as Sergiu, her tour guide, had cautioned. "Thank you," she decided to add.

Marius came through the door, his dark eyes alight with interest. He extended his hand. "Mr. Marius Brancusi, my lady. *Bună seara.*"

Nearly shivering from the intensity of his charisma, Aislinn fought the desire to run across the graveled road to the inn and safety of her upstairs room. Instead, she shook his outstretched hand, feeling the singe of power in the touch.

"Miss Aislinn Thomas." She attempted a smile. "*Bună seara.*"

"American," he stated, raising both black brows in acknowledgement of her accent. "Miss Thomas, may I inquire as to what brings you to our lovely Romania?"

"I'm, um… visiting."

"Ah. With friends, or family?"

"No. I'm… alone." She had not meant to admit that, but Marius Brancusi's dark eyes were so compelling she had not thought to lie.

"A handsome lady such as yourself traveling alone?" His friendly demeanor changed to disapproving.

She blinked at him. "Handsome?"

"Oh, my apologies. I have recently been in London visiting relatives. Handsome is a term you use strictly for men in America, is that not so?" His gleaming white smile made his face even more good-looking.

She smiled in return as his charm turned her to mush. "Yes."

"Ah, then let me exchange that for 'beautiful.'" He nodded as if in apology. "Still, I must be concerned for your safety."

"Oh, um, I'm fine. Really. Besides, my tour guide, Sergiu, says that Romania has some of the safest cities in the world."

"Safe from humans, perhaps, but not creatures of the night."

Her smile faltered. She smirked, assuming he was referring to the local legends of vampires. "I'll keep a lookout for bats."

For the merest second, a shadow crossed Marius' face as though he was expecting a different answer. He quickly replaced it with a captivating grin.

"Indeed. Well, it is certainly a pleasure to meet you, Miss Thomas. I see you have met my cousin, Mr. Bastian Radescu?"

Aislinn swallowed, knowing she would have to look at Bastian. Shivers cascaded along her nerve endings as she met his icy stare.

"Sort of," she mumbled, wishing Bastian was not standing so close. He looked even taller with his imposing six foot five frame exuding a deadly kind of masculinity, one she feared and yet felt strangely drawn to.

Pressure enveloped her brain as he stared unblinking. Every muscle in Aislinn's body tightened. *The nerve of him.* Pressing angry lips together, she steeled her focus to create a wall and push him out. When he did not desist, she threw him a warning glint and telepathically added, *Stop!*

When he winced, showing he had clearly heard her, he brightened and became more intrigued. His chin tilted downward and his frosty gaze became more direct. Aislinn felt a sudden longing to tell him everything about her, then realized the impulse was not hers. Alarmed at his abilities, she offered her hand to distract him.

Marius elbowed Bastian when he did not immediately respond. Bastian took her hand, leaned forward and kissed it with warm, strong lips, his glittering gray eyes never leaving hers.

Electricity shot through Aislinn's hand, up her arm and spread into places it shouldn't. Had he done that on purpose? Was it possible to flirt using power? Maybe his touch was so statically charged she was overreacting. When he raised his head, she relaxed her fingers and tugged at her hand. He did not relinquish his hold, as if to make the point that he would release her when he was ready. She was certain he was also trying to read her using the connection forged through their touch.

Emboldened by anger, Aislinn focused hard, built up psychic pressure, and shot him a piercing, *Stop it!* The fierce synaptic burst was one she had used only four times, the first by accident. She had thwarted unwelcomed advances each time using the same tactic, all successful, until now. The trick was to throw all of her body's energy into the command.

Bastian's upper torso coiled backward mere inches, not enough to disrupt his stance. A wicked smile toyed at one side of his mouth. He released her hand, and she flexed it.

"Will you be staying in Romania long, Miss Thomas?" Marius asked, his tone light as if unaware of the exchange. She was quite certain by his intense stare that he *was* aware.

She could lie about her travel plans. Marius' fathomless black eyes compelled her to answer.

"A week," she replied.

Actually, she had not decided how long she was staying, but knew it would at least be a week. She was desperate for an isolated place where she could escape life, escape grief, and put as much distance between her and her cheating ex-fiancé, Eddie, as possible. Searching travel sites, the historical region of Romania that she and her sister had dreamed of visiting had called to her.

*Transylvania.* Vampire central. A travel deal had popped up in her email for the quiet village of Teşila, the perfect Romanian retreat with its mountainous beauty, green-blue river, and charming folklore. Not to mention the fantastic price. It had to be a sign from her sister, Anya.

"Well, perhaps you will do me and my cousin the honor of joining us for dinner tomorrow night?" Marius asked.

Aislinn's eyes went wide in surprise and alarm. In the same room with two gorgeous men who appeared to have the power of persuasion? And way stronger than hers? Alarm bells were ringing. Marius allowed the corners of his lips to curl upward. The alarm bells softened to a weak chime.

"The mayor of Valea Doftanei is paying us a visit at my chalet, and my nephew is stopping by. I am sure your American charm and wit will add to a delightful evening. Since my wife is American, I am certain she would enjoy your visit as well. Shall we pick you up at 7:30 tomorrow evening then? We tend to eat late."

"Sure." Aislinn nodded and smiled. Then she dropped her smile. She had meant to say, "Sorry, I'm busy."

# CHAPTER 2

Aislinn slammed her bedroom door and leaned against it to breathe. Her heart was racing and her arms shook between chills of fear and shivers of excitement. Why did she accept the dinner date? Why didn't she just say no? She could have politely declined Marius' request, but he was so nice about it. He *was* charming.

More than likely, he was charming with persuasion. There had to be something to her inability to deny him. As bold as Bastian's scrutiny was, maybe Marius was just discreet.

And that made them very dangerous.

She exhaled and flung her coat across the bed, then dropped into the small wooden chair by the dresser. Her legs ached from touring the town of Sinaia earlier that day. She had enjoyed visiting several sites by bus, especially the majestic Peles Castle, the Sinaia Monastery, and a lovely church painted with a mural of angels fighting demons. Now her legs were quivering, especially with the added insult of three flights of stairs. She really pushed it this time.

"All right legs, just hang in there. You can rest tonight, okay?"

With so many wonderful places left to see, she needed to be more careful. Her legs had been healing for over a year, and she was determined not to resort to using her cane. It was just that everything here was so beautiful and she did not want to miss anything. Realistically, there was no need to rush. Her account would hold out for several weeks of touring and meals.

Maybe she would just stay here and not go back. Get a job. Learn the language. Even as joy filled her heart at the thought, she knew she *would* go back. The only two family members she had left in the world were in North Carolina. So were all of her friends.

She loved North Carolina. Mountains on one end, and beach on the other. She loved Romania now too. This was the perfect place to get lost in: a place full of wonder, historical charm and enchanting people. Well, most of them.

She undressed, pulled a silky blue nightgown over her head, grabbed her electronic tablet and stretched out across the bed.

Dear Anya,

What a strange evening. First, the jerk, Razvan, shows up again, totally wasted. And how is that even possible since Romania has the strictest drunk driving laws in the world? He must know somebody in high places. Especially since everybody reacted funny. I mean, this place is very traditional. Old people are respected here and everybody calls each other Mister or Miss all the time. Even neighbors. I think I'm getting the greetings down, thanks to the Romanian language app I downloaded. Sergiu pointed out the best one. Luckily, a lot of people speak English, too.

Sergiu's been the best tour guide ever. Of course, he's my first tour guide, but hey. He said I had to try the Romanian tripe soup. It's got this awesome tart cheesy taste, some veggies, and white things like pasta. You would love it. I thought about picking up the bowl and sucking down the last drops but I don't think Romanians do that. They thought I was strange enough for typing in this tablet while I ate.

So, back to dinner, two hot guys show up, and this guy Bastian—oh my gosh, Anya, this guy is hot. Not sure if he's creepy hot, or exotic hot, but definitely hot. Looks like a Greek god. No, make that a Viking god, with amazing silver-gray eyes that sparkle—he grabs Razvan's arm and commands him with persuasion to back off. Nothing like I've ever seen. Blew the socks off my abilities. And I used to get you to make me brownies. Ha! Remember?

Well, I go outside and boom, there he is, like he just materialized. His cousin, Marius—he's hot too—tall, dark and handsome kinda hot—comes out and introduces himself. Bastian starts mind probing me. Really pissed me off. He kissed my hand. I mean, seriously, he's the only guy so far in Romania that kissed my hand. Although I've heard it's not uncommon.

Anyway, he keeps up with the mind whack, so I blasted him. It always worked before, but Viking god just blinks and flinches. What a powerful mind. He intrigues me. I want to know where he came from. I think I should be scared, but they both have this air of mystery around them. Kind of an old world charm that's magnetic.

Then, of all things, Marius-looking-like-a-rich-dude asks me to dinner for tomorrow night. I think he got me to say yes. What the heck am I supposed to do? Although, he did say the mayor was going to be there, and another relative, so it's probably okay. I'll ask Mrs. Tănase about them tomorrow and see what she says. She seems to like them. Well, she likes Marius.

You'd like Marius, I think. You always liked the dark-haired guys with tanned skin and brown eyes. I'm sure I saw a wedding ring though. Oh yeah, he mentioned a wife.

Oh, I almost forgot, I just about killed myself taking that tour today. You liked the church, didn't you? I felt you there. You always liked pictures of old, painted churches. It's so beautiful here. No matter what direction I go in, it's just beautiful. I can feel you right here with me. We're finally taking this trip together, just like we planned. You and me.

Love you,
Aisy

~~◊~~

"My lord, I have a new sign," Bastian announced.

"I do as well," Marius acknowledged. "Just found it." Actually, Marius had been waiting for it. There had to be a reason his wife, Gabriella, had felt led to leave Greece and spend October in Romania. "Do you have a fix on the direction?"

"I have scented the wind." Bastian closed his eyes and breathed deep. "I have stretched out with my mind and it eludes me. Except…."

Marius frowned. "Except what?"

"The woman. Power surrounds her. Energy I should be able to define, but many sensations assault me and confuse the reading."

Marius raised curious brows, praying Bastian did not detect the rush of hope that burned in his heart. He, too, had sensed elusive traces of power about the girl, though he was more concerned with her blood. His foresight with discerning bloodline was legendary and yet he could not identify the elemental nuances of her past, or her skills, almost as if a determined presence blurred the energy. He was content to find out more when she attended their dinner. It had taken little persuasion to prompt her to accept, so she was obviously not used to dealing with those practiced in the art.

Bastian's tone held a hint of attraction, even desire, emotions Marius had not detected from him in many years. Was this a glimmer of redemption for his cousin? Perhaps. Or perhaps, it would be another false hope. Still, it would not hurt to keep him curious.

"Hmm, this could prove interesting," said Marius. "Perhaps we need to know more. See what you can find out, Bastian. Discreetly, of course."

Bastian flew low past the luminous windows of the inn until he spotted Aislinn through the partly-drawn curtains. An odd, bluish light shone on her face as she lay propped up with pillows on an antique bed surrounded by a carved, wooden frame.

Landing soundlessly on the balcony railing, he folded his immense black wings. He jumped, flapped fiercely and had to land on the rattan seat of a balcony chair when the railing burned him. Wrought iron. The metal always protested his morphed form.

Having transformed into an eagle straight from Marius' chalet, he knew better than to stay in the same form too long. He had once remained as a wolf for an entire day, and had trouble changing back. Marius had been furious with him. So furious, he had threatened to constrict Bastian's ability to morph.

"I will not allow you to escape this world in an animal form, Bastian," Marius had yelled. "Nor will I allow you to withdraw into the kind of darkness that will surely devour you."

But Marius did not realize Bastian had long resided in a dark place, desolate, despondent. For him, darkness was the ultimate escape. Or maybe Marius did realize.

Concentrating hard, Bastian reformed into a large, tawny cat. He was the only one of his kind to use the cat form. The others used eagles, wolves, dogs, and occasionally bears for clandestine observation. But he had worked at mastering the cat because humans always dismissed him as a stray. It had saved him many times.

With a curl of his thick tail around his paws, he settled into a sitting pose. White flakes of snow—or was it flower petals—wafted in front of the window. It was a bit too warm for snow, and too late for flowers. Surprisingly, his nose told him nothing as he pointed it toward several fleeting wisps.

After watching Aislinn through the blur of flakes, he realized she held an electronic tablet. Its blue glow outlined the soft beauty of her face and highlighted golden hair which cascaded in soft, lazy curls over her shoulders. Her large blue eyes glistened in the light. As she breathed gently, the silky nightgown made it easy for him to enjoy the shape of her rounded breasts, small waste and curved hips. A flowered quilt obscured his view of her legs. If he could just pull back the quilt and see the whole picture. Pulling back the nightgown would be better. He berated himself for the thought. This was a mission strictly for information.

With a soft sigh, Aislinn tilted her head back onto a pillow. Her eyes became distant, unfocused, sad. Bastian concentrated and reached, just a little. Scanning was harder in animal form. He had to sacrifice the magnitude of his abilities in order to hold the form.

Sorrow lined the girl's face, but it was the grief flowing from her heart that disturbed him. He squirmed and shifted his paws. He had not been disturbed by anyone's emotions in a long time. In truth, he had accepted that emotions were a liability and not worth his reflection.

This sorrow, however, was different. The crushing ache that emanated from loss and regret held his fascination. What could have happened to one so young? The ache grew. Her eyes glistened with tears. He knew this trap. She was thinking about her loss, allowing its stinging pain to tear at her heart. A tear dripped down her cheek. She sniffed.

*Fight it,* he instinctively thought to her. *Don't let it get to you.*

But she did not fight it. The heavy cloud of sorrow grew and surrounded her. In animal form, he could not project his power of persuasion properly.

Being so focused on her, he did something he had not done in decades. He drew in her grief in an attempt to discern its origin. Misery crashed over him in a suffocating, strangling wave. The depth of her sadness made his own heart wrench, dredging up long forgotten shadows. So long ago.

Amazed and bewildered, he tried to make sense of the burning emotions, as well as shake them off. Memories seeped in like water flooding an old, cracked, forgotten basement. He almost morphed out of form. With a deep breath, he concentrated on maintaining the cat form, expressing his displeasure in an eerie growl.

She turned her head, her blue eyes widening in surprise.

# CHAPTER 3

An animal-like growl disturbed Aislinn's heartrending memories of her parents. She turned toward the window to find two silver-gray eyes gleaming at her from a balcony chair. Her breath caught in her throat as she noticed snowflakes drifting around the cat.

"Anya," she whispered. "Did you send him?" She flew to the window and tugged until it lifted. It was not unusual for animals to be curious about her, or even follow her. Growing up, her back yard, and her room, had been full of strays, much to the consternation of her mother. But three stories up was a long way for a cat to go for curiosity.

"How did you get all the way up here, big guy?" He was the biggest cat Aislinn had ever seen. She examined the outside walls to her left and right, considering whether he could have leapt six feet from the neighboring balcony. Maybe he came from another room, although the inn's rules had warned no pets were allowed.

The tawny cat's ears twitched.

"You're welcome to come in, but somehow I bet Mrs. Tănase is not going to be happy with me." She shivered and rubbed her shoulders at the chill in the night air.

The cat stared. Its pale eyes appeared ghostly.

With calm ease, Aislinn reached for the cat's mind. She enjoyed touching animals' minds. They were so raw, honest, uncomplicated. Especially dogs. Give me. I want. Let's play. Can I sit with you? To her surprise, the simple mind of a cat did not greet her. This mind was complicated, deep, powerful, dark.

Aislinn inhaled sharply. That was not possible. How many strange things were there in this quaint village?

Men's voices echoed from the hallway that led to the four rooms on the top floor. Aislinn felt a twinge of sharp energy. Since she had locked the door, she assumed the disconcerting sensation of alarm was perhaps something brewing between the men themselves, and decided to pay them no attention. Besides, she wanted to understand the cat.

The cat continued to stare, unmoved. Its pale, shining eyes reminded her of Bastian Radescu. The more she stared and touched the mind of the cat, the more the creature resembled the gloomy, despondent, untamed energy she sensed earlier at the café.

The cat sat up straighter, its head bobbing as if considering jumping through the window.

A slight shuffle and creak was enough to turn Aislinn's head. Razvan stood in her room, his face flushed and eyes leering. With a gasp, she whirled to face him.

"What do you think you're doing?" she demanded. "How did you get in here?"

"Now, don't be unfriendly, there's a good *Zână*. Thought you might like some company."

Aislinn had a vague memory of *Zână* being in the section on insults and profanity in her Romanian language app.

"I don't want company," she stated firmly. "I want you to leave. Right now." *Leave. Leave the room. Leave, now.*

Razvan blinked several times as if confused and turned toward the door, which he had closed. Aislinn wondered if he had locked it, but decided to focus on the persuasion lest she lose control of him.

*Turn around and leave. Leave. Leave. You don't want to be here.*

Aislinn's heart pounded as Razvan reached for the doorknob. A man yelled a greeting to someone outside in the graveled road, and the sound broke the spell.

Razvan jerked back his hand from the doorknob, and strode toward Aislinn. "What are you, a witch? You do something weird to me."

Aislinn stepped sideways to position the narrow, glass balcony door behind her. Three stories up, she was too high to jump, but she could scream for help at the man in the street.

"Stop, Razvan. It's been a long day, and I need you to leave right now." Behind her, she turned the cold metal latch on the balcony door. "We can… talk… tomorrow. Okay?"

A cold shiver ran over her skin as Razvan's red-rimmed eyes drank in her scant nightgown. "What about what I need, Goldi?" With speed that surprised her, Razvan grabbed her arms and trapped both wrists in one hand.

Aislinn tried to yell for help, but could not finish as Razvan clamped the other hand over her mouth, flattening her against the balcony door. Aislinn screamed through his fingers.

21

"Scream again and I'll make you sorry you did. Just be a good girl and you won't get hurt."

Aislinn struggled and tried to kick, but her legs did little damage. It had only been a month since she was able to walk without a cane. Razvan was large and strong. Using his body weight, he shoved her onto the bed, wrenching her lower back as she fell in a twisted position, with him on top of her.

Aislinn pivoted with all her might to pull out from under his weight. Razvan pressed a knee into her left leg and she screamed in pain, the sound coming out as a muffled squeal as he tightened his hold on her jaw.

"I told you not to scream, Goldi. Want to see what else you get for that?"

Razvan's fist came up to strike her, but did not move. Pale fingers had closed over it.

Razvan appeared to rise into the air, shock and panic on his reddened face. His body shook. Aislinn realized Bastian was standing beside him, holding him by the throat with one powerful hand. Razvan's feet were no longer touching the floor. In two long strides across the small room, Bastian slammed Razvan against the wall beside the door.

Aislinn sat up, shaking from the assault but also from the astonishment of Bastian being in her room. Had he followed Razvan?

Horrific gurgling sounds escaped from Razvan's throat. His cheeks began to turn purple, his limbs dangling like some kind of over-stuffed marionette. Terror distorted his face as he stared into icy silver eyes.

Bastian bared his teeth with a low, guttural vibration. For a moment, Aislinn thought she saw canines in Bastian's mouth, but his curling lips dropped. A cold, deadly desire to kill Razvan radiated from him so strong Aislinn felt it permeate her entire being. Razvan's eyes rolled back in his head.

Aislinn scrambled off the bed and limped toward them. "Bastian, if you kill him, you could be blamed."

Slowly, he turned as if surprised she was in the room. "This human is evil. He should die."

"Okay. Probably true. I don't know about Romania laws, but sometimes in America, when you defend yourself and hurt the bad guy, you get sued."

Bastian drew his sandy brows into a disapproving scowl. "When justice is weak, criminals are strong. I do not like your America."

Aislinn licked her lips. "Hey, I don't always like the legal system either, but... Bastian, you might want to put him down."

Without taking his eyes off hers, Bastian released the shivering, limp Razvan. The heavy thud of Razvan's body hitting the floor was so loud, Aislinn was sure someone would come to investigate.

"And what, may I ask, do you suggest I do with him?"

Aislinn considered calling the police and realized she did not know what number to use. After witnessing the fear in the townsfolk Razvan bullied, she had a sneaky suspicion that involving the local authorities might not have the desired outcome.

"Use your persuasion," she suggested.

Bastian's cold eyes narrowed.

"Look, I know yours is way stronger than mine. Tell him anything. Tell him to never come here again. Tell him I'm ugly."

Bastian raised both brows and tilted his head in sarcasm.

"It doesn't matter, just get rid of him."

Razvan's head was lulling left and right. He coughed and his eyelids fluttered.

"He should die, my lady. I heard his depraved thoughts. Can't *you* feel the evil in him?"

"Yes, I do. And for what he was about to do, he deserves to die. But, I don't want you in trouble."

"I have successfully hidden my judgments for decad–… for years."

Alarm snaked through Aislinn's veins. *Judgments? Was he about to say, "decades?"* He certainly didn't *look* old enough to speak of decades. She would have to wait to find out. The priority was getting rid of her attacker.

"Um… what if we do something that helps him?" she proposed. "Like, tell him he's wicked. Make him feel the pain of others. Make him repent and change."

Amazement softened Bastian's face. Aislinn felt his strong mind reach out to hers. It was frightening and exhilarating feeling all that power.

"There is wisdom in you." He turned away and squatted in front of Razvan with fluid, cat-like grace. "Hear the sound of my voice, human."

*Human?* Aislinn questioned.

Razvan's eyes opened, then widened, spellbound.

"You have enjoyed privileges far too long. Your family has become powerful and cruel, diseased. You have allowed their evil to fill your heart and twist your mind. Now, you are repentant. On Sunday you will seek out the priest and confess your wickedness. Tell him you wish to mend the errors of your useless life."

Entranced by Bastian's silken, beautiful voice, Aislinn wanted to obey his commands as well. She shook her head to dispel the inclination.

"Every minute that you delay this," Bastian continued, his voice velvety, hypnotic, his accent softening. "You will be haunted by the pain you have caused others. In your dreams, during the day, during the night, you will see their faces. You will have no peace. No release from the cries of your victims. You will count the minutes until Sunday so that you may seek the priest's help. You will run there in desperation. You will ignore the goading of your friends. Let no one deter you."

Razvan's eyes widened even more.

"Do you hear and obey?"

Razvan nodded, his jaw slack.

"Leave this room. Leave the inn. You will never be able to return here again with evil in your heart. This lady was not here. Do not remember her, ever. She is gone from you. Do you hear and obey me?"

Razvan barely moved his mouth. "I hear... obey."

"Leave now. Follow my instructions."

Razvan scrambled to his feet, his bulky frame unsteady like a giant toddler. He shuffled out of the room and closed the door.

Bastian stood and watched the door with unfocused eyes.

Afraid to interrupt Bastian's trancelike state, Aislinn reached gingerly for his mind. Instead of emotions, words materialized into her awareness vibrating with powerful persuasion. *In the car. Down the road. Go home.* She realized Bastian was holding onto his connection with Razvan's mind, guiding him away from the inn. Away from her.

*What an incredible mind.* In awe she watched him as he remained focused and still, except for the slow rising and falling of his chest.

Seconds ticked by and she became aware of a stinging ache in her back and legs. She sidestepped and grasped the edge of the bed frame for support.

"Bastian?" She spoke softly. "Is he gone?"

Bastian turned and stared at her dreamily as if the sound of her voice speaking his name moved him.

With a jolt, she remembered the formal customs. "I'm sorry. I'm supposed to call you Mr. Radescu."

"Please, my lady, call me Bastian." He turned his muscular body toward her. "I do not mind. I long to hear it."

The yearning in his voice made her heart skip a beat. He was so open she knew he was not lying. Up close and without the coat hiding his physique, the tailored white dress shirt and gray trousers he was still wearing fit him so perfectly it nearly took her breath away. His massive chest narrowed to a small waist, and his hips....

"Are you injured?" he asked her, noting her awkward stance.

Aislinn shook her head, wishing for the second time that night that she was wearing more than a short, thin nightgown. "It's just... he hurt something in my back when he... threw me on the bed." Her legs were throbbing, but she dared not mention them for fear he would look and notice her scars.

Concerned, he stepped closer. He froze when she stiffened, and opened both his hands, palms out. "You have no need to fear me, my lady. I only wish to help."

Aislinn regarded his strong hands, then his face, questioning his intent. She had just watched him an inch away from crushing another man's throat, one-handed.

"Take my hands," he whispered.

# CHAPTER 4

Aislinn's arms were moving in response to his command. She hesitated, wondering if he was using persuasion. His mind was open to her and she could read no malice or ill intent. In fact, there was wonder there, curiosity, an overwhelming longing to know her, as though she were a bright blue flower that had appeared in the vast expanse of a white, snow-covered mountain.

He knew she was reading him, and he did not resist her.

She rested her hands in his, still wary.

"I am a healer, My lady. Or at least I was, once. Let me do my job."

*A healer?* Several words of protest crossed her mind. Before she could voice them, he had stepped closer and slid one arm around her waist, his touch buttery soft. She felt his broad palm press on her lower back as if he were attempting to lead her into a dance. While she wondered why she didn't feel alarmed at the blatant touch, warmth began to flow into her spine.

His eyes closed and mouth relaxed.

So did hers.

She couldn't help giving in to the sensations that poured through her, soothing, like warm bath water heating steadily, almost to the point of burning. Having witnessed ferocity and anger in Bastian, though chivalrous, she wondered how such a fantastic, loving vibration could now emanate from him. It felt like sunshine, wind rustling leaves, the brush of a furry cat....

"Better?"

Almost unable to speak, Aislinn's eyelids fluttered. She flexed her back and found she could move, unhindered by pain.

She wriggled slightly and looked up at him. "You're... amazing."

26

"As are you." He retrieved his hand, but did not step away. His eyes glistened in a loving way as if he was experiencing the same sensations as she when he healed her. She blushed, noting his emotions were laced with adoration and reverence... and something else.

He was blinking back tears.

"Bastian?"

"I have not been able to heal anyone in eight–... in many years." He turned his hands over, looking at them as though reassuring himself they belonged to him.

"Why?"

He swallowed, hard. "I could not feel it. I could not find it."

He looked upon her with such idolization, she could not move for the wonder of such a gaze.

As if unable to stop himself, his pale fingers lifted locks of her long blonde hair and let them fall like water. A rapt expression was on his face as if he had never seen anything so lovely, which she found odd since he, too, was blond. Then she understood. His admiration was not for her hair, it was for her, every part of her, and he wanted to touch something safe. She saw it in his eyes as they alighted on her chest and traveled up to her face, making her blush.

"Thank you, my lady." Like a lost soul, his fingertips brushed her cheek with tenderness. She knew she should protest. She should back away. She should tell him it was time to leave. That would be the proper thing to do.

Except that everything about his presence, so close, felt *right*.

She wanted to know more. She had never been with anyone else who used persuasion. At least, someone not related. The tingling in her body from the healing shifted to a different kind of tingling. She wanted to touch him, to understand him. Perhaps she could persuade him to stay longer. They could sit on the bed and talk. Get to know each other.

As if in response to her thoughts, he took her hand and laid her palm along the side of his face, pressing her fingertips to his temple.

"See me," he whispered, and closed his eyes.

Her mouth fell open. He was giving her permission to scan him? To read his innermost thoughts? Her heart thumped wildly as she closed her eyes and laced her mind with his.

One flickering flame merged with another. It was the most uninhibited thing she had ever experienced, drinking in the thoughts and emotions of someone revering her, basking in her presence, wanting her trust. Feeling his attraction and strength of will was exhilarating.

She found herself smiling. Though she wanted to stay right there, savoring his adoration, out of habit she reached further, deeper. Fear held a strong place in him. Which surprised her. What did he have to fear? Beyond the fear was something dark and savage, something surrounded by anger, hate and grief.

A wall slammed over the contact.

She opened her eyes to find him watching her with caution. He grew embarrassed. Then his emotions turned apologetic. She offered the hint of a smile. He did the same, clearly relieved.

"We all have our demons, Bastian," she said to soften the intrusion.

"Not like mine."

She might have agreed had she strayed further into the dark alleyways of his soul, but she desperately wanted to reassure him that she was not afraid. If he could but feel the joy it gave her to be with someone who knew of her abilities and did not see her as strange. For the past few years, she had dreamt of someone like him. She did not care that he had fears or inner demons. And really, all men had a dark side, didn't they?

His incredible persuasion was a talent she could learn from. And he could heal. What additional abilities he possessed she could not imagine, but would like the chance to explore. For the first time in her life, she was not alone. She was not weird.

He smiled. Though he had prevented her from reaching too deep, he had not severed their connection, and was touched by her thoughts.

His shimmering eyes bored into hers and held her captive. His desire to know her, to touch her, was so strong it felt as if he were making love to her soul through their connection. She resisted the sudden urge to be shy and glance away.

Eye contact had always made her uncomfortable, especially with strong-willed people. The stronger their soul, the more she lost herself absorbing their energy and forgot what she was going to say. With Bastian so close, so filled with the need to covet, she should have responded that way. Instead, she was entranced. Her heart was beating faster.

His smile began to fall and his facial muscles relaxed. The more he concentrated on her, chasing and touching her every emotion, the more his thoughts become raw, primal, bordering on dangerous. The sensuality that pulsed from him held a threat of possession, full of the promise of new and exciting vistas.

She drank his energy into her awareness, all the while knowing she should step away.

His hand flexed where it still held hers captive against his cheek. His fingers stroked the back of her hand as if testing to see if she would allow it. When she did not protest, his fingertips traveled down her arm, then lifted to her cheek where they brushed her skin like feathers. He was standing so close his body heat warmed her.

She swallowed and retracted her hand from his face. Unabashed, he slid his fingers down her neck, spreading them, moving to the nape of her neck, again waiting for her to protest.

She did not. Could not.

His emotions were so open and honest, even as his passion rose, she could not consider pushing him away. His emotions had become hers.

Taking a step closer, he slid his fingers around her neck and pushed back her hair. His lips parted in wonder, as if he had forgotten what soft skin felt like, what a woman felt like. Aislinn wondered how that was possible. Someone as handsome as he?

She breathed in the spicy, almost earthy scent of him. Perhaps it was a soap or shaving cream. Or maybe it was just him, wild and woodsy.

Radiant energy ebbed and flowed between them and began to build. She felt its dangerous flames heating her breasts and traveling to her thighs. Would holding him give her entire body a sensation like his hands had on her back?

"I will guard you through the night, my lady." The husky, whispered words caused every female part of her to throb.

"I... I...." Her mouth regrouped and tried to form the word "yes," but it did not come out. Exactly how was he going to guard her? "Thank you for saving me. Um, but, I...."

"You should not be traveling alone." The disapproval in his voice was a warning. "Why is there no man with you?"

"I haven't found one I can tolerate." *Oh, no.* Did she just say that?

His tawny brows rose. "Tolerate?"

"They lie so much. I hear their minds...." Aislinn clipped her mouth shut. What was she saying? She never told anyone that, let alone a *man*. It wasn't just that men lied to her—*a lot*, they seemed so immature now, focused on partying, attempting every dangerous stunt they could think up, and wanting sex without a care for the future. She was twenty-two years old and had faced the horror of a debilitating car accident, the death of her dearest loved ones, fighting for compensation in court, and a long, arduous recovery. She could barely stand to converse with a man that was under forty, or a man who had not experienced some sorrows and obstacles in life that sobered him.

"And what do their minds say to you?"

"They take one look at my blonde hair and think I'm a bimbo that will believe anything." *Oh dear.* Why was she telling him this? Was he using persuasion on her?

For the first time, she leaned away from his mesmerizing touch, though her left foot appeared to be glued to the floor. Gingerly, his hands rested on her arms before she could register that he was holding her in place. Not with true force, but wishing her to stay. She licked her lips. The feel of his palms on her bare arms made her skin shiver with desire for more. If those warm hands began touching every part of her she would be helpless to stop them. She might even show them where to go.

A small section of her brain fought to be sensible. This was not like her. She was always cautious. What she should do was say *goodnight*. But, other parts of her did not want him to leave. The parts that were tingling.

"I can assure you, I would not make such a mistake." His eyes seemed to glow. "If you were mine, I would cherish you. Beyond measure."

Her knees were turning to mush. "Cherished would be good."

"Keep your window closed and your door locked. Wedge a chair under the handle. A cherished woman should never be left alone."

She was about to say, "no one cherishes me right now," when Bastian's demeanor changed. A dark shadow crept across his handsome face. The skin around his eyes and mouth tightened. Wrinkles formed. He was gritting his teeth.

Pain shot into Aislinn's chest. She reeled from its intensity and stepped back. The bed stopped her. A knife seemed to be piercing her ribs with such force she thought she might be having a heart attack. Until she realized the pain was coming from Bastian.

# CHAPTER 5

Bastian's shoulders tensed and his head bowed. He swallowed, his upper body contorting in pain.

Was *he* having a heart attack? No, this was something else. Something familiar.

*Oh, no.* Aislinn knew this emotion all too well. Intense, debilitating grief.

Releasing her arms, Bastian pressed a hand to his chest.

"What is it?" she begged, afraid for him. "Who is it?"

Crushing heartache and regret filled the room. Cracking sounds issued from the walls as if they were expanding, stretching the wood and plaster. Thunder rumbled overhead.

Under Aislinn's feet the floor bent slightly. She repositioned her feet, wondering if Romania was prone to earthquakes or tremors.

Bastian bent forward and braced himself with a hand on his thigh. "I can't stop it." His voice was almost a sob.

Sorrow squeezed Aislinn's heart, embodying his pain. Her eyes brimmed with tears. She had only begun to champion the wracking agony of losing her family. Then, for the first time in a year, she realized this sorrow was not hers. A woman's face materialized and then dissipated just as fast. It was not her mother. It was not her sister. The person lost was his.

Aislinn drove the emotions away, pushing with all her might, forcing the energy out of her body. Instead, she concentrated on gaining clarity of his emotions.

He groaned.

Such an unbearable spike of anguish she had never encountered from another human being. It was as if a bomb had detonated inside Bastian, shoving open a sealed door. Cobwebs blew aside as a monster crept out.

"I'm so sorry. What can I do?" She stepped toward him and gripped his shaking shoulders. The feel of firm, taut muscles sent shockwaves up her arms. She had not touched a man in so long.

With a measured exhale, Bastian shuddered and tried to regain his composure. "For what do you apologize, my lady?"

"Because... it's something we say in America when we feel bad because someone is grieving. Your... pain. I've never felt anything like it. Well, sort of. Who did you lose?"

He turned away as if in shame. She felt his emotions shift. Remorse. Blame. Survivor's grief? She knew that, too. All too well. She had been in and out of consciousness as paramedics cut her out of a crushed, bronze sedan, lights flashing from every direction. The whispered words, "the others are gone," not meant for her to hear, had haunted her every day since.

Drawn by Bastian's torment, not knowing what had triggered it, she placed one hand over his, still pressed against his heart. The other she spread across his cheek. Reaching further into his mind, she reeled from the depths of deprecating shame, which flipped to intense anger, then guilt, then sorrow, and back. She knew that endless circle as well. She had nearly lost herself there once.

"What happened to you?" she whispered, resting her forehead against his chin. "Who was it? Tell me. Let me see."

He shook his head, dislodging her. He was shutting down their link. She had to do something.

"I wish I could take this from you, like you took pain from my back. I know grief, Bastian. It's a bottomless pit you will drown in. Just when you think you've got it under control, it crashes over you, like a giant wave you didn't see coming." She rubbed her hand over his, sending him thoughts of love and sympathy, wanting desperately to comfort him.

A sharp chortle of sarcasm escaped him. "You would try to heal *this*?"

"Yes, of course. Let me try. *You* can heal. With our minds together, we must be able to join energy. We can rise above the pain, relieve it somehow."

She had just met this man today, though this was the second time. Yet, she felt she knew more about him than any other man she had met before. Some of her dates had attempted honesty, but at some point became secretive. Or, they simply didn't know themselves well enough to know what was truth and what was a lie.

Bastian was painfully open, in spite of wanting to shield her from his memories. His internal battle raged like a whirling tornado. He struggled to gain control of the painful, foreign emotions. He gripped her shoulder with one hand as if to steady himself.

Aislinn was certain she could merge deeper with him and lift the sadness from his mind. She could replace the sorrow with feelings of affection and comfort. It would be like another form of persuasion.

"Let me try, Bastian."

"I do not deserve it."

"Do not deserve... what did you do that was so bad?"

He shook his head again and sighed.

"You blame yourself for something... horrible. I can feel it. I know this emotion, Bastian. It will eat away at you. If only I'd done this. If only I'd done that. That kind of thinking will destroy you."

"Too late. I failed to protect someone. Someone that I loved. I... thought I had buried that."

Aislinn swallowed a lump that formed in her throat. With all her special sensitivities she had failed to realize her family was in danger. She had been arguing with Anya over Anya's latest crush. Aislinn had heard the guy was losing himself in drugs. She and Anya were texting each other in the back seat like teenagers so their parents wouldn't know what they were arguing about. They were headed for dinner to celebrate Anya's birthday at their favorite Italian restaurant.

Just as Aislinn had hit SEND and looked up, lights lit up Anya's window. A dump truck the size of a small mountain slammed into them. If only Aislinn had held off arguing, she might have sensed the impending danger and diverted her father who was at the wheel chatting with their mother about work, trusting the green light in front of him. Now, it was too late. They were all gone.

Aislinn smoothed her fingers across Bastian's ear, into his hair, then down his neck. It worked as she intended, disrupting his thoughts, shifting his focus to her.

"Surely pain of the heart could be healed the way you just healed me," she suggested.

"Perhaps it can. I do not know. I cannot heal myself."

"What? Why not?"

He shrugged. "The curse that goes with the blessing, I suppose."

"Seriously? That's so unfair." What an amazing gift he possessed, and yet could not use it on himself? Unable to stop herself, she drew her arms around him and pressed her cheek against his chest, pouring as much love and reassurance into him as she could.

She felt his strong arms curl around her, almost in desperation. He rested his cheek in her hair. For a long while they stood, arms entwined.

Aislinn filled her very being with love and forgiveness and sent the soothing energy to him, over and over in waves. At first she felt his resistance and self-loathing, then she felt him soaking in her affection and positive energy, using it like a medicine to gain control of his sadness. She repeated the process until she felt his muscles start to relax and the air in the room lighten.

With their souls bared and merged, space became inconsequential. Aislinn realized it was not just the emotions of grief, but the intensity of them that was so foreign to him. They had frightened and drained him. How had he buried his sorrows so deep that the memories could not touch him? Was he *that* skilled?

"Let your heart feel light," she whispered. "Let it pass over you. Feel my heart. Feel how much I care. Focus only on that. Whatever happened was before. This is now. What happened was before. This is now," she repeated.

His breathing began to slow and sync with hers. She stroked his back. He stroked her hair.

"You are safe with me. Let the pain go," she murmured. "Let it float away. Breathe with me. We hold it up, and let it go, into the air, to be transformed into something else. All is well. We are together."

Her chanting had become persuasion and they both knew it. But he allowed her. How long they stood that way, she did not know. It felt like hours.

The inn and the street outside grew silent.

At some point, Aislinn felt Bastian's burden ebb and his control return. They continued to breathe together, their chests moving as one, in and out, which added a touch of sensuality that began to electrify the air around them.

"You have been a great comfort to me." He pulled part way out of the hug, but rested his hands on her shoulders, holding her close.

She smiled. "You saved me. It was the least I could do."

"So long." He shook his head. "I have not felt such emotion for so long." His voice lowered to a rough whisper, and his eyes traveled over her face. "Even what I feel for you now."

Aislinn's heart fluttered. He was smitten with her in a way that had nothing to do with gratitude.

"Have you done this kind of healing before?" he asked. Most of the heaviness and sorrow had left his face. Now it shone with amazement.

"No," she answered. "But, I knew I could... well, for you. You understand things. I knew we could work together."

He stared at her with such awe and incredulity that she had to lower her eyes.

"You are a rare jewel, my lady." Slowly, he leaned toward her.

She stopped breathing as he lowered his chin and pressed warm, full lips over hers.

Heat seared through Aislinn's skin, burning from the kiss down to her feet. So much desire rose inside her she reeled from the intensity. His enjoyment of the kiss flowed through her, mirroring her desire. Their joined resonance became so intertwined, Aislinn was not sure whose emotions she was feeling.

With satisfaction and delight, Bastian's rock-hard arms curled tighter, drawing her softness against his firm body. His mouth pressed harder, his kiss deepening. His tongue explored, tasting as though he were starved and could not get enough of her. His breath came faster and heavier.

No man had ever kissed her like that before. With lust, yes, but not with such a whirling combination of desire and reverence. Aislinn's hands slid up Bastian's chest and encircled his neck of their own accord, into his soft hair. How long they kissed in utter enjoyment she did not know, and did not care. Everything about their shared desire felt new, different, otherworldly.

Aislinn could not stop the electric currents pulsing through her enthralled body. She continued to kiss Bastian with a level of inhibition she only felt in dreams. His mouth became more frenzied and forceful. Lights flashed in her brain. So many sensations were coursing through their bodies and minds, Aislinn became confused. Was it him, or her, or both? She was tempted to pull away from their psychic bond just to know what pleasures were hers, and which were his.

Bastian relinquished her mouth to press hungry kisses across her cheek, then to her ear. He whispered, "my lady," with such longing Aislinn forgot why she had wanted to pull away.

His mouth traversed the side of her neck, licking and tasting. She felt her skin come alive under the heat of his mouth. She had always loved kisses on her neck but no other man had taken the time to discover and exploit the weakness. Bastian's ability to read her gave him an advantage and he ravished every inch of her neck the moment he detected her delight. Desire seared through Aislinn's torso, almost painfully. Her breasts were aching for his touch.

Bastian's broad hands roamed over her back and hips, and sent shivers every place they landed. One hand grasped the small of her waist and thrust her pelvis against his, causing delectable throbbing in her groin. Into the softness of her stomach his growing erection pulsed, rigid with need. In complete astonishment, she found herself wanting to satisfy him, and rubbed her body against his, sighing.

When his hungry tongue lapped the hollow of her throat, she tilted her head and moaned. He echoed the sound with a deep rumble in his chest. She had never experience merged sensations on such an empathic, etheric level. What he felt, she amplified. What she felt, he savored and intensified. Every touch was like raw, hot energy being relished and enjoyed, back and forth.

As his tongue traveled downward, his eager hand cupped her left breast as if he couldn't stop himself. His thumb rubbed her nipple through the silky material. Aislinn groaned with pleasure, shocked that she allowed him, shocked that she wanted more.

When his other hand captured her right breast, warm fluid flowed from her womanly core. She had not experienced that reaction in so long she had forgotten how fantastic it felt. How she had missed feeling like a woman.

Not sure how it happened, one strap of her nightgown fell away. Bastian's fingers encouraged it further until her breast and hardened nipple were exposed. He trailed kisses across her breast causing her unbelievable waves of pleasure. She cried out when his lips closed over her nipple. He sucked with a humming growl of pleasure. Aislinn arched her back, certain she would die from the exquisite rapture exploding in her body. They were going too fast but she didn't care. Nothing had ever felt like this, like *him*.

His fingers fell to her thigh and slipped between her legs to curl over her wet, lace panties. Normally, she would never let a man she barely knew get this far, not even after dating for a while. But nothing about Bastian was normal. She did not have to guess what he felt, or debate whether his words or feelings were true. His scorching emotions were loud and unfiltered. Oddly, she sensed concern creeping into him for his uncontrollable passion and desire to merge with her body.

But Aislinn's skin was on fire, craving his touch, aching for it. Nothing she was experiencing with him came close to what she had encountered with other men. Deliciously stinging currents sizzled over her skin and electrified her mind. His very thoughts turned her on. She wanted his hands everywhere. She wanted him inside her, filling her, making them one.

His fingers massaged the silky, damp material while his lips continued their hot stimulation to her nipple. They moaned together.

Aislinn could feel her body rising to climax, faster than ever before. Their joined resonance seemed to be causing the speed with which her body was reacting. Her knees buckled. Bastian held her torso against him with ease. She gripped his white dress shirt for support, wanting to tear it off him.

A stab of guilt washed over Bastian and pushed for space between the waves of passion that was consuming him. What was he doing? She was human. If he wasn't careful, he could harm her. No, he could kill her.

But it had been *so* long. So very long since he felt real passion. Real desire. This was more than needing physical release. He wanted *her*, body and soul. He was losing control over the desperate needy monster that raged in him, and did not want to stop. Like a beast sensing its cage was crumbling, the beast fought for freedom. *Take her. She is yours. You need her.*

No. He *did* have more control than this. He had been tempted before in his long life. His parents had drilled into him the effect he could have on humans and the level of responsibility he was expected to maintain. But, after all these lonely years he had nearly forgotten the wonder of desire and affection. She brought it out in him. She had opened a window and let fresh, spring air into the moldy dungeon of his soul.

Still, he had no right to treat her this way. She understood him, felt compassion for him. She had experienced his surge of buried grief and remorse. Instead of recoiling, she was moved to comfort him. And, she had succeeded in bringing him back to some measure of sanity, giving him hope for peace of mind. No one had accomplished that, though some had tried. Certainly, he had given up years ago.

The depths of his sorrow she had witnessed, but she did not know the depths of his depravity. Would she have the same desire she displayed now when her strong mind searched beyond his grief and found his lust for vengeance that had consumed most of his miserable life?

Could he hold off that moment? Could he enjoy her while she was here in Romania, perhaps convince her to stay?

It was taking such resolve to hide his thoughts while allowing their minds to stay open, so he pulled his energy back with painful regret. Absorbing and magnifying each other's passion had given him greater joy than anything he could remember in decades. If he did not stop, the pressure of their intense desires would need release. She was nearly there. She probably did not know what sensations were hers and what were his. He barely knew himself.

Knowing it was the right thing to do, he focused all his strength of will and removed his hand from between her legs. He felt the protest in her mind. Every part of his body, his very being, screamed for her.

*Bastian, no. Don't stop.* Her plea clawed at his mind and tore his heart.

Her eager fingers began to unbutton his shirt, sensing his decision to withdraw. She pressed warm lips into his chest. *Oh, god.* He groaned with delight. Those cute, sensual upturned lips, touching him, tasting him, so soft and warm. His chest and stomach were on fire, matching his throbbing manhood. So many long-forgotten emotions were awakening in him he could not contain them. The beast roared a challenge.

His resolve to tame the beast crumbled as she thrust his shirt open. Her hands and lips moved down his abdomen. Canines elongated in his mouth.

Against his better judgment, he brushed back her hair and pulled her up, tilting her chin. Still wanting to feel her soft body against his, he crushed her willing curves against him. She closed her warm swollen lips over his. He returned the kiss, relishing the moment, then devoured her neck, pressing his face and mouth into her delicate skin.

Her pulsing veins called to him. With a growl of weakness, he nipped at her neck, wanting to taste her, to claim her. Every touch elicited wanton groans from her. The beast inside was winning. No one else should have her, ever.

~~◊~~

Sharp teeth pierced Aislinn's neck. A small cry of shock escaped her, until the sucking of Bastian's mouth and tongue caused a rapturous euphoria that mesmerized her body and brain.

She had never allowed anyone to bite her before and could not fathom such a thing causing waves of exquisite delight to wash through her like a drug.

A most amazing drug.

She felt dizzy, non-distinct. Delectable, exotic tingles erupted through her limbs. Her body was rising, soaring.

A snarling rumble in Bastian's chest vibrated against hers, which was oddly sensual. Until she sensed the battle raging inside him, the call to retreat. Why was he arguing with himself? The confusion of his mind triggered questions to form in hers, interrupting the rapturous state she was in.

"No, don't stop, Bastian."

"I must," he whispered. His tongue was lapping at her neck, his breath hot against her skin.

With a low moan, he tilted his head back. She could feel his despair at having to let her go. She was like sweet honey to him. He was struggling with a different kind of pain. But why? She was too lost in euphoria to read him.

"Bastian," she pleaded, her eyes half-lidded.

"Aislinn, I want you for my own. Do you feel for me what I feel for you?"

"Yes. You know what I feel. We feel everything."

"Do you freely give yourself to me?"

A tiny voice in a far-away place in her mind urged her to reconsider answering that question. Was she thinking straight? Definitely not. She had never experienced anything like him. And did not want to let him go.

"Yes," she blurted in rebellion before sanity could stop her.

Expecting him to sweep her into his arms, instead, he replaced the strap of her nightgown and re-covered her breast. The backs of his fingers brushed against her skin. She moaned in protest, hoping her voice could call his hands back to her, anywhere, everywhere. She pulled on his arms. His lips brushed across hers while his hands held her face close. She made a soft sound of delight as he kissed her deeply.

"Close your eyes for me, Aislinn." His magnetic voice feathered her synapses like fine silk. She closed her eyes and enjoyed another long kiss.

"Open your mouth to me, Aislinn. Open." His tongue lapped and teased, coaxing her lips to open.

Expecting his tongue, she became disoriented when his finger came into her mouth, warm and wet.

"Taste me," he purred. The low murmur cascaded over her in waves. As if in a trance, her tongue curled around his finger and sucked. The taste was peculiar. She did not immediately recognize it.

"Drink, my love," he whispered.

*Did he say love?*

With her brain going fuzzy as if she were fainting in slow motion, questions she meant to ask would not formulate. He removed his finger and brushed her lips with his.

"Open to me. Again, my love." The command was hypnotic, entreating. His finger came into her mouth again, wet with the odd coppery taste. Though her lips closed over his thick finger, her curiosity fought for control. She tried to force her eyes open.

He kissed her eyelids as they fluttered. "Close your eyes, Aislinn. Swallow."

She obeyed. In mere seconds she began to feel limbless at the sensations exploding in her brain. Concerned at the unnerving confusion in her mind, she found the strength to pull away. She swayed.

"No. Do not pull away from me, Aislinn. Not now. Not ever."

"Bastian, what… what's happening? I'm so dizzy. I can't think." Strong, determined arms were holding her up, which was good because her legs weren't working.

Bastian pulled her toward him and let her cheek rest against his chest. With his arms wrapped around her, he did not want to move. She was the most beautiful, loving and selfless woman he had ever encountered. He had to ensure she could not be taken from him. It would cost him.

He whispered words in his native German tongue to sooth her confused thoughts. With a reluctant sigh, he ran fingers across her shoulder and through her pale, silky hair. So soft. How he wanted to touch every soft, sensual curve, explore with his fingertips, explore with his tongue, his body.

Now was not the time. He had to be sure she knew the risks. He had to be sure she was freely choosing him. Willing the beast to return to its cage with all his strength, he rested his cheek on top of Aislinn's head and kissed her hair.

"Sleep, my golden one."

"What?"

"Sleep. Dream. Be at peace. Sleeeep."

Like a fragile butterfly, her soft body went limp in his arms.

# CHAPTER 6

Aislinn opened her eyes and smiled at the high-pitched chirping of birds, which sounded loud for some reason. She glanced around the quaint wooden room with its colorful flowered tapestries, and remembered she was in Romania.

*Whoa, what a dream.*

With a chuckle, she pushed back her tousled blankets and stumbled across the wooden floor to her suitcase. Erotic dreams were not something she experienced very often. But, *that* was a doozy. Shaking her head and giggling at the ridiculousness of the dream, she gathered her robe and toiletries to clean up in the shared bathroom down the hall.

Giggles still escaped her as she returned and blow dried her hair in front of the antique mirror in her room. Until she noticed two pink dots on her neck. She peered closer.

*No, that's not possible.* She rolled her eyes. *Don't be an idiot. It was a dream.*

Of course it had to be mosquito bites. She had left her window open. They often got her on the neck and exposed wrists and ankles back in the States. Could Romania have mosquitos in October?

She hummed as she dressed in jeans and a dark purple shirt that Anya had given her. The black lace inset at the shoulders and wrists was so Anya. The air-brushed unicorns across the front was definitely Aislinn. Anya had paid a street artist to add the design for Aislinn before gifting it as a birthday present.

After pressing her hands across the painted image and inspecting her reflection in the mirror, Aislinn's eyes burned with moisture and sadness. Her chest tightened. She took several gasping breaths. It was the last gift she would ever receive from Anya.

She inhaled and exhaled several times in a familiar practice to gain control over the stab of grief.

Luckily, her attention was diverted by the mosquito bites. A multi-colored scarf thrown around her neck covered them to her satisfaction. Hearing the rain dancing across her iron-railed balcony, she snapped the hood onto her black, fur-lined coat.

"Whoa." She placed a hand to her stomach. "You're not very happy." With a sigh, she downed a dose of liquid stomach medication to quiet the gurgling irritation.

Finally ready, she braved the stairs. Down was so much better than up. The crisp mountain air and light drizzle chilled her face as she scurried across the graveled road. She paused at the door of Mrs. Tănase's café, drinking in the wonderful smells wafting from the kitchen inside. She rubbed her stomach as it growled again. This was more than irritation. Why was she so hungry and her stomach so touchy? Maybe it was the unfamiliar foods.

With her hand resting on the handle, she took two deep, calming breaths and reached in with her mind. Nothing but the emotional murmur of people enjoying breakfast. No disturbing anger or conflict. Relieved, she pushed open the door and stepped inside. As she suspected, Razvan was nowhere in sight. She was not sure how often he frequented the café. The nightmare she'd had about him seemed so real.

While she devoured a fruit and cheese pastry, she swallowed two pills to keep the ache in her legs at bay. Her left calf was throbbing. At least she was down to only three daily medications now. Her legs might be covered in scars, but she no longer had to use crutches or a cane. *Hopefully not*. She thought about the folded aluminum cane she bravely left in her room.

Sifting through her stack of brochures, she opened her electronic tablet and began to type.

> Well, Anya, where should we go today? It's supposed to be rainy and stormy off and on. Should we wait for the sun to go see Bran Castle, or would it be creepier in dim, misty light? You would probably go for creepy. But I'm thinking sun sounds better. It won't hurt to wait a day.
>
> Besides, my feet and ankles are killing me. I don't know if I can do the stairs. I heard it has secret staircases. My back feels great, though. Much better than yesterday. How about, let's do this market by the Paltinu River. Maybe I'll find something cool to wear to Marius' dinner.

Aislinn's fingers paused. She cringed and felt her insides whirl. Maybe she should create an excuse not to go. Although, it *would* be interesting to find out more about the two cousins. Especially after her outrageous dream. She giggled and started to write about the dream to Anya, but became afraid someone might walk by her table and see the suggestive words. Instead, she minimized the bright document.

~~◊~~

"What did you do?" Marius demanded.

Bastian paused at the foot of the polished staircase. Marius was approaching from the dining room, his hands linked behind him, his eyes narrowed with suspicion. Bastian had forgotten to guard his whirling thoughts, unusual for him. How much had Marius read?

He conjured a scene from Mrs. Tănase's café and pushed the encounter with Razvan to the forefront of his mind. It might work. He had shared blood with the prince when they were wounded in battle on many occasions; their bond was unusually strong. Marius might see past the disguise.

"What are you inferring, my lord?"

"I can smell her on you," said Marius, his voice heavy with accusation.

A hot knife of guilt slashed through Bastian. He marveled at the painful emotion. That, too, was new. Eighty years it had been since he felt guilt, or passion, or anything, except for several hours ago when the unwanted emotions had broken out of their dark dungeon, breathing fire into his heart and soul.

"In fact, I can feel new emotions in you." Marius stepped closer, eyeing the air around Bastian's torso. "Strong ones."

Bastian took a step back.

Marius chuckled. "Look at you. The Fearless Sebastian backing away from me? The intrepid demon and vampire slayer? Bane of all that is unholy?"

Anger burned in Bastian's throat. "You mock me, my lord."

The hint of amusement fell from Marius' face. "You're practically trembling in your boots. That is something I have *never* seen. It does not bode well."

"I am *not* trembling."

"Maybe not in your boots."

"This is not your concern."

"The hell it isn't," Marius warned. "Explain."

Bastian held his breath. How was he going to explain the amazing night? A night with an unforgettable woman. One he just met. One he could not let escape. Though the sun was up, he could not sleep for thoughts of her.

"I rescued her from the attempt of that vermin, Razvan, to molest her. She...." The feel of her skin, the taste of her lips, warmed his body as he remembered. His groin swelled in response. Marius would detect that as well. "She was... grateful."

"That was certainly honorable of you," Marius said with a deceptively stoic tone. "Please accept my praise."

"I am honored." Bastian gave a slight nod, wondering if he would get a reprieve. The hardness of Marius' dark eyes was not reassuring. "If you have no further need of me...."

"You are not dismissed."

Bastian stiffened and breathed slow and steady as he faced Marius. Definitely not a reprieve. Why did he think he could fool him? Marius had been the tribe's leader for three-quarters of a century. They had fought together even longer. Marius' instincts were always on target. As were his judgments. Which was why Bastian had taken the vow to serve under him.

Marius stepped closer. "I have lived long enough to recognize a very distinct scent. The scent of a woman. In womanly places. She was more than grateful, cousin."

Bastian's fingers flinched. Grateful? She nearly gave herself to him. He nearly took her. His cock grew even harder at the thought, protesting the seams of his pants. How he had wanted, no *needed* her sweet luscious curves and warm embrace. His hands could still feel her softness. Her passion still filled his senses. Yet, what they had experienced was much more than that. Something miraculous and unearthly had transpired between them.

"Was she willing?" There was a low threat in Marius' voice.

"Yes," Bastian answered truthfully. "But...."

"Did you persuade her?"

"No, my lord. I would not...."

"Did you *take* her, Bastian?"

"No, my lord." Oh, but how he wanted to.

"Surely, you did not bite her." The flush of red in Marius' eyes and his raspy tone left no doubt what he hoped the answer was. Bastian could not lie to his leader and friend. Marius would detect it anyway. What had happened to him? Guilt raked over his soul with iron claws. Why had he not exerted more control? Holding the woman had fired nerve-endings he had forgotten he possessed, roused passions he had long dismissed as impossible to feel. And the softness of her body....

"Bastian! Did you exchange blood with a human?"

Bastian straightened and faced his prince. "Yes, my lord."

Marius growled low, his eyes darkening. "What have you *done*? I sent you to find out more about her. Not *ravish* her."

"I have been besieged by my own distain for the last eight hours. If you wish to add to that chastisement, then do so."

"Which I should. *And* much more." Marius' jaw clenched. Thunder rumbled low beyond the mountain. The one thing he and Marius had in common. Affecting weather. "You could jeopardize the honor of our tribe," Marius continued. "I will not permit you to do that."

The two glared at each other. Bastian could not remember being in this much trouble. Not with Marius, anyway. Fury surged from Marius so that Bastian's skin felt the burn of it. Yet, he detected a conflict in Marius.

Marius breathed with effort, as if to calm his anger. "How long I have waited, hoped, *prayed* you would find a worthy mate. This is not how I imagined it to transpire."

"Then you hoped for more than I. The idea was dead to me."

"Please tell me she willingly drank your blood."

Bastian hesitated. "Not... entirely."

Marius' eyes widened. "My god, Bastian, you *forced* her?"

"No! She expressed a desire to give herself to me. There was no time to explain... everything just... we experienced something... I do not know how to explain. It was... it just happened. I could not think straight. I had no resistance to her."

Under raised brows, Marius looked stunned, almost amused. "No resistance to a human? A female? You're starting to sound like the gods of Olympus." His eyebrows fell. "How could you be so irresponsible? You know what happens to humans. Did you follow any of the steps? Invoke divine assistance?"

Bastian looked away from his cousin in shame.

"We know nothing of her bloodline, Bastian," Marius pleaded. "You could *kill* her."

"I will *not* kill her. She is strong. And she is gifted. She will not die." In the silence that followed, he added, "She cannot die." He could feel distain radiating from Marius. They had not argued in many years. Decades.

Marius shook his head. "The first woman that truly catches your eye, and all reason leaves you."

Bastian clenched his fists. "I did not... I could not... for so long I have been like a stone, Marius. More the walking dead than a vampire. I felt nothing. Not desire. Not joy. Only hatred for those who turned to darkness and preyed on the innocent. It was my only reason to exist."

"I know." Marius' voice softened. "It says little when miscreants and vampires become your only reason to exist. I have been concerned about you for many years, especially this last one. There was a time when I remembered a smile on your face."

"Do not speak of it."

"Perhaps I should. Before I met my Gabriella, I had lived for many years focused on work and responsibilities. Managing the tribe was my only reason for living. When I found her, I too, struggled with the rush of unfamiliar emotions. I know of its power. It was a constant battle to contain them. My obligations and sense of honor was all that kept me sane. You need to be very careful now. Do not disappoint me in this."

Bastian nodded. If he saw Aislinn again, he doubted seriously that being careful would be prominent in his mind.

"Perhaps if you revisited your feelings for Cecilia."

"No. Not again. Not tonight."

"What do you mean, not again?"

"I will not speak of her."

"Bastian…."

"I will not!" Bastian watched Marius' chin lift at the outburst. But Marius could not understand. Aislinn was not here to deflect Bastian's grief. He dared not risk allowing his memories to unhinge him again.

"If I feel it is what you need to do in order to reign in these foreign emotions and remember…."

"Do not." Bastian felt his canines extend. He struggled to retract them but they would not obey.

Marius' dark eyes glowed as red color bled over the white. His disapproving gaze dropped to Bastian's clenched fist. "You mean to strike me, Bastian?"

"No, my lord. I would never." Bastian's tightened fist had risen a few inches. Even that was an insult to Marius, his prince. Had the blood heat already started?

"See that you do not. You gave me your allegiance freely and you are bound."

"Yes I did, my lord. I have never forgotten. These… new emotions, however, are… strong. My apologies."

"Somehow, I think, someone else is in need of your apology."

# CHAPTER 7

Aislinn realized the insect-like buzzing was her cell phone dancing in her purse. She had not thought to unmute it during the journey back to the Inn. The quaint church near the eclectic little market full of souvenirs, local foods, and expertly embroidered clothing had been the perfect place to visit on a dreary day.

She dropped her coat and purse onto the quilted bed and retrieved the phone. One glance at the display, and she took a deep breath of strength and resolve.

"Hey, Eddie."

"Hey, how's my favorite girl?"

Aislinn snorted. "Yeah, *riiight*."

"You know it's true."

"You know you want me to *think* it's true. How's the new blonde?"

Several seconds passed.

Eddie cleared his throat. "New blonde?"

"Mmm-hmm, the one at The Gemini?"

"The Gem-i-ni?" Eddie said the words slowly as if searching his brain.

"Oh, come on, Eddie," Aislinn replied as if to a twelve-year-old. "Two weeks ago? Well, to help you out, me, Randall, Mia, Scott, and LaVanna, all decided to celebrate. I was off the cane. Randall was walking good on his prosthetic. Mia got her brace off. LaVanna had graduated to a walker, and Scott was along for the ride. Scott wanted to go to The Gemini because he loves to start out in one of those cute little booths with candles and soft music on one side, and then slip over to the noisy bar with the crazy music and dancing on the other side. We ate dinner on the sweet side. And as usual he pulled us all over to the bar. And there you were, in all your glory, slobbering all over some shaggy blonde in a mini skirt."

"Uh… oh. Hey, that was just…."

47

"I mean, look, you've been saying we're more than just friends—even since we broke up. And you *have* been a really good friend to me. You have. But, don't come on like I'm your girlfriend and you've made all these big changes, when you're always going to play, and apparently always with blondes."

"Look, Aisy, that girl was someone I was trying to do business with."

"Hmm, what business would that be?" Aislinn plopped onto the brightly-colored quilt and tugged at her boots.

"No, I mean it, Aisy. She's a client, and she'd had a lot to drink. We got a little cozy, but I was just trying to show her a good time. She's recently divorced and trying to, you know, get back in the game. It was *just* business. A smart business move on my part, actually."

"Yeah, you were puttin' on the smart moves all right."

"Okay, I might have come on a little strong. I admit it. It's been a long time since I had a girl in my arms, you know. And *not* the one I want." He paused for effect, but Aislinn did not respond. "I... probably had a few drinks too many. You know how I am when I drink."

Aislinn did know, and he was the obnoxious type, all strutting and full of himself. When she remained silent, Eddie continued babbling.

"Look, I know you have a thing about people telling the truth. But, she was gone on a flight the next day. And, you're my best friend, more than a best friend, the one I can always talk to. I... I don't want to lose you."

Aislinn felt a tug-of-war begin to rage between her brain and her heart. He *had* been a good friend. Once, he was more. But, when was she going to learn? This was the second time she had seen him with another woman, with her own eyes. Not to mention all the rumors. Friends kept telling her they saw him with another girl, in another city, another restaurant. Right when she would allow herself to feel something for him again. Each time it hurt.

Two months after the accident was the first time she had caught him fondling a blonde at her favorite restaurant in Charlotte. She had officially withdrawn from her classes at the University of North Carolina and moved in with her Gramma and Aunt Julia in Pisgah Forest. Stuck in a wheelchair and sporting two soft casts, she had been resisting Gramma's suggestion to go out for some fresh air. As usual, Gramma won.

At the time, it was disquieting to find an entire world bustling around her, walking, driving, laughing, going about their business as if nothing had happened. Her father, mother, and sister had died tragically, leaving her hollow and devastated. How could the rest of the world not be in limbo like her?

Still, it had been refreshing to get out of the house and breathe cold Autumn air. The air was about to turn foul and tainted. With Gramma guarding her like a sentry, they waited at the curb for Aunt Julia to bring the car around. Aislinn glanced at various people in the parking lot, feeling self-conscious in the wheelchair. It was the amorous couple kissing several cars away that caught her attention. Just like Eddie's car. Just like Eddie's hair. Eddie's body. It could not be him, but it *was* him.

Aislinn's heart had sunk through the pavement at sight of the can't-wait-to-take-this-further caressing. After a night of crying, she dumped Eddie with a phone call, hung up on his excuses, and refused his calls for several weeks. There were only so many sorrows a person could handle.

Why he had continued to call after she ended the relationship, she could not fathom. The first month of calls went to voicemail until he filled it up. She had informed Gramma and Aunt Julia not to allow him into the house. Aunt Julia would have caved, but not Gramma. Gramma threatened to shoot him with grandpa's shotgun if it meant protecting her granddaughter's heart.

Finally, she had answered a call just so she could tell him off—again. Secretly, she hoped he cared so much for her that he just couldn't stay away. A small voice of reason kept warning her never to trust him. Still, he *had* called, after the operations, throughout her recovery, and during her therapy. In a weird sort of way, he *had* become a best friend, always wanting to talk, and prompting her to talk about her progress, even staying on the phone through her tears.

Aislinn glanced out the window at the wrought iron balcony, hoping to see the cat, wondering if she had dreamed it as well. She held the phone to her ear, silent.

"I can't explain it, Aisy," Eddie spoke into the silence. "I just can't bear life without you. You're like my better half. You *are* my better half. And you are more than just a friend. You know I want to be. Now that you're up and about, I'd like to do more things with you. Have fun like we used to."

There it was, the now-that-I-can-show-you-off-because-you're-walking admission. He did not seem to be aware that he had never made the suggestion until now. But she had seen it in his eyes the first time she looked up at him from a wheelchair. *Damaged. Less than perfect.* And that wasn't the worst part. It was the odd way he licked his lips and frowned with worry, almost as if he were afraid because she *was* getting better. She had often mulled over that moment in her mind, trying to make sense of it.

Aislinn took a deep breath. "Two weeks is a long time not to call someone you don't want to lose."

"Aw, come on, Aisy. I am very busy right now. I've got several business ventures going on with my labs, and some new ones with a couple of bars I've invested in. If it wasn't true, would I be worrying about you and wondering if you're okay? I called because I've got a surprise. Are you ready? A week's all-expense-paid tickets to Disney World for two. You've always wanted to go. And you said you didn't want to go in a wheelchair.

Now you don't have to. Come on, let's go. Just you and me. We'll ride rides and see 3-D movies and eat overly-price pizza."

She groaned inwardly. He knew how long she had dreamed of doing that. "Um, that's going to have to wait. I hope the tickets aren't dated."

"What do you mean?" There was surprise and disappointment in his voice. "Are you... turning me down? Please, just hear me out. I can explain everything. I know you're thinking I...."

"Eddie!" she yelled to get him to stop babbling.

"What?"

"I'm in Romania."

Eddie was not one to be short on words, especially since he counted on his smooth talking and quick thinking to charm everyone around him. It was gratifying to stump him twice in the same phone call.

"You're joking, right?" Now his voice held a hint of anger.

"Nope. I'm sitting here at a cute little mountain inn. I'm watching what looks like snowflakes floating by my window. It's Anya, you know. She still does that for me. I think this used to be a house 'cause there's a living room with a fire place downstairs. It's beautiful. A little cold, being October, of course. But, full of adventure so far. Not like I planned, exactly, but...."

"*What?*" he roared.

She jerked, surprised by his anger.

He took a deep, loud breath and seemed to gain control over his anger. "Oh my gosh, I can't believe this. I remember you and Anya always talking about going there. Is that why you went?"

"In a way. One, my best friend was drooling all over another blonde at the one place I decided to go celebrate with my rehab friends. Two, I've got mobility that I didn't have before. And three, me and Anya can finally take the trip we've always wanted to. Actually, there was a four, because I signed up for tour deal subscriptions, and one popped up in my email. So I took it."

Eddie's exhale was loud and shaky. She could not fathom why her trip was so upsetting to him.

"Okay," he began, "one, I'm really, really sorry you got upset over the blonde, and I'm willing to do anything to make it up to you. You name it, I'll do it. Two, I'm very proud of what you've accomplished and that you're walking again. And three, I hope this trip will maybe... give you some peace about... everything that happened. If there was a four, it would be I wish I was there with you."

Aislinn smiled but curled it into a smirk. "I appreciate that, Eddie. Look, I've got to go. I've got to get ready for a dinner this evening. A local family invited me. We can talk when I get back to the States. I got an international deal, but this call's still going to run up my cellphone bill, and...."

"What local family?" His voice was deadly calm.

Aislinn rolled her eyes. "Just some folks I met at a café."

"Should you be trusting them? What's their name?"

"Eddie!"

"What? Why would it matter? I'm not there. What's their name?"

"You know, I'm not going to answer that. You'd probably look them up on the internet and harass them. Or worse, use one of your dad's connections to investigate them."

"Seriously, Aisy…."

"Drop it, Eddie."

"Okay, okay, fine. But, promise we'll talk after the dinner tonight, all right? You'll call me right after?"

"If I can. Bye." Aislinn ended the call before he could give his usual, "Love you, Aisy-girl." She did not want to hear that today.

~~◊~~

An hour and a half later, Aislinn admired her handiwork in the antique mirror. She had pulled one side of her hair up and decorated with an embroidered clasp she bought at the market. She used a curling iron to create draping curls. Most of the clothes she brought were blue jeans, T-shirts, and a few decorative shirts. Thankfully, she had packed two dresses at the last minute on a whim. After switching them back and forth in front of the mirror, she chose the blue one. The nylon blend felt silky on her skin and showed off the right curves, especially her breasts, but was not too provocative for a dinner. Plus, it was mid-calf length, and she could wear tights to hide her scars. Her oversized, cushioned ankle boots would ease her aching feet.

Frowning at the two bug bites on her neck, she donned a delicately embroidered scarf she had purchased at the market. The bright blues, reds and yellows accented her dress perfectly.

With fur-lined coat and gloves in hand, having been warned by Mrs. Tănase that the mountain weather was unpredictable and could get dangerously cold, she labored down the three levels of stairs to the living room and opened the door. At that precise moment, a black BMW with tinted glass pulled up to the curb.

When a tall, blond head exited the driver's side and turned to her wearing dark sunglasses, Aislinn's heart flipped. Though tingles of attraction shot through her limbs, she hoped Bastian was not alone. He stood frozen for a moment, just staring at her. A scowl grew on his face as he rounded the car and opened the passenger door with a gloved hand.

Waiting for a greeting that did not come, Aislinn slid into the front seat and swallowed when she realized no one else was present. She would be

51

alone with Bastian for who knew how long a drive. She hadn't thought to ask Marius where his chalet was. She assumed it was close.

Bastian returned to the driver's seat, his movements fluid as a cat even in the heavy brown coat. To her surprise, he removed the coat once inside the car, and threw it into the back seat. As if in a hurry, he put the car in gear and drove down the winding road, a little faster than he needed to.

Aislinn stole several glances at him, marveling at his buff chest and arms stretching the seams of the long-sleeved white shirt he wore. In her dream he had been wearing a similar white shirt.

"So, this is your car?" she asked to break the silence.

"No, this belongs to my... cousin, Marius." As Bastian drove, his scowl deepened. Sunlight waned and he removed the dark sunglasses, tossing them into a cup holder. Next, he removed his gloves and placed them in the console.

"Am I inappropriately dressed?"

Bastian's silver eyes roamed over her, and then closed momentarily as if he could not handle the sight. "You look... beautiful."

*Huh*, thought Aislinn. *What is up with that?* She had been suppressing anger at his aloof demeanor and decided it needed to blossom. "So, is it customary in Romania when you pick up a beautifully-dressed woman not to say a word to her and look like you just ate rancid meat?"

Bastian flicked his fierce eyes toward her face and back to the road. After a slight flex of his hands he took a slow, deep breath. "It has been a long time since I have been in the presence of a beautiful woman. I... forget my manners."

Aislinn felt somewhat vindicated but could not think how to respond. The green-blue Paltinu River sparkled in the last glimmers of the setting sun as they traveled beside it. The mountainous countryside beyond was breathtaking with its forest layers of green, gold and red. Snow-covered peaks glistened in the distance.

After the silence began to feel strange, Aislinn reached with her mind, anxious to understand Bastian's bizarre behavior. She cringed at the boiling turmoil that met her. Nothing in his rigid face revealed the depth of turbulence whirling in his soul, except for the firm set of his mouth. Beyond the stony demeanor, wild deliberations were battling for space. He seemed ready to explode. How was he masking all those emotions?

His driving, even his breathing, remained constant. She caught a wave of regret, followed by desire, which flipped to anger. Without question, he was feeling strong attraction toward her but seemed to be torn over what to do about it. At least that was reassuring. He did not dislike her.

"Stop zat, voman," he ordered, his accent stronger.

Aislinn caught her breath. "All right, how else am I supposed to find out what's rolling around in your crazy head? And how do you know I'm reading you anyway?"

"Why would I not know?"

She crossed her arms. "Well, why *do* you know? No one knows when I do that. Well, if you're a psychic you might."

"You are psychic?"

"No!" The word came out sharp. Years before, Aislinn had watched a girl at school being bullied because she claimed she was psychic. The girl had been so ostracized that she attempted suicide. Aislinn decided that she would forever keep her abilities a secret. Only Anya and Gramma would know.

Anya had agreed to make a blood vow with her that neither would ever tell. They had made tiny cuts in their palms and slapped them together and made the vow. At the last second, Anya had added, "Unless it's safe one day, if that ever happens." Aislinn had smirked at Anya, not believing such a time would ever be. And here she was, about to admit to a complete stranger that she had the power of persuasion and could read his emotions, perhaps his thoughts. Was *this* that safe day?

"Well, sort of," she decided to add. "I can do things since... well, we won't go there."

"Go where?"

"Never mind."

He stole a puzzled glance at her. "You are human?"

"Excuse me?" She chuckled sarcastically. "Exactly what *else* would I be?"

He did not answer, but his chin rose thoughtfully. "Who does your family hold allegiance to? Where were you born?"

"Um, USA? There's this leader called the President? Of course, we vacation on Mars every year, but we always come back." She did not hold back the mockery in her voice, since where she was born should be obvious from her accent. Marius had acknowledged right away that she was American.

Wisps of fog blew over the vehicle as if a giant was puffing on a cigar and blowing it right at them. The sun's orange glow disappeared, leaving a blanket of darkness descending between the trees that rushed by, lending an air of mystery to the winding road blurring in the headlights.

"And you have always had power?" he asked.

"Power?"

He frowned as if she were a child that should know better. "The ability to touch another's thoughts. To persuade them to do your bidding. And... other things."

Aislinn watched his chiseled face and considered her reply. *Anya, I hope I'm doing the right thing.* "The... persuasion, I've only been able to do really well for about four years. Well, I learned to do it as a teenager. But after the accident it was... kind of enhanced."

She expected him to ask about the accident, but the question did not come. Instead, she felt pressure in her head.

"Hey, *you* stop it, too."

A sly smile curved his lips. It was the closest genuine smile she had seen from him, one that changed his face from brooding to exotically handsome, like his cousin, except more rugged. She watched the smile stay on his face and found herself unable to resist smiling back.

After a few minutes he spoke. "This accident you mentioned disturbs you."

She rubbed her hands over her arms. "I don't like to think about it."

"If you wish, I could take this memory from you. Give you peace."

Her eyes widened and jaw dropped. "What? You can *do* that?"

"Yes."

"No, thank you. And don't even *think* about it."

His brows furrowed. "You wish to hold on to this sad memory?"

"No, not really. But, it's... part of my life. I have to pray about letting it go, a *lot*. But I find that no matter how horrible something is, if you try to bury stuff like that, it just creeps out when you least expect it and takes you down that... dark hole."

She knew the dark hole well. Friends had kept her from wallowing in that bottomless pit of despair by texting, sending pictures, and calling. Gramma and Aunt Julia stood by her as well, though they, too, were grieving. But at night when she was alone, the pit would threaten to swallow her like a giant open maw of despair. Then snowflakes would fall outside her window. Sometimes dust particles would sparkle around her, visible in the moonlight.

Anya reassuring her that she would be okay.

Aislinn took a deep breath. "I'd rather accept that it happened and find a way to rise above the pain. To visualize giving it away, back to God, to turn it into something else. Maybe I can find a way to turn the bad into something good."

"There is wisdom in you."

Aislinn whipped her head toward him. He had said that in the dream. She readjusted her position in the seat and stretched her legs to get the blood flowing. With his mind as sensitive as it was, she'd best not think about the dream in case he picked it up.

The fog thickened to an eerie charcoal gray and billowed around them. Aislinn could not help the unease growing in the pit of her stomach. She grabbed the armrest beside her. Bastian did not seem to have trouble navigating the perilous road. She could barely see it.

A deer on one side raised its head as they approached, but did not bolt. Despite her concern, she smiled as they passed it.

"The deer made you smile?"

"It was curious. Not as alarmed as I would have expected." Her smile dropped as she realized what she confided. She was so used to masking her abilities. With Bastian, her careful guard had lowered. Then again, she could not quell the excitement of being with someone she did not have to hide from. The relief was intoxicating.

"This mountain is a park," Bastian stated. "The animals here are protected. You speak to animals?"

*Ugh.* To lie or withhold the truth. How much should she reveal to him? Obviously, his mental talents were stronger than hers, so he must be familiar with touching the minds of animals.

"You seem to know what that's like." She tested him.

"For me, it is normal. For you, it should not be."

"And, why not?"

"Because you are human."

Aislinn felt a chill graze her skin. "And you're not?"

He glanced at her and back to the road. "I am as human as I will ever be."

"Somehow, I doubt that."

He raised one eyebrow. "And what do you think I am?"

"Well, *one*, since you've indicated that I am human, that infers that you are not. Two, that means you are something else, or part something else, maybe an alien hybrid. Three, since you're cold as an ice burg, and don't appear to have normal emotions, except for the ones exploding in your head like fireworks, which you are trying to *hide* by the way, I'd say android is a serious consideration. Obviously, your emotion program's gone wonky."

At first his face wrinkled into a puzzled scowl, but a slow smile took over. "Do all Americans speak like you now?"

"Oh, they're much worse. Sarcasm is pretty much the norm for us. You've been to the U.S?"

"Twice."

"Hmm, sounds like it didn't compute for you."

"Compute? Ah, yes, you did say android."

"I'm considering it."

"Did you consider it last night?"

Aislinn froze. She was unable to breathe. It wasn't possible. *It was a dream.* Her chest tightened.

"Last night?" she repeated.

"Do you remember last night?" His forehead wrinkled with concern.

"That wasn't a dream? You... you were really in my room last night?" She willed him to deny it, to wonder what she was talking about. But his silvery gaze landed on her neck, and then her breasts, before refocusing on the road.

*Oh yeah, that look was unmistakable.*

"I thought... I thought, for sure, it was a dream," she almost whimpered. She swallowed hard.

"Have you ever shared the same dream with someone?"

"Shared the same... what? Wait a minute, were you there, or weren't you?"

For a moment he did not answer. He took a deep breath as if deciding how to proceed.

"We were there," he said quietly. "Together."

He turned onto a dirt road. The forest seemed to close in on them.

Aislinn's stomach twisted. Her arms grew cold. Everything they did... he did... *she* did.

"But... why can't I remember it clearly?" she asked, perplexed. "Did I dream the part about Razvan?"

Bastian's face darkened, his mouth curling into a snarl. Through clenched teeth he said, "That vermin."

"Oh my god, you really almost killed Razvan? And that creep was going to rape me?"

Fierce anger radiated from Bastian with such force that Aislinn recoiled against the window. Pressure built up in the car.

"That man's thoughts were perverted and criminal. Filthy human. I should have killed him. You should not have interfered."

Aislinn forced herself to breathe. Her heart was thumping wildly. She noticed Bastian's accent had gotten stronger as his anger rose.

"Okay, not that he didn't deserve it, since he really did try to rape me and all, but...." She could not finish the sentence. The memory of Bastian's strong hands effortlessly holding Razvan's heavy frame up against the wall, the cold desire to kill flashing in his frosty eyes, made her breathing break into shaky gasps.

"I used too much power last night," he stated matter-of-factly. "You have forgotten much. Be calm. Your heart is pounding."

"How do you know what my heart is doing?"

"I can hear the song of blood rushing through your veins. Your life force fills this car." He said it wistfully.

Aislinn reverted to holding her breath again. She had never heard anything so oddly romantic and so utterly terrifying at the same time. She opened her mouth to tell him to take her back to the Inn, but the car came to a gravel-crunching stop.

She gasped and scanned the area, afraid he had merely parked on the side of the road. A warm, glowing lantern atop a black pole parted the gray fog and cast a golden hue across a rounded brick porch with manicured shrubs on either side.

Aislinn forced herself to breathe slower as she leaned forward to get a view of the enchanting house. Fall flowers still decorated the window ledges. Ivy crawled up one wall, still bright and green. Wooden shutters were held open by latches. She wanted to stare at the house and take in every inch of its rustic charm. But she also did not want to exit the car. It felt safer to remain inside. Cold air chilled her face, startling her. Her door had opened and a pale hand waited, palm up, for her to take it.

Her eyes traveled up Bastian's black dress pants and snug white shirt as they rose to meet his intense, ghostly stare. There was something possessive in the way he held her gaze. Her hand slipped into his. He pulled her up, nearly against his firm body. He appeared not to want to move. Aislinn felt his mind open to her, inviting her to enter. He was remembering last night.

His recall of her replayed in vivid detail. Her body warmed as she felt his desire surge in response to the memories.

All day, what she thought was a dream, had really happened. *What I wouldn't give to repeat that.*

Aislinn found herself fighting the urge to rise on her toes and kiss him. She swayed, unable to look away from those hungry, possessive eyes. His body was a mere three inches of air away, waiting to be touched.

What was wrong with her? She had never reacted like this to any man, so uninhibited, so wanton. Maybe that was it. He had nearly implied that he wasn't human. Maybe he wasn't. But what, then? Using some voodoo charm? She needed to get ahold of herself. He wasn't safe for her to be with. Not with her body making its wishes known, and her unable to control it.

His hand still held hers. The other fell to her waist. His fingers gripped tight. Yearning sparked in his eyes. His lips parted. He was breathing faster, his breath frosting in the air. She leaned toward him, closing the gap.

Lights from another vehicle flashed across their faces. Aislinn broke away from Bastian and smoothed down imagined wrinkles in her black coat.

Marius descended the porch steps. "Wonderful. Everyone is here."

# CHAPTER 8

Aislinn stiffened as power screamed through her body from Marius' hand on her shoulder. "Miss Thomas," he said, propelling her up the stairs and over the threshold before she could protest, "may I introduce my wife, Gabriella."

Once inside, Aislinn sighed with relief as Marius withdrew his hand in order to turn and greet the arriving guests. Gabriella shook Aislinn's hand and covered it with hers. The touch projected instant calm over Aislinn's fragile nerves. The bright-eyed woman was the same height of five foot five with a kind, heart-shaped face, vivid green eyes that seemed to pulse with light, and porcelain skin framed by burgundy-red hair that reached just past her shoulders.

There was something about the happy way Gabriella smiled at Aislinn, as though she was a sister she had just discovered, that caused Aislinn to feel at home. Gabriella handed Aislinn's coat to a young woman wearing an apron.

Bastian stepped to Aislinn's side as if on guard while introductions were made to the Mayor of Valea Doftanei, Nicolae Gavrila, and his wife, Elisabeta, followed by the mayor's brother, Lucian Gavrila. Marius then introduced his nephew, Dimitri, who rushed into the foyer, smelling of cold air. Aislinn happily shook everyone's hand, though she found Lucian's hungry scan of her clingy dress to be disconcerting.

Having been advised by Sergiu to wait to be seated when invited to a Romanian's home, Aislinn hovered while Marius took his place at the head of the table and Gabriella seated Elisabeta on his left and the mayor on Marius' right. Gabriella sat on the mayor's right and tapped the seat to her right for Lucian.

"Please," Gabriella turned to Aislinn, "feel free to choose a seat, Miss Thomas."

"Allow me," said Dimitri. He took Aislinn's arm, rounded the table and was about to place her between himself and Elisabeta, when Bastian's powerful arm slipped across her shoulders and steered her away. He elbowed Dimitri into the seat on Elisabeta's left. Bastian pulled out a chair for Aislinn at the end of the table opposite Marius.

Not wanting to be presumptuous since the mayor was certainly the guest of honor, Aislinn grabbed the empty chair at Dimitri's left, which positioned her between Dimitri and Bastian. Bastian scowled but took the remaining seat opposite Marius. He glared at Dimitri as if giving him an unnamed warning.

Aislinn wished Gabriella was seated closer to her. She could use some of the calm she felt when near her. Especially since Bastian and Dimitri were shooting silent daggers at each other.

Dimitri was handsome and charming but with a twinkle of mischief in his aqua-blue eyes. Aislinn marveled at his striking eye color, so like the pure water along a Gulf Coast beach she once visited. With a quick scan, she realized everyone in the family had unusually vivid eyes, as though tiny pixel lights gave them an electronic glow. Even the white portion of their eyes was striking. Marius' ebony eyes, though dark in color, possessed the same brilliance, reflecting the flickering candlelight like polished obsidian. The mayor's family, however, did not appear to carry the odd radiance.

Aside from eye color, Dimitri resembled Marius in facial features and possessed the same inky-black hair, though significantly shorter. Like both of his male relatives, Dimitri was fit, muscular, and possessed an air of charisma that kept Aislinn intrigued as he whispered comments to her during louder conversations.

Realizing this behavior irritated Bastian, Dimitri seemed determined to aggravate Bastian all the more, increasing his low quips to Aislinn. Bastian cleared his throat several times and dictated whispered words to Dimitri in a warning tone in what sounded like Swedish or German. Aislinn felt like she was in the middle of a feud. Their heightened emotions were causing her shoulders to tighten. Fortunately, the teenaged girl, along with an older woman, began to serve appetizers of chopped tomatoes and sausages covered in a warm, soft cheese.

Aislinn breathed in the amazing aroma, and nearly moaned. No food she could recall had ever smelled so fantastic. She must be really hungry. She fought an uncharacteristic desire to scoop all of the delectable morsels off the plate and stuff them into her mouth.

Instead, she closed her eyes with every bite, savoring the individual tastes. When her eyes opened she caught Gabriella's gaze shift from her to Bastian with a hint of amusement. Her brows rose toward Bastian as if in reprimand.

Their unspoken communication unnerved Aislinn and she lowered her eyes to observe the beautiful white tablecloth embroidered along the edges with flowers, vines and lace. Everywhere in Romania, the breathtaking embroidery caught her eye. She wanted to bring all of it home with her.

The tall candles in the center of the table highlighted the wine goblets bedecked with brush strokes of brightly colored glass. Mesmerized by the effect, Aislinn decided she might have to obtain a set, though she would have to pay to have them shipped since putting the goblets in her suitcase would not be feasible.

She found herself adoring the sound of everyone's voice and accent, especially Mayor Gavrila's as he happily embellished on all his accomplishments in Valea Doftanei and his plans for the future. He was balding and rotund, but full of energy and ideas. His equally energetic and rotund wife allowed his command of the conversation as long as she got to constantly interrupt him with her rendition of whatever story he was telling.

Their competition was amusing and endearing, and a welcomed diversion from the tension between Bastian and Dimitri.

Bowls of thick, dark broth full of onions and vegetables were served and Aislinn breathed in the tantalizing aroma. Clinks from glasses and utensils, conversations from the kitchen, even the movement of clothing was becoming alarmingly crisp to Aislinn. Her hearing had never been so acute. She wondered if it had something to do with the high elevation, or the mountains themselves.

The mayor's brother, Lucian, stared greedily at her which added to her discomfort. She wanted to be friendly, but every glance his way produced more of his attention on her. She tried to block out his loud, lustful emotions, but failed miserably. Her empathic abilities had become amplified, as if they had grown overnight. Aislinn felt like a giant vessel filling with sounds, smells and feelings. She entertained the idea of going outside in the cold just to shake off all of the unwanted input.

Fury radiated from Bastian each time Lucian's gaze swept over Aislinn. She could feel it without even looking at him. Several times she observed Bastian's hands clench around his napkin or silverware, relax, then clench again. His reaction was exciting in a new and disconcerting way. For a brief, and very bizarre moment, Aislinn found herself waiting for Lucian's inviting stare just to experience Bastian's reaction. She took a deep, slow breath and let it out, wondering what in the world was wrong with her. She had never been *that* kind of girl.

Eddie had never cared if any man regarded her. Salacious looks from other men seemed to give Eddie more satisfaction, more of an I-have-her-and-you-don't sense of pride. Bastian looked ready to pulverize Lucian, and punch Dimitri, who continued to whisper comments about the various dishes served, and about each person at the table, especially Bastian.

Aislinn tried not to react to Dimitri's wisecracks, but he was so amusing it became more difficult with each murmured retort.

The two servers reappeared with bowls of stewed beef, steamed potatoes and carrots, topped with cornmeal porridge and a dollop of sour cream. The teenage girl's long, curly black hair was swept back in a brightly embroidered, triangular scarf. Her gray-green eyes were not as vivid as Bastian's family, but possessed a similar alertness and magnetism. Aislinn found herself wishing to get to know her. The girl smiled while serving Dimitri, and it was clear that they knew each other. However, as the girl rounded the table to serve Lucian, her face became a mask in response to Lucian's suggestive smiles and perusal of her body. She nodded to his thank you but did not return the smile.

Dimitri whispered so softly his lips barely moved. "There he gooooes. Epic fail, dude."

Aislinn coughed into her napkin to disguise a laugh. Her stomach muscles continued to spasm from a chuckle, so she dove into the new dish to distract herself.

Bastian cleared his throat again, directed more at Dimitri than her. But when she made the mistake of looking directly at him, electricity crackled in her body and she felt spellbound. The hair on her arms rose. Her body warmed all over as if hot chocolate had been infused into her veins.

Bastian seemed unable to look away as well. His gaze shifted to her neck, and then to the bodice of her dress. Immediately, her breasts ached for his touch. She forced her eyes to shift away from him. She inspected the food on her plate to make sure she had not eaten shrimp or chocolate. What was going on with her body to react so carnally to a man she barely knew? Was it simply natural charism on his part, or some strange magic in the house, maybe even the family?

Vague scenes from her tryst with Bastian began solidifying into colorful snippets of memory, causing her a new kind of discomfort. What they had experienced was more intimate and special than lust, but lust was what she was feeling now. The curve of the table's corner had become too far a distance for her. A force pulled her body toward his. For the barest second, she visualized her and Bastian sneaking off into an upstairs room after the meal. She berated herself for the carnal image.

Another glance at Bastian proved to be a mistake. The longing in his pale eyes nearly took her breath away.

The sudden presence of the young girl beside Aislinn disrupted her trance. Side dishes of a green and an orange vegetable puree, and cabbage rolls stuffed with rice and pork, were being added to the table. She felt obligated to try each dish, but found she was devouring her portion at incredible speed. She deduced it must be because she was so nervous. She noted that the mayor and his wife ate heartily, but Dimitri and Bastian consumed very little of the beef, potatoes and cabbage rolls, which was puzzling since they were delicious.

Marius attempted to keep pace with the mayor in discussions concerning village matters and the politics of Romania. Aislinn was surprised to find that disapproval of political parties, especially the one in power, appeared to be universal.

"What brings you to Romania, Miss Thomas?"

Aislinn nearly choked, realizing she was being address by Mrs. Gavrila. She had been happy to listen to everyone else talk since she was still reeling from the discovery that everything she had dreamed last night actually took place. Crackling with intensity, her body seemed to be stuck in the "on" position, pulsing and burning with amplified desire every time she looked at Bastian, even if his attention wasn't on her.

"Please, call me Aislinn," she managed to say.

Mrs. Gavrila smiled.

"Well, um…." Aislinn swallowed, deciding to tell the truth, at least some of it. "My sister and I had planned to visit Transylvania someday. We actually grew up near Transylvania County in North Carolina, and had always said we would go to the original Transylvania one day. My sister was very Goth. And obsessed with vampires." She rolled her eyes playfully.

From the other side of the table, the Mayor exclaimed, "Yes, our vampires are quite the tourist attraction! We must keep them alive and well. Or, dead and well, is that, my dear?" He shot a teasing look at his wife.

Mrs. Gavrila roared with laughter.

Aislinn detected the barest touch of irritation from Bastian's direction, though she was focused on Mrs. Gavrila. It surprised and intrigued her.

"Oh, you." Mrs. Gavrila waved at her husband. "Although, not everyone agrees, and some will tell you it is utter nonsense. Do not let my mother catch you talking about vampires. She tells stories of the most awful things from my grandmother's day. Bodies being dug up… well, I won't talk about it here at the table. But, with many of the old folks, it's a very serious subject."

"Oh," Aislinn replied, surprised. "Well, I had planned to visit Bran Castle and learn all about Vlad the Impaler today, but rain got in the way." Aislinn made a slight sad face. "So, maybe tomorrow."

"Your sister, did she not accompany you tonight?"

Aislinn licked her lips nervously. Her cheeks grew hot. "In a way. She, um, passed away a year ago."

Everyone at the table froze. Aislinn swallowed at the stares.

"Oh, I am so very sorry to hear of this," said Mrs. Gavrila with absolute sincerity.

"Thank you." Aislinn hastily grabbed her glass of wine and took a long swallow.

"I think it is wonderful you followed up on the dream," Mrs. Gavrila offered.

Aislinn nodded, touched by the woman's insight. Burning tears threatened to escape the rims of her eyes. "Yes," she managed to say. "I felt it was important to follow our dream. And... here I am. I write to her every day. To Anya. It gives me comfort and helps me feel connected."

"Do you know, I did the same with my grandmother?"

"Really?" Aislinn felt instant relief.

"Yes, I did. And I kept it a secret for years. Many people I know feel we should not presume to contact those who have passed, and should assume them to have moved on to new adventures on the other side in places where we cannot reach them. But I found great comfort in writing to my grandmother, and often felt her presence. Even now at times I still do. I understand you completely."

"Thank you so much," Aislinn replied, blinking furiously to push back tears. "That means a lot. And you are right, not everyone can understand. This is our trip together. Me and Anya. Although, I haven't gotten very far. Just two days."

"We are delighted to have you visit. Do ask us about any of the sights you are planning to tour. We can give you advice on the best time to go. And if you have any trouble getting into Bran Castle, let me know. I'll get you in." Mrs. Gavrila offered a wink. "I know the wife of the mayor of Transylvania quite well."

"Thank you. That's very sweet of you."

A broad hand came across her left forearm and squeezed. She flinched slightly in surprise, but the sympathy and protectiveness emanating from Bastian was comforting. She had not felt comforted and protected since... well, since last night.

Her skin under his hand felt like sparklers had been lit. She marveled at her body's instant reaction to the man's touch. Though it was only his hand, somehow sensual magic flowed through him in that simple connection. Her gaze trailed along the stout curve of his muscled arm and lingered over his powerful shoulders and chest. Her body quivered in response.

When her eyes locked with Bastian's, she froze, entranced. Mrs. Gavrila laughed at something Lucian was saying, and Aislinn blinked several times, regretting having to sever the connection with Bastian. She did not want to appear a brazen flirt at the table. *I so need to lay off the wine.*

Lucian was asking her something about her familiarity with the Brancusi family, and Aislinn straightened. Lucian watched Bastian slowly removing his hand, then his eyes shifted to Dimitri. Aislinn had the odd feeling that Lucian had decided she was his next target, and was determining whether the two men on either side of her could be in his way.

"Oh, um, I met Mr. Brancusi and Mr. Radescu just yesterday morning," said Aislinn in answer to Lucian's inquiry.

When Lucian's brows rose, Aislinn added, "But already they feel like family to me."

A wave of power swept across the table. Aislinn inhaled at the sudden wave permeating through her arms and chest. She hunched her shoulders in reaction. Oddly enough, the wave seemed to have been generated from Marius.

Lucian did not appear to be affected. He smiled. "You must allow me to take you on a tour of Bran Castle tomorrow. I know all the secrets. I could take you places the other tourists are not allowed to go."

"Actually," Dimitri interjected, "Bastian and I were planning to take her tomorrow." Aislinn whipped her head toward him. "But," Dimitri added with a cunning grin, "you are welcome to tag along. The more the merrier, I always say."

Lucian attempted a short smile but his eyes did not engage. "I did not realize she had plans. However, Miss Thomas, there are *many* wonderful sites to see in Romania. You must visit the Black Sea. The water is quite famous for its medicinal properties. I have a boat I keep near Constanta. We could visit the beach."

So much protest emitted from Bastian that it stung Aislinn's left side as it radiated outward.

"Actually, Lucian," Marius spoke up, waiting for Lucian to look at him, "Miss Thomas will be busy with several tours she has booked in the area this week." Aislinn turned toward him in surprise but his eyes were holding Lucian's. "Your invitation is generous and appreciated, but will not be necessary." He glanced at Mr. and Mrs. Gavrilla on either side of him, and then reengaged Lucian. His voice became melodious and hauntingly captivating. "Miss Thomas is quite busy and will not be available this week." The words echoed soft and deep in the air. For a moment, the three guests did not blink or move.

Aislinn's mouth fell slightly open. Marius had actually used persuasion on three people, brazenly in front of her. With a single glance in her direction, Marius was instructing her not to disagree or question him. For a split second, Aislinn experienced awe at his ability to focus on three distinct people at the table, which changed to fear, then pooled into anger. Who was he to tell her what she was going to do, or with whom?

"So how are the October crowds this year?" Marius asked Mayor Gavrila.

The mayor blinked and launched into a discussion on tourism, emphasizing his fortuitous decisions that were encouraging more of it.

Aislinn glanced around the table with unease. Gabriella was watching her as if gauging her acceptance of Marius' command of the situation. Aislinn swallowed a hard lump that felt stuck in her throat.

"You smell like the beach," Dimitri whispered low.

Aislinn gave a slight start at the sound of his whisper. She turned to him and found herself relieved by the playful twinkle in his eyes. She barely moved her mouth in reply, whispering low so the mayor would not be offended.

"Um, probably my cocoa butter lotion. I love the smell."

"Mmm, me too. I love the beach. Mostly at sunset, though, when the heat's down."

"Yeah, me too," Aislinn responded with a nervous smile.

Dimitri leaned toward her and pointed at the salt for another excuse to whisper, "By the way, what time should we pick you up for that tour of Bran Castle? We need to go early to get tickets, isn't that right Bastian?"

Bastian took a deep breath and let it out slowly, as if to calm himself. "I would prefer to take her myself."

Aislinn marveled that Bastian had heard Dimitri's question, since she could barely hear him herself. She ate the last bit of her potatoes and washed them down with a swig of wine, then pretended to watch the mayor talk. It seemed the safest thing to do at the moment.

"Oh, no." Dimitri's hissed words held a mocking edge. "I meant *we*. You would bore her to tears."

Aislinn jumped in her seat as Bastian's anger assaulted her senses. She looked at him, alarmed. He was staring at Dimitri with murder in his eyes. Aislinn could not believe Dimitri was giggling low beside her. She turned to Dimitri and squinted her eyes to convey anger.

Dimitri raised mocking eyebrows at her. "Now, that's truly frightening. I'm quivering here."

She pursed her lips and exhaled noisily to make the point that he needed to stop. He tried in vain to suppress a grin, and turned toward the Mayor as if suddenly interested in his story about his wife's Persian cat having a litter of kittens. The Mayor asked Gabriella if she would like one.

"That's very kind of you to offer," said Gabriella. "I am afraid Marius will only allow one cat in the house, a large male tabby we've had for a while now."

Aislinn dropped her fork onto her plate with a loud clatter. She mumbled an apology. *The cat on the balcony.* Shining silver eyes. Had Bastian followed her last night and the cat followed him? Was the cat his? How *did* Bastian get into her room last night? *No, don't think about it. Don't consider it.* She focused on the Mayor's voice, but her mind could not stop racing with possibilities.

*Not human.*

Concern brushed across the front of her body. Her eyes found Bastian's. He had sensed her panic and wanted to sooth her anxiety. Heat flushed her cheeks as she recalled scenes of the heart-pounding passion they had shared. The most amazing experience of her life. Not just feeling her own desires, but sharing someone else's merged with hers and magnified. Bastian's warm embrace, the kisses, and…. She looked away and forced her breathing to slow. Deciding to be brave, she leaned toward him and felt the hair on her arms rise at his proximity.

"How did you get into my room last night?" she whispered as low as possible so that Lucian across from her could not hear. She felt Bastian's mental wall come up. He did not want her to know.

"Perhaps I should explain at a more opportune moment." He kept his voice just as soft, his lips barely moving.

"A simple answer, that's all I need. Did you climb up a staircase or… leap a balcony?"

His pulsing silver eyes held hers, and she waited. Neither moved. Aislinn's heart began pumping faster. Somehow, she knew his heart was pounding as well. She wanted to drink him in, merge with him like two separate flames becoming a roaring fire. If only everyone else would leave. Her skin was burning. Her nipples hardened and moisture pulsed between her legs.

So not like her. She had become a stranger to herself. She was the good girl, the one who wouldn't even kiss on the first date. Well, except for Eddie, whom she had not been able to resist.

Bastian's lips parted, his voice still a hushed whisper. "I suppose leaping a balcony would be the closest answer. Does that frighten you?"

Him leaping a balcony? No. Afraid she might forget where she was, afraid she might kiss those warm, luscious lips at the dinner table and make a fool of herself? Yes.

Aislinn pulled away, her eyes still on him. Desire twinkled in his frosty gaze as he opened his mind to read her racing emotions, and allow her to detect his rising desire. The moment he inhaled, Aislinn knew he had scented where she had gotten wet. How that was possible, she did not know, but she was certain his olfactory senses were as amplified as his other abilities.

And, he was pleased.

His mind shifted to memories from the night before. As if in a dream, through his eyes she watched him basking in her comfort and caring, profoundly amazed and grateful. He had leaned in to kiss her, an all-encompassing desire and need driving him further.

She blinked. How could she be so merged with him that she could view *his* recall of her? This could put having sex on a whole new strange, kinky level.

Unnerved, she swallowed and forced herself to face forward, which was almost painful. She turned her attention to the head of the table. Gabriella had been watching. So had Marius. They coyly averted their eyes to the mayor.

In that moment Aislinn realized Dimitri was also watching her with heightened interest, as if he was completely aware of the whispers she had exchanged with Bastian and the desire heating and crackling in the air between them. She hoped he did not have Bastian's enhanced sense of smell. Her cheeks grew warmer at the thought.

With another rough clearing of Bastian's throat, Dimitri returned to scooting food around on his plate, which Aislinn had noticed before. She watched him bring his napkin to his mouth and saw something dark in the center of his napkin. He had eaten some of the cheese, most of the soup and vegetable purees—everything except the meat and stuffed cabbage. For a young man of twenty-something, that was light eating. She supposed he could be a vegetarian.

Hoping he could not sense her curiosity, since he was part of this strange family, she watched him take another bite of food, chew, then lift the napkin to his mouth. Aislinn caught her breath. Dimitri definitely pushed the food with his tongue into his napkin which he balled up. As he lowered it to his lap, Aislinn began to feel real fear. Why would Dimitri bother to pretend he was eating solid food? Old conversations Aislinn and Anya had shared together about vampires blossomed in her brain.

*Not human.*

Icicles snaked through Aislinn's limbs. Bastian had told her very little about himself, unlike most men who incessantly chattered about themselves. His body had been completely covered under the blaring sun when he picked her up, the garments being discarded when night fell, though it was cold. He had a German-like accent but aside from being Marius' cousin, and his years of burying debilitating grief, Aislinn knew nothing else. She tried to disguise her apprehension by breathing steady. Then she remembered the marks on her neck.

Her mouth went dry. She was afraid to sip any more wine. *No, no, no. It can't be. It's the Adams Family—vampire version. This whole dinner could not be a well-orchestrated sham. It just couldn't be.*

The mayor chatted away, but Aislinn was oblivious to what he was saying. Peripherally and in her mind, she could tell Bastian's attention was on her. He had sensed her alarm. Curiosity and concern radiated from him. She also felt it from Dimitri. But, how did Dimitri know what she was feeling?

~~◊~~

Bastian noted Aislinn was staring at her plate, but no longer eating. Fear billowed around her like a dark cloud. And it was growing.

*Bastian,* Dimitri thought to him, *I think she spotted the meat in my napkin.*

*I feel her fear,* Bastian replied with regret. *Her heart is racing.*

*Dimitri,* Marius' mental voice was sharp. *You should have been more careful. She was curious but now is afraid. I do not want a scene at this table. Bastian, speak to her. Calm her fears.*

*She is afraid, but she restrains herself.* Gabriella's voice joined into the mix through Marius' connection. *She remains a lady, if nothing else. She will not cause a scene if she can avoid it. Dimitri, take your napkin to the kitchen. You have got to work on your telekinesis. That food should be in the trash can.*

*Hmm, this girl gets more interesting all the time.* Dimitri smirked at Bastian. *Are you sure you like her, Uncle? Because, I'm just thinking....*

*Do not incur my wrath, boy. She is not one of your shallow acquisitions. She is a frail human. I could kill her with a hug.*

*But, you don't want to kill her, do you Uncle Bastian? In fact, killing her is the last thing on your mind right now.*

~~◊~~

Whispers of a conversation brushed Aislinn's mind. She stole a glance at Bastian, who was glaring at Dimitri. Aislinn turned to observe Dimitri who, with a total lack of concern, was casting Bastian a playful challenge. He averted his eyes at her scrutiny. Were they speaking telepathically? She was certain of it. If so, these people possessed amazing abilities that truly transcended what she knew of psychic gifts.

Aislinn regarded Marius and Gabriella. Marius' expression was one of parental stiffness, his gaze stern toward both Bastian and Dimitri. His attention returned to the mayor, who continued to chatter, unaware of the tense undercurrent at the table.

What excuse could Aislinn produce in order to leave the dinner? She had no idea where she was, and had allowed herself to be brought in Marius' car. She realized the folly of her absolute trust. She could always use the GPS on her phone, and call a cab.

"Mayor Gavrila," she asked as the mayor stopped to take a sip of wine. "I was curious, do you and your wife live nearby?"

"Fairly close, actually," he replied. "It is about a forty-five minute drive to our estate in Valea Doftanei.

"That town is near me. I am staying at an Inn along the river in Teşila."

"Why, that's only about fifteen, twenty minutes from our home, depending on which road you take."

"Oh, that's wonderful."

"I do love driving up this way with the scenic Bucegi Forest and the mountain roads," the mayor interjected. "My wife prefers the safety of the valleys."

"I do indeed," Mrs. Gavrila agreed.

Fingertips alighted on Aislinn's knee under the table. Instantly, raw currents seemed to singe the skin up her thigh. To her complete shock, her left leg actually leaned into Bastian's touch of its own accord, a magnet finding its perfect polarity. Aislinn jerked it back, terrified at the urges overtaking her.

*Aislinn, do not leave with them.* Bastian spoke directly into her mind, the words clearer than any she had ever heard. In the past, emotions she detected from people often blurred into thoughts. But this was different. Clear. Precise.

Aislinn inhaled in surprise, her chin shaking. She stiffened and managed to contain her shock. She stared at the dishes in front of her, afraid to look at him. Hearing him with such clarity was incredible and exciting, until she realized he had given her an order. His abilities were alarming her by the minute. Even so, who was he to tell her what to do?

"My poor Elisabeta," said the mayor. "She gets motion sick, so she does not enjoy the mountain drives as much."

"*Oooo*, those winding turns!" Mrs. Gavrila placed a hand to her stomach. "Last week we attended a dinner in Bucharest, and Nicolae was driving too fast, and…."

"I was not." The mayor brandished an indignant but mischievous smile.

"Yes you were. When we arrived, I had to request a shot of brandy to settle my nerves. And I do not even *like* brandy!"

Everyone chuckled.

Aislinn decided to show Bastian he was not giving her orders.

"So, I had thought of riding with you to the inn to save Mr. Radescu the trouble, although it sounds like I might be losing my dinner on poor Mrs. Tănase's doorstep."

Mrs. Gavrila roared with laughter.

"Now, Miss Aislinn," Mayor Gavrila began, "I assure you I would do my best to expunge my reputation and deposit you safely at the inn. Of course, if I do not, my good wife might kill me, so I would be doubly motivated."

Mrs. Gavrila giggled and rolled her eyes at her husband.

"Perhaps, I should drive," Lucian suggested. His eyes were boring through Aislinn. "You will be in good hands, I assure you."

"Yes, perhaps you should," Mrs. Gavrila agreed. "Lucian always drives slow for me."

"He does not." Mayor Gavrila argued. "I've seen him take mountain curves on two wheels."

Lucian grinned, his eyes shifting from his brother to Aislinn. "Do not listen to him. I was eighteen then."

*Aislinn, do not leave with him. I insist.* Bastian's mental voice was stronger.

Aislinn smiled at Lucian to be polite, and swallowed hard. The table was trembling under her fingers. Only then did she remember a similar sensation from the night before. She looked into Bastian's eyes.

*Do not tell me what to do.*

A slight lift of his chin revealed her attempt at telepathy worked. Her breath caught in her throat at the ferocity and ownership in Bastian's pale, otherworldly eyes. The light gray irises shimmered into glass-like prisms. The whites took on pink tones. She wanted to turn away but could not. Every part of her wanted to be lost forever in that wraithlike gaze.

Sounds in the room faded for a moment. Her heart pounded, the beats painful against her ribs. The desire to launch herself at him burned in her torso. She could not believe she had to suppress the twitching of her limbs toward his. Her willing body had become her enemy. How was she going to defy him with her hormones in overdrive? Perhaps it was an illness. Or something she ate. Could she have been poisoned?

*I will do whatever I must to keep you safe,* Bastian stated. *The mayor's brother is not safe.*

Aislinn thrilled at the effortless exchange. A hidden window had opened into a whole new world of possibilities. Her lips parted in amazement.

*He looks safer than you,* she sent back to him, raising one eyebrow.

Waves of indignation, fury, and the need to control her blasted from Bastian like a thunderstorm, enough to make Aislinn feel like she was being pushed out of her chair. She hung on to the edge of her seat as candles flickered on the table, the mayor's napkin blew off his lap, and several pieces of mail flew off a side table.

"Gracious!" Mrs. Gavrila exclaimed. "Is that a draft?"

"Strange weather happens on this mountain, I've heard," Lucian commented, scanning the room for the source of the breeze.

Marius stood up, his aristocratically polite face seething with anger for a mere second, which he quickly veiled. "It is just the wind. I sometimes forget to close all the windows. We do love the fresh air here, so far from the city." He gestured with a wave toward the unseen mountain. Movement at a window in the far hallway caught Aislinn's eye. The window opened several inches, as if to validate his claim. The mayor and his wife were watching Marius and could not see the movement from their position at the table. But she could.

Aislinn's chest quivered. *Okay, just breathe. Nobody's tried to eat me. I just need to get out of here.*

*Aislinn, no one is going to eat you.*

Aislinn let out a slight squeak and jumped, shocked Bastian had detected the thought even though she was not attempting to communicate with him.

"Why don't we serve dessert?" Marius rubbed his hands together. "Our cook has whipped up something special, and I can't wait to try it." He shot Bastian a threatening glance before smiling at the mayor.

"I'll see about it." Gabriella rose. "Bastian, would you like to join me?"

Aislinn sensed it was not a request. Bastian hesitated, but rose from his chair and followed her, his movements fluid and smooth for such a large man.

"Feisty, isn't he?" Dimitri crossed his arms and rested his elbows on the table to turn his full attention on Aislinn. "Never seen him quite like this though." He kept his voice at a whisper. The secretive look in his sparkling aqua-blue eyes intrigued Aislinn, although it shouldn't have. He seemed to have accepted that she was aware of the mystical elements of his family. Lucian, however, was watching everyone, taking in every nuance.

"He's been alone too long. Does weird things to us," Dimitri continued to whisper, his eyes twinkled with mischief.

"Us?" Aislinn blinked several times for emphasis. "Like... what weird things?"

"Makes us blow papers in the air and send candle wax across the table. You want to see him really get riled? Watch me put my arm around your chair when he gets back."

"Oh, Dimitri, don't." Aislinn placed a hand on his forearm and then quickly withdrew it lest Bastian walk in.

Dimitri chuckled wickedly.

"You know, you sound like an American," she accused.

"Actually, I've lived all over," Dimitri replied. "Grew up in Greece, but moved to England for a while, then Germany, Italy, France. Met Bastian's mother in Switzerland, my grand-aunt. Went to college in the States. So, yeah, I picked up a sense of humor. Came here to Romania when Marius decided to visit for a few weeks."

"Guess that's why I can't quite place your accent."

"Yep, it's an everywhere accent." He grinned with beautiful, white teeth.

"So Bastian is Swiss?"

"He is what you might call Swiss-German, mostly. His father moved there from Romania, and met his mother, who is Swiss-German. She has the blonde hair, and those ghastly eyes." He widened his own eyes for emphasis.

Aislinn blanched at his reference to Bastian's unusual eyes. How dare Dimitri insult one of Bastian's body parts? A slow smile spread across Dimitri's face as if he was delighted at her defensive reaction. Surely he could not hear her thoughts. He must be reading her body language.

Gabriella and Bastian reentered the room. Bastian was carrying a tray of desserts and did not look happy about it. Aislinn wondered what happened to the young girl and the woman.

Dimitri leaned away from Aislinn and made a point of scooting his chair an inch to the right as if he were moving back to his original position. Bastian fixed seething eyes on him. The outer whites of his eyes were taking on a pink shade and growing redder by the minute. Thunder roared above the house, and lightening crackled, brightening the windows.

"Oh, no." Mrs. Gavrila clasped her hands together. "They said there might be scattered storms tonight. Nicolae, we must leave before they hit."

"Of course, dear, of course."

"Hmm, perhaps I *should* drive after all," said Lucian, concern in his eyes.

"Do have a bite of dessert before you leave." Gabriella flashed an inviting smile and placed desserts in front of the mayor, his wife, and Lucian. Light on her feet, she managed to step around the table and take the tray from Bastian as he hovered threateningly over Dimitri's head.

Casting Bastian a warning squint, Gabriella added the remaining saucers to the table.

She stopped beside Aislinn. "This dessert, Aislinn, is called *savarina*. It's a rum-soaked cake filled with cream, and topped with fresh fruit. I asked for whipped cream on top since I knew you'd be more familiar with that taste. I'm sure we're both Cool Whip kind of girls." She laid a hand on Aislinn's shoulder, the touch feather-light. Aislinn felt instantly calm. Her racing heart began to slow into measured beats.

"Thanks," Aislinn said, eying Gabriella, half expecting her eyes to glow. "Anything's good with Cool Whip on it."

Gabriella smiled and returned the tray to the kitchen.

Out of politeness and goaded by a wink from Dimitri, Aislinn tried a nibble of the fruit and cream mixture. It was divine. She couldn't help letting out a long, "Mmmm." She was so enraptured by the taste, it served to deflect some of her fear. Dimitri's wicked smile and winks kept her taking spoonfuls. Which was helpful since she was trying to avoid looking at Bastian, who had retaken his seat while scooting his chair as close to the corner of the table, and her, as possible. Feeling the hair rise on her arms, Aislinn was terrified her body might move on its own.

As she finished her last spoonful, she dared a glance at Bastian. "Aren't you going to eat any?"

Bastian did a poor job of appearing indifferent. He did not return her scrutiny, but spooned a bite and placed it in his mouth, returning the spoon to the plate. He didn't actually swallow.

"Miss Aislinn," Lucian leaned forward with an inviting curve of his lips, "when you are done with your tours this week, perhaps I could show you our beautiful Valea Doftanei next week. You will love our city."

Lightening flashed at the window, followed by a rumble that shook the walls of the chalet.

"Oh, Nicolae, we must go now." Mrs. Gavrila was already standing, dropping her napkin.

Marius stood. "You are welcome to spend the night, Mrs. Gavrila. I assure you we don't mind at all and would welcome the company."

"No, no, thank you. I have an engagement early tomorrow morning and must get back this evening. Besides, I just heard this mountain park has become haunted, yes?" She cast Marius a mischievous, teasing grin which made Marius laugh.

"Wonderful!" Mayor Gavrila exclaimed. "More vampires and ghosts, always brings in the tourists."

"Yes, we have heard the rumors," Marius obliged the mayor. "Thankfully, we have not encountered any ghouls that have managed us any harm."

Mrs. Gavrila giggled. "What a shame. The publicity would be great for the town."

Mayor Gavrila shook Marius' hand enthusiastically. "A wonderful dinner Mr. and Mrs. Brancusi. Such a pleasure to share my plans for the coming year. Please accept my apologies for having to leave early."

"Not at all, Mayor, and call me Marius, please."

"Well, thank you, Marius. Miss Gabriella."

Lucian turned to shake Gabriella's hand and leaned in so close that his body lingered against hers. "Thank you for an outstanding meal, Miss Gabriella. Truly a delight."

Gabriella gave him a warm smile but discreetly took a step back. "It was our pleasure. I'm so glad we finally got to meet. The mayor has told me so much about your work at the Cascavel Festival."

"A great help he was with the festival this year," Mayor Gavrila called out while accepting his coat and hat from Marius. "Wonderful to meet you all. Bastian, Dimitri. And Miss Aislinn, just say the word and we'll send a car to pick you up. You must come see us at our estate before you leave Romania."

"I would love to," Aislinn replied. *Preferable without your brother.*

*I agree.*

Aislinn inhaled sharply. This could be bad. She needed to find a way to block thoughts she did not want Bastian to hear. She had opened a window that she did not know how to close.

The mayor and his wife said their final goodbyes to everyone. Lucian kissed Aislinn's hand and wrapped it tightly around his arm to drag her with him to the door. She wondered if this might be the perfect moment to escape, even if it was with him. She needed to be away from Bastian in order to think with lucidity, and not be overheard.

Moving like a wisp of air, Marius appeared beside Lucian and the mayor. "My cousin Bastian will drive Miss Aislinn to the inn, Mayor Gavrila." He locked eyes with Lucian. "She will be quite safe, I assure you." His voice had become deep and smooth, as if he was a doctor reassuring a patient.

"We don't mind...." Lucian began.

"Bastian will drive Miss Aislinn." Marius' hypnotic tone hung in the air, heavy and still. His dark eyes did not waiver. "She will be safe. You do not need to drive her. Be very careful driving home in the fog. Very careful."

Aislinn opened her mouth to protest when Marius' mirror-like obsidian eyes focused on hers, the whites flashing with a pink hue. He raised his brows slightly. The message was unmistakable. He would use persuasion on *her* if necessary. How she knew what he inferred by that gesture, she did not know.

"Uh... yes, of course." Lucian blinked as if lost in thought. The Mayor hovered in the doorway, his smile momentarily lax.

Marius turned to the Mayor, his words still suggestive. "I know you will get everyone safely home. You will have a wonderful evening. We all had a wonderful time."

"Yes, we did." The mayor turned without another word, as if on remote control. Lucian followed him.

"Thank you for joining us, Miss Aislinn." Gabriella put an arm around Aislinn's shoulders, her expression sincere. "It was very nice to meet you." Again, Aislinn felt calm travel through her, relaxing her tight shoulders. Instead of enjoying it, she felt a slight stab of fear.

"Um, yes, me too," she stammered, realizing her suspicions about the family's combined abilities were true. "I just wish I had the chance to see the whole house."

"You are welcome to spend the night, you know." Gabriella smiled. "I'd love to give you a tour."

A chill ran up Aislinn's spine at the thought of spending more time in the house, though she was certain Gabriella was just being polite. She watched the mayor and his wife heading toward their car. "Perhaps another time. Thank you for your hospitality, Mrs. Brancusi. And, Mr. Brancusi."

Marius nodded, his eyes softening. "It was our pleasure." He opened her coat to assist her putting it on. "And please, call me Marius."

"Do call me Gabriella, please," Gabriella added, giving Aislinn a warm hug, again bringing calm to her anxiety.

"Thank you." She stuck her arms in the sleeves of her coat and stepped forward to pull it out of Marius' hands, leery of him touching her shoulders like he had when she arrived.

Bastian was waiting for her at the door. Tall, handsome and brooding, his steeled expression appeared absent of emotion. Aislinn was not fooled.

Not with this strange new connection they had. Gusts of turmoil swirled inside him like an imprisoned thunderstorm.

Through the partially opened front door, Aislinn watched Lucian getting into the driver's seat of the mayor's car, and felt a sudden desire to run after him. The barest turn of Bastian's head warned her against it.

With a nervous sigh and a roll of her eyes, Aislinn suddenly felt sorry for her ex-boyfriends who could never hide their true feelings or intentions from her. Now, she was in the hot seat, attracted to a man who was aware of everything she was thinking, even when she did not want him to be.

Resigned to her fate, she walked in silence to the black BMW, turning for one last look at the charming house. Marius and Gabriella stood on the porch and waved. Gabriella hugged herself to ward off the cold air.

Aislinn raised a hand to them in farewell as Bastian reached for the passenger door. With a sudden jerk, he raised his right forearm and frowned darkly. Marius did the same. He and Bastian shared a meaningful look of trepidation. Gabriella's eyes widened with concern. Dimitri suddenly appeared beside Marius, flexing his left arm.

*What in the world?* Aislinn thought.

Marius' eyes flared. "Dimitri goes with you."

Without hesitation, Dimitri skipped down the stairs, his face all business.

Bastian opened Aislinn's door and gestured for her to sit. As she slipped into the seat, she found him examining the woodland around the house. Dimitri practically flew into the seat behind her, slamming the door.

Marius was also glancing warily at the woods as Bastian started the motor. Marius and Gabriella watched them drive away with worried faces. Bastian steered the car down the graveled driveway and onto the winding road.

Aislinn could not shut out the tense, alert concern radiating from Bastian and Dimitri, their earlier competition absent.

"All right, what is going on? Are you guys going to leave me in the dark?"

Neither man answered. Both continued to study the forest through every window.

Aislinn crossed her arms and raised her voice. "Any time!"

She watched Bastian regard Dimitri through the rear view mirror. Whispers brushed Aislinn's mind.

"Okay, let's just leave the blonde bimbo in the dark. She doesn't have a brain anyway, right?"

"Aislinn!" Dimitri exclaimed, letting loose a half-chuckle.

"Why do you goad me, woman?" Bastian shot her a disapproving glare.

"Who do you think you are?" Aislinn turned her attention to the road. "And I ain't your woman."

In spite of the declaration, she could not help shifting her eyes to observe his magnificent chest heave an angry sigh. She schooled her eyes away, frustrated that she could not resist gawking at him.

"I wish to keep you safe," Bastian stated. "The mayor's brother is… quite flirtatious."

"I'm not talking about Lucian. And, besides, the mayor and his wife were in the car with him. What did you expect him to do, slide over in the back seat and grope me?"

When Bastian did not reply, she refocused on the road. "You just wanted to keep me with *you*."

After a few seconds, he spoke. "There is that."

Momentarily silenced by the honest admission, and a little pleased, Aislinn continued to stare straight ahead. The hair on the back of her neck rose. She scrubbed her neck nervously and detected the brush of telepathic whispers again. What *were* they talking about? How was Bastian able to block her from hearing him, even though he could clearly hear her when he wanted to?

The tension in the car rose and thickened like hot steam.

At a dangerous, sloping curve in the road, fog rolled over the car, not just gray in the headlights but black as soot. Aislinn's hands went to the dash. Her heart thumped wildly. Bastian drove as though it were a bright clear day. She did not know what he was, but an ability to drive in zero visibility without going over the side of the mountain was a talent that was truly frightening, albeit one she would like to possess.

He glanced at her. "I know this road."

"Nice try."

His lips pressed together.

She crossed her arms again. "Remember the part about how I hate guys that lie? That part certainly wasn't a dream."

With a rise of his chin she sensed an internal war between telling her the truth and telling her too much. "It is not my intention to lie."

"But you do."

"Not entirely. I *do* know this road."

"It wouldn't matter if you'd been driving it since the day you were born. With fog this thick, it takes more than just knowledge. And besides…."

"Bastian?" Dimitri's voice was low and tense, his eyes darting to each window.

"I feel them," Bastian replied.

Before Aislinn could ask what they were talking about, a massive set of bat-like wings, wider than the car, swooped up the windshield.

Aislinn cried out in fright. "What was that?"

Something landed on top of the roof with a heavy thud. Four-inch talons cut into the car with a metallic screech. Aislinn screamed and recoiled.

A gleaming sword shot up through the roof, between the talons, and an unseen creature howled in protest. Dimitri pulled the sword out of the roof, looking pleased to find brown liquid on it. Aislinn stared at him and the sword, horrified. A dark shaggy ball of fur and spikey wings rolled off the roof next to Aislinn's window. One three-inch claw clamped onto the side mirror.

With garbled cries of terror, Aislinn fell toward Bastian, fighting the seatbelt straining to hold her hips in place. She dug her fingers into his shirt and felt an electric spark race up her arms.

Eerie sounds echoed around the vehicle as the creature let go of the side mirror and evaporated into the night. Bastian's control of the car never faltered though he gritted his teeth with the effort.

"Should we turn around?" asked Dimitri.

"I am considering it. Might be worth it to draw them away from the mayor."

"I don't think they're after the mayor."

"What are they?" Aislinn's voice sounded like a squeak.

"Enemies," Bastian replied, scanning each car window. Aislinn knew instantly that he was afraid to tell her the whole truth. He swerved down a side road, jerked the car to a stop, and backed up to return the way they had come. With a train-like roar, the car became engulfed in screeching, growling creatures, their combined weight making the car shudder and groan. Glass cracked beside Aislinn, and she curled into a ball.

Car doors opened. Aislinn whirled to see Bastian and Dimitri leaping from the car, both welding swords. She had only a moment to wonder where they had hidden swords as the creatures dove at them.

Unable to look away from the ghastly scene, afraid they were going to die, Aislinn watched both men slice into the creatures with measured precision, their movements almost a dance, choreographed, as if practiced and planned. Aislinn's fear for their safety was quickly replaced by awe.

Her heart leapt at the sight of Bastian's muscular body welding the sword, aiming his strikes and ducking at the right moments to avoid claws and teeth. Time seemed to stop as the men pierced, slammed, and punched the creatures so fast, Aislinn could barely register their movements, or what the hideous beasts looked like before being rendered in two. The carnage was macabre. Blood, hair and heads flew. Feathers and fur rained around the car and disappeared in wisps of fire and smoke.

While the men fought in the light of the headlights Aislinn noticed several dog-like creatures racing up the hill toward them. Her entire body shook at the sight.

With sudden realization that the men had not spotted the horde of yellow eyes and teeth, Aislinn decided she was not helpless. Taking a deep breath and saying a quick prayer, she stepped from the car and stood to the left of the headlights.

"Aislinn, *no!*" Bastian called out.

Pressing both hands to her head, Aislinn screamed, *Stop!* with her mind, the loudest mental yell she had ever attempted. She poured every ounce of raw fury into the command, drawing out the word in waves of energy aimed toward the four-legged creatures. Like hitting an invisible wall, the creatures back-stepped and pivoted, shaking their heads. Some turned in circles, others staggered and looked confused.

Dimitri flew at them waving his sword like a machete, and plowed them over. The demonic canines scattered in several directions, two lying dead, several wounded, emitting nerve-searing squeals.

A vice-like hand grabbed her arm. "Aislinn, in the car! Now!" Bastian ordered.

"No, I want to help!" Aislinn stepped back as an eight foot tall, ape-like creature with brownish-white hair and long arms appeared behind Bastian. Reacting to her widened eyes, Bastian pivoted, but the creature swiped a paw, carving bear-like talons across Bastian's chest and right shoulder. Bastian grunted but had his sword up and across the face of the creature in a flash of movement.

The ape shrieked in pain but attempted another wild swing of the splayed claws. Bastian switched the sword to his left hand and blocked the hairy arm. Growling like a bear, the mass of muscle and hair knocked Bastian over the car hood as if he were weightless.

With a look of recognition and triumph in his red eyes, the creature bared his teeth and reached a long, shaggy arm toward Aislinn's throat. She only had second to wonder why it wanted her before a sword point ripped through its chest from the back. Aislinn screamed at the same time the beast let out a megaphone roar of pain that rattled the trees like a sonic blast and vibrated the earth under Aislinn's feet.

Bastian came into view twisting the sword, gritting his teeth in fury. The ape disappeared, leaving Bastian holding an empty sword, dripping with inky black blood and fur.

Aislinn's breaths frosted the air, ragged and halting; her entire body was shaking. The creature had disappeared right in front of her. Not ran, or jumped away, but vanished from visible existence.

Feeling her knees dissolving, Aislinn slid against a headlight and down the grillwork, grabbing at the bumper to keep from collapsing into the dirt.

A dark, winged silhouette landed in front of Bastian. Aislinn screamed again and threw up an arm. Bastian readied himself in a fighting stance, but straightened as the folding wings evaporated and Marius appeared in its place, a fierce, dangerously red gleam in his dark eyes. He took one look at Bastian's chest and said, "Guard her. Dimitri, you're with me."

"I can fight one-handed," Bastian complained, stepping forward.

"No. We will finish this."

Bastian muttered in protest and leaned his buttocks against the car hood near Aislinn. Blood poured from his chest, soaking crimson into his torn, dirty shirt.

Wanting to help him, Aislinn managed to pull herself to a not-quite-standing position. Bastian kept his eyes on the whirling shadows still determined to attack or devour them from all directions.

Aislinn's instinct was to stem the flow of blood from Bastian's wounds, but her hands would do little to help. Bastian appeared more upset about not getting to fight than any discomfort from his wounds. Instead of grimacing in pain, he seemed to be watching the battle with regret.

Something heavy thumped onto the car, making it rock. They both whirled to discover a badger-like creature bubbling and morphing as though trying to turn into a human. With a snarl, it scampered over the roof toward them. Bastian threw his left arm backward and broadsided the creature with his sword, hurling it into the forest. Then he went back to his position of leaning on the bumper and scowling while watching Dimitri and Marius fight the rest of the battle.

Something wet was running down the side of Aislinn's mouth and she swiped at it with her hand, afraid it was some bodily substance deposited by the Bigfoot-like creature. She recoiled at the sight of blood across her fingers. Was it Bastian's, or from the last creature?

With a single leap, Dimitri was beside Marius and the two sliced at anything that moved, which included several small bat-like animals flitting about their heads, and a few of the dogs that resembled malformed hyenas attempting one last lunge. Marius was powerful and exact with every swipe of his blade. Green, yellow and red fluids splashed through the air and Aislinn had to duck from the onslaught of the splatter. Marius leapt from the side of trees, using his legs to pivot and project his body, catching the teeth-baring beasts by surprise.

Just as quickly, he and Dimitri circled and sprang from the ground in powerful, graceful movements as if aware of what each other was planning to do. In two minutes, the creatures had scattered, or lay dead and turned to ash. Smoke wafted up from some of them, while others became a blowing ash cloud. On one of them, the smoke boiled and bubbled into the ground. Aislinn's stomach roiled.

"You should have let me finish." Bastian's face was set and angry as Marius returned to the car.

"Not necessary to waste a wounded man, especially my Assassin." Marius almost smiled.

"I am fine." Bastian insisted, scowling deeper.

"Let's clean up." Marius and Dimitri tore off their shirts and wiped multi-colored fluids from their hands and swords. Bastian did the same, but with careful movements since he had to pry blood soaked strips off his chest.

Spellbound by the incredible physiques before her, Aislinn longed to assist Bastian in removing his shirt, to do something helpful. She reached a hand toward him only to freeze when he turned his back to her. Confused and disappointed, she leaned against the car and folded her arms, anger affording her the strength to stand.

Marius nodded at Dimitri. "Stand watch." While Dimitri surveyed the pitch-black forest, Marius stepped off the graveled road, kicked leaves and brush aside, and dug his hands into the dirt. Aislinn grimaced when he held up fists of darkened earth and spit into them. Even worse, he held out both hands to Dimitri, who also spit into the clods of dirt. He marched over to Bastian, who had succeeded in removing the last of his tattered shirt and was wiping his sword with the remains.

Aislinn drew back in disgust at the sight of Marius applying the saliva-moistened dirt to Bastian's gruesome, gaping wounds, turning him toward one headlight for a better view. Though the site was grisly, the vision of Bastian's pumped chest and shoulder muscles made Aislinn's body warm all over. He could have stepped out of Muscle Magazine except... her mouth fell open as she realized he was completely covered in some kind of shimmering paint, like pale gold tattoos. To her astonishment, so was Marius and Dimitri, though their skin was darker than Bastian's and the tattoos glistened in more of a copper shade as their bodies moved. She had not noticed any tattoos on them before. Like round brushstrokes, the rune-like waves swirled and reflected the headlights as though fine glitter had been applied to the ink.

Dimitri had the least, with only his shoulders and parts of his neck and arms adorned in the winding symbols, barely discernable when he shifted away from the lights. Marius' chest was completed gilded, and his arms were covered down to his elbows. But Bastian—every inch of his stomach, chest, and arms all the way to his wrists glowed with gold.

Aislinn certainly hadn't noticed *that* last night. How could she not have seen them? She had kissed his chest. Of course, it had been dark in the room, with no light to reflect the shimmer, and she had only managed to open the front of his long-sleeved shirt. He had stopped her before she could remove it. She wasn't thinking straight last night, either. *Not thinking at all* was more like it.

In fact, she was *still* not thinking straight, wishing she could reach up and touch Bastian's chest despite his bleeding wounds. She clenched her hand to curb the untimely urge.

Marius continued to spit into his hands and smear mixtures of dirt and saliva onto Bastian, who frowned as though irritated and impatient, displaying no sign of pain.

Aislinn felt her body sway again. Her stomach lurched and she pressed a hand against it to quell the nausea.

"Always my sword arm." Bastian flexed his right shoulder and glowered.

"Of course." Marius grinned. "You can't get off that easy."

Bastian smirked with a half-smile.

Aislinn's mouth fell open. How could they be smiling? Joking?

"Let's go." Marius slapped Bastian's good arm.

"Yeah, *that's* going to sting in the morning." Dimitri slapped Bastian's stomach with back of his hand.

Aislinn felt her legs give way.

Bastian's uninjured arm was around her before she hit the ground. She heard Dimitri utter, "Whoa," and felt two smaller arms lift her up. She tried to speak but her mouth would not respond properly. Her vision had turned fuzzy.

"I'll put her in the back," Dimitri was saying. "Where's that blood on her face from?"

"I've got her," Bastian protested. "She is fine."

"Wow, you *are* stuck on her, aren't you Uncle?"

"Just keep your hands off her."

"Hmm. Got a mate sign showing up yet?"

"I have not looked."

"Bastian, let Dimitri help," Marius commanded. "You're going to open those wounds."

As dizziness and nausea threatened to overwhelm Aislinn, Dimitri gently belted her into the back seat. She could barely hold up her head. Their voices sounded so far away. Bastian draped his left arm around her protectively and pulled her close. She was so queasy she was afraid if anything else moved her body, she would vomit over him.

He was a safe and warm place at the moment. Even the possessive way he held her close and pressed his chin against her hair was comforting. She allowed her body to slump against him and felt tingles dance like rain over every place their bodies touched.

When they arrived at the chalet, Gabriella was waiting for them. So were four other men, standing on the steps at attention, each with a sword in his hand, two of them also holding undecipherable objects.

Aislinn tried to get out of the car on her own, not wanting to be a burden, but her legs would not cooperate. They had turned to rubber. She concentrated on taking deep breaths and gaining control, resorting to placing her hands behind her knees and forcing her legs to the edge of the seat toward the open car door and Dimitri's waiting hands.

"It's okay, I've got you." Dimitri's voice was soft and reassuring as he lifted her from the car.

"I can take her." Bastian loomed beside them.

"And get dirt and blood all over her? What a romantic *you* are."

"I don't want you touching her."

"So sue me."

"What happened to her face?" Gabriella demanded.

"I think it's from her nose," Dimitri answered, carrying her in his arms up the porch steps.

Gabriella directed Dimitri to a bedroom at the top of the stairs where he deposited Aislinn carefully onto a quilted bed. He wasn't even breathing heavy.

Aislinn felt like a limp, rag doll. Fight scenes kept swirling in her mind. Willing her limbs to work, she managed a wobbly sitting position. "I'm okay, really you guys. My legs are just… weak."

"Can I get you something to drink?" Gabriella looked concerned as she stood by the edge of the bed. She laid a hand on Aislinn's arm. Aislinn felt warmth and tranquility flow through her limbs. She peered into Gabriella's bright green eyes, and they both knew she understood this was Gabriella's gift.

"No, I'm good now," said Aislinn. "Actually, a cold soda would be great. My head really hurts. But… he's the one wounded, not me. He needs to lie down. I'm sure he's going to need stitches. We should get him to a hospital."

Dimitri chuckled.

Aislinn managed to glower at him, thinking this was nothing to laugh about.

"Are you dropping mud and blood all over my carpet?" Gabriella tried to sound cross as she eyed Bastian's chest, but her tone was teasing.

Aislinn gaped. What was wrong with these people? Why didn't they see Bastian's wounds were serious? These men just fought the stuff of people's nightmares on a level that would take a hundred people to dream up in their sleep.

"What's this?" Gabriella lifted Bastian's injured arm and pressed a thumb near his wrist, close to a reddish spot. His face went blank and eyes widened. The symbol-like swirl was more visible than the others, as if from a different brick-red, ink. It resembled a heart shape with curls similar to a Celtic knot.

Bastian cast a sharp look of alarm at Gabriella. "That's not…."

"Oh, yes it is," Gabriella argued with a twinkle in her eyes.

Everyone turned toward Aislinn.

"What's wrong?" She felt guilty, but had no idea why.

"*Oooo*, and here I thought it was all about Andromeda." Dimitri tilted his head sideways in mock puzzlement. Bastian responded with an icy, warning glint.

Gabriella's tone turned serious. "You need blood."

"Gabriella." Marius sounded reproachful.

"Well, it's a little late to hold back now, isn't it?" She gestured a hand toward Aislinn and challenged them all with a high-browed glare. "You think *maybe* she might need a few explanations?"

All three men exchanged glances.

*Bastian.* Aislinn spoke telepathically, hoping the others would not pick it up. The effort made the area behind her eyes sting. *I want the truth.*

Though his pale eyes softened, he shook his head.

"Okay, not answering me is almost as bad as lying," she spoke out loud.

"No, it is not." He sounded insulted.

"Yes, it is. I want to know what those things were and why they were after you."

Marius' face formed a thoughtful frown. "You saw them?"

"Of course I saw them! Why would I not see them? They were everywhere."

"Well, you just get more interesting all the time." Dimitri was giving her a crooked smirk though his eyes were dreamily inviting.

Bastian took a step toward him. "If you do not stop…."

"Bastian." Marius halted him with one word and turned to Aislinn. "You should not have been able to see the creatures, only shadows. Except for the Yeti. They can render themselves corporeal to anyone."

Aislinn frowned in disbelief. "Okay, that makes no sense." Still reeling from the shock of the entire bizarre evening, she shook her head, and was sorry she did as painful lights danced in her eye sockets. She held her head still with one hand. "Look, I don't care about being able to *see* them. I want to know *what* they were and why they were after you. And… and where the hell did you get swords? And when did you get tattoos? Why didn't I see them last night?"

Gabriella lifted her head to Bastian with brows raised even higher. "Only a drop, huh?"

Marius, Gabriella and Bastian exchanged questioning glances. Aislinn was sure she was hearing the faint hissing of telepathic communication.

With anger and frustration rising, Aislinn shouted. "Stop shutting me out, people!"

"Wow, don't aim that shot at me." Gabriella leaned backward.

"Sorry." Aislinn winced, aware that her skull was burning with unbearable pressure. Her upper lip felt wet, and she rubbed at her nose. More blood fell across her fingers.

Marius reached out, grabbed Aislinn's chin, and turned her face toward him. "What did you do?" he demanded, which frightened her.

"You should have seen her on the road," said Dimitri. "She threw that psychic blast at a hound horde, and they stopped in their tracks."

"Do not use that talent for several days, Aislinn. You need to heal," Marius instructed. "I suspect you have quite a headache, don't you?"

Aislinn could not find words to answer, though his ebony eyes seemed to compel an answer from her.

"Yes."

Gabriella gently removed Marius' hand from Aislinn's chin as if sensing that his fierce gaze was frightening her. "Looks like there is more to you than meets the eye, Aislinn Thomas. You're not related to the Parkers of North Carolina are you?"

"No." Aislinn wiped at her bloody nose again. "Well... I don't think so. Anya and I had just started tracing our family tree when... before the accident."

"What accident?" Gabriella asked.

"When I was injured, and my whole family...." Aislinn felt a familiar lump in her throat.

"You did not tell me *you* were injured," said Bastian with an air of concern.

"All right. Enough of this," stated Marius. "Bastian, I want you in bed. Dimitri and I will prepare it. Miss Aislinn, it is not safe for you to return to the inn tonight. Please accept our hospitality. We need to attend to Bastian, and you need to rest. Gabriella, call Mrs. Tănase so she does not worry. She often checks on her guests. Dimitri, position the men around the perimeter."

"I want to help, too." Aislinn draped her legs over the side of the bed and grabbed the bed post for support. It was not enough and her ankles wobbled the moment her boots touched the floor. Dimitri had his arms around her, but just as quick, Bastian's left arm shot between Aislinn and Dimitri, forcing Aislinn back onto the quilt.

Blood spurted from one of the mud encrusted slashes across Bastian's chest, depositing crimson globules on Aislinn's arm. Aislinn gasped but did not feel the revulsion she expected to. Normally, the sight of blood made her queasy. The sudden urge to lick the blood, however, did make her queasy. Tendrils of fear crawled up her neck.

Telepathic whispers flew around her. She could not interpret them, but everyone started moving and she suspected the commands came from Marius. She had learned that Romanian families usually had patriarchal heads and elders were respected, but Aislinn did not think this family was Romanian at all. Gabriella certainly wasn't. And Marius' accent sounded

Grecian. Their responses to Marius' commands felt like something more, almost military.

"May we have a moment, please?" Bastian was looking straight at Marius. Marius hesitated, but nodded, and everyone left the room.

Surprised and puzzled, Aislinn said, "For heaven's sake Bastian, what is going on?"

"Aislinn." Bastian sat on the bed and drew her as close as he dared, his left arm around her shoulders and his hand tightening around her waist. His face was inches from hers. "Do you trust me?"

"No."

A light chuckle escaped him. "Fair enough. I need to help you right now. I care… very much about you. Do you care about me?" His silver eyes bore into hers with hope, and she nearly lost herself.

"Um…." She wasn't entirely sure how to define what she felt, other than unabashed sexual attraction and the shock of watching him fight creatures she did not know existed. Then there was the age-old fear of confessing true feelings before a man was ready to hear them. "I… well… I mean… I do care."

His lips were suddenly on hers, soft and tender at first, then with urgent passion. The room disappeared. Her hearing was taken over by loud heartbeats in her brain. She slid her arms up his and curled her body toward him, but halted as she realized she would be touching the mud-covered wounds on his chest. Then, in horror, she remembered her bloody nose.

She pulled away. "Bastian I've got blood all over my face." She rubbed both hands over her lips, mortified.

"I don't care what's on your face." He tried to claim her lips again.

She rubbed her neck scarf across her nose and chin. He kept scooting her hands away with his jaw. "Bastian…."

He pressed warm, sensuous lips against hers, and she acquiesced. His kiss became more demanding. She gripped his arms, frustrated that she could not run her hands all over him. The etheric connection between them blossomed, drawing their pulsating energies into each other.

In mere seconds, her body was on fire with the same sizzling, electric sensations from the night before. Their combined sexual desire billowed into a flaming aura, melting away her resistance like butter. If only he was not injured and they could lie down together.

"My lady," he whispered.

"Yes."

"You are tired."

"A little."

"You are exhausted. So very tired."

"Yes." Aislinn began to feel heavy. Her limbs relaxed. Her eyelids flickered. Maybe they could just rest together on the comfortable quilt.

"You wish you could sleep." Bastian's crooning voice was a soft caress, stroking her mind.

"Mmm-hmm."

"Let us sleep now, my love. Sleep. Sleeep."

In a faraway place, Aislinn felt, for the merest second, like she was falling, just before darkness engulfed her.

# CHAPTER 9

Above Aislinn's head, beveled ceiling panels spread out from a diadem like a flower. It was quite pretty.

And she had no memory of it.

Sparse moonlight flickered on the walls through lace curtains from a window to the right of a four poster bed she was lying on. With the clearest vision she had ever experienced, she could make out a dresser, bookcase and vanity in the dark room. Even the village scenes in two paintings on the walls were visible. She blinked several times, trying to make sense of the new-found clarity. The room smelled funny, as if unused, and she could smell... people. She inhaled deep and slow. She had never smelled people unless they were very close, or wore perfume, which she had always been hypersensitive too. She sat up.

"Ohhh." She groaned and placed a hand to her head, trying to remember why she had such a fierce headache. The bottom of the bed and the curve of the bedpost triggered a vision. She remembered sitting there.

Bastian. Bastian had sat there, too. The image became clearer. His amazing body was covered in soft golden tattoos. She warmed at the thought of his beautiful body. Massive shoulders, roped arm muscles, taut chest and... mud and blood.

*Blood?*

Breath caught in her throat as she recalled the terrifying events of the night before like a horror movie she wished she could forget. A shiver ran the length of her spine and she wrapped her arms around her chest, rocking at recall of the gruesome scenes.

Was it still the same night? Or was it the next day? She reached out with her senses and winced. Her brain was still tender, so she took several steadying breaths and reached with calm, consistent focus like smoke wafting from a candle with a hidden purpose.

Marius and Gabriella's chalet. That's where she was. They were awake. So were two other men she did not know. Dimitri she could detect. Bastian she could feel the strongest. Her breasts tingled at the sensation and her womb clenched. She wanted to touch him. To fondle him. To own him.

*Good grief, what is wrong with me? This has got to stop.* She needed to talk to a woman. She needed to find Gabriella.

No, she needed to find *him*. As she threw off blankets, she hesitated. Why did she have to find him? The aching need was like a powerful magnet pulling at her. It was almost painful. She perused the memory of his handsome, brooding face and his magnificent body. Oh, that body. Her mouth watered, surprising her. Had he done this to her? She was not the demure, cautious Aislinn she had always known. She exhaled a slow breath, thinking she needed to write to Anya. Her thoughts jumped right back to Bastian.

Watching his body move, leaping in the air and slicing with blurred speed through vile creatures that had glowing eyes and wicked teeth was the most amazing thing she had ever witnessed. That should terrify her. It only made her hungry.

She rubbed a hand over her heart. Something was very, very wrong with her. She had been given some kind of drug. It was the only explanation.

Maybe she was dreaming. Only a few times had she actually been aware she was in a dream, and then tried to control it. This attraction felt too vibrant and real. And just as wrong. The creatures had certainly not been a dream.

She deflected the memory of dismembered, demon-like creatures to keep her stomach still. Though she wanted to revisit the sight of Bastian fighting, she did not want to dwell on the battle.

The pull for him grew. Instead of analyzing it further, she slipped out of the bed—and realized she had someone else's pajamas on. A pale pink camisole top with lace trim, and draw string bottoms that went to her ankles, fit perfectly. It must be Gabriella's. Aislinn's head jerked up. Who the heck undressed her?

Of all the scenes from last night, she recalled no one messing with her clothes. If Bastian… wait, she remembered a kiss. It was a great kiss.

She touched her mouth and realized her face was clean. Someone must have washed off the blood. If she was in the hospital, that would not be weird. But in someone else's house, that was weird.

She rubbed fingertips along her mouth, recalling the feel of Bastian's firm, full lips claiming hers. Delightful sensations had rippled through her body. Slowly, whispered words seeped into focus, mesmerizing, hypnotic, his velvety deep voiced chanting, *sleep.*

*Oooo, that man!* When she found him she was going to give him a piece of her mind. That was twice he sent her to sleep using persuasion. Without her permission! Not that *she* ever asked anyone for their permission. But still.

And just *what else* had he done after that? Could he have had his way with her and wiped the memory from her awareness? Did he decide to clothe her because he felt guilty? She was tempted to take off the pajamas and check her body to see if it looked messed with.

Just as quickly, she realized that being swollen and sore might be the only signs. After Eddie had asked her to marry him and coaxed her into giving up her virginity, she was bleeding, so that instance was unique. The second and only other time, she remembered feeling tender the next morning. Though Eddie had worn protection, she did recall distinct scents he left behind. The memory caused a stab of pain in her heart. She had given in to Eddie's charms, so certain they would be together, forever. The very next weekend, her visit to her family had ended in tragedy.

"What if something happened to one of us, like a terrible accident, and we never got to love each other?" Eddie had crooned. At the time, she had chided him for the fatalistic question, and thought it romantic. Neither could have known his fateful worries would materialize. And she could not have foreseen that his betrayal would be the second blow.

There had been times when she had considered taking her own life. She wanted to be with her family. She did not want to be the sole survivor. But she knew her family would not have been happy about that choice. Her father had always said, "When you fall down, Aisy, you get back up. You always get back up." When she had fallen off a pony once, as a child, though she cried and pitched a fit, her father refused to let her leave their friend's ranch until she got back up on the pony. She was so angry at her father that when she remounted the animal, she curled her legs around its round belly, determined she would not fall again. It was then she realized she had not really become one with the pony. Her fear and separateness had caused her to be stiff and led to her falling off. She never thanked her father for forcing her to remount even though she later knew he had done her a favor. If only she could thank him now.

She shuddered, and forced the pain of the past away. She needed to think about now. And right now her mind was full of unanswered questions.

If Bastian had touched her, it could have been hours ago. She didn't feel as if she had been ravished. Her nerves felt raw and sensitized, ready and waiting for... *something ravishing.*

Exposure to him, and to his crazy family, had caused changes in her. It was time to find out why.

She padded across the floor in bare feet. Wow, did her legs hurt. She pushed open the door, thrilled it didn't creak, and tip-toed down the hall.

The house had an old and new smell. Old walls, old wood, new furnishings, new people.

Heading toward the back of the rectangular-shaped upper floor, with a staircase spiraling down to her left, she passed a door to her right, but felt no presence. She continued across the bend in the landing and to the other side where she noticed three more doors, some distance apart.

At the first door, she reached out with her senses. Dimitri slept there. He was not actually in the room, but his things were. Her heart beat faster. She had experienced hints of such knowing before, but clearly her awareness was heightened, growing.

Before she took a step toward the second door, she knew Bastian was in the room. Awareness of his energy was absorbed with her entire body, into her very bones. She considered knocking, but if she was mistaken concerning her perceptions, she could have a really embarrassing moment with a stranger. The door chilled her skin as she laid her palms and cheek against it. Yep, he was in there. She grinned at her newfound talents.

Carefully, she turned the knob and stepped into the dark room. It smelled earthy. Moonlight was sparse through the partially drawn curtains, but Aislinn could make out his long silhouette on the bed.

Except that his pale limbs were a sharp contrast against what appeared to be a brown blanket folded over a white one, which left her puzzled. She inhaled deeply. Dirt. Dirt and spices and Bastian. Not what she was expecting to smell.

Bastian's eyes opened and glistened like diamonds in the moonlight. Aislinn's heart pounded in her chest. He made an instant connection with her mind. She did not resist the invasion. He raised his left arm in entreaty.

She could barely resist catapulting through the room like Wonder Woman and landing on his gorgeous body. Every inch of his frame, even his arms and legs, called to her like some exotic food she longed to taste.

As she padded toward him, she caught a side smile forming on his face.

"Get out of my head, Mr. Radescu."

"I do not think so."

Nearing the side of the bed, she took his outstretched hand. A spark arched at their touch, the light visible but not painful. His masculine fingers curled over her dainty ones.

She leaned forward, braced her left hand on the dark blanket, and froze.

It was not a blanket. It was truly dirt she had smelled. Cold, grainy and full of tiny leaves. She gasped softly and stuck her fingers in again to verify it was actually dirt. She stood up. Her eyes shifted slowly to his.

"What are you?"

He took a steady breath before answering. "It would take too long to explain right now."

"Yeah. See, that's not going to work. I need to know."

His hand tugged, still laced in her fingers, but she stood her ground, fearing the reason real dirt was on his bed, and why he needed it.

"I need this to heal."

"Why?"

"It is a long story."

"Looks like we've got all night."

"No. Dawn is coming. I can feel it."

Aislinn gasped softly, panic clenching in her gut. "You can *feel* the dawn?"

He nodded, pulling harder at her hand. She resisted.

"You know, you sound suspiciously like a vampire."

"My lady! How could you accuse me of being a vampire?"

"Uh, *one*, you're lying in dirt. Two, you... can feel the dawn coming. And three...." She halted, a sudden memory shaking her. "Okay, I have to ask you this. Because, now I'm remembering something that occurred to me during the dinner. There were two small marks on my neck this morning, well, yesterday morning. Did you... *bite* me?"

His fingers tightened on hers. "Yes. I should not have. I fear I have wronged you. Can you find it your heart to forgive me?"

Aislinn stared at him. "What kind of wrong are we talking?"

She remembered the breathtaking, delectable sensations that had raced through her willing body. Her brain might not remember clearly, but her body certainly did. Could he have used persuasion to make her enjoy it? Not that she would consider that a totally bad idea.

He gazed at her with such entreaty, she felt weak at the knees. Plus, no one had ever offered her such an eloquent apology. She took a deep breath.

"Okay, why *did* you bite me?"

Several seconds passed before he spoke. "I could not resist." He exhaled as if that was hard to say. "Everything about you called to me. I have not felt normal emotions in a long time. Except anger. But now I know it was grief hiding behind the anger."

"I remember. You... that was powerful, what you felt. I've never experienced anything like it. Well, I have, for myself. But, not like the explosion you did."

His thumb stroked the back of her hand and sent warm currents up her arm. "Many years ago...." He paused and glanced away. "It is difficult for me to speak of it."

Part of Aislinn wanted to lie next to him, and comfort him. Part of her also wanted to retreat. She swallowed, waiting to see which desire would win. One glance at his prone body and the answer was clear.

*Touch him.*

Remembering the loose dirt, she pulled away from Bastian's grasp, ignored his protest, and examined the edge of the white sheet. It appeared to be a straight sheet hanging over the bed. With both hands, she grabbed the hem and folded it over so that it rested on top of the dirt and along the edge of his body. To his delight, she climbed onto the bed and snuggled against the length of him with her head on his shoulder.

Alarmed at her body's lurch toward him, she waited for the strange sensation to calm down. But the abnormal pull only rose higher, becoming a boiling, aching desire on a level completely foreign to her.

Shamelessly, she ran a hand along his chest, careful not to disturb any of the wraps of white gauze encircling his shoulder and chest. He inhaled at her touch. Her fingers itched to go further, but she dared not.

With a grunt of pleasure, he curled his left arm around her shoulder and positioned his head so he could look at her. "You're making this very hard."

"Making what very hard?"

His mouth formed a hesitant smile, but it dissolved. "Letting you go."

She pushed up on one elbow. "Excuse me?"

"I cannot expect you to stay after giving in to the song of your blood without your permission."

"Well... but... hmm, *song of my blood?* Now that's an interesting term. Um, what if I liked it?"

He blinked. "You liked it?" A smile spread across his face, one that made him resemble both a lover and a predator.

She quelled under the intense scrutiny, and rubbed an index finger over one of the swirling tattoos to deflect his attention. In the scant moonlight the tattoos had a pearlescent shine to them, almost like his eyes, except with a golden sheen as if gold dust had been ground into caramel ink. His chest rose in a deep breath and his eyes sparkled as he watched her fingertip trace the design across his pectoral muscle. He continued to breathe faster.

"I did," she affirmed, wishing she had the nerve to lean down and lick the spot she traced just to see what the tattoo tasted like. His sharp intake of breath alerted her that his mind was still threaded into hers and had caught a whisper of her desire.

"I liked everything about you," she continued, keeping her hand still. "Sort of. Which doesn't make any sense. See, that's the problem. You're crazy. You're different. You're very bossy. I still don't have even half of my questions answered, and I think I'm scared of the answers. But... I want to be near you."

"That is my fault."

"What do you mean?"

Looking guilty, he avoided her scrutiny. "By taking your blood and giving you mine, you can now hear my thoughts, and I yours."

"What? But, I didn't bite...." She remembered his finger in her mouth and gasped. "That strange taste. Oh my god. That was your *blood?*"

"Yes." His eyes looked strained.

"But… how did you get it? You weren't cut or anything."

"I pricked my wrist. My nails are sharp when I want them to be."

She glanced at his strong fingernails. They looked normal except for the tips being more pointed than square, and curved on the ends. "Okay, seriously weird. But then, everything about you is seriously weird. Do you… bite all the women you decide you like?"

He frowned with insult. "My lady, I have not seriously considered a woman in many years. You are… different. Something about you calls to me. Marius is very angry. I did not follow the steps."

"What steps?"

"It does not matter now. I have wronged you. You are with me because of the blood call."

Her eyes narrowed. "Okay, definitely not feeling a call for your blood." Even as she said the words, she remembered her strange reaction to his blood the night before. *Major ew*, she decided. "I did actually think of you when I woke up."

He smiled with sadness, though his ghostly eyes danced with sensual desire. "Part of me is sorry. Part of me is not."

"You think all this craziness I am feeling for you is… is…."

"Our attraction is more," he insisted, squeezing her tight. "I have not felt this way since…."

As his voice trailed off, Aislinn watched lines of grief return to his face.

"Okay, I think this is a story I need to hear."

He turned away.

"Come on. Seriously, Bastian. I think you need to tell me about this. It would explain a lot."

A deep sigh of resignation escaped him. He reached over with his right hand to link with her left hand resting on his chest. "Many years ago, I had a woman. We were to be mates. We had taken most of the steps. The blessing and vow of loyalty to our prince was only three days away. Demons attacked relatives of ours, like those you saw earlier, except some were in human form. Very old. Two were possessions. Very dangerous. You kill a demon, it disappears. You kill a human, the body stays. I had to help."

After a shaky breath, he continued. "In the midst of the battle, I heard her cry in my mind. I rushed back, but they had…." His fingers clenched. "They had killed her."

"Wow, Bastian, I'm so sorry." She cringed at the ache in his heart.

"It was more than I could bear. They had… touched her. Then, severed her head."

Aislinn exclaimed and recoiled, unable to imagine such a scene. His rush of anger and horror added to her revulsion. She pulled back from their mental connection.

Bastian closed his eyes, his face full of pain. "It is something I cannot heal. The one thing they *knew* I could not heal. I flew into a rage. From that day forth, I battled creatures of the night and traitors to the blood with a vengeance I never felt before. I became our tribe's Assassin. Other leaders called Marius requesting my assistance to track down their vampires and destroy them. I was unstoppable. People called me Fearless Sebastian. I fought without fear because I did not care if I died. I wanted to die."

Aislinn felt like she'd been kicked in the gut. She strained to reinforce the mental wall to block his raw emotions. Tears were welling in her eyes from the impact of his grief, but she was also shivering from his fierce retaliation leaking through the memories.

"I'm so sorry for you, Bastian."

He gave her a token squeeze of his left arm still curled around her, but fixed his gaze straight ahead, at nothing in particular.

"So your name is really Sebastian?"

"I go by Bastian, now."

Aislinn considered pressing him for an explanation but something else was bugging her. "You said 'their vampires.' So, you actually can turn into a vampire?"

"If we hunt humans as prey. Such a one has to be destroyed." His voice became a hard whisper.

"Hmm, there's that *human* distinction again, *Mister* Alien. You did drink my blood, after all."

"That was different. I wanted... it was for a blood bond."

"So biting me is good, biting someone else is bad?" She leaned closer, watching his wonderful full lips and wanting to kiss him, despite her reservations and their bizarre conversation.

"Correct."

"So, how long has it been? I mean, since you drank someone else's blood? Besides mine."

"Last night," he replied, his voice turning serious.

"Last night! Whose blood did you drink?" She held her breath, afraid of the answer.

"Marius. He insisted, since I was injured. It speeds the healing. All warriors do this."

Aislinn exhaled, but not entirely with relief. "At least it wasn't a woman."

"No. Never women. There are few female warriors anyway. We cannot risk them."

Aislinn blinked several times. "Risk them?"

"We are also very jealous."

"Yeah." She smiled. "Kind of saw some of that." She watched him smile in return. "You know, your accent's not as strong now as it was before."

His eyes glittered like moonstones as they scanned her face. "Whenever I am angry, Dimitri says, 'Uh oh, here comes the mad German.'"

Aislinn chuckled. "Sounds like something he would say. Especially after last night. At dinner?" she teased.

"I told you we get jealous."

"Mmm, hmm, and he seems to know just how to do it."

Bastian clenched his arm tight around her, squashing her stomach and breasts against his side. "You are someone to be jealous of."

She let the compliment wash over her like scented water. "Now *that* was a really nice thing to say." She leaned toward his lips, and halted. "Wait, I thought you said you were letting me go."

"I do not wish to let you go. Marius has not given permission. Our way of life could be a danger to you. Our mates can become targets."

"Whoa. News flash." She pushed up further on her elbow. "If I became your mate, I'd be a target?"

"It is only fair that you know all the risks. Marius insists on that."

"Marius hasn't told me squat. Are you saying I'd be a target of the creepy... uh, animal things that attacked us earlier tonight?"

A shadow crept over Bastian's face as he nodded.

She lowered her voice to a whisper. "Are you worried because of the woman you had before?"

"That will *never* happen again!" His eyes flashed. His head and shoulders lifted from the pillow and both hands clenched her ribs.

"Bastian, you're hurting me."

"I am sorry."

"Okay, I believe you." She rubbed her hand across his abdomen, sending calming energy. *Don't worry*, she sent to his mind. *You worry too much.* His shoulders relaxed and his head fell back onto the pillow. Fear remained in his eyes, and he erected a block as she attempted to sooth his mind.

"You're holding back on me. What else are you afraid of?"

Even as he blinked she knew his response would not be a complete disclosure. "I do not wish to let you go," he replied.

"I'm right here beside you, so, it's a moot point right now, okay? You need to chill out."

The barest smirk toyed at the corner of his mouth.

"So, back to the blood-sucking thing." She continued to stroke his chest, wishing it wasn't covered in mud. "You drink the blood of animals?"

"Every two days."

"Oh! Ew!" She sat up.

He grinned at her reaction, pulling at her arms to bring her back to him, which she resisted. "It is a fate I am stuck with."

"But why? That's so seriously gross, Bastian."

"I need Marius' permission to tell you more about our people. We have difficulty with normal food."

She scowled. "Oh, come on. You can't even tell me about your food without his permission?"

He watched her expression as if enjoying it, but did not respond. His fingers toyed with her long hair.

"So, how much of a say-so does Marius have? I mean, does he dictate everything in your life? Who you can see? Where you can go?"

Bastian sighed. "I think I have told you too much, already. He is angry that I formed a blood bond with you. Believe it or not, he is concerned for you."

"For me?"

"Yes. I have been… in a state of darkness for a long time. Marius has been troubled. He feared I would turn evil, not from a human blood craving, but from enjoying the killing of vampires. Killing for defense of our loved ones is acceptable, honorable. Killing because you enjoy it is a step down a path of no redemption."

"And you think you were headed down that path?"

"You saved me from that, I believe."

"I did?" She brightened. "How so?"

"That night, in your room. You were feeling sadness. It reminded me of what I had forgotten. What I had buried. Then when I healed you I had to call on things I had not felt in a long time. Goodness. Light. Joy. Love. So, all that grief I had pushed down, it exploded inside me like a thousand knives. I could not control it."

"I remember. You looked like you were in shock." It was alarming to her that he had managed to completely block all those emotions, apparently for years. Of course, she functioned every day knowing her own grief for three family members lay just under the surface.

"Because I felt your pain, I remembered my own," he said.

"I almost feel guilty."

"No. Do not feel that." Tugging with his arm, he coaxed her torso back against his chest. "My heart feels much lighter. So, thank you, my lady."

"You know, I love it when you call me that."

"You do? Then I shall call you that always."

She giggled. "I like this. Relaxing with you and talking. Even though I'm supposed to be mad at you."

"You are?" Rolling toward her, he brought his mouth firmly against hers. Aislinn's skin prickled like sparklers as he kissed her. How she loved those full lips that expressed want for her so badly. She allowed herself to enjoy his heavenly mouth with complete abandon. Their tongues lathed each other in rhythm, exciting their bodies.

He rolled closer. His right knee curled over her legs. Even that small movement felt sexy. Until he groaned and stiffened.

"What's wrong," she asked, alarmed. "Are you okay?"

With a low growl of protest, he returned to his prone position. "Yes. No. The healing hurts. We cannot take much pain medicine. Our bodies override it." He sighed. "I must stop."

"Stop what?"

"Kissing you."

"Why? I'm not touching any of your wounds."

He grinned. "I have *many* uninjured places that you could touch."

"Oh, really?" Aislinn raised her eyebrows.

"I am on orders to lie still. If I give in to my compulsions, that's not going to happen." He stared pointedly at the ceiling instead of her.

"Why do you obey his orders? Who is he?"

"He is my…." Bastian faltered.

"Oh, don't stop there. Remember, not telling me something is almost as bad as…."

"No, it isn't."

"Yes, it is."

"No, it isn't."

"Yes, it is."

With a blur of movement, he covered her mouth with his again, preventing her from arguing. She kissed him back, then giggled and pulled away. His left arm flexed and he forced her body as well as her lips back to his. Before she could protest, his tongue glided along her bottom lip and she felt heat all the way to her groin. She moaned and slid her palm down his chest to his rippled abs, then slid lower and touched soft cotton. There was a drawstring.

"What are you wearing?" She would have assumed they were boxers except, with her enhanced vision, the cloth resembled a skirt with faded patterns and swirls. She was not sure whether to untie it or lift it.

While her head was turned, he pressed hungry kisses into her cheek and neck. She moaned in appreciation. His left hand slipped under the edge of her camisole.

Aislinn glided her fingertips over the soft material, toward his rising erection. She had never experienced the urge to grab a man's crotch, certainly not after knowing him only two days. Now she wanted to grab every part of him.

"We wear it when we are healing," he murmured between kisses.

"Oh." She kept her head turned to give his anxious lips better access to her yearning neck, reveling in his sucking kisses that sent shivers of arousal through every cell of her body.

"Oh my." Her fingertips nearly touched their intended target. "You still think what I'm feeling is because of this so-called blood bond?"

"Mmm-hmm. But I hope it is more." He trailed kisses across her collarbone to the strap of the camisole, which he pulled at with his teeth.

Aislinn slipped one leg over his thigh. "Well then," she decided, "for heaven sakes, bite me again."

With a sudden roar he pulled away and nearly knocked her off the bed. She slipped in the spilling dirt and landed on the wooden floorboards, on her rump.

He sat up, his legs swinging over the edge of the bed.

"Woman, do not ever say that unless you mean it." His chest was heaving. His eyes were glazed and full of unbridled lust, which was frightening, and exhilarating. It was the sexiest thing she had ever seen.

"But I... I...."

"Aislinn, understand what you are asking, what you are committing to. Because, I will hold you to it. I will claim you as mine and never let go." He looked like a man drunk with love about to ravish his woman.

"Bastian, what I experience with you is like *nothing* I have ever experienced with any other man. I don't understand what all this means, or what all your... rules are, but...."

The door opened. Marius stepped into the room. For a moment, he did not speak as he stared at them, black eyes glistening. They stared back.

# CHAPTER 10

"Miss Aislinn, we need to transport Bastian to another location." Marius' tone left no room for argument.

"To a hospital?" Aislinn asked, hopeful.

"In a manner of speaking. Would you give us some privacy, please?"

Aislinn bristled. Didn't he get that backwards? Why was he so dismissive? And why should *she* leave?

*Aislinn, please.* Bastian spoke into her mind.

Angry and resentful, Aislinn got to her feet, brushing off dirt. The temptation to lean forward and brazenly kiss Bastian was strong, but she lost her nerve in front of Marius. She felt like an errant teenager caught sneaking through a window. Marius did not acknowledge her as he stepped aside so she could walk past him. In fact, he seemed to be glaring at Bastian. She glanced back at Bastian and blew him a kiss. A hint of a smile toyed at the corner of his lips.

She crossed her arms, getting angrier by the minute as she descended the stairs with careful movements. Until she smelled food cooking.

*Oh my gosh, what a fantastic smell!*

Gabriella was in the kitchen stirring eggs in a frying pan. She was wearing a green T-shirt and gray, draw string pants.

She turned and offered Aislinn a smile. "*Bună dimineața*, Aislinn. Of course, I can just say 'good morning' to you, since you're American."

"Good morning. Smells amazing in here." Her stomach growled in response to the wafting aromas.

"Thanks. Thought you might be hungry."

"How did you know? Can I help?"

"Actually, I've just finished the eggs. I've got sausages and fried potatoes already on the table, and there's cinnamon buns in the oven. I usually have a mixture of Greek, German and Romanian cooking, some cheese dishes and pastries and stuff. But I thought you might like an American breakfast. Although, I can't get grits here."

"Ha! I would have been real surprised if you did. Now, come up with sausage gravy on biscuits and I might not leave."

Gabriella chuckled and nodded in agreement. "You know, that's something I've never served Marius. 'Course it would be a bit heavy for him." She smirked in thought. "If you would just grab two plates from that cabinet?" She indicated the cabinet to Aislinn's right, so Aislinn grabbed the plates and waited.

"I thought you guys had a cook."

"Only on special occasions." Gabriella spooned the scrambled eggs into a bowl and led Aislinn to the table. "They left before dessert last night."

"Oh. Well, thanks for cooking."

"You are welcome."

"Why only two plates?"

"Oh, the guys won't eat much of this, though Bastian likes eggs, mostly raw. They'll have some beef broth and smoothies in a while." She sat at the long oak table where they had dined the previous evening. She indicated a seat beside her.

Aislinn sat and stared at her. "That's it? Broth and smoothies?"

"Well, they ate something earlier."

"Ate... what, exactly?"

Gabriella sighed and kept her expression neutral. "Aislinn, how about we enjoy our breakfast, and then talk about the serious stuff?"

Aislinn pressed her lips together, feeling rebellious. She dared not let Gabriella know all that Bastian had divulged. "Okay." She grabbed her fork. "As long as we *do* talk about the serious stuff."

"Fair enough. Want some jasmine tea? It's my favorite."

"Sure."

Gabriella dropped a tea bag into a mug and poured steaming water over it.

After several minutes of enjoying eggs and sausage, Aislinn asked, "Um, how did I get your pajamas on, exactly?"

Gabriella presented a mischievous side smile. "Well, Bastian wanted to help. But, I wouldn't let him. And, he had just put you to sleep, which, if you're anything like me, I assume you were quite pissed about when you woke up."

"Oh, yeah, I was. The *nerve* of him doing that without my permission." She scowled and poked at one of the tangy sausages, then let out a long "*Mmmm.*"

"That must have been hard for you to dress me," she commented after swallowing two more bites of heaven. "I was zonked."

"I worked as a nurse's assistant. I know how to turn a body to get clothes on and off. And… well, I guess it's okay to say. I had Bastian TK your clothes off and over to a chair. Then I made him get out."

Aislinn choked on the sausage. She swallowed a mouthful of hot tea to force the sausage down. "Tee-kay?"

"They can move things telekinetically. When I first met Marius, he would make all sorts of things, like flowers and chocolate, appear in the air and plop into my lap. I used to call it conjuring, but he says he can't conjure something out of air. He's just transporting something that is."

Aislinn stared at her, mouth open, envisioning a bunch of crazed wildflowers and chocolate pieces popping into the air. "And that didn't freak you out?"

Gabriella opened her mouth and hesitated. "I was a little more informed than you. But not by much."

"And you're saying… Bastian saw me naked?"

"No. No. I stood in the way, and told him to transport your clothes to the chair and then turn around and get out. He kept trying to see around me, so I had Marius give him an order. Which he had to obey, of course."

"Of course?"

Gabriella looked straight at her, her face unreadable. "Yes."

Aislinn shifted her gaze across the room and through the window, where golden rays were appearing, casting a warm glow on a small garden of squash and pumpkins. "I think I need a drink, and something stronger than tea."

Gabriella chuckled lightly. "I'm curious. What did you say to Bastian this morning when you realized he put you to sleep? The first time Marius did that to me I chewed him out for five minutes."

"Actually, I *was* ready to kill him," Aislinn admitted. "But when I saw him in the bed, I… completely forgot. Darn, I meant to give him a hard time about that. How are you supposed to keep a guy in line when every time you look at him you forget why you were mad at him?"

Gabriella's green eyes twinkled. "Yeah, that tends to happen with these guys. While I was telling Marius off, he grabbed me and kissed me and… well, that was the end of that rant."

"What is it about them? I take one look at Bastian and…."

"You're mush." Gabriella finished for her.

"Yes! Oh my gosh, I've never seen such sexy men in all my life. I mean… don't get the wrong idea. I…."

"Don't worry." She chuckled. "You'd have to be dead not to look at my Marius. Or Dimitri."

With relief, Aislinn continued. "I know almost nothing about Bastian. Yet, I look at him and the world stops moving. I touch him and all reason goes out of my head."

"The good news is, they feel the same way about us. They go crazy when we're around."

"Yeah, I guess. Bastian certainly seems to. There's so much I need to understand."

"You have time. Don't rush it. It could be too much at once. Take it one day at a time."

"Hmm, sounds like the voice of experience. Actually, I learned a lot about patience when I went through physical therapy. You can only rush so much. By the way, you seem to be different from them. I mean, you feel like me. And... you're American. So... what exactly are these guys?"

"Well, Marius will give his consent to explain it all soon. As the leader, he has a say in who is told what. And... he usually likes to do it himself."

Aislinn frowned. "Everybody obeys his orders like he's the king or something. I mean, I get the whole patriarchal family thing, but Marius doesn't look a day over 35 to me, so, what's up with that?"

Gabriella smiled secretively and chewed on a fried potato before answering. "Let's just say, this family, and others like us, cannot survive without a strict code of leadership. It's too dangerous. They've learned the hard way. Marius *is* very much like a king. You may hear people refer to him as Prince Marius. As a large family tribe, we have to stay connected, we have to be focused, or we die. Marius stays focused no matter what happens. Except for one time I remember."

"What time was that?"

"When he met me."

Aislinn gaped at her. "When he met you?"

A slow smile brightened Gabriella's face. "Yeah. These guys live longer than normal people. We'll get into that later. They don't just go in and out of relationships like other people, except when they're young and experimenting with chasing after girls. But after that they, um... kind of grow up and get focused on their missions, and get trained. They reach a place where they need a specific mate. When they find that woman, they receive a sign. Like a tattoo."

Aislinn gave a soft intake of breath. "Last night. I remember. You guys were staring at his wrist, at a red mark, and then you stared at me."

"Well, well," Gabriella smiled and raised both eyebrows. "You can see them already. You *are* progressing fast."

Aislinn felt butterflies dance in her stomach at the realization that Gabriella expected her abilities to grow. In a soft voice she said, "I could see all of them last night. Marius, Dimitri, and Bastian. The marks shine like gold." She looked down at her near-empty plate, then back up at Gabriella. "The one on Bastian's wrist was red, though."

Gabriella sipped her tea. "The mate sign is a warning. Often they are so caught up in the whole warrior thing that they almost forget about a real relationship. Then, that woman suddenly appears, and *whammo*. They're knocked off guard. They act pretty insane. They can be vulnerable and lose focus. Sometimes we have to save them from themselves. Marius was overwhelmed by emotions when we met. He was so shocked by their intensity. Then again, so was I."

"That's kind of the way Bastian is. And me. Wow, what a relief it is to finally talk to you." Aislinn pressed a hand to her stomach to quell the butterflies. "Um, if a guy loses a mate, can he have another one?"

Gabriella's hard stare indicated Aislinn's question could only come from knowing more than she should.

"Yes. It happens. Especially if… they lose a mate early in life."

Aislinn averted her eyes to her plate.

"They are very protective of their women," Gabriella added, almost as a warning.

Aislinn reached for her cup of tea. "Maybe that's why he got injured."

"What do you mean?"

"Well, he got mad last night when I didn't stay in the car. That's when this giant hairy thing attacked us. Looked like Bigfoot. I've never seen such long claws. And those long, creepy arms." She shivered, nearly spilling her tea.

"That's what got him, huh? It's rare for one of those to attack. They use fear as a weapon. I can't believe it got a good swipe at Bastian. He's a legendary warrior."

"Well, he *was* kicking butt." Aislinn felt pride at the memory, then felt her body warm. "What a sight he was. The way he moved. I'll never forget it. He and Dimitri fought like they had rehearsed it. All the movements and the power. And then, *ew*, blood and guts."

Gabriella nodded knowingly.

"Anyway," Aislinn continued, "I saw that 'hound horde' as you guys called it coming at them. I got out to help and yelled—you know, with my mind—to stop them. I hoped I could do it strong enough, and it worked. Bastian grabbed my arm and told me to get in the car. That's when the hairy Bigfoot thing got him."

"His concentration was on keeping you safe."

Aislinn fought a stab of guilt. "Weird about that, though. Him acting like he recognized me."

"What, Bastian?"

"No. The Bigfoot creature."

"It spoke to you?" Gabriella looked alarmed.

"No, but I heard its thoughts. Or, maybe emotions. It was like, 'there you are,' as if it was looking for me. Then it reached out for me. I mean, seriously, why would it care who I was?"

Gabriella lost some of the color in her face. She let the air out of her lungs. "I need to let Marius know about this. Did you tell Bastian?"

"About the Bigfoot? No. Just you. Didn't think about it 'till now. Of course, I'm still trying to decide if this is the longest running nightmare or the best dream of my life."

Gabriella gave a little smile, but her eyes remained worried. "I think the cinnamon rolls are done. I'll go check."

Aislinn held the cup of herbal tea close to her lips and inhaled the fragrance.

*Aislinn.*

Bastian was calling to her. Not actually her name, and not in desperation, but with a deep longing, as if his heart ached for her presence.

Breathing slow and steady, she focused on the connection and closed her eyes. Steam from the cup wafted around her face as the energy of Bastian filled her mind. He was boxed in somehow, resigned to his fate. She explored the sensation, and became alarmed. Something was closing in on him, yet he was not afraid. She turned toward the foyer, aware his location had changed. Was he in danger?

She returned the cup to the table, and followed the pull. Wandering toward the front door, she passed the staircase and noticed a closed door on her left. She opened it a few inches. A small lamp was lit beside a chair. Hundreds of books lined the walls of a long room. She opened the door further and stepped inside, entranced. The bookcases stood eight shelves high. A very new-looking rug with thick, maroon and white stripes inlaid with flowers lay on the floor and there were several high-backed chairs and a desk. A wonderful scent hung in the room, as if someone had lit incense.

The connection to Bastian was evaporating as she explored the room and the old books, so she closed her eyes and thought only of him. The pull was to the far left corner. Puzzled, she walked the length of the room to the last set of wooden shelves. The edge of one shelf unit was jutting out.

*No way.*

She grabbed the edge of the bookcase. It swung open with ease, and made no sound.

Pausing to adjust to the darkness, Aislinn followed a golden glow that flickered and outlined an old wooden staircase. Voices echoed below. Closing her eyes again to be sure she could feel Bastian, she opened them and descended the stairs, her heart thumping.

Clearing the last stair and stepping onto a mixture of stone and concrete, she gasped. A three-tiered candelabra rested on a small table in the corner, its flickering glow outlining Marius kneeling over a large rectangular opening in the stone floor. He was chanting, holding a long, rosary-like string of beads in his hand. Bastian was lying in the dirt, his arms crossed over his chest. His eyes were closed.

"Oh my god!" Aislinn exclaimed.

Dimitri whirled and strode toward her. "Aislinn, it's okay."

"He's not dead," she insisted. "He's alive! I heard him. What are you doing?"

"We know." His fingers caressed her shoulders in a soothing gesture. "We know."

"Then what are you…?"

"Aislinn." It was Bastian's deep voice.

She forced herself to look at him. His opalescent eyes were open. Her body began to shake.

"Come, Miss Aislinn." Marius gestured with his hand. He nodded to encourage her.

"Oh, crap." Gabriella loomed at the top of the stairs. She descended slowly. "I know you weren't ready for *that*. Sorry, girl. Maybe I should have told you more."

Aislinn considered running back up the stairs.

Gabriella held up a hand. "Don't be scared."

Aislinn swallowed. "Don't be scared? They're burying him!"

"Honey, you need to decide right now how much you want to know. Do you want to know it all, or do you want to know nothing? I think you've already figured out if Bastian wants to erase all this from your mind, he can do it. The choice is yours. Knowledge or blissful ignorance. If you want, you can just go on with your life and walk away."

"No!" Bastian protested.

Aislinn felt his protest in her soul. She examined each person. "Right now, you're looking like a bunch of vampires or something to me."

"Hey, we are *not* vampires." Dimitri's hands shifted to his hips, his voice full of disgust. His indignation unnerved Aislinn, but also sobered her.

"Then what are you?"

"We will explain shortly." Marius interrupted. "Are you brave enough to come over here or not?"

Challenged with bravery, Aislinn stared at Marius and swallowed. She took a step forward and paused. Bastian was sitting up.

"No, Bastian." Marius' hand hovered above his chest. "I want you still. You need to be healed and ready."

Aislinn was no coward, but her arms shivered with fear at the eerie sight. She attempted to calm her mind so she could focus. Her empathic abilities had grown enough to read the motivations of these people. After several seconds of reaching into them, she was sure they meant her no harm. They also meant no harm to Bastian.

She took a deep breath, walked forward and stopped three feet from the rectangle of dirt Bastian was laying in. Her limbs felt like rubber. She could not control the quivering in her body.

Marius smiled with satisfaction. "Good."

Bastian was watching her with entreaty and longing in his pale eyes. They did not sparkle like usual but looked gray and ghostly. His chest and right shoulder was swathed in a fresh layer of mud where each slash was. He wore the kilt-like garment she had seen earlier. Except that in the light of the candles, she could make out ancient-looking runes.

"Miss Aislinn, we need to do this in order for Bastian to heal, especially during the day. The wounds from the Yeti are not healing as fast as I would like. There is a little infection. Of a kind I have never seen. Bastian needs the soil." Marius waited and watched her reaction.

Aislinn tried to force her shaky voice to sound calmer. "The soil is full of bugs, and mites, and all sorts of creepy crawly things. He could get more infected. And how's he supposed to breathe?"

"We are… like plants, in the sense that we have the ability to pull nutrients from the soil and the herbs we have placed in it," Marius explained. "It is old knowledge. Bastian's body knows what to do. We are weaker during the day. I need him whole and fit. We sense battles coming." Marius scooped a handful of dirt which had many colors of leaves and flowers in it as if to show her there was nothing to fear. Which did not work.

"Okay, just for the record, still sounding like vampires."

"But not." Marius insisted. "Once Bastian is covered, he will lower his heartbeat and his breathing and concentrate on pulling what he needs from this earth and these natural medicines."

"I thought he couldn't heal himself."

"This is different. We can all do this. This takes time, and we know how to help him. By sundown the wounds will have sealed well."

Aislinn did not miss the "we" part that excluded her. Avoiding Bastian's face, she stared at the dark soil surrounding him, and at the dirt in Marius' hand. Visions of the worst funeral of her life swam before her. From the side of a wheelchair, she could see her own hand dropping handfuls of dirt, one, two, three, onto rectangular coffins hovering over gaping maws in the ground. Her mother, father, and sister.

Violent tremors began at her shoulders and traveled down to her feet. Dimitri stepped close and wrapped a comforting arm around her quivering shoulders. Bastian sat straight up in the dirt.

"Dammit, Bastian. I do not need this energy down here." Marius frowned. "Dimitri, go upstairs."

"But, sir," Dimitri protested.

"Just do it."

With rebellion on his face, Dimitri turned toward the stairs.

"No!" Aislinn protested. "I want him here."

"Why?" In a wave of fury, Bastian vaulted to his feet and stepped out of the earthen bed and onto the stone floor. Dirt and greenery rained onto the floor. Marius murmured several curses and stood. Mud fell from one of Bastian's wounds. The skin underneath was pink and swollen and caused Aislinn's stomach to turn. She recoiled at the anger and suspicion in his face.

"Because he... um... makes me feel less afraid," she explained.

"Humph." Dimitri crossed his arms and glared at Bastian in defiance. Bastian looked ready to hit him.

A ray of light cascaded through the decorative grill of a small round window on the far wall near the ceiling.

"Bastian, I need you in the ground." Marius fixed his black eyes on Aislinn. "The sun is rising higher. Miss Aislinn, stay or go upstairs."

Aislinn bristled at the command. He wasn't *her* prince. At movement from his hand, her gaze lowered to the dirt resting in his palm.

"Marius, I had to bury three family members. I don't think I can stand by and watch this. But... will I be able to reach him? Will he still hear me?"

She shifted her focus to Bastian. To her surprise, anger left his face. He was pleased that she wanted to hear him. She wanted to lose herself in those yearning eyes, so full of desire for her.

"Miss Aislinn, if you keep communicating with him, he will not close down," said Marius. "He will take much longer to heal."

Bastian's eyes still held hers. "I will hear you at sunset. Call for me."

"Miss Aislinn?" Something in Marius' sharp tone made Aislinn want to obey him like the others. She was torn, but knew she could not watch Bastian be buried in the ground. She turned and forced her wobbly legs to move. Each step up the staircase was heavy and painful. Her calves throbbed, more from shock at the scene behind her than from weariness. A powerful tugging in her chest made her feel ripped from Bastian as she moved further away. Perhaps she should not have forgiven him for taking her blood.

She passed through the library and into the foyer where the rising sun cast a rainbow of lights through a stained glass design of flowers and vines above the front door. Gabriella stood beside her.

"I think I need to lie down." Aislinn did not look at Gabriella. "Maybe I need to go back to the inn."

"If Marius or Dimitri drives you, it needs to be now or wait closer to sunset. Full sun is dangerous for them. They are weaker in full sunlight."

Aislinn turned to Gabriella. "Still sounding like vampires."

# CHAPTER 11

Golden rays danced through the tall trees and splashed onto the windshield, warming Aislinn's arms as the forest rushed by. She felt heavy and sunken into the leather seat like a discarded coat.

"Aislinn, would you please get me the gloves in the dash box?"

She opened the box, found two pair of black gloves and handed one to Dimitri. He deftly inserted his hands as he drove, and pulled the sleeves of his black hoodie down over his wrists.

"Wow, the sun really does bother you."

"Yeah. It's a pain."

She snorted. "You definitely spent time in America. You sound like one of us."

"But not." He shrugged and smirked. "Since college life was often night life, that part wasn't difficult for me."

Aislinn frowned. "I never thought about how weird that would be. Did you take all night classes?"

"No, but in bright sunlight I had to be in full gear if I went from one building to another. Sunglasses, hat, jacket, gloves. The whole nine yards. I didn't attend during the summer."

"What about sun screen?"

"Sun screen is meaningless. We can't wear anything with chemicals in it. Any lotion or stuff like that has to be of very pure ingredients, like cold-pressed or flower-infused oils. Although, I've tried a couple of the sunscreens made for babies. They work… a little."

"Humph," she commented thoughtfully. "Were you weak in the sun even with coats and stuff?"

"By our standards, yes. To everyone else, I was just a normal human. I did not engage in day sports though. Practices were often during the day. That would have zapped too much of my energy."

"Dimitri, are you aliens?"

"Not for about five thousand years now." He shot her a teasing grin.

"Please tell me you're not five thousand years old."

"No. I'm just forty."

"Forty!" Aislinn gripped her arm rests.

His brows flitted playfully.

"How old is Bastian?"

"Hmm, let me think how badly he'll kill me for telling you."

"Dimitri."

"Let's just say he's way, *way* older than me."

"Holy crap."

Dimitri chuckled.

"Not funny, Dimitri. Still sounding seriously like vampires, just for the record."

"Now, have I ever drank your blood?"

"Uh... not that I *remember*," she answered with flippant sarcasm. "But then, I wouldn't actually *remember*, would I?"

"Eh, I'm good at persuasion, but Marius and Bastian are better. They've been doing it longer." He swerved sharply to avoid a rabbit scampering across the asphalt, and jerked the car back onto the road with precision.

Aislinn grabbed the dash for added support. "Oh my gosh. My heart can't take any more." She leaned her head back on the seat and pushed her hair off her neck since the sun was warming the car.

"Whoa, did Bastian drink your blood?"

Aislinn blanched as Dimitri stared at her neck. She pulled her hair forward. "Eyes on the road, buddy."

"You're not answering. That means he did. *Oooo*, no wonder Marius is pissed."

"Why should Marius care? It's none of his business."

"Everything is Marius' business."

She turned to look at him. "Not relationships, surely."

Dimitri nodded. "Especially relationships. Didn't you take history?"

"Of course. What's history got to do with it?"

"Well, Marius is like a prince to us. Did relationships matter to kings and princes?"

Aislinn blew air from her lips and rolled her eyes. "Okay, I see what you're getting at. Kings controlled who had permission to marry. Well, depending on how high up you were in court. The commoners always worked for a Lord, and had to have his permission."

"So you do know some history. I had to take it, too, but *years* of it. Ugh."

"Maybe Marius will see me as a commoner and buzz off."

"Ha! Not if Bastian's interested in you."

"Why?"

"He's our Assassin."

"Assassin?" Aislinn's eye widened in shock.

"Vampire hunter. And sometimes Marius' body guard. He was once our strongest healer, but that was years ago."

"He healed *me*."

Dimitri whipped his head toward her. "What? When?"

"Two days ago. Well, he… you see… it's a long story."

Dimitri kept glancing from the road to her, as if waiting for her to continue.

"I'll tell you later." She chewed on her lip, thinking that would have to be one *very* amended version.

"Something tells me that's *quite* a story," he teased.

She decided not to comment further.

"Aislinn, this is *huge*. I've got to tell Marius. Anyway, Bastian's high up in the tribe as Marius' right hand man. Plus, he's an amazing warrior. Goes at it with a vengeance. People were calling him Fearless Sebastian before I was born. If Marius hadn't showed up last night, and Bastian didn't get wacked by the Yeti trying to save you, Bastian would have probably taken out most of those ghouls and not had a scratch. He's pretty badass."

"Hey, you were pretty badass, too."

He grinned wide.

After a few silent minutes, Aislinn decided to push for more information. "Dimitri, where did your people come from?"

Dimitri took a deep breath. "I'm not allowed to tell you without Marius' permission."

"Oh, good grief. I am so tired of this. Maybe I need to go straight to Marius and ask his almighty permission."

"Hey. I don't make the rules. But… pace yourself, Aislinn. To be involved with this family means a kind of loyalty you may not be prepared to give. Nothing of what you've seen can be shared with anyone. And I mean… *anyone*. Not even a family member. Not even a best friend. Are you capable of that kind of secrecy?"

"Of course." Aislinn felt insulted that he would ask.

Dimitri gave her a measured look. "Think long and hard before you really answer. Keeping secrets is difficult even for the best of humanity. Most humans tell at least one person. I've known two people who we trusted, and then found out they were telling some close friends. Marius and Bastian had to go erase their memories and plant new ones. Their power of persuasion is pretty strong."

"Yeah, tell me about it." Aislinn jumped when her phone rang and buzzed in her pocket. Gabriella had loaned her a pair of jeans and a green

T-shirt since blood spatter and who-knew-what had to be washed out of her blue dress.

"Hey, Eddie." She answered the call, feeling anger rise in her gut.

"How's my girl?"

"Not your girl, Eddie. Your friend most certainly, but, *not your freakin' girl, okay!*"

She heard a soft, "*Oooo,*" coming from Dimitri's direction.

"Good grief," Eddie exclaimed. "Aisy, what's wrong with you?"

"Nothing," she snapped.

"Aisy?" Eddie's tone turned serious. "You sound really upset. You don't yell at people. You never yell."

She closed her eyes and sighed. "I know. You're right. I'm just… it's been a really bad day, okay?"

"Okay. Now you've got me worried."

"Why'd you call?"

"Girl, you're gonna break my heart," said Eddie.

"Yeah, your heart looked real damaged when you were with the shaggy blonde."

"Whoa. Are you still on the blonde?"

"No. The blonde—no, the *second* blonde—is old news now."

"You're a blonde by the way."

"Not *that* kind of blonde."

"Ouch. Not sure what the distinction is."

"I was never easy, Eddie. Not even for you. Until you asked me to *marry* you of course." She noticed Dimitri swerve slightly in the road, and correct himself.

Eddie sighed. "Don't remind me. That's still on, you know. I remember when me and you…."

"Don't even go there, Eddie," she said through gritted teeth. "That was a long time ago. That was before the first blonde fiasco. Before I realized we could never be more than friends."

"Aisy, what is *wrong* with you this morning? You are so different."

"You have no idea. Maybe I'm seeing clearer."

"Who were you with last night?"

"None of your business. You don't get to ask."

"You know I've tried to be the best friend I can to you." Eddie was breathing heavy, as if trying to control his own anger. "I'll do anything for you."

Feeling a smidgen of guilt, Aislinn took a deep breath. "Yes, you have been a good friend, Eddie. And you genuinely seem to care about me. But, it would make me more comfortable if you would just call me Aisy and not 'my girl.' Okay?"

"Hmm, I'll think about it."

"And what is all that noise? You sound like you're standing next to a tractor-trailer engine at a truck stop."

"Oh, just some interference. Listen, Aisy, I was trying to break this easy, but, I've got some bad news."

"What?"

"Your grandmother had a bad fall last night, and now it looks like she's got pneumonia real bad.

"Oh my god! What happened?" Aislinn sat up. "Where is Aunt Julia?"

"I think she was out with friends or something and got back late. She found your grandmother on the sidewalk. Looks like she was getting the mail and collapsed. You know they're at the end of that mountain road, except for the other two houses over the old bridge. No one saw her."

"Oh my god." Aislinn's stomach clenched with fear. Tears stung her eyes. "How did you... how did you find out?"

"Saw Aunt Julia's post on Facebook while she was at the hospital. We're friends. You know, she always liked me."

"Yes, she did." Aislinn swallowed tightly. "Wait a minute, why didn't she call me?"

"I told her I would call you this morning. I told her about you being in Romania, and we knew the time would be all different. And, she was afraid you would jump on a plane and come rushing back."

"She's right. I am going to jump on a plane."

"Now, just hold on," Eddie cautioned. "It's not like they've called the family in or anything. The doctor said...."

"Eddie, this is *Gramma*, okay? She and Aunt Julia are all I have left. I need to be there. I'll look up flights and stuff when I get back to the inn. I'm on the way there now."

"Okay, but wait for my call before you book anything."

"Eddie, I may need to grab the first thing I can. It's going to be ridiculously expensive."

"Just wait. Please. She may come jumpin' out of that bed like a Pop-Tart. You know her. She's pretty tough. No reason to rush."

"I'll get a better deal if I book now."

"Just wait until tonight, okay? I'll call you with an update, and I'll even book flights for you. Let me use my mileage points."

"Well, all right. But, you call me the minute anything changes. I mean it. No matter what time it is."

"I will. I promise. I'm here for you, okay?"

"Thanks Eddie. I owe you one."

"I hope so." His tone sounded contrite, but had an odd hint of satisfaction. "Bye, sweetie girl."

"Ugh." Aislinn ended the call and let her head drop back to the headrest.

"Okay, nothing else can happen, Dimitri. Just so you know. Nothing else can happen."

"Um, okay." Dimitri responded. "I'll do my best. You're going back to the States?"

"Yes. My grandmother is...." Her throat caught.

"I heard."

"You heard the whole conversation?"

"Mmm-hmm."

"You guys have super hearing too?"

"Yep."

"Oh good grief."

"I sincerely hope your grandmother gets well."

Aislinn turned toward her window. She blinked and sniffed to get control of her emotions. She and Gramma had always been close, even before the accident.

When Aislinn turned twelve, Gramma Cardeia acknowledged her unusual abilities and helped her learn to control them, to use them. It was their secret, though it was mostly a game when she was young, one her mother thought was silly, and discouraged. Gramma had told her it ran in the family. Gramma could sometimes see things in the future. She did not like Eddie from the start. "That boy's a snake in the grass," Gramma had said.

Dimitri slowed and turned in front of the inn. "Aislinn, I don't know if you realize this. But... I have to ask you something really personal." He put the car in park.

She noted his brilliant, aqua-blue eyes were full of concern.

"Did you drink any of Bastian's blood?"

Aislinn blinked. "What?"

"This is important, kiddo. Did you?"

What if Bastian was not supposed to tell her any of this? Would Dimitri know if she lied? She decided to be as honest as she dared. Her stomach twisted. "Not like he did. I didn't bite him or anything. But, he... put his finger in my mouth, and he confessed today it had his blood on it."

Dimitri whistled softly. "Okay, Marius is probably doubly pissed."

"Why? Nobody explains anything to me!"

Dimitri raised a hand to quell her anger. "A blood exchange is the first step in the bonding rite."

"Excuse me?" *You are with me because of the blood call.* That's what Bastian was trying to tell her earlier.

"In our family tradition," said Dimitri, "a male has to stake his claim by taking the female's blood. If she agrees, he gives her a bite mark that everybody can see. She takes his blood as well. By drinking each other's blood, you created, or *he* created, a blood bond. You can hear him and he can hear you, telepathically, right?"

She nodded, avoiding his eyes.

"Between warriors this is no big deal, and it is a great advantage in battle. But for a male and female, it's a whole 'nother ball game."

"And… how many steps are there to this bonding thing?"

"Um, five that I know of. You have to have three blood exchanges, spaced out a little. Although, for a pure human to convert, there are more steps. And that's only if they have permission from the tribe's leader to try."

"Of course." Aislinn threw a hand into the air, and tears began to well in her eyes. "Of course. It's just one more thing. I told you not one more thing could happen."

"Hey, hey." Dimitri took her hand in his and squeezed. "It's okay. Really. Brace yourself, honey, 'cause there is one more thing."

Aislinn closed her eyes and tears dripped down her face.

"Okay. Look at me for a minute. Please?"

Under wet lashes, she glared sideways. "If you use persuasion on me, I swear to God…."

"No." He shook his head. "I won't do that. I'm here for you, okay. Like a brother."

Aislinn sniffed. "I never had a brother."

"Well, I'll be yours, okay?"

She nodded and more tears fell. "Kay," she managed to mumble.

"Of course, that means I can't flirt with you and drive Bastian crazy. But, I could make the sacrifice."

Aislinn laughed in spite of the tears.

Dimitri took both of her hands in his. An odd little shock zipped through her hands and into her body. Her eyes widened.

"Don't worry. It just means that I really am like a brother to you now." He smiled and then the smile dropped. "I don't know if this blood bond you have with Bastian will be strong enough—doesn't sound like you got much blood—but, the more distance you put between you and Bastian, the more you will feel the pull."

"Pull?" Before he answered, Aislinn knew what he meant. She remembered waking and wanting to be near Bastian. No, *needing*. She had left the bed and found him, despite her misgivings. Later, when she left the basement, the pull was even stronger.

"Mmm-hmm. It will literally tear at you, at your insides. All the mated couples I know can't be very far from each other. Physically. Not just mentally."

Aislinn stared at him. "Okay. I take back forgiving him."

Dimitri attempted a quick smile. "A few miles is okay. Even across town for a while. But, I'm pretty sure America would be *reeeally far*, if you know what I mean."

Aislinn shook her head. "I'm going to kill him."

Mrs. Tănase patted Aislinn's hand. "It will be all right, Miss Thomas. When you get home, your grandmother will be getting along well for sure. I feel it in my bones."

"I hope so, Mrs. Tănase." Aislinn sniffed. "There was so much I wanted to see here. I was going to tour Transylvania and Bran Castle today. That was the *most* important thing. And I thought about traveling to Germany or Switzerland, or maybe even to Russia. I always wanted to see Moscow."

"Well, then, you must come back. I tell you this, if you come back to see us, Mr. Miclos and I will give you fifteen percent discount. How is that?"

"Aw, that's really nice of you, Mrs. Tănase, really. I hope I can come back soon. I love Romania. This was way too short." She scanned the dining room full of content, murmuring diners. This was where she had first seen Bastian. Her eyes watered at thoughts of all the places she had planned to see. She and Anya. Their dream cut short.

Even more than that now, she had wanted to get to know Bastian and his strange family better, despite her fears.

But... Bastian would have to wait.

"Thank you for lunch, Mrs. Tănase. I'm going to rest in my room for a while. I'm waiting on a phone call."

Aislinn basked in the warm sun on the breezy balcony with her coat wrapped tight and her electronic tablet poised in her lap. It was time to connect with her friends. Mia had seen Aunt Julia's post about Gramma and had emailed her twice, volunteering to go to the hospital or bring food. LaVanna was miffed that she had run off to Romania without her, and emailed playful threats on her person for when she returned to their therapy clinic. Randall had posted "you go, girl," and sent her a private message saying it was about time she left Eddie in the dust. Scott, ever the "all-for-one-and-one-for-all" guy, chastised her for not making it a group trip.

Resisting the urge to tell her friends about Bastian was hard. She longed to share her incredible story and get their take on it. LaVanna would squeal and want the hot details. Mia would bite her lip and tell her to be careful. Randall would congratulate her but would want to look him over, and Scott would be planning a party. Would she ever be able to hear those endearing reactions? Would she ever be allowed to share the really cool things—well, crazy things—about the new man in her life? Dimitri was right. This secret was going to be tough.

After flaunting an anemic version of her adventures, Aislinn dialed Aunt Julia's cell. Thankfully, Aunt Julia did not sound hysterical. Worried—but not hysterical. That was a good sign. Aunt Julia tended to exaggerate everything. Gramma was on a heavy dose of pain medication, so Aislinn could not have the one thing she really wanted—to talk to Gramma.

Instead, she did her leg stretches and exercises as her physical therapist had taught her, took a short bath, packed her suitcase, then began searching for flights. Blood bond or no blood bond, she needed to get to Gramma. It was only a tiny taste of blood, anyway. It wasn't like she actually *drank* his blood. Did she even swallow?

She rolled her eyes at the realization that she was debating whether she swallowed her not-quite boyfriend's blood. When she was near Bastian, when she was touching his magnificent body, even the thought of tasting his blood seemed natural. Here in the middle of the day, the idea was demented. There had to be something he was doing to her to make her lose all sense of reason. Maybe he was using persuasion and she had just grown used to it. Perhaps, distance from him was what she needed. Time to clear her head.

Her stomach growled. She glanced at the Romanian time she had added to her tablet. 5:15 PM. It was still three hours before sunset, when Bastian would awaken. Aislinn rolled her eyes again in self-chastisement. She could not believe she actually had to think about sunset in order to talk to her secret, vampire-*ish* boyfriend. They all insisted they weren't vampires. Apparently they were all lost in the same delusion.

She could call Gabriella. Did Gabriella keep the same schedule as the men? Aislinn realized she did not have Gabriella's number. In fact, she did not have anyone's number. She hadn't thought to ask. Bastian never indicated he had a cellphone. Of course, for them, with everyone's mind a mere thought away, who needed cellphones?

A firm knock on Aislinn's door made her jump.

She frowned and slipped through the narrow balcony access and paused at the locked door to her room. After the Razvan nightmare turned out to be real, she feared opening it.

"Who is it?" She laid her cheek and palms on the wood to reached beyond and sense the visitor. The energy was oddly familiar, but fuzzy, as if being blocked.

"Mr. Miclos," came a muffled voice.

The voice and accent sounded wrong, but Aislinn opened the door... and froze.

"Hello, Aisy-girl." Eddie stood with his hands resting on his hips and a wide grin on his tanned, handsome face. He was wearing a light blue polo-style shirt and jeans.

Aislinn's mouth fell open. "What the...? What are you doing here?"

"Worrying over my best friend." His brilliant green-gold eyes sparkled with mischief and confidence. As usual, his thick brown hair looked to be styled by a professional, with a few sexy locks hanging loose over his forehead nearly to his brows. "Where's my hello?"

"But... what... oh, my gosh, you *flew* all the way over here? Are you nuts?"

"Are you okay, sweetie?" For a moment, he looked concerned, and shifted his examination to her room as if reassuring himself she was alone. When she continued to stare at him in shock, he said, "You know, you've changed me somehow. I'm not usually the sensitive type."

"I... uh... what?"

"Aren't you going to invite me in?"

"Oh." Aislinn stepped back. But in a country where traditional rules of conduct were still respected, she might be seen as a "loose woman" to invite a man into her room. "You know, maybe I'll come out."

"Aisy, I came all this way for you." His voice held such entreaty, such yearning, new even for him. He leaned his hands on either side of the door frame. "You're worrying me even more. You seem distracted, out of your element. I hope no one has been mistreating you. I won't put up with that."

*If you only knew.* "I appreciate that, Eddie. I do. Let me come outside." She stepped into the hall and closed the door. He did not retreat, so she found herself boxed in, nearly against his chest.

A loving gaze met her eyes and her heart skipped a beat. Though he had grown increasing suggestive in the last two months, she had assumed it was because she was close to being able to walk on her own, and he probably found it more acceptable to be seen in public with her. Still, he *had* continued to end his phone conversations with, "Love you, Aisy-girl."

The term of endearment had moved her in the beginning, and sometimes still, but she had never encouraged him. Something about the change in him had insulted her, even before the second blonde. She was not good enough while she was in casts, on crutches, or finally a cane, but now that she was free, she was suddenly acceptable? More desirable? If he truly loved her, the mobility aids wouldn't have mattered. If she had confronted him, she knew he would fiercely deny it, and then she'd have to wrestle with whether to believe him. She couldn't discern Eddie like other men. A hazy wall surrounded him that confused her senses. Only his words and actions could be weighed.

And a man's actions spoke louder than any flattering words. Not that loving, sexy words whispered in her ear weren't wonderful. She would take them any day. But still.

Eddie rested his hands on her shoulders experimentally. "I had to assure myself you were all right." His voice grew tender. "I know this trip was for Anya. Just you and Anya, together again? Have you guys had fun?"

Tears welled in Aislinn's eyes. She had not been able to write to Anya today, so busy connecting with friends and Aunt Julia, and checking flights. She swallowed and crossed her arms. "Yes. Sort of."

Eddie's smile was warm. "That's really very sweet, you know that." He slid his hands to her elbows so he could uncross her arms. Then he took both of her hands in his. "Your memory of her makes her so real and present, even to me."

Emotions bubbled over inside Aislinn. She tried to swallow them, push them down, but could not gain control. She fell against his chest, blubbering.

Eddie wrapped lean, muscled arms around her and laid his head against her hair. Aislinn let silent tears fall. At least he understood about Anya. He had been there, with phone calls and sympathy.

"It's okay, baby. Let it all out." He stroked her hair and rocked her as she cried. But she did not cry for long.

Murmurings invaded her mind, like whispers on a wind. Bastian was not supposed to wake until sunset. For some reason, his mind was stirring, as if he had detected her strong emotions.

What if he could sense Eddie with her? She had to keep Eddie's presence a secret from him. Knowing Bastian and his unwavering jealousy, he would probably hit Eddie and ask questions later. Eddie didn't deserve that. Well, when she found him with the shaggy blonde, he did.

Aislinn straightened. "I need tissues." She opened the door and went straight for the box on her dresser. "Come on in, nobody's seen us. They probably won't know."

Eddie chuckled as he stepped inside her room and closed the door. "Why are you worried about what these people think?"

"Because this is not America, Eddie, where everybody drops rules and politeness. They still have traditions here. I kind of like it. It has a certain... I don't know...."

"Strangling effect?" he offered.

"No!" She glared at him reproachfully. "It's respectful, and honest, and charming. And by the way, call people Mister or Miss unless they invite you to use their first name."

"Hmm, stuffy."

"It is not."

"Okay, fine." He raised his hands in defeat. "I see you're in love with these people."

*Little do you know.*

Aislinn grabbed another tissue and blew her nose while Eddie glanced about the room.

"This is a small room," he commented.

"It's not small, it's... quaint. I don't need much."

"You don't even have a TV in here?"

"Wouldn't matter. Many of the programs aren't in English. And, I wanted to go out and see places anyway. I've got some movies and books saved on my tablet just in case."

He glanced at the tablet on her bed. "You still writing to Anya every day?"

A spike of grief stabbed Aislinn's heart and burned her eyes. The "yes" came out garbled while her face started to crinkle in pain again.

"Awe, come here, girl." He pulled her against him and hugged her warmly, breathing deeply of her hair. She had always loved him doing that. He liked the coconut-scented shampoo she used.

He inhaled again and pulled back to examine her face. With a troubled knit of his brows, he brushed back her hair from her shoulders and touched fingers to her neck.

Immediately, she stiffened and tried to pull back, realizing he had touched the spot where Bastian had bit her. Eddie's fingers dug into her arms.

"Who have you been with?" he demanded, shaking her.

"What? Stop that!"

"Who have you been with? I can smell him on you." His face was dark with anger, something she had never seen.

"You can't smell a *guy*. That's crazy, Eddie." She tried to pull away, but he had a bruising hold on her shoulders.

"You know I have an extreme sense of smell. That's why you use that coconut shampoo I like. And that cocoa butter lotion, which you're wearing now."

It was true. Eddie had always possessed the uncanny ability to tell her every restaurant she had visited on any given day, and told her so when he used to pick her up for dates or get-togethers with friends. After meeting Bastian's bizarre family, Eddie's ability did not seem so strange. Except... Eddie shouldn't have it.

"Anybody can smell perfume, Eddie," she argued. "Besides, I took a quick bath a couple of hours ago. You couldn't possibly...."

"I can still smell him." His expression was fierce, and frightening.

"That's impossible, Eddie. Get a grip. And get your hands off me!" Aislinn slammed her forearms outward and jerked free of his hold, which surprised both of them. She shot him a look of fury to mask the quivers of fear dancing in her stomach.

She added a roll of her eyes, hoping sarcasm would deflect him. "You're being a stupid jerk. I met some people, okay? They're Romanian. Well, I'm not sure. Their accents are all different, but...."

"And you like one of them?" His lips pressed into a hard line. The whites of his eyes seemed to pulse. He took a step toward her.

She backed up. "Eddie. Stop it! I've only been here for two, maybe three days. Give me a break." His actions were reminding her of Razvan's attack. She began assessing how fast she could turn and grab the door. Or run to the balcony and scream.

If she had to, she would wake Bastian with a scream.

Eddie lowered his eyes and took a slow, deep breath. He shifted his gaze to the window and then back at her.

"Hey, look, I'm sorry." He raised his hands, his expression contrite as if he had flipped a switch. She had seen him do this before, to deflect an argument. It usually worked. He gave a half-smile and sat on the edge of her bed. "My trip was about surprising you and making you feel better."

He looked down at the floor and shook his head as if ashamed. He lifted his head and regarded her with a sorrowful, unblinking gaze. "I don't seem to be doing that. You deserve to be treated like the lady you are. Don't worry about me. I've gone so long without sleep—24 hours—and I am just being grumpy and weird." His voice softened and drifted through her like an unseen radio wave. "Know this, Aisy. All I want is what's best for you. Please believe me. You have no need to be alarmed. Just be calm. Take a deep breath."

Aislinn realized she was, in fact, taking a deep breath as he instructed. Her shoulders began to relax. That seemed unwise. A part of her brain struggled to stay alert and angry. She found herself wanting to believe him.

"Feel at ease," he crooned. "Believe in me. I've just missed you, that's all. It's so good to see you again. You look beautiful. I'm hungry. Aren't you hungry?"

"Uh... yes. My stomach's been growling."

"Let's go eat."

~~◊~~

Norma Burch strolled into room number 324 with her face set. Her heart pounded against her ribs. "How are you today, Mrs. Cardeia?" she asked in case the old woman was conscious. There was no response from the silver-haloed face. Norma carefully slipped a needle into the woman's I.V.

"There we go Mrs. Cardeia, medicine to make you all better." Norma capped the syringe and dropped it into her pocket so she could throw it away in the next patient's hazardous trash bin, just in case this one was checked. They never were, but she was taking no chances. She dutifully refreshed Mrs. Cardeia's saline and morphine drip, and took her vitals.

Before leaving, she glanced at the old woman to be sure there was no awareness. She was not doing anything *really* bad. It would not be permanent. The chemical would only make the woman sick, and Norma was getting so much in return. The handsome man she met at the séance party at Margaret's house had offered the promise of youthfulness and vigor. For over twenty years Norma had fought the ravages of unwanted weight gain, wrinkles and varicose veins, only to have her husband leave her for a younger woman.

After showing before and after pictures of other people he had helped, the man guaranteed the one thing she so desperately wanted: to look younger and to be thinner. The handsome man had been drawn to her, he said, because of her warmth and intriguing personality. He was a distributor for a black market that bypassed approvals and exorbitant prices to give men and women products guaranteeing the beauty they had a right to recapture. Now, she would get hers.

No money was exchanged. It was a small task. Make the woman in room number 324 sicker. It would help the man finalize an important deal that he needed, and no harm would be done. All of the effects of the drug would last a mere 48 hours. The old woman would get better, eventually, and Norma's life would change immeasurably.

"This is beautiful, Eddie. How did you find this place?"

"Ha! I plugged in 'most scenic restaurants in Bucharest.' That's my big secret."

Aislinn laughed as Eddie raised his wine glass and flashed a handsome smile. The food was excellent and Eddie was unusually delightful, all earlier anger absent. Aislinn wondered briefly if Bastian would ever take her to a restaurant. Gabriella had insinuated the men ate broths and smoothies. Bastian had confessed to the animal blood. Not normal menu items. At the dinner, Bastian had not appeared to enjoy his food. Still, he ate some, so did that make him not a vampire? So far, he was meeting most of the criteria.

"Hey, you want to take that tour of Vlad the Impaler's castle tomorrow?"

"Oh, uh, that would have been great, Eddie. But, uh, I kind of made previous arrangements. But it doesn't matter," she amended quickly when he opened his mouth to voice a protest. "I need to make sure Gramma's okay first. That's why I packed my bags. I can't stand her being in the hospital. I mean, what if she…" Aislinn could not finish the words. "I just need to be there. Maybe I'll come back here someday soon. Next time I'm going to see Bran Castle on the first day, so Anya and I can share our dream together. I was so close."

His eyes warmed. "You're so sensitive and thoughtful. If you make a promise with somebody, you keep it. Even if they're gone."

"Anya's not *really* gone. Not to me. I can feel her with me often. Writing letters keeps us connected. The veil between this world and the one beyond is so thin. She stays near me on purpose, because she knows I need her. And, she sends things in the air."

"Oh, the imaginary snowflakes?"

"Not snowflakes, really. Well, sometimes. When we were little, whenever flower blossoms or dandelion seeds floated in the Spring air, she would say it was Faeries flitting about. So we pretended that's what it was. Now, everywhere I go, when I think of her, or I get depressed, she sends little pieces of white things like tiny flower blossoms in the air all around me." Aislinn swallowed and blinked back tears. "Day before yesterday it looked like snow, just at my window, nowhere else."

"I can see why you're important. You are innocent and fearless when it comes to the spiritual world. You really *do* feel Anya, don't you?"

"Yes. And… why did you say, 'I can see why you're important.' What did you mean by that?"

A slow smile grew as he scanned her face, hair and the light green sweater that outlined her body, making her blush. He looked hungry and possessive.

His phone rang. "Oh, sorry, meant to put that on vibrate." He greeted the caller, but after a moment, his face grew concerned. "Mmm-hmm. Okay, listen, we'll be there as soon as we can. You take care. You know my thoughts are with you, right?" He paused. "Don't panic, you'll end up having to take more blood pressure medicine. Just take a deep breath. We're on our way. Okay, bye."

Glancing at Aislinn with furrowed brows, he reached across the small table and took her hand in his.

"What's wrong?" she asked.

"That was the hospital. Gramma's gotten worse. They've asked for family to come in."

"Oh my god." Aislinn's face burned. Tears spilled down her cheeks. Eddie squeezed her hand. With a jolt, she felt Bastian's mind.

*Aislinn!*

*No, no. I can't talk right now. Sleep, Bastian.* She pressed a hand to her face and concentrated on closing her mind.

*You are upset.*

Aislinn choked. A sob escaped her. She could not block her emotions from him.

"Listen, sweetie-girl." Eddie rubbed his thumb across the back of her hand. "I've checked all the flights, just in case. I booked us on two, depending on what happened with Gramma. One leaves in a few days, and would have given us time to take some tours. But now... well, the other one leaves in two hours. Let's run. I'll pay a cabbie to collect your bags. I know you need to be there as soon as possible."

Aislinn vaulted from the table.

# CHAPTER 12

With a loud *thunk*, Aislinn dropped her overstuffed purse onto the turn table full of luggage to be examined. Eddie followed with his suitcase.

"Eddie, I feel so bad. You just got here."

With an affectionate grin, Eddie rubbed her shoulders. "Hey, you just owe me another trip here. No matter what happens, we come back and really see Transylvania. Deal?"

"Sure." Aislinn sniffed, trying to keep her face from scrunching into an uglier cry.

"Hey, stop that." Close to her ear, his voice was soft and tender. He drew her against him and kissed her hair. "Feel calm. Everything's going to be fine. You're with me."

She attempted a smile as she pulled away and stepped through the scanner. The attendant waved her on when nothing beeped.

*Aislinn?*

Aislinn fought to keep her mind still as she and Eddie headed down the corridor which led to their terminal. A fishhook felt lodged in her heart, each step becoming painful as a cord pulled on it, tearing flesh.

*Aislinn, what is wrong? You are still upset. I must know.*

*I'm fine, Bastian. I have to go somewhere for a while. You just rest. I'll be back, at some point.*

*No!* A rush of genuine fear blasted through her. Somehow she knew he had burst from the earth, though the sun had not completely set.

"Watch out," Eddie warned as Aislinn nearly ran into a small child that had raced across the terminal right in front of her. "You seem distracted, like you're in a daze or something."

"I'm sorry. My mind's going in a million directions."

"Look, they're already lining up to get on the plane. Let's go."

They raced toward the attendant as the last person was given back his passport. After being approved, they scampered down the ramp and into the open hatch of the plane. Eddie was stuffing his suitcase into the overhead bins when Bastian's voice seared into Aislinn's brain.

*Aislinn, where are you? Your direction feels wrong!* Panic bolstered his mental projection.

"Ow." Aislinn clutched her head.

"What's wrong?" Eddie asked as they settled into their seats.

"Uh, just a headache. I need to rest my head for a minute." What she needed was to be still so she could talk to Bastian and explain her situation, hopefully with Eddie distracted.

But Eddie claimed her hand after they buckled their seatbelts, and drew the back of her hand to his warm lips. She gave him a flat smile as he gazed into her eyes. Brilliant green was the main color encircling his irises but with an outer corona of gold like a solar eclipse. How ironic that both of the men in her life had unusual eyes and had kissed her hand in the span of three days.

Like a channel of light, Bastian's powerful mind traveled through Aislinn and connected with her visual awareness of events around her. Aislinn gasped, shocked that he was capable of such a thing. She pulled her hand away from Eddie, but it was too late. She knew the moment Bastian saw him. If it hadn't been so frightening, it would have been wondrous, as if a prickly ghost had passed through her. The blast of anger that followed made her cringe.

*Who is he?* Bastian demanded.

*Just a friend. Stop it, Bastian. You're making my head hurt.* She pressed both hands to her throbbing head.

*A friend does not look at a woman the way he looks at you. He wants you.*

"Relax Aisy." Eddie was saying. "I'll take care of everything. Want me to ask for something for your headache?"

"Sure, thanks," Aislinn said through gritted teeth. She sat back to view the waning sunset and rows of lights outlining the runways.

*Bastian, look, my Gramma is really, really sick. I have to go to her.*

*You are traveling?*

*I'm on a plane.*

*No! My lady, no.* The intensity of his heart-rending protest ripped through her skull.

"Ow!"

"Wow, you've really got a bad one." Eddie waved a hand at the stewardess. "Can we get some ibuprofen? And water?"

*Aislinn, no. Please, wait for me. I will come to you. Just wait.*

*Look, Bastian. It's going to be fine. I can always come back.*

*I will go with you.*

*No. Stay and heal.*

*You wish to be with this human alone?* She winced at the ferocity of his suspicion, and rubbed her temples.

*No. Eddie is just taking care of me. That's all. He knows my family, and he's going back with me. I have to be with Gramma.*

*I can take care of you, Aislinn. You do not need anyone else. You do not need him.*

*You need to heal, Bastian, and you can't go out in the sunlight.*

*I can be in sunlight. I am not at full strength during the day. I am like a normal human. But we can have a life in the sun if that is what you wish.*

Aislinn found a sad smile playing at her lips and swallowed against the tightness in her throat. It was a sweet compromise he was offering. She squeezed her eyes shut with guilt. She had been running from the sun her whole life. She was the one stuck under an umbrella at the beach while her darker-skinned friends ran around playing Frisbee. She was the one reapplying layers of sunscreen while her friends splashed in the ocean without a care. And here she was giving him a hard time because he could not be larger-than-life while he was in the sun.

*We have only just found each other, my lady,* he implored. *You are so ready to throw that away?*

*No, Bastian. No. I am… very fond of you. And I want to get to know you better. But, Gramma and Aunt Julia are all the family I have left. Gramma is very dear to me for many reasons. She was the one person who understood me. I must be there for her. What if she dies and… and….*

*This human was in Romania with you?* He had switched so abruptly it took a moment for her to reply.

*Eddie… came to see me. I didn't know he was coming. He was concerned about me, I guess. He travels a lot… actually.* Stumbling over the explanations, Aislinn asked herself questions she had not had time to consider. Everything had happened so fast. Why *did* Eddie come? Was it because his feelings had grown and he simply wanted to be with her? Why had he booked them on flights for this evening with no way of knowing what would transpire? How did he discover what inn she was staying at? Aislinn realized Bastian's connection was so strong he was following her line of thought.

*He came to get you.*

*I don't think so, Bastian. His family is powerful, but….*

*Yes. He did.* Bastian was certain. Aislinn realized she was not going to deflect him from the idea. Eddie could not have come to 'get her' since he had no way of knowing Gramma would take a turn for the worst. He did actually travel a lot, and was always talking about his adventures and deals.

*Look, maybe it's all just a weird set of circumstances,* she suggested.

*My lady, I live in a world that is not what it seems. Angels and demons surround us, mere breaths away. Every thought is a doorway. Demons are only happy when humans are in turmoil. It's what they do. I tell you, this does not smell like circumstance to me.*

*Seriously, Bastian, you think Eddie's a demon?* Aislinn almost chuckled at the idea.

*I believe he might be.*

*Bastian!*

*I will check on him. I have a visual imprint of his face.*

*Fine. You do that.*

*My lady, my heart aches for you already.*

Aislinn stomach clenched. It was one of the most romantic things any man had ever said to her. Waves of his sadness washed over her. She envisioned him doubled over in pain.

*Bastian, I will not forget you. Then again, I don't have a choice, do I? Since you're in my head, and in my blood?*

*I would like to believe I was in your heart.*

# CHAPTER 13

*Bastian, what is going on?* Marius' angry voice shot into Bastian's mind. He hurled up the basement stairs, three at a time.

*Marius, tell him not to drop dirt all over my library,* came Gabriella's stern voice into the connection. Gabriella's telepathic abilities had grown so much over the past few years that having a three-way conversation with he and Marius had become almost commonplace, though it should be impossible.

Bastian looked down at his body. He turned on the basement stairs and brushed off the remaining clods of dirt, then sprinted through the library and flung open the front door. He knelt in the doorway and concentrated on the eagle form. He nearly shook with the effort to calm himself in order to reach the state of consciousness he would have to maintain. When the alternating dimensional weightlessness and disembodiment kicked in, he launched himself off of the porch and began flapping his immense wings as they were still forming. He swerved just in time to clear the roof of Marius' BMW. His right shoulder ached. It was too soon for the repairing muscles, but he ignored the pain.

*Did he just leave the front door open?* He heard Gabriella ask Marius.

*Bastian, I am waiting for an answer.* Marius' tone was harsher. Soon he would be yelling at him, which could be quite painful. But Bastian did not care.

His right wing faltered. He pounded the air to get as high as possible to use the updrafts. Cold wind burned through his feathers as he pointed his body and plunged down the mountain range toward the Paltinu River like a bullet. Lights below guided his frantic search for the inn.

Panting with his beak open, he landed on the rattan cushion of the balcony chair and stared into the empty room. She was truly gone. His heart burned with rage and loss. All this time, he had lived with a bleak, soulless heart, except for his vigilance against the demonic world. He cared nothing of wealth, land, or clothes, to the point that Marius had to take over his affairs and keep a constant watch over him. For which he reciprocated by watching over Marius, and later, Gabriella.

A breath of fresh, cocoa butter-scented air had blown into Bastian's dark world, and now it had wafted away just as easily. He decided he no longer loathed his actions of that first night with Aislinn. It was a good thing he had taken her blood and given her his. Now, he could find her anywhere.

~~◊~~

"Bastian, clothes!" Gabriella ordered, getting to her feet. Marius and Dimitri stared at him from the dining room table. No doubt, the three had been discussing their concern since he had launched into eagle form before the sun had completely set. It had been easier to ignore their voices while in animal form.

"Marius, you can yell at him later," Gabriella added when Bastian raced up the staircase wearing nothing but the loin cloth. Normally, his clothes morphed with him, becoming fur or feathers. Desperate to check on Aislinn, he had forgotten additional clothing. There wasn't time.

Folding the loin cloth carefully onto a chair lest Marius berate him more than he already planned, Bastian jumped into the shower. As the water washed away the residual dirt, Bastian explained to his three companions what had transpired, and sent them the visual of the man who had swept Aislinn out of the country, away from him.

*And you couldn't tell me before you flew out of here?* Marius yelled, sending a painful spike into Bastian's mind. *I could have used other connections and resources to check on her while you wasted time!*

*Uncle Bastian, I know him.* Dimitri sounded puzzled.

*From where?* Bastian grabbed a towel.

*He was at the Appalachian gathering a couple years back, when they invited me, for sparring. Some of their lines are pretty watered down, you know. But many warriors are close to pure-blood and have our abilities. It was fun meeting warriors as strictly devoted to the cause as we are. We had several matches. I didn't fight with him, specifically, but he was there, for sure.* Dimitri closed his eyes and sent them all a visual recall.

*That looks like him!* Bastian grated his teeth as he threw on clothes. *Wait until I get my hands on him.*

*Bastian, you take no action until I verify his identity,* Marius commanded, still fuming. *Last year we were in America and met with the Appalachians. I did not see him. Did you?*

*No,* Bastian answered. *But Duke had asked me to teach him how to hunt vampires, so we were gone most of the visit.*

*Well, this was the year before,* Dimitri clarified. *I only remember him because he asked me a lot of questions. He seemed to want to know about our family and our skills. He wanted to know our loyalties to the mission.*

*And, what is his loyalty?*

*Not really sure. I got the feeling he was at a crossroads. He was searching. He had refused a blood vow to the Appalachian tribe because of his father's objections. All he would say was that his father headed a branch of the family that kept to themselves.*

*I heard Aislinn call him Eddie,* Bastian offered, as he descended the stairs two at a time, shoeless, and entered the dining room.

Dimitri regarded him with concern. "When I drove Aislinn back to the inn, she got a call from a guy she called Eddie. She was really angry until he told her about her grandmother being in the hospital. Oh, my gosh, I just remembered something. There was this loud sound in the background, like an engine. I bet that dude was on a plane when he called."

Bastian clenched his fists. "I knew he came to get her."

"If it's the same guy," Dimitri added, "the Appalachians call him Edward. One of the guys later said Edward had made a lot of mistakes, and they were all concerned about him. Said his father was really tough on him and leading him down a dark path. His father didn't want him hanging with the Appalachians. I was going to ask more about him, but someone had just managed a slice into his opponent and we all got distracted. You know they drink lots of beer?"

"Believe me, I know." Gabriella raised her brows. "Although the Parker brothers told me that they often abstain now because of its weird effects."

"Well, didn't see any abstinence while I was there! I tried some of their local beers, actually."

"Dimitri," Marius admonished.

"Hey, I was game. There were no battles pending. Didn't really care for the taste—I still like wine better—but, got into a wrestling match and found I was definitely not as sharp. He almost knocked me on my butt."

"So, this Edward is of the bloodline." Bastian stared out the window. If Aislinn's companion was this Edward, then he could not have missed the claim mark on Aislinn. Yet, he had not inquired about her mate. If he had, Bastian would have read it in his scan of Aislinn's thoughts. She wanted to keep Edward a secret from him, and Edward did not reveal his origins. Certainly, he was not to be trusted. Perhaps Aislinn was not to be trusted. Why would she keep this secret from him? How many other secrets was she keeping?

Bastian held up his right arm and stared at the mate sign on his wrist. It was turning maroon at the edges, getting darker. Was this for her, or could there be someone else? No, his body craved *her*. But then, he had created a blood bond, so he would feel that anyway. Still, there was something about her from the moment he felt her scan burn through him at the café. His heart had leapt at the sight of her trying to hide behind brochures. She was so innocent. So new to his tumultuous world, one he had now dragged her into. There was no going back.

"So, how dark is it?" Gabriella asked, with the hint of a smile on her face.

Bastian should have known she would be watching him examine the mark. His skin pulsed beside the new battle sign glowing beside the mate sign, and he noted the unmistakable dot of red.

"My battle sign is not yet set."

"Wasn't talking about that sign, and you know it."

Marius raised his right arm, and Dimitri his left.

"Mine is more pronounced," said Marius. "Two blood spots. Not good."

"Mine's darker too, and a little red." Dimitri frowned. "Guess I'm in for trouble."

Bastian raised his chin and exhaled. "So, the battle with the horde last night was not the end of our current battle call."

"No." Marius agreed. "There is definitely more to come. And I fear it involves her."

Gabriella pressed her teeth into her bottom lip. "There's something very weird about all this. I can feel power coming from several directions. I think it goes beyond this Edward."

"And," Dimitri raised both brows at Bastian, "one of us is hiding a mate sign. What about Edward? What if he has one? Okay, I have to ask this." Dimitri held up a finger. "Has any two guys ever gotten a mate sign at the same time? I mean, for the same girl? I know they've gotten them at the same time before for other girls, but…."

Everyone glanced at each other.

"Actually," said Marius. "I do remember one story. There were two warriors who showed up at a sparring match. They both discovered a mate sign had appeared. They were attracted to the same female warrior. She showed some interest in both of them, but was not ready to give up her warrior life. She left, and though the two warriors pursued her, she spurned them both."

Dimitri perked up. "So what happened? Did they ever get mates again, or was she it?"

"One died in a battle. He was a great loss. The other's mate sign faded, but reappeared nearly ten years later. The woman he took was a good woman, and bore him three sons and a daughter. But also, she was at that sparring match, ten years before, trying to get his attention. The two warriors were so distracted by the beauty of the female warrior, neither had considered the other woman. So, was the sign for the same woman, or was one of them meant for the woman he had not noticed?"

Gabriella dropped an arm to the table. "Now, *that's* an interesting story. Why didn't you ever tell me?"

Marius shrugged. "I did not think of it until now."

"I do not like this." Bastian began to pace. "It does not feel right. His presence is a problem."

"It's not going to feel right to you anyway," stated Marius. "You have a blood bond with her. You have no choice but to go to her."

"Hey, can I go too?" asked Dimitri.

"Why?" Bastian stiffened.

"I believe we all should go." Marius rose from his chair. "I will leave Armand in command until we return."

Gabriella stood as well. "There's something I forgot to tell you."

"What?" Marius and Bastian asked at the same time.

"Aislinn told me the Yeti recognized her, as if he was sent to get her. The one that attacked Bastian."

"*What?*" All three men exclaimed at once.

"She said it was like his mission was to 'find her.'"

Bastian felt a stab in his chest. "She's a target. We're not even mated and she's a target." Memories of the past threatened to engulf him. The pain of that night speared his heart anew and caused bile to rise in his throat. He placed a hand to his heart and closed his eyes.

*Not again.*

# CHAPTER 14

After landing in Munich and changing to a bigger plane, Aislinn began to feel heavy and fatigued. Rejecting Eddie's attempts to draw her closer was wearing her out. He tried to coax her into watching a movie on the seat display. She dared not watch anything, especially if it contained drama, which she feared would make her weepy. She wanted to sleep but her fears would not allow her.

Every few minutes of the flight, Aislinn's stomach cramped and pressure engulfed her heart. Part of her discomfort was the two incidences of turbulence they had encountered. With the emotions of so many worried people pressing in on her, Aislinn's nerves were shot. There was no denying that her abilities were enhanced. An enhancement she was not enjoying. Eddie found a documentary about wildlife in cold climates and Aislinn consented to watch it with him.

After that, Eddie managed to doze on the plane. Sleep eluded Aislinn. Her arms and legs were agitated and constantly repositioning, almost on their own. She finally realized it was not from muscles constricting, but from the yearning sensation in her belly.

*Bastian?*

*I hear you, my lady. My mind and body are in agony. I expected to miss you. I did not expect to miss you so badly.*

Aislinn smiled. What a hopeless romantic he was. How she had longed for that in a relationship, but was always sorely disappointed. Eddie had been charming at the start, but Bastian's intense longing was endearing on a far greater scale.

*I miss you, too, Bastian. I keep seeing you in my mind. I even miss your voice. Your real voice.* She enjoyed his projection of pleasure, though their connection felt stretched by the distance.

Eddie stirred. "Hey, sweetie-girl. You doin' okay?"

"I'm fine," Aislinn replied flatly. She removed her hand from the armrest so Eddie couldn't grab it. He had used every opportunity to get cozy. Bastian's growl of objection felt like it was passing through her and making the plane vibrate.

Eddie gently grasped her chin and turned her face toward him. "Are you sure?" His green-gold eyes, brilliant as ever, narrowed.

"Stop it, Eddie." Aislinn protested, pulling away.

"*Oooo*, someone's grumpy."

Eddie had always been a blank page for Aislinn, his emotions and motivations hidden. That oddity had thrilled her when they first met. But now, with her empathic radar newly enhanced, she sensed suspicion and possessiveness radiating from him as though he heard her telepathic exchange with Bastian. Which was impossible.

Aislinn forced a smile to ease his concerns so he would leave her alone. Eddie blatantly snatched her hand and brought it to his lips.

Bastian's reaction caused a sharp stab in Aislinn's chest, and she began to squirm.

"Eddie, you said you were here to make me more comfortable. You are not."

"I'm sorry, sweetie-girl," he whispered. "It's just so nice to be beside you again. I was there for you when you were ill, and I promise I'll be there for you while Gramma is ill." He squeezed her hand in both of his, as though he were about to release her. Instead, he turned her hand palm up and planted a long kiss in the center.

Aislinn barely masked a gasp. The warm throbbing of her female parts shocked her. Why was she reacting to Eddie? Everything she had felt for him before seemed to blossom. She found herself thinking of kissing him, which made no logical sense.

*Bastian, I gotta go. Bye.* She had to cut him off. She could not take another emotional outburst from him. Throwing up a mental wall was difficult, but she concentrated on it.

Reeling from desire spreading through her body, she realized Eddie was still planting little kisses in her hand. She swallowed, and pulled her hand free.

"Sorry. Couldn't resist," he said. The sly look on his face made him appear not sorry at all. There was no denying his attraction and desire for her. *That* she could feel growing stronger. This was why she had avoided being in Eddie's presence after they broke up. If friends were getting together, she consented to him joining the group. Any attempt at an intimate date, she had refused. She had to be able to resist him.

Her physical attraction to Eddie should be governed by her inability to trust him now. Sure he was handsome and had a gorgeous body, but she had dated handsome men before. The more handsome they were, the more arrogant they tended to be. Eddie had been arrogant, but also magnetic and intriguing. His bad-boy edge had captured her attention and made life interesting. Until everything fell apart.

Pressure filled her head like hot steam and she came alert.

*Bastian?* She had already forgotten to maintain the block.

*I cannot stop thinking about you. Please do not close your mind to me.*

Aislinn smiled as she gazed out the airplane window at a world of clouds. Then her smile dropped. *Oh crap.* He might have heard all her thoughts about Eddie.

"Eddie, don't." She had placed her hand on the armrest, and he was in the process of reclaiming it and lifting to his lips again.

"Are you sure that's what you want me to do?" He rubbed a thumb across her knuckles as she tugged. To her utter astonishment, the sensation sparked a carnal response in her.

She jerked her hand away and stuck it inside her coat. "I need to rest. Stop that."

The look of satisfaction on Eddie's face was unnerving. It was as if he knew her body was responding.

Bastian's outburst of rage jolted her, followed by his mental threats to dismember Eddie. She turned back toward the window. It was going to be a long flight.

~~◊~~

"Alexsey Cardeia. Can you tell me what room she's in?" Aislinn's stomach twisted into such tight cramps she feared she would vomit. It had seemed an eternity getting to the hospital. She held the side rail for support as the hospital elevator rose. She could have held onto Eddie, but she dared not touch him. Her body was not cooperating with her mind. Eddie seemed to know, and hovered beside her, making sure their arms touched.

Medicinal and cleaning odors assaulted her as she hurried down the hallway of doors, searching for room 324.

"Aislinn!" Aunt Julia exclaimed in a muted voice as they entered the room. Aislinn ran to hug her. Then she cast anxious eyes upon her grandmother lying in the bed, pale and lifeless, and burst into tears.

"How you doin' Julia?" Eddie embraced Julia, then slipped an arm around Aislinn. "It's okay, Aisy-girl. It's going to be okay."

Relief washed over Aislinn as she held Gramma's hand and rubbed her arm, noting it was warm and full of life. The steady pulse beat was strong. But she looked so wrinkled and pale.

"It's just the most awful thing," Aunt Julia wailed and wrung her hands. "The shock of my life, I tell you. Poor thing just a-lyin' there on the sidewalk. Thought she was dead."

"Julia!" Aislinn exclaimed. She did not need that visual right now.

"You know, it was strange." Aunt Julia sniffed and shook her head. "George Baxter came back into town and looked me up. Said we should go have some lunch. I was so excited. Haven't seen George in over twenty years." She beamed. "Didn't even know his wife had passed away. Mama told me to go ahead and have fun. She was happy for me. Wouldn't you know, the one time I get away…." A sob caught in her throat.

"Don't blame yourself, Julia." Eddie laid a comforting hand on her shoulder. "Sometimes there are circumstances beyond our control. We just have to go with it."

Aislinn realized she *had* secretly blamed Aunt Julia for not being there when Gramma fell. Feeling guilty for the judgment, she wiped tears and faced her Aunt. "You've been with her for the last three years, Aunt Julia, taking care of her every day. It would be wrong for anyone to blame you for the one moment Gramma fell. I mean, realistically, you could have been asleep upstairs and not even known."

Aunt Julia stifled another sob, but Aislinn could feel her relief.

"Julia, why don't you go home and get a few hours of sleep," Eddie suggested. "Me and Aisy will stay here and watch over Alexsey."

"Well, that would be a comfort, it would. I am so tired. Would still like to visit with you for a while, though."

"Of course. Of course." Eddie took her hand in his and gave it a squeeze. Aislinn noticed Aunt Julia was still charmed by him.

*Well, he can definitely be charming,* she reminded herself. *You fell for him once.*

"We know how devoted you are." Eddie cast adoring eyes on Aunt Julia.

"How long have you been here?" Aislinn asked.

"All day. I was so scared she might…." Aunt Julia's face drew tight as she tried not to cry.

"It's okay, Aunt Julia. You and me both."

Aislinn turned to her pallid grandmother, kissed her cheek, and tried to read the energy surrounding her. She didn't like the unsettling sensations of illness. The imbalance blossomed and billowed outward into a dark portent that Aislinn could not decipher. She concentrated on her grandmother's face. *Concern. Danger.* Perhaps she was reading concern because her grandmother was worried about her own health. Eddie began rubbing Aislinn's shoulders and it distracted her concentration.

"She's going to be so happy to see you." Eddie's voice was soft.

Aislinn worked hard to keep from crying again. An oxygen line was blowing air into her grandmother's nose. Aislinn gently straightened the tubing and brushed back her white hair.

"It's been such a rough day for her." Aunt Julia was wringing her hands again. "They don't know what happened. The pneumonia was nearly gone.

But, suddenly, she just took a turn for the worse during the night. She actually looks much better now than she did this morning."

"She does?" Aislinn was surprised.

"Yes. She has more color than last night when she was feeling so poorly."

Aislinn sighed and chose to sit on the side of the bed. "So, who's this George you were talking about?"

Aunt Julia began a colorful tale of her outing with George Baxter. Aislinn could not help being happy for her aunt, watching her face light up as she talked.

Aislinn also noticed she had dark circles under her eyes. "Aunt Julia, you look so tired."

"I tried to sleep in the recliner, but I was so worried, I just couldn't. Gracious, it's way past lunch time now."

"Go home and get some rest. Really, Eddie and I are here. At least get a couple hours of sleep."

"Well, if you're sure then. I feel better knowing you two are here."

"Absolutely," said Eddie. "We'll call you if anything changes."

Aunt Julia kissed and hugged Aislinn and Eddie before leaving.

Aislinn gazed about the room and eyed the recliner. Eddie stepped toward it.

"Come here." He patted his lap after sinking into the stuffed recliner.

Aislinn rolled her eyes at him. "You would jump in there first."

He grinned wickedly. Aislinn reexamined Gramma, hoping to see a flicker of awareness in her face.

"Aisy, let's rest and watch her together," Eddie suggested, reaching an arm toward her.

Still unnerved by the unhealthy appearance of Gramma, Aislinn opted to join him. He pulled her into his embrace and slipped an arm under her legs in order to curl them over his lap. "Now, I can finally have a PDA without the world watching."

"Eddie! I'm sitting in here with my Gramma sick in the bed and…"

"I know." He gave her a squeeze. "I'm just teasing. I know how you feel. I've known for a long time." He brushed fingertips along her arm. "Just relax."

The hair on Aislinn's arms rose. She ignored the sensation and lay against him. "I can't lose her, Eddie. I'm not ready. Maybe thirty years from now I'll be able to accept it, but not now."

"Well, she'll be a hundred years old by then, so, yeah, you might have to prepare."

Aislinn gave a half-hearted chuckled. "No, just ninety-eight."

~~◊~~

Marius laid a firm hand on Bastian's arm. "Bastian, don't you dare leave this plane." He sent power into the command as a hint of retribution should Bastian disobey. He had to find a way to rein him in.

"I have to get to her," said Bastian, his face set. His knees bounced in irritation. "That man is preying on her. He knows she's in a blood heat and will react to any man that touches her."

"You can't possibly hold an eagle form for that many hours, and we're too high up. You will be exhausted by the time you get to her and useless to protect her. Not to mention the fact that you'd decompress the plane if you found an opening."

"Yeah," Dimitri chimed in, "and I'm not carrying your luggage all the way to Cirillo's compound."

"I do not care about clothes."

"I know you don't. That's why Gabriella has to buy them for you. I heard she bought you a real pair of blue jeans."

Bastian heaved a noisy sigh of irritation and stared passed Dimitri toward the oval window. He crossed his arms.

"Get your big fat arms outta here." Dimitri complained.

Marius smiled to himself as Bastian unfolded his bulky arms and dropped them into his lap. The memory of his own state of mind when he met Gabriella was still clear. The overwhelming need to protect and cherish his newly-discovered mate overrode everything else. He was jealous of everyone and everything that took her attention from him.

Even now, glances from other men on the plane cast toward Gabriella, sitting to his right in the aisle seat, made his arms flex in a desire to hit each of them square in the jaw. He had never grown comfortable with other men admiring her lush curves and beauty, and probably never would. In fact, he needed to switch seats with her. He should probably allow Gabriella to calm his nerves.

Bastian's affection toward Gabriella was something he had never worried about. Bastian's heart and passions had been dead for so long that he merely acknowledged Gabriella's existence in a sisterly way. Of course, Bastian's incredible loyalty would never allow him to feel anything more. Only now, with the presence of Aislinn igniting true desire in Bastian did he show any recognition that Gabriella was even beautiful. At one point, Marius caught Bastian watching him and Gabriella with a curious jealousy, no doubt wishing he had what they had.

For so many years, he had watched Bastian spiral into a bottomless pit of purgatory, waiting only for the next battle, or the next report of one of theirs going vampire. He was so good at finding vampires, other leaders had requested his help when one alluded them. Each time Bastian returned triumphant. But the satisfaction lasted only a few days. He did not laugh, he refused parties and dinners unless Marius ordered him to attend; he sat alone in the dark, or spent the day as an animal in the woods if he was not needed. Marius had arranged for many women to visit, or to be at certain gatherings, hoping one of them would trigger a mate sign. But to no avail. Not even beautiful Andromeda, who he was quite certain Bastian had actually kissed, had been able to crack the walls around Bastian's heart.

He felt bad about that, knowing that Andromeda fell in love with Bastian. She pined for him still.

Marius took a deep breath and vowed to insure that Bastian got the woman he wanted. The woman he needed. He would have to tread carefully. If Aislinn's body rejected Bastian's blood and spiraled into illness, there would be hell to pay. Other tribal leaders would surely hear of it and render judgement that he had lost control over his cousin. Marius had never lost control over a warrior.

Aislinn had looked piqued and weak the night before. It could have been the shock of the battle. But it could also have been a reaction from Bastian's blood. He had to force Bastian to be cautious. Humans were known to die three days after a blood bond was formed, even when they appeared to be making the transition. He could only hope that Aislinn contained some percentage of their bloodline, or some inner strength that would carry her through the changes.

Even at the chalet, Marius had touched Aislinn's shoulders and punched hard into her energy to find the subtle gossamer threads that would give him a hint of her ancestry. But his scan was again blocked. An energy he could not define was fighting him.

Later, he and Gabriella had both held Aislinn's coat and concentrated after Bastian had put her to sleep, but both had agreed a strong spiritual presence continued to keep their prying energy at bay. What presence would go to such lengths to block them? And why? Gabriella was certain she felt close relatives circling, protecting Aislinn. But Marius had detected darker presences as well, as if a battle was being waged around the girl, unseen.

If demons had been summoned to attack Aislinn, or thwart her progress, the picture was far greater than a mere blood bond. Marius closed his eyes and concentrated. A picture of Cirillo Markos, The Appalachian, appeared in his mind; a great bear of a man with piercing brown eyes flecked with gold and green.

*Commander Cirillo Markos*, Marius spoke his full name, the all-important etheric address. *This is Marius Brancusi. Can you hear me?*

A few seconds passed.

*Prince Marius?* Cirillo answered, surprised. *I hear you. What do you need?*

Marius smiled at Cirillo's addition of "Prince," a title most American leaders did not acknowledge. But, Cirillo was a man who granted as much respect as he demanded. And he knew that if another tribal leader called to him through a blood bond across the ocean, it was serious.

*My Assassin, Bastian Radescu, has claimed a young woman by the name of Aislinn Thomas. She is from your realm, but her bloodline is unknown. She told an innkeeper in Romania that she is traveling by plane to return to the state of North Carolina because her grandmother is gravely ill. A man named Edward, also of your realm, but not of your allegiance, accompanies her. We are uncertain of his intentions.*

Cirillo seemed to be thinking. *Marius, I know of a young man named Edward whose family resists allegiance. Edward Hawthorne. We have not seen him in two years. Do you wish me to investigate him?*

*That would be greatly appreciated. Gabriella, Bastian, Dimitri, and I are traveling by plane as well.*

*Do you wish me to try and locate Edward and Aislinn?*

*That will not be necessary. Bastian knows where the young woman is headed, and will scent her once we are on the ground. I can give you more details once we arrive. Our first priority is the wellbeing of this woman.*

*Understood. Marius, we will be happy to accommodate you and your family at my compound in King's Mountain.*

*You have my gratitude, Cirillo. Please express my thanks to your mate as well.*

*I will. We look forward to seeing you.*

Marius sighed deeply. The thrum of a battle brewing not only tingled within his bones, but the battle sign on his arm was fluctuating and shifting color intensity. A struggle was growing, looming. Whether within hours or days he was not sure. But he wanted to be ready.

# CHAPTER 15

Eddie hovered over Alexsey Cardeia. After five hours, he was tired of waiting in the cramped hospital room and wanted Aislinn to himself. They had crashed for a while in the easy chair, but Aislinn was adamant that she would not leave until she could speak to Gramma. Only making the old woman better would allow Aislinn to let go. That, and a few other things he had planned.

From his mother, he had learned some healing ability, and alchemy, which had elicited meager praise from his father. Healing would be painful, but it would work to his advantage. Aislinn had left for the ladies room. He placed a hand on the old woman's chest just below her neck, closed his eyes and concentrated on empowering her body to flush out the toxic drugs. He called upon the spiritual energies around him and focused on blue healing light, love, and joy.

*Oh, god, how that hurt.*

The spiritual world was not fooled. The positive energy tugged at him to return, calling him like dawn brightening on the horizon, splashing color into a dismal sky. He didn't want any part of the light. He did once, years ago. But he had not been good at it. Fighting demons and creatures of darkness brought him acceptance from the Appalachians. But his father warned he was getting too close to the goody-goodies, which would make him worthless. And make him an enemy of the family. "Don't risk the family," was his father's motto.

Eddie winced as he allowed the energy to build around him. It burned and attacked the darkness within him. Each draw on the pulsing energy caused the pain to grow exponentially. With all his might, he gathered as much of it into his hands and passed the light into the old woman. Again he grimaced and shook as he drew in energy, and projected it into her. He made a third attempt just before the door creaked.

Eddie removed his hands and gasped for air. Quickly, he threw up a wall to deflect Aislinn's empathic ability. A sympathetic but hopeful expression smoothed into his face as she appeared around the corner and approached the bed.

"No change," he said. "But I have a good feeling about her. I think she's going to get better."

"Really? You think so?"

"Yes. I really do. Hey, you want something to drink?"

"I guess."

Eddie rested a hand on the side of her face and drew her close to kiss her hair. He dared not go for her lips. He calculated her acceptance of him and knew he was slowly winning. Time and experience had taught him to be cunning and careful. He could not let her fall under the control of anyone else. Too much was at stake.

Projecting charm and persuasion, he sauntered down the hall and approached the nurse's station. "Hello. Sorry to bother you, but, could I get a soft drink?"

"Sure." The nurse had that mesmerized look he was familiar with. Even without persuasion, women had always found him attractive and he used it to his full advantage. Fortunately, he did not have to assert himself here since the nurses at this hospital were friendly and accommodating.

"Here you go," said the nurse, eyes wistful as she handed him a cup of dark, fizzing soda with ice.

"Thank you." He gave the nurse his most winning smile and watched her melt with adoration. Humans were so easy to manipulate.

"Sure," she responded dreamily. "Just let me know if you need anything else."

"I will." He could feel her watching him walk down the hall. It did not stop him, however, from taking a capsule from his jeans pocket and opening it over the iced drink. He stirred the contents with his finger, then licked it to be sure the sparkling drink would disguise the drug.

Aislinn was pacing when he returned to the stifling room. "Sweetie-girl, you need to relax."

"I can't relax. Gramma's just lying there. I can't think straight. My nerves are all a jumble. My stomach hurts. I've got to… I need to… I don't know what I need." She flapped her arms to her sides.

"Here, I got you something to drink."

She waved a hand. "No, I don't want anything."

"Come on." He laid a hand on her shoulder to keep her still. "Just a few sips? Please?" He tilted her chin up and gazed into her bright blue eyes, using the barest touch of persuasion, layering it with desire. "You must be thirsty. You haven't eaten for hours."

"All right." Aislinn sipped the soda, and then kept sipping.

*There you go, girl. That's right.* He smiled inwardly. It would not take long for the drug to take effect and make her pliable.

Aislinn resumed pacing while she sipped the cold soda. He watched her with anticipation.

A doctor stepped into the room and Aislinn shouted, "Dr. Bradley!" The doctor held out his hand but she surprised him with a warm hug. Eddie felt a sharp pang of jealousy as a cheerful smile leapt across the doctor's face.

"I'm so glad to see you!" Aislinn exclaimed. "I didn't know you were Gramma's doctor."

"Well, I was in the emergency room when she came in. We got to know each other pretty well when you had your surgeries last year. Plus, I filled in for Dr. Peters when she had that ankle fracture and blood clot a few years back. I know your grandmother, Miss Thomas. She's a fighter."

Aislinn smiled. "That she is, doc."

"She has a mild fracture in her hip, fortunately not in a vital place, but I want her in a soft cast for at least six weeks. Mostly because I suspect you'll have trouble keeping her in a wheelchair. Probably as much trouble as I had keeping you in one."

Aislinn grinned sheepishly, and stepped out of the way while the doctor listened to Mrs. Cardeia's heartbeat and lungs.

"Her breathing is better and the pneumonia is nearly cleared up. She's stable and we're making her as comfortable as possible."

"I just wish I could talk to her," said Aislinn.

"Well, she became agitated yesterday. Kept mumbling things like, 'I have to help her, she's in danger,' and she kept trying to get out of bed. Your Aunt said she must be reliving the accident that killed your family. She seemed delirious, but I couldn't find any medical reason for it. She shouldn't have had a reaction to the medicines we were giving her, but I changed them anyway, just to be safe. I also prescribed something to calm her nerves. This morning she was better, but became a bit agitated again, so we had to give her another dose. We did a CAT scan but everything looks clear. I've ordered a toxicology test to see what she had in her system."

Eddie breathed in sharply. *Not a good idea.* The doctor's eyes flicked to his, and Eddie concentrated. *No need for a toxicology test. No need. She will be fine. No test. No test. No test needed.*

To Eddie's surprise, Aislinn glanced sharply at him. He offered her a comforting smile. Could she have detected his persuasion? Her abilities *had* been growing over the past year.

She swallowed, looked confused, and turned back to the doctor. Eddie knew by her quivering lips she was trying not to cry.

"If I could just hear the sound of her voice, I'd be okay," Aislinn said. "I know Gramma would be calm and get better if she could see me. I just know it."

Eddie cursed silently and slipped around the other side of the bed. With a smooth gesture, he laid a hand on Alexsey Cardeia's arm, giving the appearance of leaning over her with concern. He focused on her mind and sent all the power he could muster into her. *Alexsey. Wake, old woman. Wake. Hear my voice. Wake!*

"I have a surgery this afternoon," said Dr. Bradley, pulling a card from his pocket and handing it to Aislinn, but I'll be by later to check on her. Call me if you need me or have any questions. My answering service will contact me right away if it's an emergency. I changed her antibiotic and gave her something for the inflammation." He frowned. "I'm not sure if we'll be doing additional tests. The staff will be keeping a close watch on her. And I'll be here very early tomorrow morning as well. I have every reason to believe she will recover. Like I said, she's a fighter."

"Thank you, doctor." Aislinn's voice shook.

As the doctor left, Eddie noticed Alexsey's eyes flutter. *Wake, Alexsey. Wake. Come out of it!*

"Aisy, I think she's waking up."

"Gramma?" Aislinn rushed to her side. "Gramma, can you hear me?"

The old woman's puffy eyes wavered but finally focused on Aislinn. A slight smile curved her lips.

"Gramma," Aislinn sobbed with relief. "Are you okay? How do you feel?"

The woman took a soft breath, and cleared her throat. "Better, I think." Her words were slurred but understandable.

"Gramma, I can't *wait* to get you home. You're going to get better, you know that?"

"It's good to see you Aisy. I was so worried about you."

"Why were you worried about me? You're the one that got hurt."

"I felt something. Something that…." The woman's eyes fell on Eddie and her facial muscles dropped.

She had never liked him, no matter how charming he was to her. She sensed too much and his persuasion had little effect, for some reason. Alexsey Cardeia's grandfather had been an orphan, as well as her husband's father, Aislinn's great-grandfather, but Eddie suspected they were both possibly of the bloodline. Whose line, he wasn't sure. Aislinn definitely had a hint of the gifts. He had to work hard to block and confuse her scans of him whenever they were together. He had resorted to wearing charms as well. But with Alexsey Cardeia, Eddie was less successful at blocking her perceptions.

"It's great to see you awake again, Gramma Cardeia," he said, mostly for Aislinn's sake.

The woman stared at him with brilliant blue eyes, identical to Aislinn's.

Eddie gathered energy about him, held the smile on his face, and tried to block her ability to read him. In her weakened state, she would get nothing but what he wanted her to.

The old woman turned back to Aislinn and smiled. "Weren't you in Romania?"

"I was, Gramma, I was. But, I came back the minute I heard you weren't doing well."

"Oh no, you did not."

Aislinn grinned. "Oh yes I did. Don't worry, Gramma. You fight this, okay? I want to take you home tomorrow. So, you fight this. Guts and determination changes the body's direction, remember Gramma?"

The woman nodded and gave her a weak but happy smile.

*Oh, brother.* Eddie turned away, uncomfortable with the love between them. He folded his arms while they chatted away.

Aislinn flinched as a firm knock echoed on the hospital room door. She hopped off Gramma's bed and opened the wide door. To her surprise, a tall, cocoa-brown-skinned man with closely-cropped, curly black hair stepped into the room. He looked to be about twenty-five years old.

"Alexsey Cardeia's room?" he asked.

"Yes," Aislinn responded.

"I came by to see her. Heard she wasn't doing well. Oh, Duncan Hill." He held out a hand.

Aislinn shook the firm hand and stared in wonder. Everything about him reminded her of Marius and Bastian, from his broad shoulders to his firm arm muscles fighting the seams of his yellow shirt. He moved with an easy, balanced grace. Aislinn could almost envision a sword in his hand. His brown face possessed a strong jaw, and his eyes shimmered like hot copper rings filled with molten gold.

When Aislinn continued to stare at him, he said, "Oh, I'm a relative. Her aunt is my great-grandmother. I think you and I might be second or third cousins or something."

"Oh, wow, it's nice to meet you. I didn't know I had any other relatives." Aislinn felt her heart skip a beat at the thought of meeting relatives she knew nothing about. How wonderful it would be to have more family. She would not feel so alone. Why had no one told her?

"Well, people tend to lose touch after a couple of generations. And one side of my family was born overseas. But hey, family's family."

"Absolutely. I'm excited just to know you exist."

His smile brightened his handsome face. His features had the look of African descent but also the more angular lines of an Egyptian. Aislinn felt an instant sense of trust for him. There was kindness in the crinkle of his eyes, and an atmosphere of protectiveness about him.

"Is Miss Alexsey awake?" he asked. "Can I see her?"

"Sure. Come on in."

As he rounded the corner, Gramma broke out in a pleased grin. "Oh, I know you. Penelope's son?"

"Yes, ma'am, I'm Duncan Hill."

"I remember you. Well, how are you gettin' along? A few years back you were just out of high school, but I recognize you just the same. You haven't aged a day."

"Well, you haven't changed a bit either, ma'am."

"Oh, go on with you." She waved a hand, but her grin broadened.

Aislinn gestured toward Eddie. "Duncan, this is my friend, Eddie Hawthorne."

"Nice to meet you," Duncan directed the comment to Eddie.

Eddie rounded the bed and offered his hand. For the briefest moment, Aislinn got the feeling Eddie did not like Duncan. Though Eddie smiled, his eyes held a guarded respect for Duncan, and his stiffness made him appear jealous.

Duncan, however, displayed a flat smile and furrowed brows when he shook Eddie's hand. His eyes blazed gold as they danced around Eddie's frame looking around him instead of at him. "You look... familiar."

"Oh, I just have one of those faces," Eddie replied.

Aislinn pondered Eddie's uncomfortable reaction. Her stomach began cramping. She pressed a hand against her abdomen and realized she was feeling dizzy and disoriented. She wondered if this was another effect from the pull of the blood bond. She was so tired of the tug on her heart, she had resorted to blocking Bastian out. She groaned as her head began to swim.

"Are you all right, Aisy?" asked Gramma.

"I don't know. We traveled all through the night. First to Munich, then to Washington. We couldn't get an international flight straight to Charlotte for some reason, so we had to take another plane to Charlotte. I couldn't sleep at all, though."

"I tried to get her to sleep, but, without any luck." Eddie shrugged.

"Why don't you two go get some rest?" Duncan suggested. "I'll be glad to sit with Mrs. Cardeia for a few hours. We have a lot of catching up to do. I assure you I will guard her with my life."

"Well, um... " Aislinn stared at him. There was something in the intensity of his golden eyes and the promise in his voice. She had no doubt he would do as he said, as though he had been appointed a guardian and would not shirk from that duty.

"Go on, Aisy, you go get some rest now," said Gramma. "You look like you haven't slept in a week. I won't break."

Aislinn smiled. She had known she would be okay if she could talk to Gramma and judge her responses. Now that she had, a great relief came over her followed by overwhelming fatigue.

"Come on, Aisy," Eddie encouraged. "We'll get some rest, then come back later."

Aislinn felt lightheaded and strange. The events of the last three days must have taken more out of her than she realized. "Okay. Sounds great. We'll be back, Gramma." She gave her a tight hug and kiss on the cheek. "I love you."

"I love you too, dear."

"Bye, Gramma." Eddie waved. Gramma raised a few fingers off the sheet but did not smile. Aislinn wished Gramma didn't dislike him so much. But, Gramma was protective and Eddie had hurt her months ago. She would have to explain later all that Eddie had done for her, and being such a good friend throughout the trip. At times he had been a pest, but he did seem truly concerned about her.

"Nice meeting you, Duncan." Aislinn shook his hand again, hoping he would be there when they returned. "Hey, let's get together soon so I can find out about your side of the family. It would be nice to have some more relatives."

"Will do."

For a moment, Aislinn thought she spotted a reflecting gold tattoo peeking from under the short sleeve of his yellow shirt when he waved.

# CHAPTER 16

"Eddie, I am going to throw up."

Eddie glanced at Aislinn's pale face as he drove. He didn't want her to be sick, just disoriented and compliant. "You need to lay back and rest."

She obeyed and pulled the lever on the side of the seat to push it back. "If I tell you to stop, you'd better be quick, because I'm going to be puking."

Eddie reached over and pressed a hand to her shoulder. "Just ease back, Aisy. Just breathe. Calm your stomach." He sent as much steadying energy as he dared without undermining the effects of the drug. She pressed her cheek against his hand. *Good. That's my girl. Warm up to me.*

With relief, he pulled up to the winding road that led to the back of three old houses converted to student apartments for the nearby colleges in Brevard. This was a new apartment for her in anticipation of starting classes in January. Since he had hired someone to follow, he knew which apartment was hers. First building on the left, the small suite with the back entrance.

She stood by the car like a zombie while he retrieved their luggage from the trunk. "Come on, girl. Follow me." He grinned inwardly as she complied. *Excellent.*

He had to take the keys from her to unlock the deadbolt when she fumbled with them unsuccessfully. A loud *squawwwk* made him jump. Fearing a shape-shifter, he scanned the darkness and spied a crow eyeing him from the small dogwood tree beside her kitchen window.

*Aislinn and her stupid animals.* She was always surrounded by them.

"Buzz off," Eddie hissed, flapping a hand toward the bird.

It gave a short *cawww* of protest, so Eddie moved faster, afraid the bird would fly at him. When the lock slid open, he urged Aislinn inside.

Glancing to make sure no humans observed them, he hauled in their luggage and dumped it on the floor, closing the door fast.

Aislinn stood in the small living room, staring at her couch as if she did not recognize it.

"What?" She mumbled. "No. I think I'm just sick."

"Who are you talking to, sweetie?" *Crap, the other guy must be trying to communicate with her.* Well, he would get nothing but disconnected nonsense. Eddie needed to work fast to undo the hold the other man had on her.

"Here, sweetie-girl." Eddie took hold of Aislinn's shoulders and drew her close. "I think the exhaustion is hitting you. You need to rest."

Aislinn nodded. Her eyes looked vacant. "My legs."

"What about them?"

"I can't move them."

"That's okay. I've got you." Eddie swept her into his arms and headed to the bedroom. With care, he laid her limp body on the green and brown quilt Gramma had made, and began removing her shoes.

A high-pitched, wining growl permeated the silence. Eddie jerked his head up in alarm only to realize a calico cat was sitting outside the windowsill. It placed a white paw on the glass as if signaling to be let in. Golden-lilac eyes stared into his with the look of more than a pet.

*A familiar?* Too much knowing in those eyes.

"Eddie? Something's wrong. I can't think straight. I feel... weird."

"Hey, don't worry, sweetie-girl," he crooned as he dropped her shoes and socks. Excitement rose as he touched her skin. "Just lie down. I've got you. You're all taken care of."

He closed the curtains on the window and heard an additional *wrauwl* of protest beyond the curtain. *Well, you're outside and I'm inside, cat. Deal with it.*

He crawled onto the bed and lay prone beside Aislinn, getting worried he might be interrupted. He brushed hair from her face and bristled at sight of two tiny marks on the left side of her neck. How dare someone else try to claim her! She was his. She had always been his.

Her very life was in his hands. *He* decided whether she lived or died. Though, she wasn't actually supposed to live. Despite his best efforts, she had survived the car accident. Six months later, she had survived the poison he had arranged to be put in her glass at a party. The girl next to her had knocked the drink over and everyone laughed. The other girl finished the last sip and was in the hospital for three days.

On the drive to a bus trip, Aislinn, Aunt Julia and Gramma Cardeia miraculously got a flat tire. He went through a lot of trouble to arrange that bus to collide with another, which sent it rolling over an embankment. But the three women never made it to the bus.

So many plans. Yet, someone—some force—always seemed to be keeping her alive.

Tenderly, Eddie kissed Aislinn's irresistible soft cheek. Now was a good time to use more persuasion.

"Aisy-girl."

"Yes." Her eyes were half-lidded.

"You know I care about you."

"Uh-huh."

"You have feelings for me, still. So strong. I feel them. Don't you?"

She hesitated, but nodded.

"Show me, Aisy-girl." He kissed her cheek again, then planted soft kisses on the other cheek. He used his senses to read her, to gauge his progress. "You're feelings are growing stronger, aren't they? You realize how much you care for me. How much I care for you."

She nodded again, her eyes nearly closed.

He positioned his body half way on top of hers and braced his elbows to hold his weight. The suppleness of her female curves underneath him was intoxicating. His cock had grown hard throughout the car ride in anticipation. Now it was painfully bulging in his jeans. He rubbed her cheek with the back of his fingers, feeling the confusion roiling in her brain.

*Give yourself to me, Aisy-girl. You're mine. You're mine. You've always been mine.*

"Who? Don't listen to who?" she murmured.

Eddie gritted his teeth. The other man was breaking through. His mind must be very powerful. Well, he could forget about it. Eddie had her now and he knew how to make her his forever.

"That's what I'm saying, sweetie-girl," Eddie cooed. "Don't listen to the other voice. Just listen to me. Listen *only* to me." His lips hovered over hers as he whispered. "You want to kiss me, Aisy. Don't you?"

She nodded.

He closed his mouth over her sweet lips. She responded and he felt a thrill rush through his chest and groin. Carefully, he nurtured the passion, kissing her deeper, caressing the sides of her face with his fingertips. He inched his body over hers.

*You want me, Aisy-girl. Desire for me is rising inside you.* She groaned. His body ignited at the feel of her soft, compliant curves squirming underneath him.

A gentle sigh escaped her as he trailed kisses down her throat. He pushed her hair out of the way and licked the tender skin. The stranger of the bloodline had bit her on one side, staking his claim. Eddie would claim her on the other. There would be nothing the other man could do to undo that mark.

Now that Eddie was feeding on other women, his canines were working properly. At first, he had been unable to make them cooperate, cursing his watered-down bloodline. But practice and help from a demon had paid off. Plus his cousin, Helmer, possessed the amazing ability to sniff out bloodline. Whenever Helmer found a girl he could control, he invited Damian and Eddie to feed off her in order to strengthen their own abilities. It was an amazing secret, and explained why the vampires they knew became the way they were. Why they grew stronger. More powerful.

Pressure throbbed in Eddie's mouth as he felt the stretching, like knives sliding through sheaths.

The flow of life pulsed under Aislinn's skin and assaulted his nostrils with sweet promise. And something else. He felt the resistance, like opposing polarities of two magnets pushing, resisting. The closer his fangs hovered, the more the coding of the other man's blood warned him she was claimed.

He laughed mentally at the feeble warning and pierced the plump vein in just the right place. Her body arched under him. She uttered a small blissful sound of surprise. He slipped a hand beneath her dark blue sweater to unhook her bra. With satisfaction, he listened to her moan as he sucked blood into his mouth and relished the feel of her firm breasts under his eager hands.

The hot, life-giving liquid rushing into his system was exhilarating, more vibrant than from any other woman. Indeed, she was special, as the mage had predicted. Her blood tasted far richer than he was used to. Exquisite and intoxicating. If he had only known, he would have imbibed sooner.

His father had overreacted and ordered him to kill her. The mage could not perceive how Aislinn would affect his family, only that there would be consequences. As long as Eddie kept her under his spell, he could prevent her from doing any damage. That was all that mattered. If he could control her, he could control the consequences. His father couldn't argue that.

The buzzing sensation in his head reminded him that her blood was tainted with the Ketamine drug, so he withdrew lest his mind become confused. He knew the drug was fast-acting, although his body would metabolize it much faster than hers. Regretfully, he drew his tongue over her skin. The sealed wound looked red and puffy.

*Good.* He smiled with satisfaction. If the other man in Romania decided to come for her, there would be no doubt whom she had chosen.

"Eddie," she murmured in a dreamy voice.

"I'm here sweetie-girl." Her face displayed the languid ecstasy he had come to relish from the women he took blood from. The endorphins in his glands sent ripples of delight coursing through their veins. Of course, since Aislinn's eyes were closed, it could also be the enhanced effect from the drug. He had used it before, but the last two girls had passed out on him.

He growled with sensual delight as he pushed up Aislinn's sweater to run his hands up and down her breasts and kiss the soft mounds. How he had longed to own these beautiful, full breasts again. She had not consented to seeing him without other friends around for nearly a year. He undid the button on her jeans and paused, remembering his goal.

Extending his nails, one ability that *had* always worked well for him, he pierced open the skin on his left wrist and pressed it against her mouth, watching drops of blood fall onto her lips. "Drink, sweetie-girl. Drink for Eddie. You know you want this. You've *been* wanting this, haven't you?"

To his surprise and delight, she swept her tongue across her lips. Her mouth closed over the tiny slit on his wrist. He sighed with pleasure as he felt the sucking sensation on his skin. She seemed close to losing consciousness and he feared the blood would go no further than her mouth, which would probably still work, but he was taking no chances.

"That's it, Aisy. Just a little more. Swallow, Aisy. Swallow it for me. Yes. That's it." He watched her throat contract and knew she had complied. He brought his wrist to his mouth to lick the wound so it would close.

Why hadn't he thought of this sooner? Well, he *was* preoccupied with killing her. After her injuries, she wasn't much of a threat, so consumed with mourning. Months later, she was focused on getting well and being able to walk again. That had presented a problem. With every phone call and every visit to the physical therapy center he hated for its positive energy, he had monitored her friends for any hint of unusual abilities. He saw none. If they were of the bloodline, they were dormant like Aislinn, unaware and unconnected.

He was never sure about that LaVanna. Along with beautiful skin the color of milk chocolate, she had remarkable taupe eyes that seemed to glow whenever she looked at Eddie, as if she were putting him on notice not to mess with her friend.

Mia was always polite, even sweet to him, but he felt a sense of danger around her that he could never define. He assumed it was her faith. She tended to lean away from him when he got too close, perhaps sensing his proximity to demonic energy.

Randall was always cool. Scott was the most fun. Still, they kept wary eyes on him. Why these friends were so protective of Aislinn, he did not know. Even her physical therapist, Harper, never warmed up to him.

While Aislinn had stayed with Gramma Cardeia and Aunt Julia during her year-long recovery, he had less control over her. Though Aunt Julia was easy to manipulate, Gramma Cardeia was on her guard and never left them alone. Even the one time he managed to get into Aislinn's room, he had felt power vibrating in the house, and Gramma Cardeia had showed up at the door, her mere presence letting him know she intended to stay until he left.

When Aislinn broke up with him, there was no getting past the front door. The essence of ethereal guardians was always strong, though he could not discern who or what they were, besides the usual menagerie of stray dogs and cats always attracted to Aislinn. He had no doubt Gramma Cardeia had called in her own reinforcements of the spiritual kind.

Unfortunately, he had not obtained the ability to extend his canines until months after Aislinn's accident. It gave him greater status with a few of the Appalachians he kept in contact with. If only he had claimed Aislinn before she left for Romania.

Even when he was planning other ways to kill her, he hadn't been able to get the feel of her tight body and the sight of her pretty face out of his mind, no matter how many girls he took. But now? Now, she was *his*. There was nowhere she could go without him having access to her mind. Nowhere she could go that he could not find her. Smiling with triumph, he slid open the zipper of her jeans.

A loud crash erupted in the living room. Before he made it to the bedroom door, a hand reached in, grabbed him by the shirt and flung him across the room. He smashed into the wall and felt powdery sheet rock raining over his body.

# CHAPTER 17

"You son of bitch!" The massive, tawny-haired man took one look at Aislinn unconscious on the bed with her sweater up and stomach exposed, and turned back to Eddie with menacing, silver-gray eyes.

*Oh yeah, that look is unmistakable.* Eddie was certain this was the one who had tried to claim his girl. Well, he was too late.

With a quick toss of his head to shake the sheet rock out of his hair, Eddie scrambled to his feet, poised to fight. Two years had passed since he had fought one of the blood, and he was rusty. Two more men stepped into the room. The second one, he recognized. Dimitri Melas.

"What did you do to Aislinn?" Dimitri demanded.

Could Dimitri be the one? No, the crazed, silver-eyed man, whom Eddie was beginning to think looked familiar, came at him in one swift stride.

"What did you do to her, vermin?"

Eddie ducked as the man's right fist aimed for his face, but faster than Eddie could prepare, the man's left fist hit him in the chest with rib-cracking precision. Eddie gasped for air, pivoted his body and swung both a leg and a fist at the larger man. Though he managed two blows somewhere into the man's rock-hard chest and thigh, with a growl of rage, the other man hoisted him into the air in a prone position and body slammed him into the floor. Eddie felt blood in his mouth and wondered how many bones were fractured. Pain was roaring in his ears.

Before he could test his limbs to see what was working, he felt his body lift into the air vertically and hammer sideways back into the sheet rock. A vice-like hand closed over his throat, with part of the man's arm and chest pressing him into the shattered wall.

"Going to kill one of your own, Olympian?" Eddie managed to mumble through clenched, bloody teeth.

"You're not one of mine." The enraged, blond-hallowed face was inches from his. "I'm going to ask you again before I break every bone in your body. What did you do to her?"

"She's asleep," Eddie managed to spit out.

"I can feel her mind, vermin. She is *not* asleep."

Eddie knew the man was not allowed to kill him without proof of misdeeds. But he didn't have any doubt that the man would follow through on his threat of bone breaking.

"I gave her something to help her sleep."

Dimitri was leaning over the side of the bed. "She's out *cold*. And, her shirt's up. Damn, her pants are unzipped."

Eddie watched Dimitri pull Aislinn's dark blue sweater down gently, almost lovingly, and wondered for a brief moment if he could have been the one that tried to claim her and that this man was simply a pissed off relative.

The larger man's fingers tightened over his neck. Eddie struggled to breathe and pushed with all his strength against the body pinning him. Something about the man's face sparked a memory. Eddie had seen those eerie mercurial eyes in a painting once, in one of his mother's books.

"Hey, knock it off down there, will you?" a young man's voice called from the apartment above. "Or I'm callin' the cops."

"Sorry, we were just exercising," came a woman's cheery voice. "Got some new equipment. We'll be done in just a minute. Just need to set it up. Sorry!"

The stern, dark-haired man standing in the room whirled at the sound of the woman's voice. "Gabriella?"

"Good thing I didn't stay in the car." A stunning woman with burgundy hair stepped into the room.

"Woman, I told you to wait in the car."

"And when have I ever listened to that order, Marius?"

"Marius," Eddie managed to sputter, hoping he was wrong. "The Heracleidae?"

"Yes." The man squashing him practically snarled. "And I am Sebastian of the Heracleidae. Bastian, in this century. Who the hell are you?"

*Oh, crap. Not them.*

"Bastian, let him talk," Marius commanded. Bastian's fingers loosened but only enough for Eddie to speak and breathe.

Eddie coughed, blood spattering from his mouth. "I am Edward of...."

Marius grabbed Eddie's left wrist and squeezed. Power shot through Eddie's arm like an electric current.

Marius dropped Eddie's arm and stated with a flat voice, "You're Alcmaeonidae."

"Yes," Eddie affirmed, shocked that Marius was able to discern that with a quick scan. "And you'd better have a good reason for attacking me." Eddie desperately hoped this would have the effect he intended. Otherwise, these pure-blood Olympians could kill him quickly and explain later. His father had told him he was related to the Alcmaeonidae, specifically Cleisthenes, a king who led a revolt against the Dorians, from whom Marius was rumored to be related, hopefully not holding a 2,000 year old grudge.

His mother had insinuated that they carried Heracleidae in their bloodline as well, but his father had always silenced her, not wanting to acknowledge the connection. "We're the brains of the species, they're the brawn," his father had often repeated.

To Eddie's relief, Bastian relaxed his grip further and stepped back, allowing Eddie to stand on his own, which was difficult. Eddie tried to mask the fact that he was leaning on the crumpled wall for support. He pushed his aching body up between exposed wall studs.

"Well, Edward," Gabriella spoke as she examined Aislinn. "What did you give her? I worked in the medical field, so don't lie to me. Her pupils are dilated."

Eddie considered what lie to tell.

Marius loomed before him. "Speak when my mate addresses you, Edward of the Alcmaeonidae."

"It was a sleeping pill."

"Nice try, Edward," said Gabriella. "I want the name. If I take a vial of her blood to a lab, and take the results to a council meeting, what will that present to them?"

Ketamine and gamma hydroxybutyrate, formulated in his private lab. Not something he wanted revealed at a council meeting. Perhaps if he twisted the truth, she would let it drop. If memory served him, she had been mate to Marius for nearly ten years. She might not have kept up with modern drugs. He could come up with a pharmaceutical she had never heard of. Then again, Marius might know if he was lying. His perceptions were known to be strong.

"Ketamine," he confessed since it was a half-truth. "But just a pinch. Enough for her to sleep. She was exhausted."

Gabriella's eyes narrowed. "That's known for two things, Edward. Anesthesia and date rape."

"Son of a bitch." Bastian shoved his left hand into Eddie's chest. "Can't get a woman by yourself, eh vermin? You had to drug her?" Bastian's right fist aimed for Eddie's face.

Eddie pivoted his body, but Bastian's fist had followed the movement and caught Eddie's left eye socket before plunging into the wall. Eddie shook off the stars bouncing behind his eyeball. Bastian had his hand around his throat again and squeezed with obvious intent.

"You smell like a vampire." Bastian accused through gritted teeth. "It's a scent I know very well."

"Bastian, don't kill him." Marius ordered, sounding annoyed.

Bastian released him, but hovered like a lion waiting to devour him.

"Yeah, listen to your *prince*." Eddie spat blood out of his mouth.

"Yet," Marius added, his black eyes narrowing at Eddie.

Eddie decided it was probably best not to piss him off. Marius Brancusi led all of the pure-blood families in Greece and several countries in the Balkans. If memory served, Sebastian was related to him, had fought by his side for nearly a century, and was one of the most feared vampire assassins of all time.

*Fearless Sebastian. Of course.* His father had warned him and his brother about him when they were teenagers. "Watch the biting, boys, or the Fearless Sebastian will come after you." If only Eddie had persuaded Aislinn to reveal who she had befriended, he would have known what he was up against. Now he needed to think fast. No one but his brother, his cousin, and his father knew how far into darkness he had strayed, but Bastian's keen senses had already detected the vampiric energy flowing through him. Eddie *had* actually cut back after watching a good friend begin to take on the gray pallor of a vampire. His looks mattered way too much to him for that.

Perhaps if he convinced these people they were treading on his territory, his home, they would back off. Aislinn had allowed him to move some things into her previous apartment a week before the accident. After that, she moved in with Gramma. This apartment was new. But, they wouldn't know that.

"It was only to relax her," Eddie explained, wiping a hand across his bloody mouth. "Her nerves were shot after travelling for hours. Her grandmother is very ill. And it was all I had. I was looking out for her. Something I have done for the last year and a half, for your information. This is our place and she's *my* girl. So who are you to question me?"

Gabriella straightened, marched over to the closet and yanked the double doors open. "Okay, Edward, where's your clothes?"

He was afraid of that. But to his surprise, he spotted a blue cotton knit jacket he had once loaned to Aislinn. "That's my jacket right there. The blue one."

Gabriella grabbed a sleeve and breathed deep. "Smells like her, not so much you. And both scents are weak."

"We had an argument right before I could move my stuff in. That's why she went to Romania."

"Humph." Gabriella raised both eyebrows and returned to Aislinn's side. With care, she examined Aislinn again, touching her lips. "She has blood on her lips and a new claim mark on her neck. Since I know Bastian staked his claim two days ago, and there was no other mark on her, would you like to explain that?"

There was a roar from Bastian. "How dare you try to claim my mate!" Bastian grabbed Eddie by the shirt and threw him into Aislinn's bookcase. Books tumbled out of it onto Eddie's head and arms like a rock slide.

*Damned books.* Aislinn was always collecting books.

Marius stepped forward. "Bastian, I want to hear what he has to say. While he's conscious, if you don't mind."

Eddie tried not to look relieved, because he wasn't sure he could survive another assault from this Herculean brute. Every breath and movement was painful. It was time to call in reinforcements. Eddie took time to cough and draw air into his aching ribcage while he chanted deep within his mind. *Orthon, hear me. Orthon. Come forth. Do my bidding. Call the creatures of darkness. If they want Olympian blood, there is a feast here. Call them. Tell them the spirits of the underworld will reward them for a victory. I will give them humans to claim. Call them.* The ancient summoning chants rolled through Eddie's mind and he repeated them three times, focusing on the dark places inside himself that he frequented too often.

Eddie lifted his head and glared at Bastian's suspicious, ghostly eyes. "She's not yours, Sebastian."

"The hell she isn't."

"I claimed her last year. The mark faded."

When Bastian's chin lifted, Eddie knew he had him. Claim marks could fade after a few months unless the male constantly reinforced them, making the marks permanent. Most males did reinforce them.

"Then why did she know nothing of claiming, or our people?" Bastian asked. "And I scented no man in her blood?"

"I kept our people a secret from her. She wasn't ready. And it's been a year since I claimed her."

Gabriella snorted with sarcasm. "Oh, that's honorable. If you already claimed her, then why was it easy for her to leave you and come to Romania? And, where is your mate sign?"

Eddie tried to roll his shoulder back into place, and winced. "We don't get them anymore. The marks aren't part of our line."

"Wait," said Dimitri. "That's not true. There were many warriors at the Appalachian gathering that had tattoos."

"So, maybe *they* got the right genes. Guess I wasn't the lucky one." All the bitterness of being considered second class, of not being one of the elite warriors, shot through Eddie like a poison arrow. Hate for these men coiled inside him like a venomous snake. Deep in a forbidden place in his mind, he chanted, *Orthon, call them. Call all of them. They will be rewarded. You can take them. There are only three.*

Vile tentacles, malicious and depraved, snaked through Eddie's soul as the demon rose. Eddie detested the repugnant octopus-like sensation but welcomed the strength of will that filled his chest and flowed into his arms. He could only hope that the Heracleidae were so angry they would not sense the demonic presence rising.

"No Olympian allows his woman to leave," Bastian stated. "Or leaves her unprotected in a foreign land."

Then Eddie remembered. The story of Sebastian. His mother had told him all the old stories. "But *you* did once, didn't you, Fearless Sebastian?"

Marius' arm shot out against Bastian's chest to prevent another assault. Bastian seemed close to discarding his leader's arm and attacking Eddie. He stood with fists clenched. His face was burning red with rage. Veins in the whites of his eyes were bleeding crimson.

Dimitri moved to Bastian's side. "I overheard her conversation with you, Edward, on the phone. She was angry."

"Women get angry all the time."

"Not like that. She accused you of being with another woman. An Olympian would not do that, either."

"Oh, really? The first Olympian's did."

No one spoke for a moment. Eddie's words had the ring of truth, and they could not refute it. Zeus' absurd sexual escapades were legendary.

Marius spoke up. "That was five thousand years ago, Edward. Our tribes forsook that behavior long ago. It should have been hard for Aislinn to leave you, yet it was not."

"She's hardheaded. Like I said, she left on her own because she was mad. I had no choice but to follow her... because of our bond."

The subtle lidding of Bastian's pale eyes did not escape him. *Aha,* thought Eddie, *gotcha.*

"Yet, she never missed you," Bastian countered. "And spoke only of being alone, and of men she could not trust. Men who lie."

"You had gotten in her head, Olympian. I had to get you out. She didn't miss you, either."

"Yes, she did. I felt her confusion, and her pain. She called to me constantly as you traveled." Bastian's voice lowered to a deep-throated threat. "And *you* knew I was there. I saw you."

Dimitri flinched and pulled up the sleeve of his left arm. "Whoa. We've got trouble."

Bastian stepped back, flexed his right arm, and pulled out what appeared to be a large knife hilt from his pants pocket. A gleaming sword burst into the air from the hilt leaving a pure, sweet note singing in Eddie's ear. How Eddie had longed for one of the blessed swords that engaged at the presence of evil or imminent battle. But only the arrogant pure-bloods got those.

Marius pulled out a sword hilt as well. The bladed flashed into the air so fast it took him by surprise "I wonder if they are after Aislinn, or after us."

Though the demon had done Eddie's bidding and called upon the resident creatures of darkness, he suspected the sword might have been triggered by the close proximity of the demon rising inside him, wanting control. As a low-ranking demon, Orthon could not walk the Earth and partake of its vices without a body, so Eddie loaned him his in return for favors.

~~◊~~

Aislinn heard raised voices, worried, angry. Emotions around her were thick. Though she was whirling in a gray fog, she fought for consciousness. Odd sensations were pulsing in her veins and turning in her gut as if she had eaten strange food and her stomach was deciding whether to get rid of it.

Becoming aware that she was in a prone position, she concentrated on moving. But her limbs refused to respond. With effort, she managed to open her eyelids. She blinked to clear her vision.

Eddie was leaning against her bookcase, with white powder all over him and blood on his face. Dimitri, Marius and Gabriella were there. Bastian loomed threateningly closed to Eddie, with only Marius' arm holding him back.

Nausea wafted through Aislinn and she groaned.

"My lady." Bastian was instantly beside her, his large hand caressing the side of her face and hair. She could smell him. Spicy and woodsy and alive.

Why was he here? Was she back in Romania?

"Bastian?" she managed to speak.

"I am here, my lady. You are safe, now."

"Get away from her." That was Eddie's voice. Eddie? For hours, or was it days, Eddie had taken care of her. She had wanted him. Or did she?

Eddie's voice materialized in her mind. *I am your mate, Aisy. Forget him. You are mine now.*

"You filthy vermin!" Bastian whirled.

How had she heard Eddie telepathically? How had Bastian?

In the brightness of the room, Bastian's quick movements caused her eyes to dance and she lost focus. She blinked furiously to clear her blurry vision and make sense of the impossible scene before her.

Marius was blocking Bastian's access to Eddie, his hands gripping Bastian's massive arms, which surprised and frightened Aislinn since Bastian always obeyed Marius' commands without question. The bunched muscles and predatory look in Bastian's face was as fierce as a rabid animal.

"Bastian!" Marius's raised voice was strained but firm. "As much as I would like for you two to settle this, the choice here is Aislinn's."

Gabriella spoke up. "It could be ten hours before she shakes off the drug. And even then, she will be confused. This will have to wait."

*Drug? What drug?*

"In the meantime," Marius continued, "we have demons to fight. Bastian, look at me. Bastian!" Marius lowered his chin, his eyes turning red with intensity as if aiming them at Bastian.

Bastian grunted and stepped back as if stung. He turned his attention to Marius, looking stricken with betrayal.

"Listen to me, Bastian," Marius ordered. "Whether they're here for Aislinn, or for some other purpose, we don't know. But we've got a job to do. Edward, do you have a weapon?"

"In the car," Eddie replied, straightening.

*Oh, wow, Eddie's going to fight for me?* Aislinn began to wonder if she was dreaming. All of these people should not be in the same place.

Bastian was glaring at Marius, a warning edge to his voice. "I will not leave her unguarded."

"Then neither will I," Eddie declared.

"You'll have to." Marius continued to stare at Bastian while addressing Eddie.

"Why?" Eddie complained.

"Because I know Bastian. And he will not leave his mate. Not this time."

"I care as much for her as he does, probably more. And I claimed her before. She's my mate."

*What?* Aislinn's mind reeled. *What was Eddie saying?*

"That fact is yet to be proven," Marius stated with suspicion. "But right now we need another fighter to handle the perimeter. We have two women to protect, one of them is down, and we need to make sure the demons do not make it into this building and attack innocent people in order to distract us. If they're not already in a body, they will jump into one and have people fighting with each other. Are you with us, or not?"

Aislinn focused long enough to hear Eddie reply. "I'm with you."

~~◊~~

Eddie flew to his car, glancing around the parking lot for signs of demons as he went. None had solidified yet, but he could feel them. Orthon fought for control, wanting the thrill of using Eddie's body. Eddie jerked his arm to reclaim it. *Not yet. I have things I gotta do in order to keep my cover.* Orthon roared in frustration, causing Eddie's legs to wobble.

Wrenching his long knife from under the front seat, and recovering two smaller ones from a hidden panel in the passenger cushion, Eddie headed down the sidewalk between two of the three-story buildings housing students. Eddie glanced up at some of the metal balconies. The college students often occupied them at late hours. Fortunately, the air was too cold.

The hair on his arms stood on end as he paused at a safety staircase around the corner from Aislinn's door. Tiny pinpoints of light flickered to the right about ten steps away. Eddie shifted, his body tensed to react. Marius leaned out of the shadows of the adjacent building so Eddie could see him. Eddie had forgotten that pure-bloods' eyes often glowed in artificial light like wild animals in the woods.

He had only a moment to marvel at seeing the glow for the first time, when a fast moving shadow rushed him. Knowing the demon would have to solidify before striking him, Eddie raised the long knife and readied himself for the liquid disturbance of the shadow that would indicate where it was going to strike.

His blow to the creature's arm struck at the same time Marius' sword speared its chest. A scream of agony hung in the air after the creature disappeared, leaving a burnt smell behind. Smoke was curling up from Marius' sword. *Of course.* Marius no doubt periodically had it rechristened with holy water. None of Eddie's weapons were blessed. Would they be able to hold a blessing now? Eddie doubted they would.

Just another reminder, always another reminder that he was not pure-blood, that he could not compete with the Olympians at the top, with his father, or with his brother, or even his cousin whom his father praised. His path into darkness and deviancy had pretty much doomed his aspirations with the Appalachians. He no longer cared what they thought. Fighting now would insure his proximity to Aislinn long enough to take her away. His father was going to be pissed.

Screeches from the graveled area behind the building drew Marius and Eddie. Four small creatures with black wings were rushing Dimitri, who pivoted and slashed to dislodge them. One plummeted to the ground but not before catching its talons in Dimitri's blue jeans. As the creature dematerialized its arm to break free, it sunk its teeth into Dimitri's leg. When Dimitri swung his sword, the creature collapsed into black smoke.

Eddie and Marius ran toward Dimitri, but mid-stride, Marius turned to point his sword at Eddie. Eddie slid to a halt in the grass. Had he been found out?

"Guard that entrance," Marius ordered, pointing his sword toward the back door leading to Aislinn's apartment.

Relieved, Eddie obeyed him, especially since he feared one of the demons could expose him at any moment. Orthon fought for control again, and Eddie tripped, but recovered.

"Ugh," he heard Dimitri exclaim behind him. "I hate imps."

As Eddie positioned himself at the corner of the building, he turned in time to see a tall, humpbacked, ogre-like demon step out from behind a small shed on the property and lumber toward them. A twisted look of hunger distorted its gruesome face. Eddie decided Dimitri and Marius could have the creature all to themselves. It was the first ogre Eddie had actually seen, but he had been warned of their strength by his father. Their smell alone could undo a warrior's resolve.

From behind the ogre creeped a skeletal hag with filthy, shredded clothing, unkempt hair and scabby skin. Eddie's stomach turned, and the hair of his arms stood on end. With a hiss and an unearthly laugh, the hag leapt toward Marius, whose stance proved he was ready for her. Dimitri was sizing up the ogre. Even humpbacked, the huge creature towered two feet above him.

The dimwitted ogre struck first, its club-like arms swinging, its beady eyes eager to hurl something. The hag was flaunting suggestive comments to Marius. Marius pulled a crucifix from under his shirt and the hag snarled and hissed. Eddie knew it would prevent her from controlling Marius' mind. The hag proceeded to flaunt all the horrific ways she was going to enjoy licking and dismembering Marius' body.

The combatants circled each other. Orthon fought for control of Eddie's limbs again. Eddie squirmed and jerked to recover. The hag noticed his movements at the edge of the concrete walkway.

She pointed at him with a bony blackened finger.

Eddie gasped and ducked around the corner. He could not let the hag give him away. Shuffling in the darkness made him turn. A green creature with a hideous face and red eyes spoke, his breath foul. "We are here…."

Eddie sliced at the creature's head before it could say something loud enough to reveal him. The rest of its body wobbled in a hideous flailing of decrepit arms and flying hair. The head rolled and hit the ground with a thud. Eddie grimaced and stabbed the heart of the creature. Fire engulfed the head and body. Laughing erupted around Eddie, from where he could not discern.

*Devils' laughter.* Eddie gasped. His mother had warned him of this. "When you hear it, you'll know you've gone too far," she had told him years ago. Now he understood. He had betrayed a demon he had called to do his bidding. The act was so diabolical, evil had laughed in appreciation of his darkness.

Backing away from the horrid smell in the air, and the fear rising inside him, Eddie returned to the corner of the building, near Aislinn's door. He watched the hag fall at the point of Marius' sword and burst into gray and black flames. Smaller half-formed demons rushed at Marius. Turning as if to retreat, Marius whirled and beheaded one of the creatures, his movements a blur even to Eddie. In a continuous movement, Marius dispatched the rest of the demons so fast, their faces showed surprise as they dissolved.

From the stairs near Eddie, something with wings dropped, obscuring the moon and stars. Eddie slashed with his knife, nicking part of a wing. The creature gave a garbled hiss, seeming to sense Orthon. Instead of pursuing Eddie, it rose in the air and flew toward Marius.

To the left of the yard, the ogre howled in rage as Dimitri swung his sword several times, catching the ogre's arms with each attempt to grab him. A crashing sound in Aislinn's apartment made Eddie jump. He took a step toward the door. A swarm of flying imps squealed and surrounded him. Their screeches hurt his ears.

Gabriella screamed, followed by an unnerving growl that echoed off the buildings. Eddie swung in several directions to deflect the imps. "Go out there, you idiots," he whispered through clenched teeth. He pointed toward the grassy area where Dimitri and Marius were battling.

Finally free of them, he leaped toward Aislinn's door, but halted. Bastian might take the opportunity to use his sword against Eddie. Shards of glass blasted from a window on the other side of Aislinn's door, and Eddie ducked. A massive brown shape somersaulted and disappeared before landing.

Eddie plastered himself against the brick wall, ready for what might follow. He could see Bastian's hand and sword extending from the damaged window.

Out in the yard, Marius was fighting several human-shaped demons. Dimitri was now chasing the ogre. They disappeared into the woods at the edge of the property. Eddie decided to remain where he was to keep an eye on the door to Aislinn's apartment as Marius had instructed. Shadows flitted in and out as demons laughed and played with becoming corporeal, as if the fight was mere sport. Some disappeared into other apartments.

The flock of imps descended onto Dimitri as he trotted out of the woods toward Eddie. Eddie pointed to an area above Dimitri's head. Dimitri ducked, whirled, and dispatched the imps two at a time. It was amazing, even for Eddie, to watch the Olympians fight. He had only been in one true demon fight, but it had been several years earlier, and many lectures later from his father to cease assisting the Appalachians.

Feeling a close presence, Eddie whipped his head in a half-circle in time to see a dark shadow begin to solidify near the side stair around the corner. Like floating ink it hovered toward him in the open air. Fear washed through Eddie as the creature hesitated out of his reach. Eddie realized the demon sensed Eddie wasn't his target. If it ignored him and headed toward the two Olympians, Eddie might be discovered.

Lightning quick, he threw his knife toward the inky shape. The creature howled in rage and turned, focusing yellow eyes.

Eddie reached for one of his smaller knives, expecting the creature to jump at him. Instead, it materialized into something resembling a bear-like wolf. Eddie crouched. The creature was faster than he expected and scrambled up and across the bricks above him, defying gravity, to push open Aislinn's broken door. Eddie leaped toward the shape, grabbed one of its wolf-like legs and slashed the other with his knife. The creature curled its body backward, and a mouth full of teeth aimed for Eddie's face. Eddie grabbed the wolf's throat and squeezed with all his might. Hideous teeth were snapping like an alligator at his eyes. Eddie kicked forward into the creature's belly. With a horrific growl, all four sets of claws began to shred Eddie's shirt.

Dimitri's sword appeared through the center of the creature. Its limbs recoiled. The hairy midsection appeared to be melting. With an unholy howl, the creature evaporated, blowing ash and a black substance into the air.

The black dust billowed as if exploding. Eddie coughed and backed against the door frame to catch his breath. He hadn't seen action like this in so long. The thrill of fighting with Prince Marius and Dimitri was like a drug. He had fought evil again, had been part of a team. After the damage Bastian had done to him, he was amazed he lasted this long. He was tougher than he thought. He was tougher than his father thought.

"You okay?" asked Dimitri. Eddie nodded at Dimitri to show him he was all right. Dimitri nodded in return and leapt toward Marius as if expecting more demons.

Orthon roared and Eddie momentarily lost control of his face, the roar escaping his own mouth. To his surprise, a similar sound came from inside the apartment. Bastian must be fighting something.

*No, Orthon. Later,* Eddie commanded. *Later! Later you can have it.*

Eddie placed both hands to his head and focused, coughing as if to expel Orthon.

"Are you all right?" It was Marius beside him.

"Yes. It's just this… black dust."

After slapping Eddie on the back, Marius led him and Dimitri into the apartment. Bastian was wiping his sword with a towel. Black dust littered the floor around the bed Aislinn lay in. She appeared unconscious, resting in Gabriella's protective arms.

"Saw some action in here I see," Marius said as Bastian handed him his towel.

"Another Yeti came for Aislinn." Bastian replied, his eyes shifting to Eddie.

*A Yeti?* Eddie questioned. *No one commands a Yeti.* He certainly hadn't called for one.

~~◊~~

Eddie turned onto a side, unlit street where he knew prostitutes frequented. Of the girls available, the best choice was a thin woman with stringy blonde hair. Her face appeared aged by wrinkles and blotches, the unhealthy ravages of meth use. As he suspected, she was thrilled to be chosen and asked for a paltry $35.00.

In a secluded area, Eddie allowed Orthon to experience human lust and the thrill of biting the woman's neck to take her blood. It took sheer will to prevent the demon from consuming too much. The blood was drug-tainted, and Eddie did not want to have to explain a dead body. Nor did he wish to have trouble controlling his own, though his body would metabolize the drug quickly.

Having met his obligation to the demon, Eddie used as much persuasion in his voice as he possessed to blur the woman's memory. Orthon protested the command to retreat, wanting to torture and kill her, but Eddie chanted until he regained control. He deposited the woman on a different street, leaving her dazed and confused, but with $100.00 in cash.

He sped away to rejoin the Olympians. They had looked suspicious when he told them he had to make a quick stop for a friend. Bastian had wanted to hit him again when he boldly reassured Marius that he had no choice but to follow Aislinn, since they were bonded.

Eddie thought he had perfected the art of resisting a psychic scan, but when Marius had tried to read him, he nearly winced at the incredible power projected from the Balkan leader. He was forced to turn and make a quick exit to his car, calling back over his shoulder that he would be mere minutes behind and would catch up.

The hour-long drive proved grueling since he had to chant the entire way to shed all traces of the demon's energy in order to pass through the gates of The Appalachian's compound, and survive.

The wards stung like a thousand bees as he drove through. A garbled cry escaped him as he curled into a ball. Fortunately he was alone in his car, so none of the others saw him cringing and fighting to regain control of the vehicle. He wiped tears of pain from his face as he parked.

One thing was certain: he was not leaving Aislinn in their hands. He was fighting for his claim.

# CHAPTER 18

One disjointed scene after another assaulted Aislinn's dreams. Faces slipped in and out. People were yelling. Fighting. Confused, she forced the images to retreat, and sat up in complete darkness, her head swimming. The room did not smell familiar. For the past week of her life, she had been waking up in unfamiliar places.

Inhaling experimentally, she realized she could smell everything from the comforter and sheets to the books and furniture. It smelled like a man's room. But whose?

She threw off the comforter. She was wearing blue jeans and the navy-blue, long-sleeved sweater that she had worn at the hospital. No wonder she was uncomfortable. At least someone had not undressed her this time. Able to see the furniture in the dark, she padded barefoot across the floor and peered out the door. Somewhere, food was cooking. It smelled divine.

A wooden balcony railing stood in front of her and she realized she was on the second floor of a spacious home. The long avenue of shiny hardwood laden with throw rugs reminded her of the upper floor of Marius and Gabriella's chalet. Except this was not the chalet. It was way bigger. Light from a single lamp in the hallway below cast long shadows up the curved staircase. To her right, an open door revealed a bathroom, so she headed there.

She flicked on the overhead light and cried out. Wow, her eyes were sensitive! She held both hands over them until they could adjust. After thirty seconds she decided squinting would have to do. Through lashes, she surveyed her appearance in the bronze-edged, oval mirror. The person staring back at her was frightening. Her blonde hair looked like someone had turned her upside down and used her for a broom. She attempted to smooth it down and spied a brush on a small set of glass shelves. Groaning at the knots, she brushed through it until she was sure she wouldn't frighten anyone else. Several washcloths sat in a wire frame on the opposite wall so she grabbed one, soaked it in cold water, and washed her pallid face.

Pushing back her hair to wipe her neck, she stopped. Leaning forward, she blinked several times to be sure she was actually seeing a bite mark— on the *other* side of her neck.

"*Oooo*, that *man!*"

She slapped the wash cloth onto the sink and vaulted from the room. At the balcony railing, she paused to listen as a low, familiar voice rose from a room downstairs. The commanding tones belonged to Marius. Bastian would surely be with him. Rather than alert him by calling out, she would simply find him and give him a piece of her mind he would never forget.

Marius' voice grew more distinct at the foot of the stairs. Aislinn walked across a large foyer inlaid with rich walnut herringbone and parquet designs, giving the wooden floor a three-dimensional effect.

Leaning at the edge of a partially-opened door, she spied Bastian sitting in a high backed chair looking stern, with rows of books behind him. Marius was talking about battles.

Taking a deep breath, she marched into the room ignoring everything but Bastian. She stopped in front of him and pointed at her neck.

"What the hell did you think you were doing?"

Bastian stood, his face proud and grim.

Feet shuffled. Lots of feet. Aislinn turned. Over twenty-five people that she had not been able to see from the doorway, most of them men, were staring at her. She could not believe she had not sensed their presence. She was so filled with anger toward Bastian, there was no room for anyone else's emotions.

"Hey, Aisy-girl."

Aislinn whirled, wide-eyed. "Eddie? What are *you* doing here?"

Bastian spoke. "He, my lady, is the one who bit you last night."

"*What?*"

Eddie swaggered toward her. "I was just claiming you again, sweetie-girl, like I did a year ago, remember? Me and you?"

"What are you talking about? I kicked your butt out a year ago!" Anger rose like a fire-breathing dragon in her gut. Its rage filled her, pulsing in her muscles, ready to spring.

"You were angry, I know." Eddie lifted a hand as if to appease her. "But last night you said you cared for me, don't you remember?"

Garbled scenes raced through Aislinn's mind but none registering such a statement. Oh how she wanted to wipe that arrogant, over-confident look off his face.

"I most certainly did not," she declared. "And you... you *bit* me? You're one of *them?*" She gestured toward Bastian and Marius.

"Not exactly, my lady," Bastian protested, glancing away as if disgusted by the idea.

"Yes. I am," Eddie answered boldly. "And I claimed you as my own."

The impudence of his tone, the shock of his inclusion into the secret world of this strange, blood-sucking family, and the audacity of thinking she could be claimed like a piece of meat on a buffet line was too much, especially after twice betraying her with his charms on other women.

"You son of a bitch. How *dare* you!" She punched Eddie's already bruised face as hard as she could. Though the blow pushed his face to the side, he pursed angry lips and flexed his jaw muscles to shake off the sting. Boldly, he faced her, his fierce green-gold eyes showing no remorse. In fact, he looked ready to ravish her.

Bastian stepped toward her. "My lady, I...."

"And you're not much better!" She pivoted on one foot to face Bastian. "Biting me and not explaining anything? Who do you people think you are? You think you own anyone you want?"

She glanced from Bastian to Eddie and focused psychic energy. "You can both go to *hell!*"

From the way Eddie flinched in surprise and had to take a step back, along with men on either side of him, Aislinn realized the psychic power she shot into the declaration worked better than she planned.

"Whoa." A young man's voice murmured from the group standing along the opposite wall of bookshelves. "Glad *I* don't have a mate sign right now."

Aislinn whirled and opened her mouth to throw a choice phrase in his direction when Marius stepped into her line of vision. "Miss Aislinn." His tone was a chastisement. "You are a guest in the home of Commander Cirillo Markos, who graciously offered us protection here."

"Well, I'm *sorry*," she quipped with sufficient sarcasm. "I didn't *ask* to be here. And I didn't *ask* for anybody to bite me. Or *claim* me, or whatever the hell you call it. I don't even know where the hell I am. But you know what? I am *out* of here." Aislinn passed the line of men and cleared the doorway in swift strides. She paused midway across the beautiful foyer, torn between trudging up the stairs in hopes of finding her purse, and marching out the front door in the middle of the night.

"No Bastian," she heard Gabriella's voice behind her. "Let me handle this."

Aislinn turned to face Gabriella. She did not want to insult her, but was unable to quell the righteous fury consuming her. She could not remember the last time she was this angry. Well, maybe at Eddie a few times.

Gabriella smiled and stepped toward her. "I'm liking you more every day, Aislinn Thomas. It's three o'clock in the morning. Your purse and suitcases are upstairs. I know you're angry right now, but hopefully not at me."

Aislinn swallowed back her rage and chose not to speak, instead taking deep breaths to calm the beast she had become. Gabriella was part of this crazy nightmare, but she had been a warm glow in the darkness from the beginning.

"How much can you remember from last night?" Gabriella tilted her head as if curious.

Aislinn forced the strange jumble of images to coalesce, but became confused with the order and timeline. "I was at Gramma's. I mean, I was in her hospital room. I... met a relative. Duncan. Then I got sick. Eddie drove me back to my apartment. And... and... I remember walking through the door but everything's, like, gray from that point, except faces flipping in and out. Voices were yelling. Weird growls and stuff. Fighting. You were there."

"Just so we can't be overheard, let's go up to the room where your things are."

"My stuff's up there?"

"On the side by the wall. You may not have seen them."

Thoughts of her purse, cellphone, and clothes spurred Aislinn on. She sighed at sight of the long, curved staircase. As she labored with each step, she realized she was able to mount the stairs with more strength than she remembered. Gabriella slowed to keep pace with her.

"Are you okay?"

"No, I am not okay. But that doesn't have anything to do with this. I was in a bad car accident a year ago. The one that killed my family. I was in casts for a long time and had to use crutches. My legs had titanium pins in them. I can walk on my own now, but for some reason steps are still hard for me. Although, I feel a bit stronger today."

"Oh." Gabriella's voice sounded sad. "I glimpsed scars on your legs at my house, but I didn't want to pry."

"Well, I usually wear long pants, or tights. You should have seen me at the inn in Romania. All the first and second floor rooms were taken, so I had to deal with the stairs every day. That was tough, especially after touring."

Slowing halfway up the staircase to take a breather, she decided to change the subject. "So, whose place is this again?"

"Cirillo Markos leads of one of the Eastern U.S. tribes. We refer to him as The Appalachian. His title of Commander is the American version of Prince, so you need to understand that he and Marius are equals. Cirillo's leadership covers Maryland, Delaware, the Virginias, and the Carolinas. Tennessee and Kentucky, too, I think. They are a mixture of many races. This is the home of his great-grandfather, who came to the U.S. in the late eighteen hundreds, after the Civil War. He has managed to unite several pure-blood tribes and scattered remnants of the weaker bloodlines into a cohesive family. Marius and Bastian respect him for that."

"What... state are we in?"

"North Carolina."

"Oh." She sighed with relief. "I'm not far from home then."

"We were at your apartment in Brevard, but knew it would be safer here. This place is guarded with warriors and wards."

"Wards?"

"Yes."

Aislinn gave her a disbelieving shake of her head. "Are we talking... magic?"

Gabriella smiled, her eyes twinkling. "Something like that. Ancient knowledge. The important thing is that everyone here would fight to protect you."

With that sobering thought, and Gabriella's presence calming her nerves, Aislinn began to feel guilty for her outburst in Cirillo's library. *Just four more steps, four more.* Grateful to reach the top, she crossed the balcony and entered the bedroom she had slept in.

"Aislinn." Gabriella found a chair near the dresser and sat in it. "I need to ask you some personal questions, girl to girl."

Aislinn felt irritation sparking to life again. It was not that she minded Gabriella, but she was still feeling somewhat violated. Wary and apprehensive, she sat on the bed.

As if she were giving a quick, matter of fact report, Gabriella explained the last seven hours of Aislinn's life. Aislinn listened, wide-eyed, her mouth agape.

"And that is all I know from my perspective," said Gabriella. "Do you recall having a conversation with Edward about your relationship with him, or consenting to a claim?"

"No!" Aislinn insisted. "I mean, a few weeks ago, before I caught him with another woman, which he swears was just some needy business client, I had let my feelings for Eddie grow again. I let down my guard, started to consider him a boyfriend again. He kept calling and sounded so... in love with me, I guess.

"Then I saw him with this woman at a bar. Me and some friends went there to celebrate our victories. It was a year ago all over again. I mean, he was rubbing her arms and whispering stuff in her ear, and... had that... *look*. You know. Like he was ready to take her right there on the floor or something.

"So you were not living together?"

"What? *No.* I mean, if you had asked me a month ago, I might have considered it. But, not after I saw him at that restaurant."

Gabriella kept her expression neutral. "Okay. What about now?"

171

Aislinn shook her head. "It sounds strange, but, Eddie just showed up in Romania, and then my Gramma took a turn for the worse. Next thing I knew, we were running for a plane. We had already agreed we were just friends. Well, I stated we were just friends. He probably didn't agree. Three planes later, we finally made it to the hospital. I can remember most of what happened in the hospital, and I remember meeting a guy named Duncan, who came in to visit Gramma. Then I got so sick. In my apartment, all I have is, like, flashes of weird pictures. Eddie was leaning over me and whispering something. Oh, my gosh."

"What?"

"I think I kissed Eddie." Aislinn stared across the room and touched her lips. "I don't know why, but I remember kissing him. Voices were in my head. Some of it sounded like Bastian. And... some of it sounded like Eddie. Except, I couldn't remember who Bastian was. I think I woke up and saw you, and Dimitri. Bastian and Marius too. You were all angry. Eddie was... all beat up."

Gabriella smirked. "Bastian and Edward had an altercation."

"Oh, no. It's a wonder Bastian didn't kill him. That's why I didn't tell Bastian about him."

"Oh, Bastian *wanted* to kill him, but Marius wouldn't let him."

Aislinn snorted. "Well, thanks to Marius on that one." Sorting her thoughts, Aislinn left the bed and began to pace, wishing there was a rug on the hardwood floor for her sensitive feet.

"I vaguely remember talk about battling demons. I think Marius was organizing everybody." She paced again, and turned to Gabriella. "I don't remember Eddie biting me." She shook her head. "My mind is... blank. And how can he be biting me, anyway? Is he part of your family of... of... whatever you are?"

Gabriella took a deep breath. "Not specifically my family group. Marius' leadership includes our people living in Greece, Albania, Bulgaria, Romania, and several other countries. The Balkans, basically. A very difficult task considering the history of the region. Here, the eastern part of U.S. is comprised of three tribal leaders. The Plymouth leads the northeast, The Augustine leads Florida, Georgia and Alabama, and in the middle is, of course, Cirillo, The Appalachian. There are two main families of the bloodline in his realm who have not given their allegiance to Cirillo, but they respect him and keep to themselves. Edward, I believe, is in one of those families."

Aislinn stared in disbelief. "Gabriella, it's like there's a whole hidden world here. And I'm in the middle of it." Her voice cracked with a sob. Her chest hurt. She worked her facial muscles to gain control. "Why do I feel like crying? My emotions are, like, so whacked right now. Is there any way you can ask Marius to give you, or someone else, permission to explain all this to me? I'm dying here."

"Certainly." Gabriella gave her a brief smile and closed her eyes, which Aislinn was not expecting. After 20 seconds of silence, Gabriella opened her eyes and stood. "Marius will see you now."

"What? No. I'm not going back down there."

Gabriella reached for Aislinn's hand. "I am so sorry for the way things happened. If you want answers, grab them while you can. Marius has explained to Cirillo your situation and your need to understand what has been happening to you. Cirillo is concerned about… certain events, especially the attack on the way to the inn, back in Romania, where you sensed the Yeti was after you. And then, last night, we had to battle demons. Another Yeti came after you. Rare. Very rare. No one commands a Yeti."

"What?"

"You were out of it at the time. Believe it or not, Cirillo is quite indignant about the way you were treated, and welcomes the opportunity to give you some explanations."

Aislinn cringed. "I *was* kinda rude, wasn't I? Gabriella, I've never made a scene in my life. I was taught to always be a lady, no matter what. But the rage I felt when I saw that other bite on my neck—that was like nothing I have ever felt before. And I hit Eddie!"

Gabriella crinkled her brows. "My emotions were very heightened when Marius and I created a blood bond. They call it the blood heat. You've had a blood bond from two different men. That's unprecedented. Your passions will run very high now."

Aislinn rolled her eyes. "Just one more thing. Always one more thing. I didn't even know all those people were in there. I should have felt their presence. When my emotions are strong, my empathic abilities don't work. But I can't believe I was so angry I couldn't feel them."

"So." Gabriella rose to her full height. "Go in there like a lady, offer your apologies, and charm the pants off them."

Aislinn laughed. "I'm so glad you're here."

Gabriella winked. "So am I."

As the two women entered the library, voices fell silent. Aislinn did not look at Eddie or Bastian, but kept her eyes straight ahead where Marius sat in a chair beside Cirillo's desk.

Gabriella graciously led her to Cirillo Markos who rose from behind the large desk. Gabriella introduced them properly. Cirillo shook Aislinn's hand firmly, then leaned forward to kiss her cheek, and then the other.

Aislinn gave a shy smile. She had seen a few people greet others that way during her trip, but never in America. Cirillo was stocky, at least six feet tall, with short, graying black hair, and the type of piercing gaze and stern face Aislinn associated with police officers. She noticed his eyes were the color of milk chocolate with splashes of gold and green, amazingly brilliant. *Figures.*

"Mr. Markos," Aislinn began, wondering if she should have addressed him as Commander. "I apologize for being rude earlier. I was… very upset, and had no idea where I was, or what had been done to me."

"No problem, Miss Aislinn. I understand completely. Please, have a seat."

Across from Marius and Cirillo, Bastian stood and offered his seat to her with a chivalrous gesture of his hand, though his eyes still portrayed a hint of displeasure and restrained anger.

Unable to discern whether his anger was directed at her, or the whole twisted situation, Aislinn contemplated refusing his chair. His rugged, handsome face and incredible physique made her body warm all the way to the soles of her shoeless feet in spite of trying to stay distant from him. He was wearing a white, short-sleeved shirt and—Aislinn gasped softly—blue jeans. It was the first time she had seen him in blue jeans and he filled them out nicely. Very nicely.

*Oh no, shift your eyes.* She did not want the room full of men to catch her staring at Bastian's crotch and thighs. The thought of sitting where he just sat was oddly appealing since she couldn't, and probably shouldn't, touch him.

Wordlessly, she sat, feeling the strain of tearing her gaze from him. With easy grace, he rounded the chair to stand behind her, as if on guard. Out of the corner of her eye, Aislinn noticed Eddie glaring at Bastian with hatred.

*Good grief.*

*Aisy-girl, just relax. I'm here with you,* Eddie's voice crept into her awareness.

Aislinn leapt to her feet. "Don't you *dare* talk to me in my head! You were *not* invited."

Eddie blanched, apparently surprised she would reveal the private exchange in front of everyone.

Cirillo spoke. "Edward, please do not exacerbate this situation. Marius, I would like to forbid either of them from telepathically communicating with Miss Aislinn until she willingly gives her permission. By creating a blood bond, with or without her consent, they have brought her into this family, and we owe her our protection and guidance."

"Agreed," said Marius. "Bastian, will you comply?"

Aislinn could hear the unspoken protest in the way Bastian let the air slowly out of his lungs. She swallowed as seconds ticked by. Hesitating to obey one of Marius' requests caused tension to rise in the room.

"Yes, my lord," Bastian answered stiffly.

"Edward?" Cirillo's piercing eyes left no doubt what he thought about Eddie's actions. "You have not sworn allegiance to my tribe. But you are in my home and under my jurisdiction. Will you comply?"

"Yes, sir." Eddie's voice had a sulky edge to it.

Aislinn felt her shoulders drop in relief. She eased back into the chair. Oddly, she felt protected by a man she barely knew. It was then she noticed Dimitri scowling at Eddie from across the room. Her heart lurched at his brotherly protectiveness.

Marius spoke. "Cirillo, with your permission, I would like to begin an explanation to Miss Aislinn that will give her a framework for the behavior of…" he shot a disapproving glare at Bastian, and then Eddie, "our two warriors."

Cirillo gestured a hand toward Marius. "Be my guest."

Marius gave him a nod of appreciation. Gabriella sat on the broad armrest beside Marius. Marius slipped his arm around her waist. "Miss Aislinn, I will start at the beginning. At least, as much of the beginning as we have. Five thousand years ago our ancestors landed on a mountain called Olympus. They were not from Earth."

Aislinn's lips parted and her face went lax. Her jests concerning Bastian being an alien came back to her in twisted, ironic recall. She glanced at some of the men in the room. Her attention stopped at a young woman who was probably around nineteen or twenty. They all looked human enough. Except, they were absolutely gorgeous. Fit, toned, alert, with an air of magnetism she had come to associate with Marius' family, and Eddie. All of them had brilliant eyes; even the darker hues, browns and navy blues shone with gemlike luster. The room crackled with the energy and beauty of them. Aislinn swallowed at her body's heated reaction to the nearest men.

"So, you *are* aliens?" she asked.

"*Were* aliens," Marius clarified. "What you know of as the Greek gods, were our ancestors. They were a race not just technologically advanced, but mentally and physically advanced, at least compared to the humans of that time."

"So, you are aliens… and gods?" Aislinn raised both brows with a hint of sarcasm.

Marius smirked tolerantly. "Our ancestors were the slaves of an intelligent and domineering race. Cruel, really. Alterations had been made to our ancestors' DNA in order to enhance their abilities, yet keep them in bondage. After all, our masters did not want weak slaves. They wanted strong, talented ones who could do all the work. The masters were telepathically powerful, very large beings, but grew increasingly lazy. So, the manipulation of energy, telekinesis, telepathy, and longevity, were all genetic modifications encoded into our blood. Shifting into other forms, however, was a talent we learned here, from the Fae."

Aislinn widened her eyes. "Fae? As in Faeries?"

"Not the tiny winged people you are thinking, but a race of beings who can shift dimensions and change shape. They can be tricky to work with, but a long time ago, an Olympian freed a princess from the clutches of an Unseelie Fae who was also a warlock. A story I will tell you another time. But in exchange, the Olympian requested the secret to shape-shifting.

"The universe is a busy place, physically and dimensionally. Our ancestors knew of Earth from merchants and travelers who visited our original planet. We believe our DNA either came from humans, or was combined with humans. Because of the likeness, our people hoped they could hide on Earth and not be discovered.

"They planned for many years. When their chance to escape came, they took it. They confiscated a ship and landed on mountain Olympus, in Greece, and the people of Earth believed them gods. They had strength, they had *chariots* that flew, and weapons that shot lightening and flame. Our people went from slaves to being gods with absolute power. That became a problem. I'm sure you know what is said about absolute power." He waited for her to answer.

"Absolute power corrupts absolutely." Aislinn obliged him.

"Precisely. Our ancestors were taller and stronger, which added to their mystique, but they also did not age like humans, appearing immortal. I am 128 years old. Bastian is 123."

Aislinn fell back against her chair as if struck. She whirled to examine Bastian. There wasn't a gray hair on him. He appeared no older than 35 to 40 years. In fact, he looked magnificent.

Broader in the chest than Marius, and taller, Bastian resembled a wrestler on steroids. Except for the silver eyes, which clearly looked alien. He watched her quiet assessment of him. She could tell his mind was open to her, wanting to know what she thought, and was probably able to read her, but he did not dare speak telepathically.

Aislinn's neck and chest heated at his intense gaze. The rest of her body followed. Desire to run her hands all over him, and feel his hands on her, was so acute she clenched her fists. Reluctantly, she returned to facing Marius to detach herself from the rising lust, puzzled that it was so fast and fierce. "Your passions will run very high now," Gabriella had said. That was becoming a gross understatement.

Marius' resemblance to Bastian was in facial features only. Though muscular as well, Marius was slightly shorter, though still tall at six feet. His black wavy hair and dark eyes gave a Spanish look to his face, whereas Bastian resembled a Nordic Viking.

"As I said," Marius continued, "power became a problem. We were created with high passions, thus the need for leadership. On Earth, leadership broke down. Humans were playthings."

He tilted his head. "We believe in the almighty creator of the universe. We do not need people worshipping *us*. For our ancestors, it became a necessity, however, because the worshippers would capture blood from animal sacrifices, and give it our ancestors, believing them gods because they could ingest it."

Aislinn stared at him. "They only drank blood?"

"Our digestive systems were damaged, purposely. Our captors believed that if we could only ingest fluids such as water, juices, broths, but mostly the blood of other creatures—which forced us to eat often—then we would be dependent on our captors for sustenance. In this, they were correct. Even if we escaped, our ancestors could not survive in the wild on their home planet. But the problem was solved when the people of Earth took care of their needs.

"There were many battles between other extra-terrestrial groups visiting here. Some of them were called the Titans. All were considered gods by the humans when my people arrived.

"One of our ancestors had amassed extensive knowledge of manipulating DNA from assisting his master. He toyed with genetics for fun, creating half human, half animal creatures, which was unconscionable. He also discovered that when humans ingested Olympian blood in small amounts, spread out over time, our encoded DNA aided in creating compatible humans, if they were strong enough. Reproduction became much more successful. Less need for interfamily unions."

When he paused, Aislinn took a deep breath. "Like Hercules, half-god, half-human, and gods marrying their sisters?"

"Yes. I'm pleased you know your ancient history."

"History was one of my favorite subjects."

"Good. As time went by, the bloodlines, and therefore the abilities, became watered down. Wars got in the way. Zeus and the original ancestors eventually died. Plagues and natural disasters decimated our numbers.

"Bastian, Dimitri and I celebrate our history as the descendants of Hercules. Some in my tribe believe we are of Perseus because it was he who decided he wanted no part of using humans as servants and worshippers, and fought against such tyranny. For that dedication, his descendants were both blessed, and cursed. Demonic beings and sorcerers, even fallen angels, attacked my people. We interfered with their desire to temp humans and feed off their suffering. And, we kept other Olympians in line so they did not abuse humans.

"Because of the great deeds our people did, often saving whole villages from dragons and tyrants alike, they were...."

"Dragons?"

"Yes, there are few left, now. Each of us has a patron saint and an angel we rely on. By pledging ourselves to the task of fighting all forms of evil, we are blessed, and also use blessed weapons. You saw some of those on the road in Romania."

"The swords. Where did you hide them?" Aislinn asked.

Marius smiled secretively. "We carry their hilts. The blades appear in the presence of evil."

Since he did not elaborate, Aislinn asked the question she was having trouble with. "So, if you guys really live that long, how do you fool everybody?"

"We've learned to fake our deaths. I died, officially, in 1941 during World War II. Bastian died a few months later."

Aislinn felt her muscles tighten and her mouth fall open.

"Only Olympian families know the truth. We move to another country, sometimes come back as a relative. Even change tribes if necessary. We also change our names. Brancusi is not the surname I was born with. There are remnants of our bloodline in every country, nearly every culture. Though we live hidden lives, there is no way to be a force for good among humans without becoming part of communities, and part of a tribe. We must have strong leadership and strict cohesion.

"To bring you up to the present, we plan reunions and council meetings every few years with the other tribes. Probably should do it every year." Marius glanced at Cirillo, who nodded, his expression stern as if this was an issue he felt strongly about.

"Modern technology keeps us in touch. Of course, the blood bonds worked for centuries, but as many Olympians continue to mix with humans, or abandon the cause, abilities and knowledge are often lost."

Aislinn imagined orgies of people biting each other's necks in order to communicate. "The blood sharing thing—everybody here does that?"

"Bastian, Dimitri, and I, and... let's see, two of these here," Marius gestured toward two men in the room, "along with Cirillo, have been in battles together and offered each other blood in order to give strength when wounded, and to communicate. Sharing blood gives us a telepathic connection, even over distances. The Vow of Allegiance is one of our ceremonies where subjects offer their blood to their tribe leader to allow instant communication. And compliance."

Aislinn recoiled at the statement. "So, wait, everybody who is part of your... group, kingdom, whatever, lets you drink their blood so you can talk to each other?"

"The men, yes. The women, no. A man and woman cannot exchange blood without creating a blood heat. The hormones engage. There is no stopping it." The intensity of his gaze made Aislinn feel as though he were waiting for her reaction.

"Yeah, been there, done that," Aislinn murmured in a sour tone. "So, who made you leader?" Emotions rose in the room, and she felt them this time, mostly concern for Marius' reaction, and at her irreverence. Instead of cringing, Aislinn decided to allow the emotions to wash over her. She breathed through them. The blood bonds were giving her a new appreciation for her abilities.

Marius' chin rose slightly. "A leader is chosen in many ways. Birthright, abilities, and maturity. Code of honor. Dedication to fighting evil. We do have a Council of Elders who gets involved. A leader makes a vow of leadership, guidance, and protection for his people."

Aislinn examined Marius and Cirillo briefly. They certainly held an air of unquestionable leadership about them. In the quietness of the room, Aislinn realized she could hear women's voices echoing from somewhere nearby, along with the clang of dishes and pots. Some of the men noticed too, and turned their heads toward the library door in anticipation.

Aislinn inhaled enticing aromas, but focused on Marius. "Are you saying that all of these people have given a Vow of Allegiance?"

"Yes, to Cirillo," Marius answered. "They respect me as a tribal leader, of course."

"And... these people obey either of you without question?"

"That is correct." Marius nodded.

"That explains a lot."

Marius looked curious. "Why do you say that?"

"Because Bastian and Dimitri treat you like a king. They obey your commands instantly."

"As they should."

Not sure how to respond, Aislinn opted to fight that battle another day. "You think... I could be descended from you? Your people, I mean?"

"I believe so. Genealogy has become one of our obsessions in recent years, though there are many records we cannot recover. We often explore stories of children with exceptional psychic or warrior abilities in order to trace their bloodlines. If they have even a small amount of Olympian blood, by the time they are thirty-five they usually discover they must eat pure, unprocessed food in order to heal. We become health nuts, you Americans would say." His lips twisted in a half-smile. "I, however, possess the ability to intuit an Olympian bloodline by reading someone's energy. You..." he pressed the tips of his fingers together, "have eluded me."

Aislinn quelled under his scrutiny and wondered why her blood would be any different.

"But no matter," he added. "I am close to figuring you out by way of your family."

He waved a hand toward the bookshelves in the expansive room. "Most of us, well, certainly the leaders, have libraries in order to remember history, and to track our families. In your case, we have uncovered a hidden genealogy that may explain your abilities."

"Really?" Aislinn sat up with interest.

"Your grandmother's bloodline is part Grecian, Romanian, Swedish and German, as is Bastian. I understand your grandmother's grandfather, your great-great-grandfather, was adopted, and contacted by someone of the blood late in life and told of his connection to a warrior people with special abilities. This also happened with your grandmother's husband's father, your great-grandfather on the other side, who was also adopted and knew nothing of his origins. There may also be Portuguese and Celtic in your line. Lines that are possibly Olympian. And, today we are hearing of an African and Egyptian connection through your great-grandmother's sister.

"Your grandmother shared these... family secrets... with your mother and father, but your mother thought the stories were nonsense and did not want you exposed to the idea."

Aislinn felt a chill run through her limbs. Marius had intimate knowledge of her mother's preference that she not be told of the "gypsies and fortune tellers" in her grandmother's ancestry.

"Have you been investigating me?"

"Yes." His tone held no apology.

"So, I'm... actually... part of this?"

"You are now. It would explain why two blood bonds did not kill you."

She blanched and swallowed, her mind rushing through memories and family conversations. "Well, just for the record, I've been psychic, but never had fangs."

Several listeners laughed good-naturedly.

Cirillo smiled. "We don't all have the fangs, darlin.' My immediate family does. Some of us, and I won't mention names...." He glanced about the room, his eyes landing on one man with straight brown hair. "Have been known to claim a mate by using a temporary henna tattoo to keep with tradition." The thirty-something man was jabbed in the arms by two others, and grinned sheepishly. Aislinn noticed there were several races represented. All had lean, athletic builds as if they exercised often. Even the young woman was fit and shapely.

"And, we have many who do receive the battle signs," Cirillo added. "For those who do not, we have a ceremonial congratulation, and take them to a shop that does the tattoos for us. They use a special ink."

"Oh." Aislinn glanced at Eddie. She had seen a light tattoo on one of his shoulders, which he always insinuated was from a time he drank too much and went on a dare. Eddie's eyes became proud and possessive. She quickly shifted her attention to Cirillo. "Do I understand that you get these tattoos from every battle? They just... show up?"

"For the most part, yes," Cirillo answered. "We ask our angel for protection *and* for the marks that give us warning of impending battles. The marks lighten when the battle is over. Many humans cannot see them. For those of the weaker bloodlines who feel called to be warriors, we have often invoked spiritual assistance for other means of warning them. Some can simply feel the battle coming."

Aislinn scanned the room, noting any tattoos shining on arms, then swiveled in her seat to examine Bastian. His short sleeves revealed honey-glazed tattoos that ringed the collar at his neck and were visible from his elbows to his wrists. She remembered them shimmering on his chest in the moonlight when he was wounded, and later when he rested in the bed of dirt. The golden sheen on the tattoos was unlike any ink she had ever seen. They were definitely brighter to her now, as if her eyes had grown an extra lens.

"Have you done nothing but fight battles your whole life?" she asked Bastian, her voice softening.

There was silence in the room. Aislinn could feel the others collectively holding their breath. With her enhanced senses, she detected admiration and awe for Bastian. Some thought her question impertinent. She had dared to ask a super hero why he rescued people.

Bastian regarded her with a look of stalwart conviction. A hint of desire sparkled like diamonds in his silver irises. Even now, under her scrutiny and that of the onlookers, he could not hide it.

Her body warmed in response. Her heart beat faster.

A strange cloud of light shrouded everything in Aislinn's peripheral vision. Its brilliance obscured every object and person from view except Bastian. Aislinn blinked. The bright light pulsed. Like an ethereal, blessed hand the warm light reached through her body and touched her heart. She gasped softly. It was as though she were being given a sign by some unseen angelic force as to a purpose. Something was supposed to happen. Bastian was connected to it. So was she.

As it dissipated, Aislinn swallowed and slowly turned, feeling shaky, not knowing whether to share the experience with anyone. The expressions of the men and women in the room did not convey any knowledge of her encounter. They continued to radiate such respect and veneration for Bastian that moisture formed in her eyes.

She straightened and addressed Marius. "Could I be taught to fight like them?"

An eruption of protest filled the room, causing her to grab the arms of her chair. Bastian's voice was the loudest. Cirillo raised his hands for quiet.

"Gracious, child," Cirillo addressed her. "Whatever for?"

She nodded toward the fit young woman. "She's a warrior, isn't she?"

"Zoe, my granddaughter, was trained along with her brothers, partly because she enjoyed helping them practice, but mostly because it would take an act of God to keep her out of it." Several chuckles bounced around the room and the young woman smirked with triumph.

"However," said Cirillo, "as a rule, we try to keep our women from fighting."

"But think how much more you could do," Aislinn argued, "if both women and men were warriors."

"For many of the stronger lines," Marius interjected, "losing our mate can mean the end of the bloodline, and our time as a warrior. Losing one… takes out two."

Aislinn felt a tremor of foreboding. "Why?"

Marius took a deep breath, his eyes flicking toward Gabriella. "Because losing them is losing half of ourselves. Many Olympians have been known to give up on life and waste away. A few even turned vampire in their grief."

"Vampire?" She resisted the urge to turn and look at Bastian.

"If we remain engaged in worthy tasks, we endure. But, if we give in to anger, vices, despair, especially the temptation to drink the blood of humans as a way of… enslaving or killing them, then we become evil's tool. Grief and loneliness from the loss of a mate can cause a madness which some do not recover from. Such is the intensity of our bonds."

Aislinn remembered Bastian's confession. Did she save him from such a fate? She felt a stab of pride at the thought.

"Plus, if the female is of the blood," Marius continued, "her ability to bear children is vital. Many of our family lines have died out altogether over the centuries. Allowing our mates to fight—physically—is risking our future."

"Okay. That kinda makes sense," said Aislinn. "But it does take men to make babies."

Gabriella nudged Marius with an elbow and winked at Aislinn.

"Yes, that is true," Marius responded. "But we can't carry and give birth to babies, now can we?"

Aislinn smiled. "Okay, you got me there. But, I did help fight demons in Romania. Those dog things."

"Yes, but you compromised Bastian." Marius' eyes blazed with judgement.

"Hey, that's not fair. They didn't see those creatures coming."

"They would have, Aislinn. Believe me. If a hound horde was coming toward Gabriella, nothing in this world would matter to me except protecting her. Do you understand what that would mean in the middle of a battle, one I was leading? I would no longer be connected to the other warriors with me. I would no longer be concerned for my own safety.

"Most of our females possess psychic abilities. You have shown abilities along those lines. Those can be used to fight in many other ways. Not to mention the charity and volunteer work our women perform for our communities, helping to mend and change lives. There are many ways to be a warrior for good."

Aislinn thought of her grandmother and the secret moments they shared talking about extra-sensory abilities. "I was psychic even as a child. In little ways. I remember what it was like to know things and have people think I was crazy. My grandmother warned me not to tell anyone. My mother didn't like it."

"Which is why many of our children are homeschooled. Being in public school is too much for them. Especially if they are pure-blood and get angry and their teeth extend."

Aislinn straightened. "You *do* that when you get angry?"

"Yes, though not until the age of fourteen or fifteen. It's a trait of my particular bloodline, but many here in American have shown it as well. Strong emotion brings it on."

Aislinn couldn't help sweeping the room with her eyes. "Does everyone here have to drink blood?"

"My bloodline carries the intestinal limitations," Marius answered matter-of-factly. "We hunt animals, drink their blood, and set them free."

"Good to know. I *think*. What if you're stuck and there are no animals around?"

"The circumstances have to be dire. Only in life or death would we take blood from a human. That is our rule."

"But...." Aislinn was hesitant to ask, then decided not to back away from the question. "I was bitten, twice, by people who thought I was a normal human."

A slight shuffling of feet swept through the room of onlookers. Aislinn quelled under the onslaught of mixed emotions. Disapproval and curiosity was evident, especially toward Eddie. She also heard Bastian's slow, heavy intake of breath behind her. Most of the warriors in the room still felt respect for Bastian, as if wanting to believe he had a good reason.

Marius' eyes darkened with an icy glint. "I have already shared my... objection with Bastian. I will leave it up to Cirillo to address the issue with Edward."

"Which we will do today, Edward." The cold stare Cirillo shot toward Eddie unnerved Aislinn. Though Cirillo had been pleasant with her, his penetrating gaze hinted at a side of him that made him a formidable leader and opponent.

Marius took a controlled breath and twitched his lips with a slight agitation. "Sharing a blood bond with a mate is a different issue entirely. Both Bastian and Edward have expressed their belief that you are more than human, which is a good thing, for them, and for you. I have no reason to believe Bastian or Edward have succumbed to 'the devil's laughter.'"

Guilt and fear was the last thing Aislinn expected to hit her with a jolt. It took a moment to realize it was Eddie's sharp emotions she was receiving. *The new blood connection.* Before, he had always been a mystery because she had trouble reading his emotions. She dared not look at him and give away her new awareness. Alarm snaked through her veins. What was going on with Eddie to feel such guilt, aside from taking advantage of her?

"The devil's laughter?" she prompted, hoping for some insight.

Marius raised his eyebrows. "If we prey on humans by taking their blood, we violate those humans. And in a sense, the dark side wins. Or... *laughs.* Many have been known to hear it."

Aislinn considered his words. "And, you punish your people when one of them becomes like that? Well, a vampire?" Again, a blast hit her from Eddie, one of overwhelming fear.

Marius stretched his legs. "That's where warriors like Bastian come in."

All eyes in the room shifted to where Bastian stood behind her chair. Aislinn swallowed but did not turn around.

"He is our tribe's Assassin," Marius clarified. "Each tribe has one. Bastian has never failed to... shall we say, bring to justice a vampire who has been sentenced."

Aislinn dared not ask for details of the "justice," for fear of the answer. The site of Bastian easily choking the breath out of Razvan, and his displeasure when she stopped him from finishing was a vivid memory.

"Do you have any other questions?" Marius asked.

Aislinn thought quickly, not wanting to miss any opportunity to understand these strange people now in her life, especially Bastian. She was baffled by Eddie's inclusion since he had never told her, but could have. And, she had eaten normal meals with him many times. Though, come to think of it, he always ordered soup, and occasionally fish, but never beef or heavy foods like lasagna.

"I'm sure I'll have many questions later. But there's one I can think of, and, I probably shouldn't ask it, but, will you and Bastian have to hunt animals in order to... drink their blood? I mean... while we're here?" Her shoulders stiffened in anticipation of the answer.

Marius' lips curved in the hint of a smile, but he regarded her with a steadfast gaze. Aislinn had the feeling she was being tested to gauge her tolerance and acceptance. "We will hunt, if we need to. We have a gland behind our fangs which releases endorphins into the bloodstream of animals when we bite them. It relaxes them enough for us to take a minimal amount of blood. Elements in our saliva help to seal the wound so it does not continue to bleed when we are done. Then we release them."

A predatory shadow appeared in Marius' black eyes. Imagining him and Bastian catching a deer and sucking its blood made Aislinn grimace. At that same moment, she remembered how she felt when Bastian bit her. It was one of the most glorious sensations she had ever experienced. And he had known it would happen. Anger flared in her chest. He had known the bite would cause her to be willing, would cause her to enjoy it. Was he any better than Eddie? How she wished she could talk to her grandmother about this. Gramma would give her a clearer perspective.

Marius' eyes took on a threatening gleam. "There is one last thing I need to mention. Be warned that if you in any way endanger the existence of our people, or our mission, by sharing this information with anyone—and I do mean anyone—I will erase all knowledge of us, including Bastian and Edward, from your mind, blood bonds or no."

# CHAPTER 19

Cirillo straightened from where he had been leaning on his desk, and reached out a hand to Aislinn. "Miss Aislinn, since you asked about being a warrior, I'd like to show you something."

Aislinn accepted his hand, anxious to take her mind off Marius' threat. Cirillo led her to one of the tall bookcases lining the wall, and pressed an area behind them.

With a humming *whirr*, two of the bookcases pivoted in a complete circle. Aislinn's eyes widened as she realized there was a hidden room and staircase behind them. The bookcases closed before she could see more. Spread across the back of the bookcases was a giant map comprising parts of Virginia, West Virginia, North and South Carolina, Tennessee, and North Georgia. Scattered over the states were thousands of pins and flags of many colors like multicolored beetles.

Cirillo's eyes gleamed. "The gold flags are churches. Yellow is for youth or senior centers, halfway houses, soup kitchens, any place where good people endeavor to help others."

He pointed to several green flags. "Green is for schools. We designate a white star for colleges, because people are choosing to go there, and they remain a general force for good, even if the college is not faith-based. Knowledge is power. A yellow star designates a faith-based school, because students are usually less traumatized there than public school and feel a greater sense of belonging. Morals can be freely taught."

With a circular gesture of his palm, he indicated other flags. "Police stations are navy blue, fire stations are light blue with the little flame symbol you see there. My son started that. Hospitals and clinics are purple, court houses and political areas are tan. Brown encompasses ecological groups, animal rescue, various types of people who make a difference for the planet in their own way. All of these colors designate forces for good."

After a satisfying intake of breath, he pointed to a red flag. "These flags in red and orange and gray X's depict areas where there are forces for evil. This one right here," he tapped a red flag with a question mark, "is a cult-like group we don't know a lot about, but when we walk by the property, we can feel oppression, suffocation. Some of these orange flags you'll notice have writing on them designating gangs. Uh, oh." He peered close to an orange flag with a black and white skull.

"Looks like my grandson stuck a skull on this one. He must have overheard us talking about that gang. Many gangs rule entire neighborhoods and towns, not only promoting fear, but drawing vulnerable people into their twisted ranks where they lose themselves in a false delusion of family. Red flags with white X's on these two streets show areas where cops suspect there might be slavery or forced prostitution rings. We've got people looking into those."

Cirillo raised both hands toward the map. "*This* is our war map."

Comprehension dawned as Aislinn examined the bright flags. *A war map between good and evil.* She felt a lump in her throat, and a strong desire to be a part of it, to make a difference in the world.

"You can still be a warrior, even if it's helping only one person at a time," he suggested. "The more churches, help centers, areas for hope and aid in whatever form, the greater the impact against evil."

Aislinn swallowed, full of emotion. "What about these gold and silver stars?"

"You have a good memory." He smiled and pointed to one. "This is where you are right now. Family lines committed to the cause are designated with gold stars. Their homes and compounds are marked. Families who do good work, but do not fully know who we are, have the silver stars. Because we know who *they* are."

Jovial voices echoed from the foyer and all eyes turned in that direction. Three handsome young men strutted into the library, one yelling, "Heard there was a battle brewing and you couldn't find any decent warriors!"

Cirillo gestured with a dismissive arm and a smirk. "And here come the royal brats."

Everyone erupted with greetings for the three men, the loudest being Gabriella who squealed with delight and ran to embrace them, kissing each cheek. When the men spotted Marius and Bastian, the tallest of the three slapped a red-haired boy on the shoulder and said, "I thought you were lying about the Hercules dudes."

"That's Heracleidae," Marius responded with a smile and shook the man's hand, offering him a kiss on each cheek.

"Same difference," said the man with a grin. "I can't pronounce it anyway. I'm just happy to see you again, sir."

His eyes brightened when he spotted Bastian. "Bastian, good to see you again. I'm getting better." He kissed Bastian's cheek and surprised him with a hug. Aislinn was surprised to see Bastian smile.

Gabriella introduced the young men to Aislinn as her third cousins, the Parker brothers, Duke, Earl, and Baron. Baron corrected her with "Barry," and the others laughed and commented that he was messing up their trio. All three had brown hair, were of medium build, and could almost pass for triplets. Duke was clearly the oldest and most outspoken. Duke and Baron had dark, navy blue eyes, but Earl's were a shocking turquoise.

After watching several people giving the newcomers mock bows and exaggerating their names, Aislinn asked, "So, you're not really royal, you just sound royal?"

"Absolutely," Duke replied. "Not a royal bone in my body, unless Mom got it on with a prince and didn't tell me."

"Hey, speak for yourself," said Earl. "I, my lady, am the Earl of Charlotte—North Carolina that is—at your service." Jeers followed his declaration as he reached for her hand and kissed it.

Aislinn chuckled and offered him a curtsy, adding an outward flair of both arms.

"Okay, I'll take her," Earl declared to the room, waving one arm and wrapping the other around Aislinn's shoulders. Amidst protests, he pretended to lead her out of the library. "The rest of y'all can hold the fort, okay?"

Catcalls and laughter continued, and Aislinn giggled. This house was going to be fun after all.

A massive hand on Earl's arm halted his attempt to continue abducting Aislinn. Earl stiffened and turned, his bright eyes still in a mood to play. His other hand had tensed in an instinctual, defensive posture. Aislinn realized he must be well trained, like the others. She turned to look for the owner of the arm, which put her and Earl's faces only inches from each other.

"Let go," was all Bastian said, his accent thick. His eyes flashed dangerously white, most of the silver-gray color absent as if squeezed out by anger. He seemed to be holding back the extent of his emotions with extreme effort. His deadly, threatening gaze caused a shiver to run through Aislinn. She also felt an excited craving for him, which surprised her since she was enjoying Earl's flirtations.

"Whoa." Earl looked shocked. "The Fearless Sebastian wants…." His eyes slid to Aislinn's neck, making her blush. He released his hold as though burned. "Why didn't you tell me you had a claim on our fair damsel here?" Earl's tone was somewhat teasing, but held a wary respect for the towering Bastian. Earl glanced again at the fresh claim mark as if fascinated.

Aislinn held up both palms toward Earl and warned him. "Don't even go there right now."

Gabriella touched her arm. "Come on, Aislinn, let me introduce you to some of the women." Grateful for the distraction, Aislinn followed her out of the room feeling a slight tug as she cleared the doorway. Pressing a hand on her stomach, she leaned back to find Bastian still standing as if frozen, his keen eyes on her, ignoring Earl who was shooting side glances between her and Bastian.

For a split second she spied Eddie's brooding face, and her stomach ached even more.

Gabriella noticed her hand on her abdomen and gave her a sarcastic smile. "You just left a room with two men bound to your blood. I imagine the pull is stronger for you than normal."

Aislinn rolled her eyes. "There's a normal?" She decided to keep to herself the realization that Bastian's possessive posturing to Earl had caused her body to lurch with carnal desire. Veins were pulsing in discrete places. The blatant lust had intensified with one glance at Eddie. As Gabriella had suggested, her body was indeed protesting being separated from both of them.

*Just one more thing*, she found herself thinking as she followed Gabriella down the long foyer. She should not feel a pull at leaving Eddie, but she did feel it.

"Gabriella, do you feel that, um, pull, every time you walk away from Marius?"

Gabriella smiled to herself. "Yes. Even after ten years."

Sounds of activity and jovial voices rose as Gabriella turned left into a vast kitchen full of women bustling about with pots and dishes, preparing food and talking.

"Hey, Lady Gabriella, you up for some breakfast?" A robust woman with graying dark blonde hair in an unraveling French braid was grinning at Gabriella as she clapped a metal spoon on the edge of a large steel pot.

"Ma Beatie, stop calling me that. I'm not an official Lady here in America."

"Yeah, but it sounds pretty dang good, doesn't it?" The woman chuckled heartily in a husky voice. "And you're married to a prince, so you ought to get some kinda title out of it."

Gabriella smirked. "Gabriella will do just fine, thanks. Besides, you're the real First Lady here."

Ma Beatie snorted and waved a hand. "Me? I'm just a country girl."

Gabriella leaned forward conspiratorially. "Ma, I am not fooled. You could lead armies."

An appreciative smile brightened the woman's face and elicited another chuckle. "Have the big boys fed since they got here?"

"No." Gabriella shook her head. "I'm sure they'll make do with whatever you've got."

"Heck, I got a cow out in the barn they can seduce."

Several women laughed raucously, and Ma Beatie chuckled at her own joke.

Expecting Gabriella to be offended, Aislinn was surprised when she rolled her eyes and smirked at them.

"I think they'll refrain, although I never know with those three. If they have to, they'll retreat to the woods and go after a deer just to blow off some steam."

"Georgie tried to talk Bastian into catching a wild pig last time," declared Ma Beatie. Several high-pitched guffaws exploded in the room.

"Ew," said Aislinn to Gabriella. "I'm not kissing him if he does."

All the women halted movement, and eyebrows rose. Some leaned past others to get a better look at her. The only sound was pots bubbling.

Ma Beatie paused in the act of wiping her hands on an apron. "You his girl?"

"Uh, well... I... sort of."

"Well, either ya are or ya aren't, honey." Ma Beatie turned to Gabriella. "Does he got a mate sign?"

Gabriella sighed. "Yes. *Finally*."

"*Hooo, hooo*, he's gonna be fun this trip. A mate sign for the old ice-prince. Well, girl," Ma Beatie addressed Aislinn, "as handsome as that boy is, you'd better make up your mind. 'Cause there's lots here what would love to have 'im, ice and all."

Several *oooo's* and giggles rang out, followed by knowing glances and eye-rolls.

Aislinn blanched at the suggestion, scanning the various women to see if any looked conspiratorial. To her absolute shock, she could feel her own fists tightening, tensing for an attack. Her teeth clenched. *Good grief*. Had they turned her into some kind of animal?

One girl with long black hair glowered and her dark amber eyes squinted. Could she be after Bastian? It had not occurred to Aislinn that she might have to fight to keep Bastian. He had made his desires clear. But what if his mate sign *was* for someone else? Or some other woman *thought* it might be. Was that possible? Her insides twisted in an uncomfortable, defensive way. Anger began to rise, which was beginning to be the norm.

"Ma, let me officially introduce you," said Gabriella. "This is Aislinn Thomas. Aislinn, this is Beatrice Markos, Cirillo's wife."

"Nice to meet you, Mrs. Markos." Aislinn offered her hand.

Ma Beatie took a step forward and shook it soundly, nearly bruising Aislinn's hand. "Nice to meet you, girl. Just call me Ma like everybody else does. You look a far sight better than you did a few hours ago."

"Um...." Aislinn searched for a suitable reply. "Thanks for your hospitality."

"You're surely welcome. You hungry?"

"Actually, yes."

"Good, cause we got lots of fixins' here. Let's get this show on the road, ladies. Oh, let me introduce you to the rest of the beauty queens." She pointed to each woman and called out their names, eleven in all, who offered greetings as they spooned food into serving bowls. All of them smiled except for the dark-haired girl, who was introduced as Hera. She looked to be about sixteen or seventeen.

Aislinn helped carry bowls through two glass doors, one in the back of the kitchen, and another where the expansive foyer ran the length of the house and ended at a large, sliding glass door. Four long wooden picnic tables stretched across the largest screened-in porch Aislinn had ever seen. Several colorful lanterns along the ceiling shed light on the tables. A bug zapper glowed in one corner occasionally exploding wayward insects. Outside the screens, the darkness disguised what property lay beyond.

"Well, let me call in the troops," said Ma Beatie after all the food was out. Aislinn jumped as a sharp clanging assaulted her ears from the kitchen. To her astonishment, Ma Beatie was ringing a triangle-shaped, metallic object in the corner. Aislinn recalled seeing such a bell in an old western movie.

In a stampede, the men charged out of the library and spilled onto the porch, through every conceivable doorway. Two young boys and three girls also joined the table, followed by four younger preschool children, whose eyes brightened at all the food. Aislinn wondered what they were all doing up at four o'clock in the morning.

Gabriella grabbed Aislinn's elbow. "Come," she ordered, and led her toward Ma Beatie.

"Ma...." Gabriella ducked her head and whispered. "I want Aislinn in a place where Bastian and Edward can't fight over her."

"Gotcha," Ma Beatie replied, her mouth twisted in wry humor.

Expecting Ma Beatie and Cirillo to sit at the head of the row of tables, Aislinn was surprised when they positioned themselves in the center. Cirillo motioned Marius and Gabriella to his right, with Bastian and Dimitri following.

"Aislinn, please sit on the other side of Dimitri," Gabriella ordered.

"Hera," Ma Beatie whispered and pointed. "Sit there, on the other side of Aislinn. Thank you."

Wordlessly, they all obeyed. Aislinn bristled as the girl with the long black hair plopped onto the bench, her body rigid and eyes averted. Aislinn considered offering her a greeting and just as quickly decided the girl deserved no courtesy. Whatever her beef was, she could just wallow in it. This, too, was uncharacteristic for Aislinn and she found herself a bit dismayed. She had never turned down an opportunity to be courteous with someone she just met.

To Dimitri's left, Bastian was casting him a warning glare.

Dimitri leaned toward Aislinn and whispered softly. "Oh, the fun I could have with this."

"Dimitri, don't you dare," Aislinn hissed. "I don't want Bastian riled up."

"Hmm, leaning in his direction?" Dimitri's brows were raised.

Aislinn gave him a crooked smile.

"It's supposed to rain today, anyway."

Aislinn frowned. "What's that got to do with Bastian?"

"Aislinn, haven't you noticed? Bastian's emotions affect weather. That's something he and Marius have in common."

Her mouth fell open as she stared at him. She recalled the odd timing of thunder rumbling just outside her room when Bastian was besieged by the unveiling of his hidden grief. Then later, at Marius' chalet, thunder struck, lightning flashed, and the house shook as they argued about her riding back to the inn with Lucian.

"Sorry." Dimitri's eyes twinkled. "One more thing."

When his mischievous expression altered to one of dislike, Aislinn followed his line of sight and realized Eddie had rounded the other side of the table and rushed to position himself across from Aislinn, nearly knocking over Earl Parker who was aiming for the spot. Earl cast an apologetic glance at Ma Beatie before sitting down.

Cirillo stood and everyone quieted. He bowed his head and gave a prayer of thanks for the food. Everyone followed with a hearty, "Amen."

As soon as Cirillo sat, bowls began circling the table and conversation buzzed. Surveying all the dishes, Aislinn decided to pace herself and spooned a small portion of the hearty beef stew, sweet potato casserole, creamed corn, green beans, black-eyed peas, turnip greens, mashed potatoes, gravy, and several vegetable purees which someone had gone to great lengths to make colorful in layers within glass bowls. When coleslaw, carrot ambrosia, and several fruit purees were passed to her, she realized she had no room on her plate.

Discreetly, she eyed the minuscule helpings of solid foods Marius, Dimitri and Bastian chose while heaping ladles full of meat broth and vegetable and fruit dishes, spooning them into bowls waiting by their plates.

Several conversations took place across the four tables and Aislinn listened intently in order to learn as much as possible as she ate the delicious food. Marius and Gabriella engaged Cirillo and Ma Beatie in conversation about their projects and plans and what was happening with other tribes.

"So," Earl addressed Aislinn, "I've never been to Romania. What's the food like?"

"Delicious," she answered with a smile. "Different, but delicious. I had to use my Romanian language app a *lot*. There was this fruit-filled pastry at a little café that was awesome, and something called tripe soup."

All three Parker brothers exclaimed at once.

"You actually ate tripe soup?" Earl asked in disbelief.

"Yes, it was awesome," said Aislinn, puzzled. "Why, what's wrong with it?"

Duke was grinning with sheer delight. "It's beef stomach. You know that, right?"

Aislinn blinked several times. "I thought it was some kind of pasta."

Barry guffawed and slapped the table.

"I swear to you that's what it is," Earl said. "Nobody here in America eats it."

"Wait a minute," Barry raised a hand. "*Somebody* does. I've seen it at the grocery store."

"In Aislinn's defense, gentlemen," Gabriella spoke in a reprimanding but lighthearted tone, "you haven't lived until you have tasted tripe soup in Romania. There's nothing like it."

"Not gonna happen." Duke shook his head.

"I'm game," Earl declared. "I'll try anything. Once." He pointed at Aislinn. "Aislinn, hold me to it."

"The *polenta* and *sarmale* in Romania were quite nice as well," said Eddie. "Me and Aisy had some in Bucharest."

Faces froze and voices halted.

"So, Duke, Earl, how are those self-defense centers for youth coming along I've been hearing about?" Dimitri asked, breaking the silence.

Aislinn was relieved when the brothers began talking over each other as they updated him on their work. Aislinn glared at Eddie but his eyes held a blatant challenge.

Duke and Dimitri shifted to a discussion on France, where Duke wanted to visit.

Not wanting to interrupt, Aislinn tapped Dimitri's hand and pointed to the salt. He handed her the shakers of salt and pepper.

"She can't have pepper." Eddie's voice was sharp, and the Parker brothers stopped talking to look at him. Aislinn and Eddie locked eyes. Aislinn had no doubt he was choosing that moment to show everyone, especially Bastian, how much he knew about her. Even as she glowered at him, tingles ran across her skin. She averted her eyes in hopes of quelling the unruly reaction.

"Is that so?" Dimitri's voice was purposely light as he glanced at Aislinn and smiled.

"Unfortunately," she answered, and snatched the salt to shake it over her green beans.

"Why unfortunately?"

Eddie answered for her. "The medication she takes causes inflammation in her stomach. She can't eat peppers or tomato sauce either."

Aislinn slapped the salt bottle onto the table causing speckles to shoot into the air. "I am quite capable of answering for myself, Eddie."

"Just looking out for you." Eddie offered one of his charming side grins and raised brows which usually worked magic in any crowd. Aislinn did not miss the strange, possessive gleam in his hazel eyes. She wondered if the blood bond he created was having weird effects on him as well.

Controlling her irritation, Aislinn turned to Dimitri. "I used to love pepper. After the accident I had to take a lot of medications, especially pain pills. I still take some of them, for inflammation. It led to my current condition which… limits my intake of spicy foods, and pepper."

"Now, *that* would kill me," said Barry from across the table. "I live for spicy food."

Aislinn grinned at him in appreciation.

Earl pointed at his brother. "Seriously, I watched him eat a whole jalapeno pepper once. It took him a full minute before he grabbed a beer out of the frig. We were timing him. I lost the bet."

Several people scoffed at the story, which got the brothers arguing over who had eaten the hottest pepper.

A foot rubbed against Aislinn's leg under the table. One sharp glance at Eddie and she knew it was him. Her body grew hot with desire, which enraged and infuriated her. It was *his* fault her body was reacting this way. His foot continued to rub.

"Stop it, Eddie!" She slammed her fist to the table and threw a psychic push into the command, which caused both Eddie and Earl to jerk backward and look wide-eyed. Aislinn felt guilty that she had hit Earl.

Bastian leapt from the bench seat, causing two glasses of tea to topple over. As his foot landed on the tabletop, Marius stood and yelled, "Bastian!" with a hand extended toward him, which was the only thing that kept him from vaulting over the table at Eddie.

Several men had gotten to their feet from reflex, including Eddie.

Cirillo also stood. "Edward. A word." He exited through the sliding glass doors behind him and into the foyer without looking back. Aislinn watched Eddie uncoil from the bench and follow him, his face sullen and flushed. Before clearing the frame of the door, he cast a possessive look toward her, then raised his eyes in a clear threat at Bastian.

Before Bastian had taken more than a step forward, Dimitri sidestepped to block him. "Uncle…."

Bastian pushed past him. "I am answering that challenge."

Marius placed his body squarely in front of Bastian. He spoke low. "Bastian, not here, not now."

The room held a strained silence. Aislinn could feel everyone waiting, worrying that Bastian might not back down. To her surprise, she also felt a thread of anticipation from some of the warriors, as if they were delighted at the idea of a fight.

Feeling guilty for disrupting the cheerful meal, Aislinn pulled her legs over the bench and stood in front of Bastian. Her plan was to say something to divert him. After all, he was just defending her. With fists clenched, Bastian heaved heavy breaths as though it were taking tremendous strength to obey Marius.

Watching him breathe caused Aislinn's focus to shift to Bastian's incredible body, taut, powerfully built, and smelling woodsy and masculine. Thoughts about his rebellious behavior needing to be under control evaporated. He was magnificent, delicious. She wanted to remove his shirt and taste him.

Bastian swallowed, his lips parting as their eyes met. Electric currents burned through both of them at his hungry, possessive gaze. Their minds opened to each other without conscious thought.

The room seemed to disappear. A strange wildness danced within Aislinn, bereft of inhibitions and rules like an untamed nymph aching to follow a satyr into a dark, mysterious forest. She knew she should not let the wanton desire rise but was so fascinated by it, she ignored all caution. What would it be like if Bastian and Eddie fought? The fight would be fantastic, thrilling. How she would love to watch Bastian's body move, and all the power behind each punch. All her life, she had hated to see people fighting, could not even watch a boxing match, and here she was, breathless with anticipation.

Her skin radiated like glowing embers. The more she gazed into Bastian's glimmering, eager eyes, the tighter she melded her emotions to match his, and the more her body reacted. Her breasts seemed to swell and ache for his touch. Part of him was swelling as well. She felt like a feral wolf in heat, not a human. Moisture pooled between her legs. If not for the room full of people whose alert emotions she could still feel, she was quite sure she would let Bastian and Edward fight it out, and bed whichever Olympian won, right on the porch floor.

Any provocation toward Bastian, a nod, a gesture, a mental call, and she was certain he would push Marius aside, run into the house, and crush Eddie's throat, just like he would have Razvan's.

The excitement at the power she possessed burned in her veins and pounded in her head. She knew she should stop, knew she should break the bestial trance. But she could not make herself stop. She wanted Bastian to fight Eddie for her. Then she wanted his hands roaming, hot and wild....

"Aislinn," said Gabriella. "Right here. Look at me. See me."

Aislinn bristled as Gabriella blocked her view of Bastian by stepping between them. Aislinn was forced to look into Gabriella's vivid green eyes.

"Pull it back down, Aislinn," Gabriella whispered, the movement of her mouth barely discernible. It was just enough for Aislinn's advanced hearing to detect, and possibly those who were closest, but not everyone.

Embarrassment flooded through her and she felt her cheeks grow hot. She wasn't a wolf. She wasn't a wild, carefree nymph. She was a *human*.

"Yep, big boy," said Ma Beatie, getting to her feet and patting Bastian's thick arm, "knew you were going to be fun this trip. How 'bout some of my banana pudding? You loved it last time."

Bastian's eyes softened as he focused on Ma Beatie. He took a deep, slow breath. "That would be fine, Frau Beatie."

"Good. Come help me get it."

Bastian's eyes widened in surprise, but he complied and followed her to the kitchen. Several women jumped from the table to join them. A growl escaped Aislinn's throat and she felt her muscles coiling for action.

Gabriella pressed a hand into Aislinn's shoulder, and Aislinn felt calm weave its way through her taut nerves. "Let it pass, Aislinn," she whispered low. "Get control of it. The time will come to let it out."

Aislinn made note of which women followed Bastian into the kitchen. They had just better watch themselves.

She gazed at Gabriella with consternation. Relief at Gabriella's understanding instead of judgment gave her the strength to take control of her mind and body. Retaking her seat and staring at her half-empty plate, she noted that it was the second time someone had distracted Bastian by forcing him to help with dessert. She resisted the urge to laugh.

Dimitri laid a hand on her shoulder and squeezed. Aislinn jumped, then gave him a grateful, shy smile.

"Wow," he murmured, "I'm so glad I left France and joined Marius. This has been one exciting trip."

"Exciting for you, maybe," Aislinn retorted.

"Ah, I have feeling it's going to get way more exciting for you. I'm sure I heard you growl just now." When her eyes widened in dismay, he winked. "You know why they won't let them fight it out, don't you?"

Aislinn froze. "No. Why?"

"Blood heat. They'll kill each other. Everyone's always on alert when someone's in a blood heat. We can't afford to lose one warrior, let alone two. A couple hundred years ago there were these two Olympians in France who were in blood heats, and they both thought the other was after their woman. They tore each other up so bad they both died. Since then, they don't let anybody fight if they're too riled up with it." At the shock on her face he added. "Not alien, but not entirely human, are we?"

Aislinn returned to gazing unfocused at her plate. "Neither am I. Not anymore."

"Here, try this chocolate stuff Mrs. Parker sent over with the guys," Dimitri suggested, shoving a casserole dish topped with white cream, tiny chocolate chips and chopped pecans. "It's to die for."

She pouted at him.

"Sorry, probably shouldn't have said die." He spooned some on her plate.

Aislinn ate several bites slowly. It was one of the most delicious things she had ever put in her mouth. After it was gone, she felt both elated and tired.

As the noise level in the room rose with the consumption of desserts, Aislinn began to feel alone, and overwhelmed with hers and everyone else's emotions. She was not as sensitive while Bastian and Eddie were in the room. Now, with their absence, everyone's emotions were loud.

Aislinn left her seat and stole a place on the bench beside Gabriella that Bastian had vacated.

"Gabriella, I need to lie down for a while. I'm exhausted. But, I'm hoping to go visit my grandmother in a few hours. I'm worried about her. I know where I am, based on Cirillo's map, but I don't have a car here. Can someone drive me to my apartment so I can get my car?"

"We rented a car and have it here."

"Oh. Did Eddie come with you then?"

Gabriella's countenance fell at mention of Eddie. "Edward drove his own car. We can't leave you alone, Aislinn. It's too dangerous."

"What do you mean, you can't leave me alone? I'll be in the car. It's only an hour away."

"You weren't fully awake last night when the men had to fight demons. They attacked *your* apartment. Had the whole place stirred up. A Yeti came in for you again."

"What? That is so weird. And what's the deal with a Yeti?" Aislinn had forgotten to whisper and several eyes were suddenly on her.

"Bastian injured him. They normally disappear before getting wounded. We don't know why they're after you. It's highly unusual. There's no way Marius is going to let you go anywhere without at least two warriors with you."

Chills swept across Aislinn's arms.

"I have escaped death many times in the last year," she confessed. "It has baffled me. I thought I was cursed. Now… I feel like I need to look at everything in a new light."

"Tell me about these times." Gabriella frowned with concern.

"Well, of course the first is the car accident. My whole family was killed, but I survived. Barely. I was in a coma for several days, and had many operations after that. Six months later, we were at a party and this girl knocked my glass over. I had just come back from the rest room. It was the first time I'd been out without my Gramma. We were all laughing, but the girl grabbed my glass and swallowed the last sip just for fun. We had to call an ambulance for her because she passed out. They said there was a strong poison in her system. I think it was meant for me.

"Then, a couple months after that, Aunt Julia wanted to take a bus trip to visit an old friend of the family. Gramma and I decided to go with her. We got a flat tire on the way to the bus station. The bus we were supposed to ride in collided with another one. Five people died. They said the brakes were tampered with. A few weeks later, the brakes on Gramma's car went out. She swerved off the road and we ran into a pile of dirt at a construction site. If the dirt hadn't been there, we would have gone off a steep embankment and could have been killed. Sometimes I wonder if someone's trying to kill off my entire family, and I'm a loose end."

Gabriella's brows creased even more. Then Aislinn realized the tables had grown quiet. Everyone was listening.

"I think you are a target, Aislinn. We just don't know why yet. We need to consult a mage. All the more reason for you to have Olympians with you. After you've rested, we'll drive you, okay? We have one other place to visit today. I'm sure we can fit both trips in."

Aislinn shook her head. "No. You guys have been up all night. Are you on the same schedule as... them? Do you sleep during the day?"

"It depends on what is going on. I've grown to be very flexible." Gabriella gave her a crooked smile. "But, I think I'll rest for a few hours, too."

~~◊~~

Cirillo turned angry, piercing eyes on Eddie, his body stiff and unyielding. "What are you thinking, son?"

"Sir, the blood heat is just making me a little crazy." Eddie raised his hands and dropped them in frustration, putting on his best innocent face. He was intent on winning, but in truth the blood heat was driving him to react in ridiculous, desperate ways.

"Which you knew would happen when you chose to exchange blood with a woman."

"Actually, I've never done it before. And there's so much I was never really taught."

"Don't even try to tell me you didn't know about it, or you wouldn't have done it. I'm in no mood for excuses. Like I tell my tribe members after they've wrecked their car, don't tell me you didn't know alcohol would affect you. The time for restraint was while you were choosing another drink. Not when you were fumbling with keys and blurry vision."

Eddie considered how best to win Cirillo to his side. "Sir, I am in love with this girl."

"One who already has a claim on her."

"She was mine," Eddie insisted, balling a fist. "We've been engaged for over a year. He had no right."

"And if I asked Aislinn right now whether she considers herself still engaged to you, what will she say?"

"Sir, we've had our ups and downs. And she's confused." Eddie shook his head, not sure how much Cirillo knew. But he also needed to plant a seed. "She told me she didn't want to make a decision based on our blood bond. We agreed to meet and talk things out. I just... didn't want to wait."

"You agreed to my order to cease communication with her."

"We talked about all this last night," Eddie said in a rush. "She's having trouble remembering this morning. I just... wanted to do something that would trigger her memory. And... we were right across the table. There was no reason not to talk to her."

"There was every reason, and you know it. If you were officially mine, your butt would be downstairs in the brig by now." He planted broad hands on his hips, his brows knitting into a dark frown. "Besides, Edward, you had no proof that Aislinn was Olympian. You had no business biting her."

"Neither did he."

"I'm talking about *your* actions. Not his."

"Aislinn is empathic, sir. To the point of avoiding crowds. She has persuasion, too, but rarely uses it. And look at those blazing sky-blue eyes. All signs to me."

"But you know the rules, Edward. And don't tell me you don't. We verify bloodline first before recruitment or claims. Or anything else."

"Sir, actually, I *don't* know all the rules. I wasn't raised... well, like you."

Cirillo took a deep breath, examining him. His tone softened. "Why haven't you joined a tribe, Edward? You belong in mine, but I'd be happy to know you at least joined another."

Eddie took a deep breath as well, thinking how painful it would be to excise himself from his connection to black magic and demonic presences. He decided to tell the truth. "My father forbade it, sir. I regret that now. I fought demons with Marius last night. It felt good. I think you should know, my life could be in danger if I join you."

Cirillo raised his chin and eyebrows. "Your father is that much against your birthright?"

Eddie frowned. "He sees my birthright as... something different. Staying true to the family is all that matters to him. 'Protect our secrets. Don't risk the family.' That's his motto."

Cirillo seemed to peer right through him. "Edward, say the word and I will accept your Vow of Allegiance. I will afford you the protection you need, even if it means temporarily positioning you in another tribe. Don't go this alone."

Eddie was surprised when his heart skipped a beat. If he accepted, he might be free of his father's stifling control. He might have an equal chance with Aislinn. Hope brightened within him until he made the mistake of remembering the painful wards he drove through, so excruciating they had brought him to tears. Converting would be a painful business. And he was not fond of pain. Still, Cirillo might feel compassionate toward him if he appeared to be considering joining.

"I appreciate that, sir." He blinked as if he were holding back tears. "I really do. I need to think about it."

"And just so you know, if you contact that girl again without her consent, I *will* slap your butt in the brig. Vow or no vow."

Aislinn left the meal and entered the foyer. Neither Eddie nor Cirillo was in sight, although the library door was closed. She crossed the long hall and groaned at the slight pull of her body toward the library. With a disgusted roll of her eyes, she hurried past it, and halted at the curved staircase near the front door. It was beginning to look like Mount Everest.

"I don't think this staircase bites." Dimitri leaned his chin over her shoulder. "But I could be wrong."

The false grimace she shot him was followed by a smile. "Since you're my new brother, I'll tell you. My legs were shattered in the car accident a year ago that took my family."

"Whoa. Does Bastian know?"

She shook her head and swallowed the lump that rose in her throat. "I can walk now without assistance. But I can't run much, and stairs are, well, tedious. I've been up them once this morning. And really I'm getting stronger. I just don't relish the thought of going up again. Habit, I guess."

Dimitri swept her into his arms before she could protest. "Never fear, my dear sister. I shall aid you in any time of need."

Aislinn let out a *whoop* and said, "Dimitri, you don't have to do that." She looped her arms around his neck and giggled as he jogged up the stairs.

"I know that."

"Aren't I heavy?"

"Ha!" He chuckled with delight. "I'm an Olympian, remember?"

"Do you get injured often? I mean, badly?"

He frowned as he reached the top of the stairs. "Not much in the last few years. I've gotten better. But, since my uncle is—once again, thank

you—the best healer around for evil-borne injuries, I'm in good hands."
Carefully, he positioned her on both feet atop the landing.

"Evil-borne injuries?"

"What the hell do you think you are doing?" The thick accent barking up the stairs was unmistakable.

They both leaned over the upper railing to find Bastian glowering at them from the bottom of the staircase, hands on hips.

Dimitri shrugged and turned to Aislinn with mischief in his eyes. "I got nothin.' What about you?"

"Dimitri!" she chastised, knowing he was baiting Bastian.

How Bastian could move so fast, she did not know, but he cleared the stairs two and three at a time and was in Dimitri's face before she could react. "Why are you always touching her?"

"Bastian!" Aislinn admonished, and gently slipped between the two men. She placed a hand on Bastian's chest which brought his piercing eyes instantly to her. She shivered, in a good way, and knew by his softening gaze he had felt the electric sensation that always burned through their bodies at the slightest touch.

"He was just trying to help me," Aislinn clarified.

"To get up the stairs? You are a young, strong woman."

Aislinn pressed her lips together as she considered how to respond. In that moment she recognized an old fear. That she would be seen as less perfect for her injuries. Damaged. Second rate. Scarred. Eddie probably had a lot to do with that fear. She decided to amend that habit.

"My legs were severely injured in the car accident I told you about. Stairs are still difficult for me, sometimes. I have to be careful, that's all."

He looked completely dumb struck. "Why did you not tell me? I would have gladly assisted you any time you needed to climb stairs."

Avoiding his accusatory tone, she shifted focus to his chest where her hand still rested. Tawny curls escaped through the open V of the white collar. Curls that she would love to run her fingers through. Reluctantly, she removed her hand and swallowed back the rising flames. "I need to be self-sufficient. I can't think in terms of people doing things for me. I have to take care of myself."

"You know I can heal. Especially now, since…."

"Since I helped you deal with your grief?" The sweet memory of his hand on her back returned. Such a rippling bulk of manflesh loomed in front of her, his mere presence causing all of her nerves to dance on end, yet his healing touch was as gentle, warm and soothing as a new puppy. She swallowed, deciding she'd best stop thinking about that.

"Dimitri says you can only heal evil-borne injuries."

"That does not mean I cannot try."

Her nostrils filled with the scent of him, musky, along with the heady scent of a forest, wild and inviting. She nearly forgot Dimitri was there. She could not let the thrilling sensations take over again or Dimitri would witness something she didn't want him to.

"I think you should know, most sports are out of the picture for me. I have trouble hiking. I don't... run much." She watched for a reaction in his sparkling silver eyes, waiting for that slight hint of disappointment or disapproval.

"Dimitri." Bastian spoke without removing his eyes from Aislinn's. "Would you give us a moment please?"

"Sure." Dimitri sauntered over to the top step and winked at Aislinn before descending.

Aislinn returned Bastian's scrutiny, reading a mixture of anger and pride toward her.

"You actually think that your inability to run, or climb stairs, has any bearing on how I feel about you?"

Aislinn's eyes widened. "You don't mind? Really?"

He exhaled with frustration, his hands going to his hips. His eyes scanned the air, at nothing in particular, and then dropped to her. "You have a giving heart, Aislinn. I felt it that night in your room at the inn. You freed mine. I can feel things I had forgotten how to feel, even though... I can no longer hide the painful memories. Still, I could not even *remember* passion, let alone feel it. That seems to be getting the better of me. You are mine. Whether you choose or not, the answer is the same for me."

He took a step closer, his chest stopping short of brushing against her breasts. His voice became gruff. "You were meant for me. You have everything I need."

Aislinn reeled. *Everything he needs?* But, they barely knew each other. A few of his words eerily mirrored some of Eddie's, but Eddie didn't make her tingle like this. Her heart was threatening to pump out of her chest. Her skin grew hot. Just like earlier, during the meal, her body quickly became an inferno. Carnal ideas danced across her mind. Delicious touches to consider. With several deep breaths she debated whether to calm her roused body, or let go.

Bastian molded a hand to her cheek as though steadying her face so he could kiss her. He leaned closer. She found herself rising on her toes.

Then his eyes narrowed. "Until you decide, do not make assumptions about what I think or feel. We have much to learn about each other."

With that, he turned and descended the stairs. In shock, she gazed over the balcony and watched his six-foot-five bulk cross the foyer and disappear down a narrow hallway to the left that she hadn't noticed before.

Aislinn forced herself to breathe and placed a hand to her chest. Her body didn't seem to care that they didn't know each other very well. It was ready, willing, and able to know him.

# CHAPTER 20

As soon as her head hit the pillow, Aislinn's mind whirled with events and choices. She could not believe Bastian left her kiss-less on the balcony. Every moment they had experienced together, even just being in the same room, she replayed and reviewed, weighing her decision. Part of her wanted to draw out making a choice. Wait for her anger to subside. Make both men pay for their secrets.

They both deserved it. Neither had explained what the rules to claiming were. The fierce way she had rounded on Bastian after thinking he had bitten her again without permission, bothered her.

Discovering that Eddie was the one that had bitten her to force another bond was as much a shock as discovering Eddie was an Olympian. Really, it was Eddie she was most angry with. She had enjoyed Bastian's touch from the beginning. That first night, their brief encounter, was still special to her. Magical. It ranked highest on her top-ten list of amazing moments. Yet, since Eddie had entered the picture, she had spurned Bastian as well as Eddie in order to protect herself.

Memories of embracing Bastian's firm chest, corded abs, and narrow waist wafted across her mind. Reliving the feel of his tight skin under her fingers as he lay on the bed of dirt made her shiver with desire. She wanted to be with him, to feel him. What if it was only because of the bond? Would she feel this way even if they had just been introduced and he had not bitten her? There was only one way to be certain. She needed to get to know him and find some way to distinguish between what was real and what was induced.

Perhaps tomorrow. Or today.

To her surprise, Eddie's mental presence interrupted her musings.

*Aisy, if you want to leave this place, I'll take you. I'm not asking for anything else. I just want to make sure you're comfortable. I'll take care of you, whatever you want. Let's go see Gramma. She needs us.*

Aislinn balled her fists, furious that he could now invade her privacy whenever he pleased. But in preparing to mentally slap him, she realized the new connection allowed her to discern Eddie's attempt to block his emotions and intentions. He was not being completely honest. If he meant what he said, what he professed to feel for her, what reason would he have to hide his true feelings? She pressed into the connection. A wall was there, spongy, but there. One thing she *could* discern was how badly he wanted to leave this house and take her with him. It bordered on desperation.

*Eddie, you did this without my permission.*

*I asked you. You said yes.*

*I was drugged! Gabriella told me. No matter what I said—most of which I can't even remember—you knew I wasn't in my right mind.*

*You knew what you were saying. You knew it was me. You kissed me willingly.*

Aislinn paused. She remembered kissing him. But, her mind was still under the influence of the drug. Or was it?

*No matter what you say, Eddie, you could have waited until I was cold sober. You still did it against my conscious will.*

*So did he,* Eddie countered.

Aislinn caught her breath. Okay, he had her there. Bastian did get her to swallow his blood while she was not thinking straight after kissing and being bitten by him.

*It was different with Bastian.*

*How different?*

Aislinn's mind returned to that night at the inn. She smiled at the memory of being in Bastian's strong arms. The sensations of his hands touching her, his lips, the feel of his muscular body against hers, was just as clear as if she were standing again in his embrace. Her grief had triggered his. Her desire to help him had moved him. She had comforted him. Without fear, they had opened to each other, merged energies, experience each other's passions. What they shared was more real, more meaningful than Eddie's attempts to own her.

Eddie seethed, catching a glimpse of the visual. *I can't believe you just jumped into his arms. More than a year we've known each other, and you go and....*

*Stop right there, Eddie. We weren't together. Yes, we knew each other. And I had feelings for you. Back and forth it always was with you. I'd start to trust you again, to let my feelings grow, and then I'd see you with someone else again. Do you have any idea what that's like?*

*Listen to me. Those two women were nothing. I can....*

*No. You listen this time. Even when I wasn't catching you with other women, word got back to me from friends seeing you with other women. North Carolina's not that big, you know. Did you think you could play the field in Raleigh, or Charlotte, or Asheville, and word not get back to me?*

*Who said I was with other women?* His mental tone was angry and threatening.

*Friends.* Aislinn steeled her mind. She was not going to make the mistake of giving him a visual this time.

When he could not force the images, he changed tactic. *I heard Bastian had a thing going with a woman named Andromeda.*

Aislinn froze. What was it Dimitri had said? "*Oooo*, and here I thought it was all about Andromeda." Was there someone else in Bastian's life? Jealousy rose in Aislinn like a fierce beast. Whoever Andromeda was, Aislinn was going to have to break her neck. After she broke Eddie's.

*Out of my head, Eddie.*

*Aisy....*

*Now!*

When his presence dissipated, she exhaled as if the escaping breath could expel the raging beast. She had never been the jealous type. Hurt, yes, but not jealous. None of the women in the kitchen had been introduced as Andromeda. She needed to find out who she was. Find out and eradicate her. Aislinn rolled her eyes. This most definitely felt like boiling, green, deadly jealousy.

When she had seen Eddie with the blonde during her celebratory dinner, she had made her decision. Eddie would be out of her life. Over and over she had told him she did not want to be more than friends. His actions proved that was all they could ever be, unless she was willing to share him.

She was not. She had made her plans to travel to Romania the next week. To get away from him. To draw the energy of Anya's spirit around her in a place they had dreamed of. To clear her mind and consider a new future.

Then she met Bastian, and her future skyrocketed.

Eddie must have felt threatened. Why would he jump on a plane to join her in Romania? She explored the memory of his fingers brushing back her hair at the inn in Romania. He had touched her neck and became incensed, declaring he could smell another man.

Anger shot through Aislinn like a bullet and she pushed up from the pillow. He had seen Bastian's mark. As an Olympian he knew what that meant before she did. He was jealous because *someone else* got her. He had not wanted to let her go. He never bit her, never claimed her, but he could have.

The need to control her prompted his claim mark, not some unexplained rush of love and affection. Biting her while she was asleep was unconscionable. She had not consented. Except… kissing him… and enjoying it.

She bit her lip. Buried feelings for him snuck out of their closet. How had he accomplished that? Though her memories of last night were blurred, she had wisps of hearing Bastian and Eddie and being pulled between the two. She had wanted Bastian to bite her again. She had wanted to experience that heady, dreamy sensation. Had she confused him with Eddie?

Worried conversations and threats between combatants flitted like frantic moths around a flame. Gabriella's voice came back to her. *It could be ten hours before she shakes off the drug.*

*Ooof, that man.* She would set Eddie straight tomorrow. Or was that technically today? She tried to relax against the pillow again and not think of any men. Which was hard to do, since the entire house seemed to be filled with the most handsome, buff men she had ever seen in her life.

Sunlight brightened the room. Aislinn glanced around, not as disoriented this time. It was missing something though. Bastian. And Eddie. *Ugh.*

Where was Bastian sleeping? Was he spread out on a bed in one of these rooms, his magnificent sexy body looking like a marble Greek statue? She sighed at the thought.

Tree shadows floated across the white ceiling and forest green walls as a soft breeze blew outside. Aislinn's thoughts travelled back to lying beside Bastian on the bed of dirt, sliding her fingers across the smooth expanse of his defined chest and abdomen. Even in the dark, she had admired his physique and the way her body responded to every inch of his skin that touched hers, even the excitement of his arm curling around her.

Spying her cell phone on the side table, she touched the screen. 8:30 AM. Did he always sleep during the day, the whole day? It was amazing how little she still knew. The house felt quiet. In the middle of the night the house had been alive with people and conversations and eating. Picturing the house bereft of movement in the bright of day seemed backward, unless they were all gone to work.

*Bastian, are you awake?*

Though he was groggy, his warm presence filled her mind. She could sense him as surely as if he were lying next to her with his eyes open, breathing. Was he angry? The wall she felt was soft, so he wasn't really trying to block her. Concern and agitation leaked through.

*Bastian, please answer me. Don't block me out.*

*I hear you, my lady.* His mental voice sounded matter-of-fact.

*I'm sorry I got angry with you earlier. I was mostly angry at Eddie. It was all... too much.*

No response.

*Are you angry?* she prompted.

*Frustrated.*

*Why?*

*After eighty years I finally find someone who makes me want to live again, and everything keeps getting in the way. Marius hinders my actions. Edward has hindered our relationship. And... you don't even know if you want me.*

*I do want you.*

He hesitated to respond. *Then why did you reject me in the counsel room?*

Aislinn swallowed. *I felt violated. The new bite was there and I had no memory of it.*

*That vermin tried to negate my claim. I would have killed him if not for Marius.*

Aislinn breathed softly for a moment, feeling his fierce, unfiltered emotions and reveling in them, to her surprise. She smiled at her body's reaction, and at him. *You can't go around killing everyone you deem guilty, Bastian, even if they are guilty.*

After a pause, he replied. *It saves time.*

Aislinn chuckled outright. *I'm sure there are a lot of vigilantes out there who feel the same way. I don't know Olympian law, but, are you allowed to do that?*

*Not without a counsel trial.*

*Good to know. Eddie didn't have a trial. Did he?*

*Not yet.*

*How do you hold trial?*

*For serious crimes, three tribal leaders convene and evidence is brought. The leaders vote. Sentence is given.*

*Oh.* What a strange, hidden world he existed in. She recalled a documentary she had seen on gypsies and their own private justice system. Perhaps it was not so strange.

She waited for Bastian to further the conversation, but he did not. Was he holding back because of Marius' edict, or was he having second thoughts?

*Bastian, I want to get to know you. To understand you. To make sense of your world.*

Relief, joy, and desire hit her like heat from an open oven door.

*It is my wish as well,* he affirmed.

*I wish I were with you.*

After a pause he replied. *Perhaps that is not wise right now.*

Was he blowing her off? *I want to watch you sleep. I thought you would be asleep already.*

*I tried for a while, but sleep eludes me. Besides, if you join me, sleep will not be what I wish to do.*

Aislinn smiled. The mere thought of his hands on her skin ignited every nerve ending she possessed. She chewed on the inside of cheek, thinking.

*Bastian, what room are you in?* Though she could probably find him, searching such an enormous unfamiliar house was daunting.

When he did not immediately respond, she had the oddest feeling that he was distracted. She waited.

*Bastian?*

Finally, he answered. *The house to the north. There is a covered walkway. Take the narrow hall from the foyer.*

*You're not in dirt, are you?*

Mentally he chuckled. *No.*

When he offered no follow-up, she smirked and rose from the bed. He was being standoffish. But really, hadn't that been her fault? She had protested his claim in front of nearly thirty people, mostly men. She stuffed her phone in her jeans pocket and found a mauve, nylon and cotton-blend shirt, soft and supple. Since she was going to the hospital later, she grabbed her purse and navy blue hoodie. North Carolina was not as cold as Romania, but this was October. Anything could happen.

Happy to find no one on the upstairs balcony, she scurried across to the bathroom, grabbed the first minty mouthwash she could find under the sink, and gargled. She splashed water on her face and smoothed down her hair. A shower would be nice, but that would take too much time. He might be able to wait that long, but she couldn't. The ache to be near him pulsed through her body like an addiction. Parts of her throbbed for more than just nearness, but she needed to resist this man if she was ever going to truly know him.

Mindful of each step, she descended the long staircase slowly, hoping no one would notice and ask questions. What would she say, that she was exploring the house?

Across from the stairs she spied the narrow hallway Bastian had spoken of. On tip-toes she skipped down it. A tiny spyhole from a door at the end of the hall let in a beam of light. She opened the door and blinked at brilliant sunlight. An awning rose above her covering a bricked sidewalk. On the right, a five-foot-high wall of similar red brick bordered the path to a one-story house, a mere forty feet away.

Seeing other houses beyond trees, she stepped into the grassy lawn and realized four houses, including the large main house, were spaced at the corners of an expansive, diamond-shaped courtyard complete with a running track and a swimming pool glistening bright in the sun. Stone walkways with awnings, like the one she was standing under linked all of the houses. Aside from a few weathered benches, several apple trees with bright red fruit lent shade to the vast courtyard. She turned to view the house she had been sleeping in.

"Good lord-a-mighty," she exclaimed. Her eyes traveled up three stories. The main house towered above her. Stepping backward into the courtyard for a better view, she counted no less than six wide chimneys atop the roof. The house she grew up in could have fit inside the massive structure twice, maybe three times.

"These people don't think small." She shuffled across the walkway and touched the doorknob to the first house. The energy felt strong. It also felt quiet. Bravely, she entered. A small office sat to the left and a fairly small living room to the right, but straight ahead was a hallway with two doors on either side.

Marius was standing motionless at the end of the hallway. Breath caught in Aislinn's throat. A knowing shimmer in his dark eyes revealed he knew exactly why she was there. Aislinn felt her cheeks grow hot. Was he going to stand there and watch her walk into Bastian's room, or forbid her?

His dark eyes flicked to his right, and back. Aislinn brightened. He was telling her what room Bastian was in. Was this approval? Marius turned to his left and entered a room, closing the door behind him.

Aislinn took a deep breath. The door he had indicated with a glance was partially open. Should she knock?

*Heck no.*

She turned sideways and skimmed inside without the door touching her body. It was so dark. How had they completely blocked sunlight from entering the windows?

Oh god, she could smell him. His woodsy, musky scent was intoxicating. She could get drunk on that. Or would have, until she smelled someone else.

A woman was whispering. Aislinn felt the woman's emotions. Wanting. Needing. Entreating.

Standing motionless, Aislinn's vision adjusted faster than she expected. A large four-poster bed came into focus. On it sat Bastian. Beside him was a striking woman with long black hair. One of her hands rested on Bastian's forearm.

"You've changed," the woman cooed with a thick Italian accent. "There's an openness in your face I have longed to see."

"See it somewhere else, bitch," Aislinn declared. She strode forward, poised to pounce, to rake her nails over the woman's beautiful face.

The woman was on her feet, swiftly closing the distance between them. As the woman's fist rose, Aislinn sidestepped and mentally screamed, *Stop!* Her psychic yell was instinctual and strong, but contained all the fury she felt.

The tall woman stumbled back, eyes blinking in shock.

Aislinn hoped she hurt the woman. If she screamed louder, could she?

Bastian had leapt forward at the same time as the woman. He stretched his arms between the two. "No!"

"Do not interfere!" The woman yelled at him. "This American wench has challenged me."

Bastian blocked her. "She does not know our ways."

"I will teach her."

Bastian straightened. "No. I... I have claimed her."

The woman stepped back even further, teetering as if having been struck. Her full, red mouth fell open, eyes widening then flicking toward Aislinn's neck. "What?"

Bastian swallowed as if apologetic.

Empowered by the effect the claim mark produced, Aislinn took a step toward the woman, intent on giving her another psychic blast, one she would never forget.

Bastian stopped Aislinn by placing his palm on her chest just below her neck. "Aislinn, no."

Aislinn squinted menacingly, anger sizzling. "How dare you tell me...."

His broad hands gripped her shoulders. "Andromeda is a warrior. She could harm you."

Affronted by Bastian's insulting assessment, Aislinn considered her rival. So *this* was Andromeda. What a spider she was, all leggy and stringy black hair. Aislinn pushed against Bastian's hands. "I can harm her, too."

"I do not wish either of you to be harmed." Bastian pushed her back.

"I'll answer her challenge," Andromeda spoke in a haughty voice, taking a step forward.

"I said 'no!'" Bastian glared at Andromeda.

Expecting the dark-haired vixen to ignore him, Aislinn thrust aside Bastian's arm, her hands itching for the woman's throat. Bastian shoved her torso behind him and held her there using both hands behind his back, each gripping an arm. Aislinn struggled against his amazing hold, slapping the back of his rock-hard arms.

"Andromeda, please go," Bastian entreated.

"She challenged me."

"I told you she does not understand a challenge. She is new to us."

"She'll learn quickly enough."

"Andromeda." His voice softened as if addressing a wounded child. "I have chosen her."

Aislinn stopped squirming, waiting for Andromeda's reaction.

"Her?" Andromeda yelled. "This nobody? She isn't even a warrior. I heard she's *human*. I have a mate sign. Are you going to ignore that? You know I can give you full-blooded...."

"Go," Bastian said, his tone letting Andromeda know there would be no further argument.

211

Aislinn watched the woman stomp from the room and throw the door open so that it banged against the wall. Her footsteps echoed down the hall, followed by the outer entrance door banging.

Bastian released Aislinn's arms and pivoted to face her.

Aislinn pounded fists into his bare chest, so angry she shook. "My favorite thing! Finding my man with another woman! I just never thought it would be *you*."

"Oh, so I am your man now?" He fought to control her arms.

Wrestling with him, Aislinn realized not only was his chest bare, the rest of him was naked except for tight-fitting boxers. Andromeda was in here with him and he was wearing nothing but those? Her anger exploded.

"I'm going to *kill* that woman! And then come back here and kill *you!*"

Bastian pushed her against the wall, pinning her arms. She raised her knee and he threw his body against her, thwarting her aim. "It's the blood heat, Aislinn. Think! Do you normally get this angry? Have you ever wanted to kill another woman? Really kill her?"

Aislinn froze. While she might have said it metaphorically, she would have never thought to actually commit the deed. But she *was* thinking it.

"I, too, have wrestled with the heat," he confessed. "Of course...." He softened. "I have not been thinking straight since the moment I met you."

At the same time Aislinn's shoulders dropped, she could feel his erection growing, pressing against her stomach. Instead of being nervous or shy about it, like she would have before, she envisioned touching, stroking him, feeling him inside her, completing their bond as nature intended.

His silver eyes took on a milky, wanton texture. How she loved looking into their eerie, otherworldly depths, especially when he was reading her mind.

She wasn't ready to come down from her mountain of rage just yet. But if she kept staring at those eyes, she would forget how badly she wanted to stay angry. Having his male-scented body so close was taking thoughts of spider woman right out of her head. Desire snaked through her like a hungry flame. His luscious lips were only inches away. She envisioned licking him as though he were a lollipop.

"I love where your mind is right now," he crooned, pressing forward and rubbing his pelvis against hers.

"Not everywhere my mind is. I still want to kill that spider woman."

"Ready to fight for me, are you?" He grinned with salacious satisfaction. "So, am I your chosen?"

"I told you I wanted you."

"Not the same thing." His fingers loosened their grip a touch, and his thumbs began rubbing circles on the wrists he had pinned to the wall.

"You said you wanted me." She reminded him.

"Yes I did. And you spurned me, as I recall."

"Do I look like I'm spurning?"

A smile toyed at his lips. "No, you look like a woman who is either going to break my neck," his voice grew husky, "or wrap her legs around my hips and let me bury myself into her until she is sated."

Their mouths met with such force they nearly bruised each other. Bastian fisted one hand into her hair, while the other cupped her buttocks and lifted her. Her legs wrapped around him like a tree trunk and he pressed his erection against her. Aislinn moaned at the wonderful pressure his shaft exerted. She could feel lusty fluids warming her, making her ache for him.

Bastian growled against her mouth as he detected her thoughts. Over and over they kissed until their mouths were hot, tingly and swollen. Neither could slow down.

Bastian walked them toward the bed and collapsed onto it, rolling Aislinn carefully onto her side, his leg capturing both of hers.

The feel of Bastian's muscled chest against Aislinn's breasts was exhilarating. She ran her hungry hands over him in a frenzy, his arms, his chest, his back and buttocks, all the while kissing him feverishly.

He released her lips and nibbled at her neck. She groaned with delight, raking her fingers through his hair.

Covering every inch of her neck and throat, he licked and sucked until she was squirming, hoping for teeth.

Suddenly, he froze.

"What's wrong?" she asked, panting.

Bastian pulled back and propped his head alongside her with his elbow.

"My lady, you have stated that you want me. And, you are certainly showing it. But, I am under orders not to talk to you through our bond until you *choose*."

"What?" She licked her lips and squirmed, which he watched, desire glistening in his eyes. "I think I'm making it pretty obvious."

"Mmm, that you want my body, yes. But, what about the rest of me?"

"Seriously? Am I with Eddie or with you?"

"I want to hear it from you." His voice was deep, slipping over her like warm water. He pulled strands of her hair between his fingers and held them over his upper lip, breathing in the scent.

"I don't want Eddie." Aislinn swallowed as her body ached with need against his. It wasn't an entirely accurate statement. The blood bond made her want Eddie, a little.

"Still waiting," he whispered.

"Okay, I want you," she murmured. "What... what does the claiming mean to you people? You know we don't have that in our culture. We get *engaged*. And what's the steps Marius fussed about? If I say yes to you, what am I saying?" She explored his crystalline eyes, amazed that she could see them so clear in the dark.

"The first step is to establish Olympian bloodline. Marius and Gabriella believe you are part of us. You have suffered no ill from ingesting my blood."

His fingers slid down her chest to glide along the edge of her shirt. "Marius also believes you are good for me, so we partly have his blessing. That's one step. And... I already created the first blood bond. We need two more. The next one must be with your consent, so that all the world knows I have claimed you and my blood has mixed with yours."

Her body shivered with anticipation. "Okay," she breathed, wanting to re-experience that blissful sensation. "Just one thing, though. This claiming thing sounds like you own me or something. I still don't quite get it."

Abruptly, he slid a hand under her shirt, onto her bra and rested there. His eyes narrowed. "Trust me, my lady, if you accept my claim, I will own you, body and soul, and you will be glad I do." Holding her attention with his eyes, his hand began to massage.

Aislinn breathed faster. *Oh my goodness.*

"Bastian," she whispered. "Everything in me wants to touch you, to be with you and think of nothing else. Is this the bond, or is it me?"

Shifting his massive body gently over hers, his other hand began massaging the opposite breast, which made her gasp. He continued to hold her gaze, clearly enjoying her predicament.

"My lady, the bond cannot create what does not exist. It only heightens and escalates."

His broad hands withdrew, then slipped to the hem of her shirt and pushed upward. She raised her arms to let him remove her mauve shirt. She unclasped her bra. Before she had freed herself from it, he claimed her breasts with hands and mouth.

They both moaned with delight as he sucked rhythmically on her nipples. She groaned, her chin tipping back as waves of pleasure rushed through her. She plunged her hands into his hair and pressed his head against her breasts.

Their psychic bond merged into an electrifying charge that rose and filled the air around them. They moaned in unison as they experienced each other's pleasure.

Bastian continued to lathe her nipples until she was sure she would climax from it. Suddenly, he released her.

"No," she protested softly, until she realized he was unzipping her jeans. She decided to help him, and shimmied out of them. "I thought you could remove these with your mind."

"The sun is up."

"Oh. But... it's dark in here. So how...?"

"I'd rather use my hands anyway."

"Mmm. Me too."

With a rush of impatience he yanked the blue jeans off her legs, and reached for her lace thong. He slipped his fingers under it.

"What is this?"

"It's a thong." In a flash, she realized eighty years ago he and his bride probably had never seen or heard of a thong. "Just pull it off."

He did not hesitate, though he held it up in puzzlement and sniffed deeply, his eyes closing in delight, before dropping the scant piece of material. Returning his hand to its desired destination, he cupped her where the lace had been. "So little hair." His voice held wonder in it.

"I had most of it removed," she whispered, barely able to speak for his fingers reaching in, parting, exploring. She whimpered and gasped. "It... used to... drive me crazy."

"I like it." His fingers curled into her, making circles, and she groaned louder. He slipped fingers further insider her. She arched, pulling at his shoulders.

"You are so wet for me, my lady."

He removed his boxers one-handed. His erection sprang forward.

*Whoa*, Aislinn exclaimed.

He chuckled, and she realized he had read her thoughts and was pleased.

Would she stretch enough for him?

*I will make us fit*, he promised.

She gasped and got hotter at the prospect of him filling her.

*We were meant to fit, my lady. I want you to feel every inch of me*. A husky sound escaped his throat as he parted her legs with his knee. Even that gesture made her grow wetter in anticipation.

He pressed his erect tip against her wetness, and his eyes closed. So did hers.

Taking hold of his shaft he circled her opening. They groaned together. She raised her hips toward him. If he hesitated another minute, she would scream. Moving an inch at a time, he eased into her, prolonging the sweet sensation, which sent their bodies and spirits reeling, almost unable to hold onto the moment.

He whispered her name as he slipped further in, rocking until he filled her. Her mouth opened wide, giving voice to a garbled cry. Bucking against him, she grabbed his shoulders, gasping from exquisite pleasures. He pumped, in and out, exploding sensations within her. She felt a sense of rising, as if the bed had disappeared. As he continued to thrust, energy crackled around them, igniting their physical and psychic bonding.

"Faster," Aislinn begged. Bastian began to pound into her. Her climax spilled over her in waves and waves of exotic rapture.

A guttural growl escaped Bastian as he arched his neck, his lips parting in ecstasy. Gasping for air, he collapsed onto her, his forearms supporting his chest so he did not crush her. He swore something in German.

For several minutes, they basked in the afterglow, bodies and minds linked, and no desire to separate. Bastian kissed Aislinn's face lovingly. His body still shivered with the pleasure of being inside of her, of claiming her in a way he had once assumed he would never experience again with a woman he truly cared for. Their bond had enhanced every pulsing delight the other felt. And, most importantly, she had come to him. Of her own free will.

Even after their satisfying love making, he could not stop kissing her. His canines had extended and he was careful to not hurt her lips.

"Your fangs…." She must have felt them.

"They extend when I…."

"When you make love?"

He smiled. "When I make love with *you*. Even when I *think* about making love with you. Or, touch you. Or, kiss you." He kissed her mouth gently while his fingers brushed along her soft, plump breast, teasing her nipple.

That made her hum with joy.

She pulled out of the kiss and traced his lips with a fingertip, touching his canines, which caused them to ache in his mouth. "What are we going to do about that?" she teased.

"That depends."

"On what?"

"On whether this means you are consenting to being my mate. Are you?" If only he could temp her to say the words. The proclamation would be binding, though she did not know that. Words had power in his world.

"God, those are actually sexy." She touched his canines again, making him want to nibble at her finger. "Never thought I'd ever say *that*." She chuckled.

"You are avoiding my question, my lady." He raised his chin to dislodge her probing finger.

"Mmm-hmm. You're right, sir Bastian."

"Does this mean you want me to make love to you, but are not ready to commit to me?"

She stared at him with those doughy, blue eyes, and he wanted to make love to her all over again. He kissed her to show her no reply was acceptable. For now. As long as she was in his arms, that was an answer of a sort. Besides, he had already made up his mind. She was his, and no amount of jumping on planes was going to stop him from having her.

Her soft, warm hands roamed over his shoulders and back, and squeezed his buttocks.

A smile tugged at his mouth. "Are you ready for more?"

Sliding her arms between his, she rubbed her palms up his chest, kneading his muscles. He closed his eyes at her exploration, fiery tingles again spreading throughout his body.

He leaned forward and kissed her adorable, upturned lips. When she responded in kind, he kissed her with greater passion, claiming her entire mouth and tasting her with his tongue. Passion ignited between them making his heart pump faster, engorging his erection while he was still inside her. As he swelled, he moved in and out. She groaned beneath him.

His canines were aching again. He could smell her blood, hear it rushing just under her tender skin. He made his way to her neck, kissing and licking, but resisting the temptation.

With a breathless whisper, she asked, "If we exchange blood again, will it make our bond stronger, enough to make Eddie stop trying to talk to me?"

He froze. "I would rather Edward stop breathing."

She sighed with a wisp of a laugh. "Can't blame you there."

While he exhaled deeply to defuse the rage boiling in his chest, he touched fingers to her cheek. So soft.

"Do it," she whispered. "Bite me again."

"Oh my god, Aislinn." With his elbows still holding him up, he rested his forehead in the crook of her neck and shoulder, so close to the spot where he had claimed her before. "That is like letting the beast out of its cage."

"I think I can tame the beast." She pushed back his hair. Then she raised her head and nipped his neck.

That was it. He had no resistance left. He sunk his teeth into the same spot on her neck as before. Barely perceptible, he sensed the inclusion of Edward's blood in hers. It harbored no real resistance, but was a message. An unwelcome message. He growled, drew her blood into his mouth and swallowed.

She arched under him, gasping. He knew the endorphins would heighten every sensation they felt, so he merged with her mind ensuring they could both experience it.

Working his erection rhythmically inside her, he sucked more of her sweet blood into his welcoming body. Like an illicit drug, it shot energy through his muscles and nerves and into his brain. He exclaimed in German in his mind, entranced by the rush of pleasure enthralling him.

She was moaning and digging her nails into his chest muscles. He pumped faster into her sweet, swollen core, continuing to drink the amazing elixir, willing the endorphins to enhance her pleasure into an exploding inferno.

He felt his own climax building from the added embellishment of her blood. She was thrusting her hips at him in frenzied desperation, her moans getting louder. He could feel exquisite tingles shuddering through her in waves of ecstasy. It triggered his own climax and caused his body to shake as he emptied into her again. He tilted his head back, lost in delight. Dazed and sated, he lowered his head to lick her wound and stem the flow of blood.

A whisper drew him out of his dreamlike euphoria. Aislinn was urging him to complete the bond. He speared a fang into his wrist and felt the trickle of blood run down his arm.

*Bastian.* Marius' voice, soft and sounding far away, invaded his mind.

Bastian roared at the audacity of Marius. *I am with my woman!*

*Follow the ancient ritual, Bastian. Follow the steps, or she will not be your woman. You cannot rush her exposure. Give it time. It has only been three days at most.*

In a long, low growl, Bastian let the protest spill from him in Greek curses instead of German since it was Marius and he hoped he heard it.

"What's wrong?" Aislinn whispered, alarmed.

Bastian held tight to her, but the beast was backing up. Though his anger at the intrusion shook him, his Olympian brain considered Marius' words and knew the wisdom in them. There were stories of Olympians sharing their blood with humans too fast—and too much blood—without the ancient rituals and prayers of protection. Some died. Some went insane.

Taking her blood posed little threat. Giving her *his* blood did. The coding in his blood would continue to change her, enhance her.

He pressed his face against her soft cheek, fighting the desire to give her his blood.

"Hey, aren't you going to give me your blood?"

A growl blasted out of his mind and his throat. She flinched, her eyes wide. He ran fingers through her hair to reassure her. Every fiber of his being wanted to give her his blood, to bind her closer to him.

"I want to," he confessed, his throat tight. "You do not know how much."

"Then, why…?"

"Marius wants me to stop."

"What? He's talking to you *now*?"

Bastian closed his eyes and nodded.

"Holy crap, what the…? Is this what you guys do? Jump into each other's heads while you're having sex? Share the thrills?" Her voice was getting louder.

"No, Aislinn, it's not…."

"This is the most disgusting… get off me!"

"Stop, Aislinn."

"Heck, no." She was gritting her teeth and pushing hard against his chest, which did nothing to move him. "I mean it, Bastian."

"Aislinn, listen. Please." He grabbed her forearms to keep them still. "It's not what you think. Marius is supposed to look out for you. He knows I care too much." His voice lowered. "He knows I want you too much."

Her blue eyes shot icy daggers at him. "This is freaking crazy."

"To you, I'm sure it is. And do not think I like it. Right now I would like to punch him. If he was standing beside this bed, I would have. No one has the right to come between us."

Her breathing softened but her bright blue eyes were still flashing. "Okay, one, I've got two men in my head already, which is more than I can handle. Two, you've got a whole party going on in yours. Three, one of them just jumped into our bed for a ride. Doesn't that sound the least bit *wacked* to you!"

He pressed his lips together to keep from smiling, certain she would not find it amusing. "One, I do not have constant conversations going on. Marius only detected it because of… of the intense feelings I was having— *we* were having. And you were getting a bit loud. He's right across the hall. Normally, he would have closed himself off, which he can do, I assure you. Two, he approves of us, but he is worried. He believes your exposure to pure Olympian blood is too fast. I could endanger you. Edward endangered you. Three, I should have killed Edward on the spot. If I was the prince, I would have done it."

She blinked.

"Which is probably why I was not chosen to be prince. I cannot always control myself. And four…." He let his fingers slide over the puncture marks in her neck, reveling in the knowledge that no Olympian could miss it. "I still want to do it. I believe you are of the blood. There are things you can do, which proves it. I know your body could handle it."

Her examination of his face turned mischievous. Before he could stop her, she grabbed his arm and licked the blood, all the way up to the cut.

"Aislinn, *no*." He jerked his arm away.

"Ha!" She swallowed with flair, smacking her lips. "Tell Marius not to intrude on us again."

Bastian swore, then laughed. "You are the most impetuous woman I have ever met."

She grinned, touching her upper lip with the tip of her tongue.

He grinned back. "That was not very much blood, you know."

"Hey, it wasn't much blood the first time either." Her face scrunched. "Blood tastes really weird."

Bastian shook his head. "I guess we will see if it makes any difference."

"I feel different already."

"It will not work that fast. Well, not the changes."

"Huh, shows what *you* know."

"Do you feel different?"

"Um… well, I have a six-foot-five Olympian on top of me, *and* inside me. So, yeah, that's a change." She wriggled underneath him.

"Whoa, don't do that," he warned, his shaft so sensitized it was almost painful.

She giggled. "And, yeah, my senses are definitely enhanced. I can smell things I couldn't smell before. See things. *Hear* things." Her fingers stroked his jaw and slid down his neck.

He exhaled with delight. Her slightest touch felt like tendrils of delicious fire on his skin.

"I can feel you, and find you when I need to," she said. "That's fairly new."

"I am glad you found me."

"Me, too." She squinted as if angry. "Even if it *was* with another woman."

"That was not my doing. She arrived a short while ago and must have asked where I was resting. Believe me, I was just as surprised as you to see her. She flew in during the night. Someone tipped her off about the battle signs appearing. She may have even received one."

Aislinn's lips pressed to a thin, angry line. "She's got the tattoos?"

"Yes. They are lighter than the men, but work the same. Only an Olympian can see them clearly."

"Oh, so you've seen them?"

He inhaled, his gut tightening. It would not be a good time to inform her of Andromeda's attempts to pull him out of his stagnation for the last year. They had kissed several times. She had urged him to go further. His body had been tempted, but his heart had not. Another explanation would be better for Aislinn. "Around us, she tends to wear… clothes that make them obvious."

"Nice."

"So." He stroked her face. "Any other enhancements?"

"I can hear whispers when you and Marius and Gabriella and Dimitri are talking. I can't quite make out what you're saying though."

That was odd. Only seasoned Olympians could do that. "You should not be able to hear that. Not without a blood bond connecting them."

She shrugged. "Maybe it's because of our blood connection and you being connected to them. I hear their minds touching yours. There's just one problem."

"What is that?"

"I don't have fangs. So if I still want to take your blood, how am I going to get it, other than slurping your arm?" She scrunched her nose.

"I used a fang on my arm a minute ago. I can also puncture myself with a fingernail like I did before, in Romania." Raising his right forearm, careful to continue holding his weight above Aislinn, he extended the fingernail of his right index finger.

"On my gosh, your nails come out, like a cat?" She grabbed his hand to examine it.

"Mmm-hmm."

"That is so freakin' cool. I could have used that on Andromeda."

Deciding not to respond to that, he cleared his throat. Andromeda was a competent warrior. She could have hurt Aislinn, badly.

"I do not feel Marius purposely tuned in to me," he assured her, "but he has a strong mind. So, now would not be a good time to disobey him."

He lowered his head and kissed her luscious lips. "Know this, though, Aislinn Thomas. I willingly bind my heart and my life to you. I pledge to provide for you and protect you, always. I intend to adore you. For all eternity." He kissed her temple. "And cherish you." He moved to her other temple and planted a kiss. She was smiling. "And make passionate love to you until you are so sore you cannot leave the house."

Her mouth flew open in astonishment. "Oh, you!" She beat against his chest, and he chuckled.

She froze, concern covering her face. "Oh, no."

"What?"

"I just had sex with an alien, and didn't use a condom."

"My lady." He laughed low, pressing forward between her legs to remind her where he was. "I am an Olympian. You are my mate. I would be nothing but ecstatic if you were with child."

"Hey, one, you wouldn't be the one carrying it." She began to push harder against his chest which he found alluring. "Two, I love everything you said, but I haven't signed any papers yet. Three, I want my customs honored, too. And four, what the heck happens to me when I'm around you? I've only had sex with one other person and *never* without a condom."

"What other person?" Though neither of them was a virgin, anger tightened his chest at the visualization of another man touching her. His fists clenched.

She stilled. "Turns out, the other person was an Olympian, too. Though, I didn't know it. The only guys who can make me throw caution to the wind, I guess. Is it some Olympian voodoo charm you guys have?"

"I hate him more."

She smiled coyishly.

Quelling the fury that threatened to ruin the afterglow of their lovemaking, he grabbed the pillow next to them and shredded the case from it in one pull. Edward had had relations with *his* woman, took her virginity. That should have belonged to *him*. He glanced at her and she seemed suddenly afraid of the look on his face.

"When were you last with Edward?" he asked.

"A year ago." Her voice was meek. "Well, a week before the accident. He asked me to marry him. Said we would go out together and pick out a ring. I bought into the whole thing, I guess. Even let him move some things in. After the accident, I caught him with someone else. I broke up with him." Her face darkened, pain wrinkling her brow.

A year ago he could handle. "I have another reason to kill him."

She rolled her eyes, her mood lightening.

Gently, he tucked the pillow case under her buttocks and thighs.

"What's that for?" she asked.

"You and Edward always used a condom?"

"Yes." Her lips barely moved. "But it was only twice. Why?"

He pulled out of her.

"Whoa!" she exclaimed, and pressed the pillowcase between her legs.

He rolled over and stretched his arms over his head, definitely feeling better than he had in eight decades.

# CHAPTER 21

Aislinn watched Bastian's tattooed chest rising and falling, strength radiating even as he slept. Her eyes travelled over the outline of his pectoral muscles and abs, so clear even with the blackout curtains covering the windows. Her vision was surely changing, enhancing.

With a quick brush of her lips across the nearest golden tattoo, she reluctantly slid her arm out from under his. His arm twitched as if in protest and his brow furrowed, but he did not wake. They had slept together for nearly an hour. The room was dark, but her body knew it was morning. Her eyelids refused to stay closed.

Earlier, in the bathroom adjoining the bedroom, she had realized her thong was not going to be much protection from his semen escaping her. After several wads of tissues, she had searched under the sink until she found various sizes of pads in the cabinet. Mouthing an airy thank you to Ma Beattie, assuming she had placed them there for the needs of her guests, she put one into the crotch of his boxers, which she confiscated.

When he complained, she had thrown a whispered yell at him from the bathroom doorway. "Can't do anything small, can you people!"

He had chuckled at her candor. "My lady, that's eighty years of back-up."

She smiled at that now.

Careful not to make any noise, she continued to dress into her jeans and silky mauve shirt. She rolled her eyes in chastisement, not believing she'd had sex with him without considering a condom. Eddie always had condoms, and had tried many times to coax her into having sex, until she finally gave in after talk of marriage. Eddie obviously lied about being in for the long haul. Though now he was man obsessed.

A frown formed across her forehead. Was there something about both men that caused her to abandon her normal caution? She had vowed to hold off until she was with the love of her life, preferably after marrying him. Of course, at one time, she had thought that was Eddie.

Bastian claimed Olympians were monogamous. Eddie had cheated on her at least twice, albeit with proclaimed remorse and lame excuses. If Eddie was Olympian too, what did that say about Bastian's claims? What if his declarations were based on the now while his passion was high. Would his desire for her last beyond the wild rush of the blood heat?

Eddie had once made her body yearn for his, but Eddie had held back. With his Olympian abilities, he could have shared the incredible merging of minds that she experienced with Bastian.

Even as she thought it, Aislinn knew the answer. Eddie feared her having access to his mind. Feared her having some control. A wall she could not penetrate was always there, between them.

Bastian had no fear of her mind's awareness, most of the time. He was brazen and demanding, but he could be charming, if overbearing, especially with his way of claiming her. Of course, it wasn't like Bastian had done the traditional thing and asked her to marry him. If he thought he was going to get away with that just because he was an alien, he could forget it. She wanted a ring, a wedding, a dress, the whole nine human yards. Not just blood exchanges in bed. Or, fantastic, toe-curling sex in bed.

In the meager blue glow of the clock, she glanced once more at the faint shimmer of his tattooed chest as he breathed, and sighed. She did not want to leave the room, but she could not sleep. And, she needed to see Gramma. Pulling the door almost shut, afraid it would wake him, she crept from the room. She half expected Marius to be waiting in the hall. Fortunately, the house remained quiet.

*That's because all the freaking aliens are asleep.*

The walkway between the houses seemed a good place for a private conversation, so she dialed Aunt Julia. At the sound of her Aunt's voicemail recording, Aislinn blew air from her lips in frustration.

"Hey, Aunt Julia, I'm coming over for a visit. I'm about an hour away so please call me as soon as you get this message. I assume Gramma's still there. Hope they'll let her come home today. Okay, see you soon."

Gramma would know how to handle the Olympians. Gramma would be open, but Aunt Julia could not be there. Aunt Julia had always been squeamish about anything supernatural, or even out of the ordinary. Like Aislinn's mother, she had often pointedly walked out of a room if any such conversation arose.

Aislinn considered what to tell Gramma as she traversed the narrow hallway in the main house. Marius had indicated she was sworn to secrecy. How much could she say? *Gramma, I met a guy. He looks like a Greek god and—oh by the way—he is? And yeah, he's a vampire, too. Sort of.*

Then again, leaving out the part that he was an alien, drank blood, slept in dirt, and kicked ass with a blessed sword that appeared when evil was present made mentioning him at all seem lame.

As her foot hit the edge of the carpet in the foyer, she heard the heavy swish of the sliding glass door at the opposite end near the kitchen.

"Aisy," Eddie whispered, his voice sounding relieved and hopeful as he jogged to close the distance between them. He glanced around as though not wanting to be discovered. Usually a mixture of bossy and suave, it was odd to see Eddie looking contrite, almost desperate.

"Um, hi." Aislinn kept her voice polite, noting his bruises and black eye from his altercation with Bastian were changing from purple to green already. She knew he healed fast, and now knew why. "How are you?"

"I'm fine now that I can see you." He flashed a toothy smile.

"Actually, we need to talk about that."

"I know you're confused, but we...." His eyes slid to her neck and his smile dropped.

Aislinn swallowed at the hurt and shock he displayed. A dark rage crept over his face. Before she could stop him, he grabbed her shoulder, pulling her close as if unwilling to believe his eyes.

When he inhaled, she knew he smelled Bastian. She slapped his hand away and pivoted from his grasp, surprised that he let go.

"You let *him*, but not *me*?" His vivid hazel eyes were smoldering, threatening, like in Romania. His rage boiled over her in waves. More than just empathic perception, she realized their blood bond was amplifying the burning energy. She took another step back.

"I didn't exactly *let* you, did I, Eddie?" she declared. He could be angry all he liked. He lost his chance two blondes ago.

With pursed lips, Eddie shifted to view the hall she came from. "You just saw him, didn't you?"

"That is none of your business now."

"Just like some slut, you jump in the sack with some other guy?"

"How dare you call me a slut! And look who's talking. You're the worst slut I know. And don't even *try* to tell me the two blondes I caught you with were the only ones. I think you have a thing for blondes. Everybody who saw you—all across freakin' North Carolina—it was *always* with a blonde. Just never *me*."

The flair of his nostrils and grinding of his jaw confirmed her suspicion. He could not hide it from her now. Aside from his body language, the blood bond left his mind open, bare and accessible.

"That's it, isn't it?" She shook her head and snorted. "What a fool I was. I was just a number on the list, wasn't I? Blonde number what... ten... fifteen... twenty?"

"No! With you, it was different. It *is* different. Okay, so I have a thing for blondes. So what? You're the only blonde I wanted to keep. You're... special."

Aislinn seethed as she sucked in a deep breath and let it out. "You know, your honesty actually gave you away this time. That line should have been, 'It's different with you, Aisy. I fell in love.' But, that isn't what you said, is it Eddie? You wanted to *keep* me like some... prize. To own me. You were just afraid someone else would get me, weren't you?"

"But I do love you." He took a step closer, his arms reaching for her.

"No, no, no." She raised her palms, and took an additional step back. "It's too late to fix that. I can't believe I wasted a year on you. I wanted so badly to believe you had changed."

"I *did* change! I decided to keep you."

Aislinn shook her head in disbelief. "You decided to *keep* me? Like a new toaster or, or, a microwave?"

Eddie ran a hand through his hair. "No. Not like that. You don't know what I'm up against, Aisy. I've got...."

"Nope. Don't bother. You bared your soul, all right. It's twisted and it's *dark*."

When he blanched, her brows furrowed in surprise. The statement hit him harder than it should have. Fear and guilt radiated from him like an open furnace.

"You know what, Eddie? This is it for me and you. I don't want you in my head. I don't want you in my bed. And I don't want you in my life. Don't..." she warned as a hand reached for her face, "touch me."

Rage and shock colored Eddie's cheeks and neck. Aislinn felt his menacing intent a second before he stepped toward her. His fingers curled around her neck and she felt claws. Someone sneezed and Eddie froze, releasing his hands. They both whirled to find a young boy, one of the children Aislinn had seen at the meal, sitting at the top of the staircase. The boy went wide-eyed at being discovered, turned and scampered across the upstairs hall.

With a quick jerk of his head, Eddie examined the foyer as if afraid someone else might be observing them. When he turned back to Aislinn, his face held the wild, manic look of a madman.

"You're going to be sorry for this," he threatened.

Aislinn experienced his surge of fury and retaliation through their bond, foreboding and malicious.

"I don't think so, Eddie." She hoped the force of her words would prove stronger than she felt. Quivers of terror were rippling through her chest. She had never seen such a look of menace in his piercing green-gold eyes. He brushed past her and stomped out the front door. Sunlight blinded her for a moment, until the door slammed hard.

Aislinn placed a hand to her chest, breathing through the emotions. The other hand she pressed to her stomach. His dark threats still invaded her. She had to find a way to break their bond.

"Is it safe yet?"

Aislinn jerked upward to find Earl's head leaning just outside the oak door to the library, a hint of humor in his raised brows.

Aislinn sighed and made a quirky sideways curve of her mouth. "You weren't supposed to hear that."

"Yeah, but it was good. Better than cable." Though he was trying to suppress a grin, his unusual turquoise eyes twinkled. Wisps of brown hair hung loosely over his forehead as perfect as a magazine model.

"Are you the only one up?" Aislinn asked.

"Uh… at the moment. Some of them will get up around noon. Not the Hercules dudes of course, unless something bad happens."

Aislinn averted her eyes to the ornate rug. Earl had probably heard Eddie's comments about her tryst with Bastian.

"Why? You need something?" he prompted.

"Well, I really need to get to my Gramma. I called my Aunt Julia but she's not answering."

"Where's your Gramma live?"

"In Pisgah Forest, but she's in the hospital right now in Brevard. She was doing better yesterday, but I just… need to see her." She swallowed back emotion.

"I know where that is. I could drive you."

"Really?"

"Sure." He stepped into the foyer. "Although, you know, kidnapping you for three seconds almost got me killed. Escaping the compound with the Fearless Sebastian's girl might take a few years off my life. Like… hmm… all of them?"

Aislinn rolled her eyes and chuckled. "I promise, I'll place myself between you and the mighty Sebastian."

"Hmm." He rubbed his chin, examining the air above her. "Somehow I think he could still throw punches at me over your head."

"Oh, stop. I'll hit him myself if he hits you."

"I'm sure that'll do the trick." He nodded, broth brows curved in sarcasm.

"No, wait. I know. Tell him I was leaving, calling a cab or something, and you didn't want me to go alone. Besides, if you don't take me, that's exactly what I'm going to do. Gabriella said I couldn't go anywhere without a warrior. And… you're a warrior." With palms raised as if surrendering, she grinned wide and decided to leave out the part about Gabriella requiring *two* warriors.

"That I am, fair damsel. Our chariot awaits. But… let's get back before Fearless wakes up, okay?"

Eddie drove through the slow-opening iron gates, and sped up the brick drive, knots tightening in his stomach the closer he got to the looming mansion. Enrique was already headed to the driver's side as Eddie put the car in park. Not wanting Enrique to see him looking weak at the prospect of visiting his father, Eddie stepped out with swagger and a smile, and flipped the keys to Enrique.

"Afternoon, Mr. Hawthorne," said Enrique.

"Drop the *Mr.*, Enrique. You know I hate that."

Enrique smiled. "Yeah, but the ol' man likes it."

Eddie rolled his eyes. "Exactly. Now, I'm not the ol' man, now am I?"

"Yo, *Eddie*, how's it *hangin'*?" Enrique opened his arms and grinned wide.

"Ready as always," Eddie replied. "Now *that's* more like it."

Enrique's grin faltered as he spotted Eddie's black eye. "Trouble with ladies, señior?"

"Always." Further bantering with Enrique, whom Eddie had always liked, would be fun, but his father had a way of using everyone for a spy.

Ornate oak front doors opened as he approached. He nodded to Robert, the old, gnarled butler, who had been there for most of Eddie's life, and never cracked a smile.

Eddie strode across the marbled foyer, ignored the posh décor, and marched into his father's study.

"Hello, Dad."

"Edward," his father called out from behind a desk, looking surprised. "Doing okay? What the hell happened to you?"

"Been working out with some fellow Olympians."

"Looks like you lost. We talking Appalachians? I thought I told you to stay away from them."

"It's an important cover, Dad. As long as they think we're still goody-goodies, they won't come looking our way for any… questionable business."

Horace Hawthorn's eyes narrowed. "I suppose that's actually well thought out."

"Don't sound so surprised."

"Don't get smart with me. I was making deals when I was ten. You didn't care about anything until you were eighteen. If then."

*Yeah, yeah, same old you'll-never-be-as-good-as-me-speech.*

"So, to what do I owe this visit?" Horace prompted, looking suspicious.

"I need a charm. One I know you have."

"Thought you had your own supply of everything at that lab of yours. According to your brother, you're hot stuff now when it comes to spells and supplies for the black arts."

Eddie raised his chin, trying not to react to the disappointment in his father that he had surpassed his brother in something.

"Used mine up. I think you've got what I need, if I remember correctly."

"Oh? What's the problem?"

"Just some girl trouble."

"Girls aren't trouble unless you care about them."

*Perhaps you should have cared about Mom.* "This one... I just might," said Eddie. "Don't know. Not sure what I feel."

"Maybe if you had taken care of business, you wouldn't be feeling anything right now."

Eddie stared at his father's menacing blood-brown eyes, the red inner rings of the irises pulsing. He should have known his father would be spying.

"Taken care of business?" Eddie repeated, giving nothing away.

"You were told to kill that girl. She's still alive."

Eddie sighed. "I did try to kill her. *Four times*, in fact." He paced in frustration. "Someone's always helping her. It's power. Lots of it. Stupid grandmother had it all over the house. I still found ways, but... I've been thwarted every time."

"I've told you before, Eddie. You have to be persistent and thorough. You always screw stuff up. I trusted you with the job, and you let me down. Now, you could bring chaos into this family."

"Aw come on, Dad. She's obviously not the one. The mage's prediction didn't come true. She hasn't affected this family at all and it's been over a year. Besides, the stupid prediction was so cryptic it could be taken a million ways."

"I only see it one way. Eliminate her."

"Like with a Yeti or two, Dad?"

It was the freezing of his father's expression that gave him away. Eddie had suspected his father's interference, but hoped he was wrong. His father was not afraid to make deals with demons.

"Why, you seen one?" Horace asked.

"Not me. The only thing they care about is scaring people. I'm not afraid of them, so why would they come after me? But, I understand two came after Aislinn Thomas. One in Romania, and one here. What a coincidence."

"Look, I've been cleaning up after you your whole life." Horace's face took on the hard, cold stare that Eddie hated. "You didn't take care of it, so I did."

Eddie straightened. "How the hell did you summon a Yeti?"

"I've got my ways. Still lots for you to learn."

"But... a Yeti... to kill her?"

"Not kill her. Just frighten her into a little accident. Like I said, someone needed to take care of it."

"And what if I wanted her? What if I can keep her under my control? Did you ever think of that?"

His father's eyes narrowed. "You can have any woman you want, Edward. Why her?"

"Because." Eddie averted his eyes. "She's different."

"Different how? Are you in love with her?"

"No," Eddie denied, knowing it was the one factor in the prophecy he had never owned up to. "I just... enjoy her better than the others I've had." Eddie perused his father's treasures decorating the room, knowing he should be aloof and pretend to value Aislinn as arm candy and nothing more. Love was something his father saw as a weakness.

Did he love Aislinn? He often told her, but up until that moment he had not considered it to be true. When he met her, she was so sensitive she had seen through his façade of confidence and discovered a son rejected by his father, so desperate for approval. Many of his emotions, more so his intentions, he had managed to hide from her. But not his father's disappointment in him. She had seen right through that, even told him he was perfect just the way he was, that he should pursue his dreams and forget what his father thought.

Eddie stole a glance at his father and knew by his dark gaze that Horace was deciding what direction to go in. If Horace thought—even for a moment—that Eddie actually cared for Aislinn, he would arrange to have her killed, regardless of what Eddie wanted.

"So, you enjoy her," Horace stated. "Do something about it. You have her hair? Or blood?"

"I came prepared."

"Then control her so she can't be an influence that affects this family. Fail to do so and I'll kick your ass myself. Don't risk this family and everything I've built."

"Don't worry, I won't," Eddie answered, resentful for his father's threat.

"I've worked too hard to get us where we are," Horace added. "We control businesses, we control politicians, and we control cops. It doesn't get any better."

*Yeah, yeah, yeah.* "I *know* that, Dad. I used my own fangs to claim her and create a blood bond."

Horace's eyebrows rose appreciatively. "Well, you're not a total disappointment, are you? I didn't know you had managed those abilities."

Eddie smiled sideways. "I can manage a lot when highly motivated."

"Well, well. Not even your brother's managed that."

Eddie should have coveted the approval and felt satisfaction at again one-upping his brother, Damian, but he did not. He genuinely loved Damian. His whole life he hated being compared to him. One-upping his father, however, did give him immense satisfaction. It was a family relative who had confided his father could not produce fangs and had punctured his mother's neck twice with a knife tip to form their bond, though he lied to everyone else about it. Now was not the time to rub that in, since he needed his father's cooperation.

"So, Dad. The key to the potion room?"

# CHAPTER 22

Before Bastian's foot hit the first step leading to the ornate church doors, he felt it. Power and love pulsed around the building and swept over him as he ascended the stairs. Many months had passed since Marius had forced him to go to church, which was usually the case since Bastian feared his dark spiral into the desolate world of hate and revenge might cross the line between good and evil. Now....

"Feels wonderful, doesn't it?" Gabriella smiled. "Aren't you glad we woke you up?"

"It feels... good," Bastian agreed, grudgingly. For a moment, it reminded him why he fought demons. He was still scowling about Aislinn leaving with that randy Earl Parker. Gabriella had assured him Earl would honor his claim, and return Aislinn safe and sound. But Aislinn was in a blood heat and should not have left. How could she go off with another man so soon after their lovemaking? Just the thought of her looking at Earl with desire made his blood curdle.

Marius had ordered him, loudly, to accompany him and Gabriella. Invoking divine assistance was one of the steps, so at least it was a worthy deterrent from him finding and killing Earl, and locking Aislinn in a room.

As they entered the chapel, disrobing from their sun-protecting coats, hats and gloves, a priest walked down the main aisle between the pews.

Gabriella wagged a finger at him. "You felt us coming."

"Actually," the priest replied, his face glowing with an uncanny serenity that Bastian had come to associate with one who kept company with God, "I dreamed about you early this morning, so my awareness was heightened a bit."

"Father Davis, this is Marius Brancusi, my husband, Prince of the Balkans, and Bastian Radescu, his cousin."

"Ah, the Balkan Heraclids." He shook their hands warmly.

"That's Heracleidae," Marius corrected.

Bastian sighed to himself. He did not know why Marius insisted on the old tongue. He was overly prudent about such oddities. They were descendants of Hercules, that was enough.

"You still use the ancient Greek pronunciation?" Father Davis looked surprised.

"Well, *my* tribe does."

There was a twinkle in Father Davis' eyes as he offered Marius a short, tolerant smile. "Come."

Gabriella knelt and made the sign of the cross at the front altar under a statue portraying the crucifixion. Marius followed and Bastian did the same. He felt a tingle in his skin. It was a subtle reminder that his dark side was not unnoticed. He took a deep breath, even more thankful that he had met Aislinn. Perhaps Providence had sent her to nudge him back into the light.

Father Davis led them down a hallway to a side room that was sparsely decorated with chairs and a prayer altar. "In my dream you said you came to fight an important battle. Is that why you are here today?"

"In part, Father," Marius answered. "We do indeed ask for your blessing and prayer of protection, on our persons as well as our weapons. However, we have another request that is now urgent." His eyes rested on Bastian.

Realizing Marius was giving him the option to speak for himself, Bastian stated, "I plead for divine protection for a woman I wish to claim."

Father Davis' brows rose. "I did not see that in the dream. Is she of us?"

"I believe so, Father," Bastian answered with conviction. "She has had no... adverse effects from our blood bond."

"So... you have *already* claimed her?"

"Yes, I confess it is true." Not only did Bastian dare not lie in a church, he suspected the priest was unusually perceptive.

"As a Heraclid, I assume you have the ability to bite...."

"Yes, Father. I do."

Bastian could feel Father Davis' eyes boring through him.

"She showed no ill effects?" asked Father Davis in a stern tone. "Did not get sick to her stomach? No weakness or fainting?"

"It was very little blood, Father. Although...." Bastian's heart clenched at thoughts of mentioning Edward's meddling. The priest needed to know the whole truth. Anger swelled in him like a volcano about to burst. It was the blood heat, and he knew it, but it was difficult to control since he did not *want* to control it. "Another Olympian tried to claim her, Father, after me, and exchanged his blood as well."

In a frown of disapproval, the priest's eyes widened. "And she was aware of the consequences?"

"No, Father. The vermin used a drug to subdue her."

Shock replaced the priest's frown.

"Believe me," Marius explained in a dark voice, "I would have stopped him had I known. We almost succeeded. But the deed had been done. So far, we do not perceive any damage to the girl, but this is the third day. As you know, problems tend to manifest by the third day."

"You are uncertain of her lineage, and she is affected by two blood bonds," Father Davis stated, "and she suffers no illness as of yet?"

"Well," Gabriella interjected, "except for being torn between two different men and the doubled emotions of two blood heats. Her senses and abilities *are* enhanced. Her psychic abilities hint toward a fairly strong and diverse bloodline, one we may have verified through her relatives. But, we still have concerns."

"Two different blood infusions. Two men claiming her." The priest's drew in his brows with concern. "Unprecedented. Very unfortunate."

"Yes," Bastian replied darkly. "Unfortunate that he survives."

The priest rested a harsh gaze on Bastian. "Your mission is to be a guardian and warrior, fighting against the forces of evil in order to protect, defend, and liberate humans, is it not, my son?"

"Yes, Father."

"I do not believe a rival Olympian falls into that category."

"That depends upon how you look at it, Father."

"You should not have risked another's life without being certain of her chances for survival," Father Davis chastised. "Nor should the other Olympian."

"I know," Bastian replied. "And I ask for forgiveness. But she is the one, Father. She has a heart that makes mine feel again. Makes mine good again. Without her I have no reason to live."

"You are doing God's work, my son. You have every reason to live."

Bastian shook his head. "Not without her. I will not last, Father. I will turn to…." *To darkness, and possibly be lost forever*, Bastian thought. He knew he was in trouble long before he met Aislinn. Andromeda had tried, but she had not been able to melt his heart, nor his ancient rage. Aislinn was unique. She truly *felt* him, and was not afraid. And… she was beautiful. Her soft, rounded, luscious body… *No, don't think about her body. Not here.*

Though Father Davis' face was grim and disapproving, a shrewd smile escaped before he snatched it back. "Let us ask for protection for her, that she not suffer, or perish, from the changes. And, that *you* not perish for risking her."

Bastian lowered his eyes. He felt like a child being scolded. "She will not die, Father. I am certain of it."

Bastian felt humbled as the priest blessed all three of them with holy water, read scripture, and invoked the protection of saints and angels. When the priest petitioned a special blessing and protection for Aislinn's blood, Bastian's shoulders dropped with relief.

~~◊~~

"Huh, that's weird." Aislinn yanked the contents of her purse out, depositing the items one by one into her lap.

"What's weird?" Earl asked.

"My folding-brush isn't here. Oh well. Must have left it upstairs."

"Hey, there's the hospital. Know what room she's in?"

"Yeah. 324."

"Kay, let's see what parking's like here. Whoa, here comes the rain!"

With rain pummeling the car, they circled several rows and finally got lucky when another car pulled out of the front row.

They laughed as they ran to the top of the stairs leading to the main entrance. Earl shook the water off his umbrella, then paused and squinted. "Hey, lookie there. I think that's Duncan."

"Oh, really?" Excited, Aislinn tried to follow his gaze through the gray drizzle. A tall, lean, brown-skinned man was jogging two rows of cars away. She recognized him, wishing he was closer so they could call out to him.

"It's him," she said. "I met him just yesterday. Wow, was it yesterday?" She shook her head in disbelief. "He's a relative of mine. Gramma said. I didn't know anything about him. Nobody ever mentioned any distant cousins or anything. Wish they had. Maybe he was here visiting Gramma again. Looks like he's headed for his car."

Earl turned to her. "He's an Olympian, Aislinn."

"Really? Ha! We're related." She pointed a finger at Earl. "See, that shows I have Olympian blood after all."

"Unless one of his parents carries the bloodline and simply married into your family."

"Hey!"

"I'm just saying." He shrugged to tease her. "His maternal grandfather's Egyptian, descended from the Olympians who moved to northern Africa. His grandmother's Moroccan. The other side is a mixture of European lines. I met him last year. But he's been gone on a mission for a while."

"I *knew* I saw a tattoo on his arm yesterday. You know, one that has that shiny gold sheen to it."

"Look." Earl waved an arm when Duncan turned his head toward the hospital entrance. "He's staring at us kinda strange."

Duncan raised his arm to wave, then his arm slowed and his smile changed to concern.

~~◊~~

The closer Eddie got to the hospital, the more certain he was that Aislinn was there. Hopefully, none of the Olympian's were. As he strolled down the wide hall, he watched Earl Parker exit room 324 and head toward the men's room.

*Crap.* Just what he needed. What if Aislinn had announced she was choosing the Heraclid? Eddie would have to plan his comments carefully. He licked his lips and walked forward.

A brown-skinned man was coming down the hall from the west elevators. *Duncan?* Eddie cursed under his breath. He was getting surrounded.

Earl paused at the men's room door and looked surprised as he noticed Duncan walking toward him. Earl waved and grinned. A familiar pang of jealousy burned in Eddie's chest. Stupid Appalachians were so buddy-buddy and goody-two-shoes. He had wanted acceptance in their world, but he had wanted his father's approval more. Why did he wait until now to question that choice?

Duncan spotted Eddie as he neared Alexsey Cardeia's room. Eddie brightened his expression as if glad to see him. *Double crap.* Now he'd have to go mingle. He flashed his most winning smile.

Though Duncan's expression was not warm, he offered his hand. Eddie shook it firmly, noting Duncan glancing around Eddie's head and shoulders in the same odd way he had before.

Earl turned, surprised. "Hey, Edward. What are you doing here?" He eyed the vase of yellow roses Eddie carried in his left hand.

Eddie pointed a thumb behind him, toward the plaque reading 324. "Just checking on the family again. I've known Aislinn's folks for a long time. We keep in touch. Her aunt and I are good friends. Is Gramma Cardeia doing better?"

"Yes." Earl and Duncan said at the same time.

"Great, I'm just going to run in and see her. Hey, what are you two doing here?"

"Keeping watch over Mrs. Cardeia." Duncan's response held a slight edge to it, one that Eddie did not appreciate. How could Duncan possibly know anything? He was an Olympian but not an empath as far as Eddie knew. Plus, Eddie was good at blocking his intentions. Concentrating on a single good thought was the key. No one ever looked beyond the initial reading. He was the only person he knew that could fool an empath.

"Oh. Great. Great." Eddie tried to sound enthusiastic.

"I'm guarding Aislinn," Earl offered. Earl's tone held no hidden meaning, but Eddie had the strange feeling that he had just been put on notice. They were probably on Bastian's side.

"Well, I'm going to go in and visit. Nice to see you both." Eddie turned and pushed through the wide door. He could feel positive energy radiating in the room. The old woman *was* better.

"Eddie, you're so sweet." Julia rushed forward to hug him. "Mama's doing so much better. Come and see."

Aislinn's shocked face had hardened by the time Eddie made it to Alexsey Cardeia's bed. He ignored Aislinn and focused on the old woman.

"Hi, Mrs. Cardeia. You look *much* improved."

"Thank you, Eddie." She said, her eyes flicking from Eddie to Aislinn, assessing the tension between them.

"Here. Brought these for you." Eddie placed the small vase of yellow roses on the side table. Mrs. Cardeia loved yellow roses and Eddie had gone to three stores before finding them.

"Why, thank you. That was very thoughtful." A slight smile escaped her, and Eddie grinned, hoping he looked genuine.

"You're very welcome." Eddie felt an electric, almost burning sensation standing so close to Aislinn, even though she was on the other side of the bed. His heart began pumping harder, his body heat rose, and he resisted the urge to shift his throbbing arousal to a more comfortable position within his restrictive blue jeans.

In his careful plans, the blood bond had been a way to hold onto her, but he had not considered what the blood heat would do to him. For so long he had worked to obtain the Olympian abilities. Now he was suffering for the one he had underestimated.

Putting on his best sad face and projecting wellbeing, he faced Aislinn. "I'm sorry for what I said earlier. You have a right to choose who you want, and your own direction in life. I just want you to be happy. Really. That's what friends are for. And, I'll always be your friend."

Aislinn's face lost some of its hardness. "Thanks. I appreciate that." Her voice was stiff, but her blue eyes flicked to his green shirt and then to the swell under his jeans. Eddie felt shivers of desire in his chest and additional pulsing in his groin. He watched Aislinn swallow and take a deep breath, her nipples peaking under the close-fitting mauve shirt. She could fight it all she wanted, but the blood heat was still intact for her as well. She was reacting to him.

Eddie had chosen his clothes carefully. He knew Aislinn had always liked the polo-style shirts on him, especially when they showed his physique and his tan. And she had always liked this particular pair of blue jeans.

Diverting his focus from his aching groin, he addressed Julia. "Julia, how are you holding up through all this?" She was one fan that never wavered. "You look like you haven't slept in days."

Aunt Julia blushed with delight at his concern. "I haven't. Truly I haven't." She wrung her hands, her voice becoming shaky and weepy. "It's just been a time, let me tell you. My arthritis has been acting up something awful, what with this rainy weather and all this going on. Poor Mama has had a time with pneumonia."

"Now Julia," Mrs. Cardeia admonished. "Make me sound like'a invalid, you will."

"Well, it scared us all to death, Mama," Julia admonished. "We're just glad to have you back. And Eddie's so sweet to come by and check on us. You're always welcome, Eddie."

"Thank you," Eddie answered, moved by her affection.

Aunt Julia beamed. "Well, it's going to be all fine *now*, of course. Dr. Bradley says Mama can come home tomorrow morning. Though, she'll be a might bit held up for a while. Just don't know if I can keep her in a wheelchair."

Eddie glanced playfully at Mrs. Cardeia. "That might just take an act of God."

"Oh, go on with you both," said Mrs. Cardeia. "It won't take no time for this mess to heal up. I've got things to do."

"Ha!" Eddie laughed. "I knew it." He waggled a finger. "You are going to be a terrible patient."

Mrs. Cardeia waved away his comment.

Eddie stole a glance at Aislinn. She had been quiet throughout his bantering with her family. Now, her stern look was softening even more.

Wanting her to assume he had given up on her completely, he turned his attention back to Aunt Julia. "Hey, listen, if you need anything tomorrow, you let me know, okay? I can drive you, help with the wheelchair, whatever. I'm happy to help."

"Thank you, Eddie." Aunt Julia smiled and squeezed his arm. "That's so sweet."

A blue-uniformed woman arrived with Mrs. Cardeia's lunch. Julia busied herself clearing off the utility tray. Eddie decided it was now or never.

"Aislinn, I'd like to give you something. Kind of a going away present, I guess." He pulled a black velvet box from his pocket.

Aislinn stared at the black velvet box as if it was a strange animal that might bite if she got too close. It was Julia who gasped when Eddie opened the lid. Eddie knew by Aislinn's silent, doe-eyed gaze that she liked the gold bracelet immediately. Any time they had walked by jewelry stores together she always stopped to ogle the charm bracelets. And this one was gold, a rarity in itself, since most of them were made with silver-colored metals.

"Oh, that's gorgeous Eddie." Julia clasped her hands together and giggled.

"Eddie, I… this is really nice, but… I really shouldn't." Aislinn gave him a flat smile.

"It's just about being friends." He shrugged and shook his head to dispel her worries. Then he gathered power, subtle and sensual, and speared it into her with his next words. "No matter what happens, people shouldn't give up on their friends."

Her lips parted. Her sky blue eyes seemed unable to look away from his.

Eddie dropped the box on the bed and extricated the bracelet. Brushing Aislinn's side as he stepped close gave him the opportunity to conduct more power into her, the blood bond giving him license. He slid his hand down her forearm, desired firing from his fingertips, and curled the bracelet around her wrist, latching it before she could protest.

"I don't want to forget the fun times we had," he said, his voice heavy with persuasion. "No matter what happens." He raised both brows in entreaty while she gaped at his audacity—and at the glittering bracelet.

*I'm sorry, Aisy. It was just the blood heat making me crazy. You know what that's like now, so... forgive me?*

Her sharp intake of breath was followed by indecision in her surprised gaze. He held that gaze with practiced persuasion. "Please, wear it for me? Please?"

For a split second, her eyes held a faraway look. She stared back down at the bracelet; then frowned as if growing confused.

"Come on," he urged softly, drawing on the passion of the blood heat, which he knew she could not deny. "Aislinn and Eddie, best buds forever, now and always, parting never. Please?" He pressed his hands together as if in prayer, forming a comical look on his face, waiting for that all important consent.

She blinked as if trying to focus. She smirked at his antics, noticing Aunt Julia acting giddy. "All right," Aislinn replied. "For now."

*Whew.* He smiled. *Done.*

# CHAPTER 23

Aislinn fought the urge to call out to Eddie as she watched him leave. A surprising lump formed in her throat. After telling him she did not want him in her life, she had assumed that the magic of the blood bond would dissipate. Yet, like an invisible cord connecting her heart and body to his, she felt the tug as he disappeared. It left her with a lonely ache.

"Hey, I need to get back." Earl poked his head into the room. "Sorry, I was out here talking to Duncan."

"Duncan?" Aislinn asked. "He was just here."

"Yeah, but he came back in. We were talking shop. You 'bout ready?"

"Oh, can't we stay longer?"

"Uh…." He pulled out his unlit phone, his gaze at her secretive. "I'm getting a call from… my boss to be back." He scratched his head to further indicate the call was telepathic. "We can come again tomorrow."

Bastian had spoken to her telepathically earlier, enraged that she had left with Earl. He told her he and Marius and Gabriella were going to see a priest, so she countered that everything had worked out anyway. He was probably now asking Cirillo to call Earl in order to get her back, assuming she wouldn't listen to him.

Aislinn reluctantly said her goodbyes to Gramma and Aunt Julia and promised to be there next morning to help take Gramma home. She gave a soft snort as Aunt Julia and Gramma giggled like school girls when they said their goodbyes to Earl, who kissed them both on the cheek.

*Guess the Olympians have that effect on all women,* Aislinn thought wryly.

"Are you okay?" Earl pressed the down arrow beside the elevator as they waited in the hall.

"Um, sure. Yeah." It was a lie, but Aislinn could not define the whirling emotions and dizzying thoughts she was having. She got sick the last time she was at this hospital. She was feeling sick again, but more of an unsettled and isolated feeling. The pull from Eddie's absence made her stomach hurt.

Low clouds darkened the sky, though the rain had slackened to a thick mist as they walked in silence to the car.

"Want to stop and get something to eat on the way back?" Earl asked as he opened her door.

"Yeah. No. I don't know."

Earl started the car and pulled out of the parking lot. "Well, which is it? Yes, no, maybe so?" He chuckled.

"Just, um, do what you want, Earl."

"Aislinn, you seem different. Ever since you came out of that room, you've not been yourself."

"Well, what *is* me?" she snapped.

"Uh, say again?"

"I mean, seriously, I've got alien blood running through my veins, probably readjusting all my DNA. I'm being told what to do, where I can go, when I have to leave, who I have to care about. These blood bonds are doing all kinds of weird things to my guts. I want to go to my apartment. I've got my purse and my keys. I can go back to Cirillo's and get my clothes later." *Never, is more like it,* she decided.

After a minute of silence, she stole a glance at Earl, who was frowning as he drove, looking older and more serious than he did before.

"Has your apartment been cleansed?"

"What do you mean, cleansed?"

"Aislinn, demons entered your apartment and Olympians battled them in your back yard. The area needs to be cleansed. I'll check to see if it's been done."

"Are you freaking kidding me? Another thing nobody told me?" Aislinn rolled her eyes.

"Even so, you have a blood bond with an Olympian, so maybe you should contact him and let him know what you're planning to do."

"Oh, great. One more person to tell me what to do. Can't wait."

Earl glanced at her, his brown brows drawn together. "I meant that he will be concerned about you. Don't you think he cares...?"

"Yeah, sure he cares! The blood bond forces him to, doesn't it? Just put me in shackles and flip me over his shoulder like a cave man. Then he can do whatever he wants to me. Well, for your information, I have two blood bonds. So what am I supposed to do with that? Where are all your precious rules now?"

After several minutes of driving and the windshield wipers tapping a steady beat, Earl spoke in a quiet voice. "I heard you dump Edward. Did I imagine that?"

"No. I don't know what got into me. It's not his fault. It was the blood heat affecting him. I mean, they both deserve a chance, right? Hell, maybe I'll just take both of them. Make some new rules up as I go along. That'll throw the almighty Olympians for a loop."

She crossed her arms, fighting anger that would not stop growing like the urge to vomit. Her face felt hot. Her stomach roiled. She rubbed her arms, trying to dispel the odd sensation of her veins being on fire. *Olympians.* Who did they think they were, anyway? Gods that can just do what they want, keep their secrets and feed them to her one by one? Poison her with their blood?

She was stuck with another Olympian driving her where she did not want to go. How did she let herself get into this situation? All these people were new to her. None of them should probably be trusted. Eddie had been with her for over a year. He had her best interest at heart. He had made mistakes, but… he stood by her no matter what. He was a reliable friend.

Still, she mused, Bastian was an excellent lover. She smiled like a cat, shrewd and self-absorbed. Maybe she still had use for him. Or, maybe she would just run away and see if they could find her. She needed to get away, that was for sure.

"Earl, I want to go to my apartment," she stated. "If we make a U-turn up here, we can get back on Asheville Highway, and…."

"We've been driving east on Hendersonville Highway, Aislinn." Earl took a deep, slow breath. "I'm not turning back. This is a bad idea."

"Why?"

"You have no protection there. Not to mention Bastian would be very upset with me."

"So. You're an Olympian, too. Just tear his head off."

"Aislinn!"

"What? It's what you guys do, isn't it?"

Earl's face became stern. "Not to each other."

"Ha. Bastian wanted to kill Eddie. Probably would have if precious Marius hadn't stopped him. Gotta stick to the *rules*," she mocked. "Rules, rules, rules. Always rules with precious Prince Marius."

"Aislinn, do you have a blood sugar problem? Like diabetes maybe?"

"What? No! Why would you even ask that?"

"Because a friend of mine has blood sugar problems and sometimes he's not quite himself when he hasn't eaten for a while. Why don't we stop at the next exit and get you something."

"Sure. Whatever. I don't care."

With so many customers at the brightly lit McDonald's, Earl opted for a side lot where several trees and bushes formed a barrier near an undeveloped piece of land. Aislinn watched with irritation as he began to stroke his arm, something all the Olympians at Cirillo's compound had done periodically. Thunder rumbled and the rain fell heavier.

"Not good," Earl muttered. "Come on, let's get inside where there's plenty of people."

"I don't want to be around anybody. All those freakin' emotions. Just get me something. I don't care."

"Aislinn, you need to come *with* me." Earl's piercing turquoise eyes scanned the people scampering through the parking lot in the rain.

"Oh, for heaven's sake." Aislinn threw open her door, caught herself before falling over a tree root, then slammed the door behind her. As she rounded the front bumper, an arm grabbed hers. She whirled and hit whoever it was in the face with her fist. Friend or foe, she did not care. She was in a mood to hit somebody.

To her horror, the head of the man lurched back, turned red, raw, and reformed as a human face.

Aislinn started to scream but was cut off when the man snatched her flying hair and pulled. Clawing at his hand to free her hair, she was surprised when he roared in protest and let go.

Earl had grappled him around the neck and was pulling him away from her. Like a deer, Earl jumped away to avoid the swinging arms of the enraged man, or whatever he was. His skin was like a liquid crystal screen that went solid after each movement.

Exposing two sets of fangs and sneering, the man lunged at Earl. Aislinn stood frozen. Rain pounded her face as she watched them fight, not knowing what to do. Just like Marius, Bastian and Dimitri, Aislinn recognized the smooth, calculated movements of a man trained for battle as Earl dodged the man's charges while slicing across his assailant's arms with a dagger.

Nails dug into Aislinn's shoulder. She cried out and recoiled, finding the red rimmed eyes of a woman and a mouth full of teeth descending on her. Aislinn spun and tripped over a decorative holly bush, the sharp branches and prickly leaves digging into her back and shoulder.

The woman was on top of her, mouth open wide. Aislinn rolled to dislodge her, flailing with her arms and legs, finding strength in her limbs she did not remember having. The woman's long, wet, dead-smelling hair was falling in Aislinn's face. Her nails were scraping her skin. The open mouth of sharp teeth kept aiming for her neck.

Enraged that someone else was trying to bite her, Aislinn squeezed both hands around the woman's throat and kneed her in the stomach.

"I am not... in the mood... for you!" Aislinn yelled through gritted teeth as she punched the floundering woman in the eye and head, energized by the storm of emotions rising in her. The woman twisted her head in an unnatural way and would have closed her teeth over Aislinn's wrist but her head snapped back as a brown, muscled arm dragged her by the hair.

The muscled arm belonged to Duncan.

Strangely beautiful despite her red-rimmed eyes and chalky-white skin, the woman screeched like an injured animal and began swiping claws at Duncan with a speed that defied Aislinn's ability to track the movements. Ducking and pivoting with grace and agility, Duncan avoided the nails while he pulled a narrow flashlight from his jeans pocket. It snapped open into a long shining blade on one end, and a wooden stake on the other. The woman hissed and growled as they struggled.

Unnatural fury seared through Aislinn and she rushed forward. Duncan was *her* relative, and that woman was not going to hurt him.

"No, Aislinn!" Duncan warned, but Aislinn was not listening to anyone today. She grabbed the woman's ragged black dress and attempted to pull her down. Aislinn felt weightless as the woman turned a complete circle and backhanded her, which flung her to the ground. Duncan grabbed the woman's hair and arm and threw her against the car in order to place his body between her and Aislinn.

The woman snarled and darted left and right to get to Aislinn, but Duncan matched her every movement. Aislinn vaulted to her feet, determined to be part of the fight.

"Aislinn, get back!" Duncan ordered, trying to shield her from the woman's extended neck and sharp teeth. He grunted when they sunk into his arm.

The high-pitched, unnatural sounds that came from the woman chilled Aislinn to the bone. The woman tore away from Duncan to aim teeth and claws at Aislinn's neck. Duncan pushed off the car and plunged the wooden end of the flashlight into the woman's chest. As the woman's mouth fell open in an eerie squeal, he smacked her face away from Aislinn. The cry pierced Aislinn's ears like a siren before the woman exploded into a cloud of gray dust, pieces of her sprinkling over them.

Duncan leaped past Aislinn to aid Earl.

"No! Stay with her!" Earl called out.

Duncan froze and backed up.

Aislinn watched Earl spiral and plunge his knife into the strange man. To her astonishment, the man threw Earl off of him and ran across the parking lot toward a line of woods that bordered the small shopping center.

"Should we finish him?" Duncan asked, concerned.

Earl shook his head. "It's an older demon. It's taken a human host. If I kill it, we'll have to call in our contact with the bureau to destroy the body. Too open here. Besides, they're clearly after Aislinn. I'm worried about waiting."

"You all right?"

Earl nodded. "Just small injuries. Oh. She got you, man."

Surprised, as if he had forgotten, Duncan spied streams of blood dripping down his shirt sleeve. "Aw, man!" He stamped his foot and jerked his arms in disgust. "That poison's gonna make me sick."

"Come with us to the compound. Bastian's there. Dimitri says he can heal again. Probably faster than Ma Beatie. Well, it's still daytime, but the storm will help. Glad to see you, by the way. How'd you know?"

Duncan grimaced before answering Earl. "I see auras."

"Oh, yeah, I forgot about that! Barry told me and I forgot."

"When I saw you at the hospital, I saw a dark shadow hovering above you and I knew you were about to fight evil. So I followed you in. Then I saw Edward and he had weird muddy shades and darkness around him. Overhead, the colors were swirling like a full on battle was going on."

Aislinn frowned. "What do you mean?"

"Nothing happened inside," Duncan continued, evading her question. "So when you left, I followed you in the car."

"Why didn't you just tell me?" Earl asked.

Duncan wiped his stake in the wet grass and retracted the blades. "I've learned to not tell people about their auras until I know what they mean. Makes people uncomfortable. Plus...." He stared at Aislinn, his brilliant golden eyes darting around her. "When you left, she had dark gray and black bands circling around her, like a net. Never seen it before."

"Like what?" Aislinn demanded. *Something else? Something new that no one wanted to tell her?*

"Colors of evil mixed with colors of good," Duncan explained. "But like in rings, fighting for space. Closing in. Is there something you want to tell us, Aislinn?"

Thunder blasted above them, forestalling the insult Aislinn was preparing to throw at him.

"Let's get out of the rain," Earl suggested. "I need to get her something to eat. She needs food."

"I do not," Aislinn protested, crossing her arms.

"Yes, you do. Duncan, get in the back seat. I got some shirts. We'll wrap your arm."

Aislinn sat in the car, disgusted, angry, and dripping on the interior. Oddly, she did not feel cold. She watched as Earl spit into a handful of mud, then joined Duncan in the back seat to plaster the gooey mess over Duncan's teeth-punctured arm. Duncan's tattoos had a golden-coppery sheen and flickered like fine glitter against his brown skin as he donned a white T-shirt."

"You okay to drive?" Earl asked.

"No problem. It'll take at least an hour for the poison to affect me. Then I might eat you."

"Ha. Very funny. Let me give you some of my blood. It will stave off the infection." Earl shoved his wrist in front of Duncan's mouth.

Duncan closed his eyes and his lips parted, displaying elongating fangs. When Duncan closed his mouth over Earl's wrist, Aislinn said, "Ew, gross," and turned around in her seat.

"Thanks," said Duncan after mere seconds.

"No, you need more," Earl insisted.

"No. I'm not taking any more. You might need it if we run into more trouble. It's an hour's drive."

Aislinn turned to see Earl licking his own wrist to close the wound. Duncan looked slightly euphoric as he rested his head back onto the seat. Aislinn recognized that look. Even in her confused state, she realized what a boon an Olympian blood infusion must be after being wounded. At least that part made sense.

"All right, let's go to the drive-through so I can get Aislinn something," said Earl. "You go in front on the way to Cirillo's so I can be sure you're okay."

"We're going to my apartment," Aislinn corrected.

"Hell no, we're not." Earl's expression was angry and firm.

"Oh, come on, Earl," Aislinn whined.

Earl's turquoise eyes turned to ice, his jaw clenching. "How many more demons do we have to kill for you?"

Aislinn shrunk into her seat. It occurred to her that she could see anger in Earl's fiery gaze, but did not feel it. Nothing emanated from Duncan, either. Wordlessly, she turned around, pondering the absence of her ability to detect emotion, wondering if it was a good thing, or a bad thing.

Earl ordered her a burger, which Aislinn took three bites of only because he refused to leave the restaurant parking lot until she did. She wasn't hungry. After ten minutes she stared in surprise at the empty containers in front of her. She could not remember eating. Or drinking. She rubbed a hand over her face. Maybe the Olympian blood *was* making her sick. Bastian's or Eddie's? Maybe she should call Eddie.

The warble of a phone caught Aislinn's growing auditory senses even amidst the roar of the highway and the incessant rain pounding like shards of glass on the car.

"Hey," Earl spoke into his cell phone. "Yes, we're on our way back. Me and Duncan just fought a possession demon and a vampire. At least I think it was a vampire. Not sure what she was."

"Anybody injured?" asked a voice that sounded like Duke.

"Just some cuts for me. Duncan got bit by the vamp, though. Need to get him healed."

A tractor trailer passed and Aislinn could not hear Duke's response.

"Yeah, we kicked butt," said Earl. "Had to let the demon go. Had a human body. I notified Cirillo, so he's arranged to get security cameras wiped. Didn't want to stick around and wait for cleanup. Duncan got the vamp, though." He paused. "Yes, she's fine. Well, sort of."

Several voices began talking at once through the phone and Aislinn had trouble distinguishing between them even though she was concentrating on hearing what they might be saying about her.

"All right. All right. Aislinn, Bastian wants to talk to you." He held out his phone.

"What's he doing awake? I don't want to talk to him right now."

"Are you sure?"

"Of course I'm sure!"

"Okay, don't bite my head off." He placed the phone back to his ear. "Duke, she… oh, sorry Bastian, she says she doesn't want to talk right….." Earl had to hold the phone away to protect against Bastian's raging voice with a sharper than normal German accent. Earl held the phone toward Aislinn in entreaty.

"I *said* I don't want to talk to him." Aislinn resisted the urge to grab the phone and throw it out the window, baffled by the intensity of the desire. As her arm muscles tightened in frustration, the urge to defy Earl and the rest of the Olympians grew.

Earl put the phone to his ear. "Bastian, we'll talk to you when we get to the compound. Aislinn isn't feeling well right now."

Bastian's deep voice softened and Aislinn could not make out his words.

"I don't know," Earl replied defensively. "I don't see any injuries or anything. Aislinn, did the vampire scratch or bite you?"

"Would everybody just leave me the hell alone!" *What is wrong with these people? Somebody get me out of here.*

"Bastian, we'll be there in forty minutes. Tell Ma Beatie to be ready." Earl dropped his phone into the console.

*Aisy, are you okay?*

*Eddie? Is that you?*

*Hey, I felt you getting upset. I got worried. Is everything okay?*

*No, it is not okay. I have got to get away from these people. And demons came after me again. I feel like I'm in the middle of a nightmare. Why is this happening to me?*

*Sweetie-girl, I'm so sorry. It could be because those Olympians are a target. As long as you're with them, you'll have problems. I can come get you if you want. I don't owe any allegiance to them.*

*Okay, tonight. I'm not staying another night. I want to go home. My bags are ready.*

*Okay Aisy,"* Eddie replied, his mental tone laced with understanding and sympathy. *"I'll check with you in a little while. Just call out to me any time. I'll hear you.*

Aislinn sighed, then realized Earl was staring at her. She rolled her eyes. "Do all you people drive without actually looking where you're going?"

"Aislinn, I need you to tell me everything that happened in that hospital room."

"Nothing happened." She flapped an arm.

"Edward was there."

"Eddie is my friend."

"Okay." Earl's face hardened and he focused on the road.

They rode in silence for the remainder of the trip until Earl pulled onto the graveled drive leading to the compound.

A cold, stinging sensation like sharp, icy needles scraped over Aislinn.

"Ow! What the…." She examined her arms to see if they were wet or bleeding. The air felt different, energized. "What was that? Did you feel that?"

"That's the wards. They protect the compound from demons… and things. You felt it this time?"

"Yeah. Weird. Like… stinging ants. Ugh." Aislinn did not like the suspicious look on Earl's face.

"Come on in." Earl's voice no longer held the friendliness she had come to enjoy.

*Fine,* she thought. *You can all turn against me. I still have Eddie.*

# CHAPTER 24

Hating every step, and resisting the urge to turn and run, Aislinn followed Earl up the wide wooden porch steps into the expansive house, followed by Duncan. A million eyes were on her, in a semicircle. She froze, staring at the crowd. Silence hung heavy in the crammed foyer. She pulled her wet hoodie close around her.

Bastian stepped forward. Dressed in a white shirt and blue jeans, his tall, well-built frame loomed in front of her. His silver eyes looked cold, dangerously tinted pink at the edges.

"You did not answer me." His tone sounded calm, but lightening crackled above the house, making Aislinn flinch.

"Yeah, well, maybe I didn't feel like talking to you." She glanced at the waiting faces, all tainted with mistrust.

Bastian shook his head slowly, recapturing her focus. "You could not *hear* me. Just like you cannot hear me right now, can you?"

Aislinn crossed her arms. She heard nothing. In fact, she felt nothing. Not a single emotion crossed her awareness, though the room was full of Olympians with intense expressions. In five years, she had not experienced a single moment absence of external emotions, even from neighbors. It was everywhere, like an invisible crowd that followed her, calling out words and feelings that were not her own. She had learned to accept the noise and taught her mind to ignore the ramblings. But this was like being in an empty cell far underground, with no living thing for miles.

"What did you people do to me?"

No one answered. They seemed to be collectively waiting. Fear snaked through her veins.

"And *you*," Aislinn addressed Bastian, "aren't *saying* anything."

"Actually, I am," he stated flatly. "Something's blocking our bond."

Someone in the crowd moved a leg. A long, exposed leg, topped by a short black skirt.

Andromeda. Aislinn felt anger rise as she viewed the sharp, pretty face that held disappointment, distain, and vane hope. Andromeda had just better stay away from her men. Expecting the anger to grow, instead it fizzled to annoyance. Then she felt nothing. No anger. No rivalry. She had lost the desire to challenge Andromeda. How had these people changed her? Had Bastian's blood caused this?

"You know what? I'm leaving." She grabbed the banister at the foot of the stairs and pushed past two people, anxious to make it upstairs and retrieve her suitcases.

Like a nimble-footed deer, Dimitri leapt to the staircase, blocking her access. "Aislinn, please listen to me for a minute. Something's wrong with the way you're acting. I'm worried about you."

"Dimitri, I need to get away from all this and go home. I'm done. All right? I'm just done."

Dimitri impeded her progress with his arms. Bastian mounted three steps, stopping beside her.

"And if either of you tries to follow me," she pointed a finger at.each of them, "I'm calling the police."

Bastian grabbed her wrist. "Aislinn, do not…."

"How dare you!" Aislinn tried to pull her arm from his grasp, swinging the other fist to hit him, which he deftly grabbed mid-air. She jerked her arms backward with all her strength, using her body weight, finding her muscles to be stronger than ever, making him work to hold onto her.

When she pulled one wrist free, Eddie's bracelet flew through the air and crashed to the floor, beads and charms going in several directions.

"Now, look what you've done! That was a present from…." Aislinn fought to keep the room from moving. She brought a hand to her forehead, and swayed. She looped her arm over the banister for support.

"Well, now," said Ma Beatie, hands on hips, looking down. "How 'bout that?"

Aislinn watched the beads still wobbling. Three of the round charms were smoking. Like discarded, lit cigarette butts, gray smoke wafted in thin streams above the three shiny beads.

"Father Davis invoked a blessing on this house three days ago. Sprinkled holy water, too." Her eyes rose to Aislinn's. "You've been spelled, girl."

Aislinn felt a shiver run through her. What did that mean? One by one, the emotions of each person began to materialize into her awareness, suspicion, worry, concern, fear, like attendees at a hearing filing into a courtroom. The weight of their feelings grew heavy making her claustrophobic.

Bastian's ghostly eyes radiated fury. "Where did you get this?"

When she did not answer, Earl did. "Edward gave it to her. That's it, isn't it, Aislinn? That's what changed. He gave you that in the hospital room, didn't he? While I was out in the hall."

Aislinn stared at him. She could not move. Not only was she still dizzy and felt like her brain was shifting in and out of dimensions, the enormity of the implications was too much for her to process. No, Eddie was her friend. Wasn't he? She'd been thinking all the way home how he was her only friend. Besides, Eddie didn't know anything about spells. Did he?

*Aislinn, who gave this to you?* Bastian's question pierced her mind.

"Oh my gosh, I heard you," she exclaimed, one hand going to her mouth. "But, how…?"

"Did Edward give this to you?" Bastian's voice sounded deceptively calm as he lowered his chin. She felt something greater than anger emanating from him. It became a purpose, a resolve, growing so fast it was fierce and frightening. Thunder crackled above the house again, making the lights blink.

"Yes," she whispered.

"Marius," Bastian said without taking his eyes from Aislinn. "I am going to kill that man."

Aislinn's body began to shake. She slid down the railing and spokes and landed on a step.

"Not until he is officially judged, Bastian," said Marius. "I will call for a trial."

"I will not wait that long."

Aislinn glimpsed Bastian's fangs as he gritted his teeth, evidence of his rage.

"Then I will command you to stay by my side until the trial convenes."

"That will not matter."

"I will compel you."

"It will not work."

"Beatie." Cirillo stepped forward. "Would you get us a bowl to put these beads in? I want Barry and Violet working on them. Let's find out what Edward put in 'em. Earl, I want you checked for wounds. Duke, Nathan, take Duncan to the clinic downstairs. Bastian? We have a warrior to save. I am asking for your assistance."

When Bastian did not move, his eyes still fixed on Aislinn, Marius raised his voice. "Bastian! Duncan has little time left. Do not abandon your mission."

Reeling from Bastian's violent, internal struggle, and her own confusion, Aislinn knew she had to do something. He would not leave her, not this time.

"Go," she spoke in a soft voice. "Help Duncan."

Bastian's chin lifted and his eyes narrowed. New emotions warred inside him. What if she left while he was gone? What if she was unguarded? What if it was a ploy?

*I will be here when you're done,* she assured him telepathically, though she was not certain that statement was true. *Go.*

Wordlessly, Bastian turned and headed for the library, his long legs stiff, one hand resting on his right pocket where she knew he kept his sword hilt.

Aislinn slumped forward and dropped her head into her hands. People, voices and movement rose in the foyer like a disturbed fire ant nest. Emotions and conversations filled her head. Whispers of telepathic conversations brushed across her synapses like nail files in the dark.

She heard Duncan's loud protest that he could walk just fine as several warriors began hoisting him toward the library where, Aislinn assumed, they would descend the hidden stairs to whatever secret rooms were housed down there.

Earl began reporting the details of the battle to Cirillo and other interested listeners. Ma Beatie, Barry, and a pretty woman with tan skin and curly black hair were retrieving the pieces of the bracelet with tweezers and spoons, placing them in glass bowls. They spoke in low but excited tones about the possible spells used and how best to dissect and destroy the pieces. Aislinn's body jerked with each clink of the beads into the glass bowls as if they were miniature grenades exploding.

"Hey." Gabriella placed a gentle palm on Aislinn's arm and sat beside her on the stairs. Aislinn closed her eyes, accepting the serenity that flowed through Gabriella's gifted hands. "I'm just double checking. Is that the only thing Edward gave you?"

Aislinn nodded, staring at the beads and the chattering women.

"Did he utter any rhymes or poems, anything that might sound like an incantation?"

"What? No."

"Are you sure? Think back. Anything that sounded like a poem or a statement."

Aislinn puzzled over the question, then shook her head. "Just, something about us being friends forever. It was kinda like a rhyme, I guess."

"Did he ask you anything that you consented to?"

"Not really. He apologized and said he wanted the best for me." She examined her memory of the short conversation. "When he was putting the bracelet on me, he said something, and then 'please,' like asking if I would accept it, I think."

"There it was," said Gabriella.

"There *what* was?"

Gabriella took a deep breath. "Consent."

"I didn't consent to anything!" Aislinn's voice squeaked.

"Okay. It's okay." Gabriella rubbed Aislinn's arm with tenderness. "There is something you need to say to throw off any remaining effects of the spell."

Aislinn stared at her in disbelief.

"Something simple but powerful. Say, 'By the power of God, I choose to be free from this spell. I am now free to choose my destiny.'"

"I... what?"

Concern wrinkled Gabriella's red brows. "If you wish to be free of the spell, state it, Aislinn. Your words have power, and you are calling on power."

"But... who am I talking to? God? Why would I...?"

"Everyone, everything, God, yourself. It's a declaration. Like a prayer. You will learn to understand it."

Aislinn rubbed her face. "All right, what was it again?"

"By the power of God, I choose to be free from this spell. I am now free to choose my destiny. I am free. I am free. I am free. Repeating it three times reaffirms your intention and request."

Feeling self-conscious, Aislinn repeated the phrases. She was surprised when she felt lighter.

Gabriella smiled. "Good girl. Repeat it again if you find yourself thinking in ways that you did while you were under the spell. Are you injured in any way?"

"No. I need to be alone for a while. I think I'm going to be sick."

"Let's go upstairs."

Gabriella led the way to Aislinn's room. Aislinn stopped in the middle of the room, unable to decide what to do next.

"What's that funny smell?" Gabriella asked. "Are you sure you're not injured?"

"No! I mean, yes. Sorry. My emotions are all messed up."

"Do you want to talk about it?" Gabriella asked. "It might make you feel better."

Aislinn exhaled. "I think I just need to be alone for a while. No Olympians. No blood. No spells."

"Okay. That I can do." Gabriella closed the door behind her.

A shower sounded like a good idea. The bed looked better. Aislinn dropped onto the quilted bed and curled into a ball, not caring that her clothes were still soaked, and her shoulder was burning.

~~◊~~

Fitful dreams plagued Aislinn. She woke several times, shaking, but fell back into another dream again. Faces. Teeth. Hairy creatures with red eyes.

She was stalking people, scenting their blood. Through dark rooms, hideous creatures with clown masks were laughing, aware she could not escape them.

"Aislinn, wake up," said a deep voice. Fingers were stroking her hair. A hand was shaking her shoulder. "Aislinn, wake up."

She woke with a start. She was shivering, bathed in sweat, and itchy from the damp clothes. Bastian's worried face was close to hers. He seemed out of focus.

"I don't feel good." she mumbled. "Leave me alone. I need to sleep."

"You were having a bad dream. What is that smell?"

Aislinn lifted her head and scowled. "What smell?"

Bastian hovered over her, moving his nose from the left to the right. Before Aislinn could register what he was doing, he pulled her hoodie off her shoulder.

"You got scratched," he declared.

"No I didn't."

"Yes, you did. In fact...." He tore the silky mauve sleeve off her shoulder and she scowled at his roughness, trying to push his arm away. "I smell poison. I think you got bit. Just cracked the skin."

"Well, no surprise there. Everything here bites me." Aislinn expected an angry glower from him, and did not care when she received it. "You're tearing my shirt."

"Be still. Let me heal you."

"I'm fine." She jerked her shoulder away.

"No, you are not."

"Yes, I am."

"You are not."

"Yes, I am."

"Aislinn, we are not doing this again. I know that smell. You have been infected."

"Yeah, well, I've been infected by everybody," she snapped. "What's new?" She sounded like a petulant child, but she did not care.

Bastian lowered his head and brushed her lips. "My lady, what do you desire?"

Taken off guard by his abrupt change in tone, she pondered his inappropriate question. His full lips kept kissing her face in various spots. Soft beams of moonlight wafted through the curtains. With her new clarity of vision, she should be able to see him, but he was a blur.

"Do you desire touching?" His velvety voice warmed her like hot cocoa. "Or..." he purred. "Can you smell my blood? Just under the skin? Smell it, Aislinn."

Without thinking, she inhaled deeply. His male scent made her smile. So did his blood. How interesting. Like tantalizing, rushing tendrils of life, the pumping veins smelled sweet, even sensual. That was definitely new.

"Mmm." She curled toward him.

"Yesss," he purred. "You want to taste, don't you?" His fingertips brushed across her jawline, down her neck, and across her color bone. Her skin tingled under the light touches.

"Mmm, hmm," she murmured.

"Close your eyes." Like silk brushing over her body, his voice chanted. "Be still. Wait for it. Be very, very still. Then you can taste. Be so still."

Like delicious sunlight, warmth flowed into her shoulder. A warm hand was heating her skin. Some spots were tingling, almost stinging. Her blood began to burn. She grunted under the assault and squirmed. Then she began to struggle. Just as she became frantic, joy, like children's laughter, the cool sweetness of flowers, the mist of summer clouds, flowed through her limbs and she felt whole.

She opened her eyes as the wholeness dissipated.

"Better?" Bastian was smiling as though he had experienced the same sensation.

"Yes. Much."

His smile broadened as the back of his fingers brushed along her cheek. "My poor lady. So much has happened to you."

"I told Dimitri not one more thing could happen. That was a couple days ago. I think. I've lost track."

Bastian closed his lips over hers, gentle and loving. This time she responded, and reveled in the blend of physical and emotional reactions they both felt. She had missed that. She frowned as he pulled away.

"I need to make love to you so that you are too tired to go anywhere." He stood, placing his hands on his hips. "I think it is the only way I can keep an eye on you. You keep getting into trouble."

"Hey." She tried to sit up. "You healed me, didn't you?"

"Yes."

"I thought you couldn't do stuff like that during the day."

"It is near dawn, my lady. You slept through the night."

"Oh." She glanced at the dark window. "How did I sleep so long? And, what was all that stuff about blood?"

"It was a way to get you still and focused. You were infected by a vampire, the demon kind. It made you want blood. Plus, because of our bond, when you think of my blood, you will desire it."

"Seriously? Totally gross, Bastian."

"Mmm-hmm." He reached out a long arm and brushed back her matted hair with his fingers.

Aislinn pressed her lips together, angry that his ploy had worked. Why that should bother her, she did not know. At this point, she did not know what to feel, or why. "Hey, why aren't *you* angry anymore? I mean… after… everything that happened?"

"Healing takes concentration on good energy. Positive feelings. I have to put myself in that state of mind. Frau Beatie could have healed Duncan with her herbs and medical knowledge. She has some healing skill as well, like mine. But I suspect Cirillo and Marius knew I would have to forget my anger in order to heal. It took me several minutes to get there for Duncan." He leaned forward, but stopped, crinkling his face. "And right now my Olympian nose cannot tolerate that shirt."

"Hey!" She slapped his arm.

He pulled her from the bed. "Let's take a shower."

"Let's? As in both of us?" She staggered to her feet. "Oh no you don't."

"Yes." He pulled her close.

"No."

"Yessss."

The hypnotic purr in his voice was tempting, especially beside her ear.

"Are you trying to use persuasion on me again, Mr. Radescu?"

"Hmm, what a wonderful idea, Miss Thomas."

His broad hands were roaming over her back and hips sending delightful shivers up her spine.

"That's *Ms.* Thomas to you, Olympian. You're in America now."

He chuckled and gripped her waist, flattening her body against his.

"I'll call you whatever you like," he whispered, his breath hot against her cheek. He pressed a kiss into the curve of her jaw and neck.

"My lady, then," she replied.

"My lady," he murmured, and reclaimed her lips.

Quicker than she wanted, he ended the kiss and steered her toward the door. She felt oddly conflicted about the kiss, almost guilty. Just hours before, she was ready to run away with Eddie.

"I'm not going down the hall to the bathroom with you. People will see us."

"Then people will know you have chosen me."

Aislinn reeled from the statement. Fear clutched at her heart. Her thoughts and desires *had* been affected by whatever Eddie put in the bracelet, and part of her still remembered those feelings.

*By the power of God, I choose to be free from any spell. I am now free to choose my destiny. I am free. I am free. I am free,* she chanted in her head. She wondered if she should be making any decisions right now. She had been so ready to claim Bastian, and then ready to claim Eddie. Now, she was reluctant to claim anyone. Perhaps it was best if she pulled away from Olympians altogether.

Bastian's eyes narrowed. "That spell has you still."

"No, it doesn't *have* me. I just... I don't know... everything feels weird now."

"I cannot vait to kill zat man." His accent sharpened with his stab of anger.

"Shhh." She placed two fingers over his lips. "Don't say that."

"You wish to preserve him?"

"No. I wish to preserve you."

"You think that vermin has a chance of besting me?"

"No, I think Marius is going to lock you up, or something."

A slight grin toyed at his lips. "That is a distinct possibility."

As their eyes melted into each other's, he opened his mind and soul to her, reaching for assurance. She allowed him to see that she truly did not want an altercation between him and Marius, nor did she wish him to get into trouble by turning vigilante before the trial. The confusing, leftover feelings for Eddie, she blocked.

"Don't go running off and killing anybody, please Bastian? If you get into trouble, what am I going to do?"

He sighed, looking over her face as if memorizing it. "You are wise."

"Humph." She snorted. "Not wise enough. I don't know anything about your world. How was I supposed to know Eddie could put a spell on me with a bracelet? Bastian, I need to know this stuff."

"You will learn." He tried to smooth her tangled hair. "Come. Let's get you washed up."

"Hey, I'm not going in there with my clothes on." She tore off her hoodie and dropped it to the floor. "Wait a minute. I don't have a robe, and we have to go down the...."

He swooped her into his arms, ignoring her squeals and protests, and tramped down the empty hall, closing the bathroom door with his foot.

When her feet hit a fuzzy throw rug, she scowled at him. Examining his hopeful face and his chiseled physique as he unbuttoned his shirt was her undoing. Her mouth watered as he removed his shirt, exposing every taut muscle.

She surprised them both by pulling her shirt over her head. Noting the sensuous gleam in his eyes as they rested on her bra, she slowed down to take it off. The fire igniting her skin reminded her how fast the blood heat could kick in. It was so strong she didn't know if she would be able to take the time to undress.

Bastian's breathing quickened as the bra fell to the floor. Aislinn opened all her empathic sensors to draw in his reactions. It was much more fun than just feeling her own. She didn't feel *that* kind of thrill when she looked at her breasts.

His entire body quivered with anticipation and desire. The knowledge charged her like a battery. She unbuttoned her jeans and grabbed the waistband.

Bastian's chest was heaving short breaths, his lips parting as his silvery eyes roamed her body.

"You took my clothes off once before," she taunted. "When I was at the chalet in Romania. Gabriella said it was telekinesis. It's nighttime now."

A slow smile spread across his handsome face. "What if I want them to come off slowly?"

She smiled sideways.

"I have healed two people, one of them you," he said, his eyes twinkling. "Why waste precious energy." His breathing steadied, his eyes on the rim of her blue jeans, waiting.

Not the reaction she wanted. "Wait, are you telling me you can't do it because you healed people?"

"It takes a lot of energy to heal. But not so much that I cannot manage to remove your clothes if you wish." He raised one eyebrow.

"Huh. Forgot about that little detail. Well, you still have muscles. Lots and lots of …."

He removed his own blue jeans. Unable to wait, she dropped hers. The shock in his face at sight of his boxers on her changed when she dropped those just as fast. With a triumphant gleam, he reached for her. She wagged a finger, then took his hand. With the other, she turned on the water.

She felt his warm hand massaging her buttock. He pressed his erection against her backside and groaned. Which gave her a new idea for their time in the shower. She turned and stepped into the hot spray of water, then halted, realizing Bastian's hand had frozen on hers. His eyes were unfocused, staring past her.

She was about to blurt, "Well, are you coming?" but paused when wrinkles of concern crossed his chiseled features.

"What is it?" she prompted. One side of her was getting cold where the hot water wasn't hitting.

With regret, his reflective eyes met hers. His mouth flattened in anger. "I am needed."

"Now?"

"Yes. They brought in someone else who has been badly injured. Demonic wounds. Their best healer is in the hospital having a baby. Frau Beatie is asking for assistance."

"Their healer's a woman?"

"Yes. Take your shower. Things are happening. We may have work to do." He donned only his blue jeans, having trouble fitting the zipper around his male parts that were not ready to be disappointed.

"Work… what does that mean?" she asked.

But he had left the bathroom, shutting the door behind him.

"Okay, guess I'll take a shower," she mumbled toward the walls. "Alone."

~~◊~~

*Aisy-girl? I haven't heard from you. Are you okay?*

Aislinn gasped. Hot water sheeted over her face as she stood with her mouth agape.

*Aisy? Were you asleep? I couldn't reach you for hours. I can feel you now but I'm not hearing you. You said you wanted me to come get you. I'm worried. It's late. Just say the word and I'm there. I'll meet you outside the compound. Tell them you're going for a walk. Or don't tell them anything.*

Anger snaked through Aislinn's limbs and coiled in her gut, ready to strike. Her muscles and fists tightened. The blaze of fury threatened to burst from her. Any moment it was going to. The audacity of him putting a spell on her. Tricking her. She wanted to scream at him and just keep screaming.

Barely containing the combusting energy, she spoke, her mental words slow and distinct. *You put something in the bracelet. How dare you. Who the hell do you think you are?*

Eddie was silent. She felt his fear growing.

*What have they told you?* he asked. *You know they want to keep us apart. They'll tell you anything to keep you on their side, with their man. Don't get sucked into it, Aisy. You belong with me.*

Aislinn could not contain the explosion of righteous fury any longer. She screamed as hard as she could, sending the stinging, synaptic missile straight at him.

*Get out! Get out! I hate you!*

The jolt of pain that hit Eddie was satisfying. Pain was followed by rage. Wherever he was, he was yelling and throwing things.

Aislinn projected a mental wall so Eddie could not get back in. Her mind was becoming stronger. She stood panting, her hands pressed to the sides of her head, leaning on the wet wall. She had to learn how to master these new connections and intrusions. The bathroom door flew open with a bang. She let out a squeak and nearly slipped in the tub.

The curtain flew open, assaulting her with cold air. Bastian's tall frame blocked the light over the mirror, giving him a magical glow but casting his silhouette in shadow. His silver-gray eyes glinted with wrath.

"What happened?" he demanded through gritted teeth.

Aislinn backed up into the hot spray to deflect the cold air, though watching his angry face was oddly erotic.

"Eddie," she answered. "He realized I was no longer under the influ–... that the spell wasn't working any more. He was pleading with me to leave here and let him pick me up. I got so angry I just... blew up and screamed at him to go away."

Bastian's fist tightened on the shower curtain, snapping one of the plastic circles. "It was heard by many."

"Oh. Really? Sorry," she apologized in earnest. "I just wanted him out of my head."

"I will get him out of your head." Bastian stepped into the tub, engulfed her in his arms, and sunk his teeth into her neck.

Aislinn gasped at the puncture of his fangs, the stinging discomfort quickly forgotten when her limbs began turning to butter from the languorous sensations spreading through them.

Every inch of her skin came alive, becoming more sensitive to the spray of the hot water and the brush of his blue jeans against her pelvis, even the coldness of the metal button against her stomach. Nothing mattered but the delicious rapture dancing inside and over her like melted honey and chocolate.

Bastian's bite was aggressive, sucking hard at her neck.

With a groan, he withdrew his fangs and swiped her neck with his tongue. As the endorphins began to diminish, she realized he was holding onto her with one arm, and removing his blue jeans with the other. She would have helped him, but felt so drugged she did not want to move. He kicked the wet blue jeans to the back of the tub.

Hot and hard, his erection throbbed between them as he crushed her soft curves against his naked body. Instead of being repulsed by his roughness, her soul leapt with joy, the blood heat making every place their skin touched feel like tiny explosions.

His lips closed over hers. They kissed hard and fast. His tongue plunged into her mouth, triggering sparks of delight through her body. She wrapped her arms tighter around his shoulders, digging her hands into every muscle. She wanted to claim every inch of him.

Bastian pivoted to shelter Aislinn's face from the hot spray of water before he reluctantly released her lips with a luscious pull of her bottom lip. Raising a hand and extending his nails, he pierced two sharp points into his own neck.

"Aislinn... now, my love. Before he can stop us." His husky voice could not be denied. He had not used persuasion. She did not need it. She ached at the sound of his voice as much as the touch of his body.

Everything about him, the alien eyes, the stubble on his firm jaw, his wet, straw-colored hair, was like a magnet she wanted to absorb. Two streams of blood were traveling down the right side of his neck.

She did not hesitate. She clamped her mouth to his neck and imbibed. He groaned loudly, cradling her in his arms. The blood was hot and tasted sweet and coppery, not foreign like it had before. Their exchange of blood felt decadent, a forbidden fruit, all the more exciting. And now it was too late for Marius to stop them.

She did not care if they got into trouble. His blood made her stronger. She could feel her body accepting its ethereal coding. It did not hurt or damage her as Marius had feared. Instead of making her feel sick, she felt energized. Her body—her new altered body—knew what to do.

Sparks flashed behind her eyes. She rubbed her slick, naked body against Bastian's, one hand behind his neck to keep her mouth latched to it. Her skin, her muscles, her brain tingled and vibrated with delight. Bastian's blood was like ingesting a fast-acting drug, something illegal and expensive. *Olympian blood.*

~~◊~~

Bastian grasped Aislinn's buttocks and lifted her to his throbbing manhood. Parting her delicious wet folds, he rocked her onto his tip, enjoying her groans of pleasure. She was so perfect for him. Her soft, curvaceous body was made for his. Her empathic mind would always be there to calm his dark, vengeful soul. Her courage would always be a match for his. From this day forward he would keep her so satisfied, neither Edward, nor any other man, would be anything but a dim memory.

Aislinn moaned louder as he pressed deeper. Bastian's moans matched hers, lost in the sweet warmth of her body. Hearing her telepathic plea for more, he plunged inside her.

She cried out, throwing her head back. "Yes! Oh, yes." They were one, body and soul. The aching, demanding blood heat exploded with satisfaction, filling them with wholeness.

Bastian slammed into the hot, slick, walls of her core again and again, watching her grimace with absolute pleasure. She curled her body toward him, rebellious intent in her bright blue eyes. She threw her arms behind his shoulders and pressed her greedy mouth again to his neck.

With her legs wrapped around his hips, her hot, willing body swallowing him, and her mouth sucking on his neck, he nearly lost himself in the glorious sensations. How many years had it been since he felt such euphoria. With Aislinn, it was more electrifying and satisfying than anything he remembered. She sucked harder and they moaned together.

"Cease, my love," he whispered, reluctant, but knowing he had to stop her. "Lick my neck now." He pressed his cheek against hers to coax her away. It would not do to allow her too much of his blood. She was still new. "Lick my neck, Aislinn. It will seal."

Her hot, wet tongue lathing his neck was so erotic, he felt himself swell even more. Every inch of his skin prickled and burned with a fiery elation. He pumped harder. Her head fell back in response, her mouth opening in ecstasy.

Merging his mind with hers ignited the blood heat to a roaring blaze, heightening every touch and caress. Each wave of sexual pleasure they sent back and forth heightened the electrifying sensations. His climax was building fast, but he wanted her with him.

He trailed sloppy kisses down her neck and breasts, delighting in every soulful sound she uttered. As she arched her back, he dropped his head to her breast and filled his mouth with a wet, pebbled nipple. She cried out and grasped his hair, pressing his head against her. He pulled and tugged, and she urged him on by repeating *"yes"* in his mind. He latched onto the other nipple and she arched her back further.

*Come with me, my love* he urged, and pumped her luscious female body over his. *Rise with me. Together.*

Letting out a cry of exaltation, she shuddered against him.

Two more thrusts and he spilled into her. The explosion was so powerful, Bastian braced one hand against the shower wall to steady his legs. Their souls floated in another dimension of pure delight, savoring the throbbing sensations coursing through their bodies, over and over into a soft haze of happiness.

~~◊~~

"Marius, let them go." Gabriella whispered.

"He could kill her, Gabby." Marius hissed through clenched teeth. More than anything, he wanted Bastian to be happy, to have the one thing his bitter, lost cousin had believed would never happen again. But Marius was responsible for Aislinn's wellbeing, especially if she was going to be part of his domain. The consequences were grave not just for Bastian, but for the reputation of the entire tribe if Aislinn were to die.

"No, he won't kill her," Gabriella argued. "Something tells me she's anything but dead right now." Gabriella placed a hand on Marius' chest to stop him from leaving the library where Cirillo was contacting his generals and dealing with an unprecedented number of attacks on Appalachian sites. "I feel her in my future, Marius. Something she and I will do together. If she hasn't gotten sick after all this, she's not going to. She's got Olympian blood. Enough to save her and transmute the coding. No doubt of it."

Marius sighed, knowing he should probably trust Gabriella's instincts, which were usually correct. "I should have stopped him when he went up there. I'll never forgive myself if she grows ill tomorrow."

"I don't think there was any stopping this," Gabriella insisted. "Remember, in my dream in Romania I saw Bastian fighting to save his mate. At first, I thought I was recalling Cecilia, but I realized later it was a girl with blonde hair, not black."

"You saw him fighting demons to save her. That he has done."

"Yes, but I don't think it's over. I feel more. Much more. A dark cloud is looming, something very heavy and strange. I had another dream with people in bizarre costumes and masks. I could not hear you. Aislinn was there. She could not hear Bastian. Such a strange dream."

Marius encircled the soft hand Gabriella had placed against his chest and brought it to his lips, worried about Gabriella's dream. They were often prophetic. He threw up a mental wall to block Bastian's rapturous thrall. "Well, I need to get Bastian out of my head right now. They're in the shower. Let's take a walk or something."

Gabriella smiled at him, that beautiful smile that had been his undoing from the first moment he saw her and his world had changed forever.

"I've got a better idea to take them off your mind," she said. Giving him a wink, she tugged his hand and led him out of the library.

# CHAPTER 25

There was no surprise in the vivid green-gold eyes of the stark, tall woman who opened the door for Eddie. Though it had been over a year, her regal beauty and haughty bearing were as striking and ageless as Eddie remembered. Today, however, there was a softness he did not remember, as if a warm light was replacing the sadness usually residing there.

"Hi, Mom," he said.

"Eddie." She pulled him inside, wrapped her arms around him, and held him as only a mother could. Then she pulled out of the hug with a worried expression. "What's wrong?"

"Well, first, how *are* you?" Eddie offered his most charming grin.

"I'm fine. But that's not why you're here." Olivia Hawthorne's sixth sense was still as sharp as ever. This was one time Eddie did not want it to be.

"So? I can still ask how my mother is, can't I?"

After a wry smile, Olivia said. "Of course. Come in."

"Hey, Clare, how are you?" Eddie called to his brown-haired, burgundy-eyed sister, who was descending the stairs with barely-authentic disinterest. Black and red streaks ran through her hair, black eyeliner circled her eyes, and lipstick the color of red wine made her look *way* too old. A black mesh shirt with red lace over a black bra and multi-holed blue jeans completed the Goth effect.

"I'm good," she answered flatly.

*Damn, when did she grow up? And gone Goth?* A sudden yearning to be in touch with his sister again surprised Eddie. When his parents split eight years ago, Clare, still a child, went with their mother. Eddie and Damian, and later their cousin, Helmer, remained at the mansion with their father, though Eddie really wanted to live with his mother. It was just that he had yearned so for his father's approval. He knew his father would have considered him weak, a mama's-boy, if he had chosen his mother.

"How's school?" Eddie asked.

"Good." Clare's face was expressionless.

"Yeah, I hated it too."

A hint of a smile twitched at the corner of her mouth.

Another trait that was different than most Olympians, his father had not bothered with home schooling, believing his sons unable to produce fangs, and wanting them to endure the harsh environment of public school to "toughen them up." Still, Eddie was surprised his mother had not given Clare the option.

Eddie turned to his mother. "Are you getting along okay, Mom?"

"Yes. I still have my work at the women's charity league. Clare and I help with the soup kitchens and several halfway houses. And… of course… we have friends and family who look after us. Keep us sane." Olivia smiled.

"Well, I could definitely use some of that."

"You'll never get what you need from the Alcmaeonidae, Eddie. They value their wits too much."

Eddie blinked. She was probably right, but his family's branch of the Alcmaeonidae kept the dark arts, and he wanted power. His grandfather's creed had always been to feign a moral and religious life, but remain neutral in the true fight between good and evil in order to preserve the prosperity of their families and businesses. Hiding the arts they shared and preserved was the unspoken part. At least, according to his father.

"There are some good ones out there, Mom."

"But your father's not one of them."

Seconds ticked by as they stared at each other. He wished she hadn't been so blunt. It was an old argument. Eddie stole a glance at Clare, who was watching them as if anticipating a fight.

"Mom, I need your help," Eddie implored, shifting his stance. "You were always good at potions, and there's one I need that I've never used before."

Olivia studied him. Eddie kept his mind focused on the potion and ingredients he needed, hoping she could not read past it. They both knew he excelled at potions, and owned several labs full of forbidden ingredients and chemicals, so asking was akin to admitting he was way over his head.

"Eddie, you can't make a woman fall in love with you. Nor should you have to."

A spike of anger flared hot in Eddie's chest, but he contained it. She had seen past his block. It was probably the blood heat making his wall too soft. "I know you've always said that, Mom, but I just want a little help with this girl. She's… special."

Olivia continued to stare until her brown brows raised and her face softened. "You love this girl?"

Eddie nodded, lowering his eyes, embarrassed. Love, however, was not entirely what he had in mind. He rubbed his hands together. "Sometimes love just needs a push." Another charming grin was in order, and he flashed his best, hoping this would placate his mother despite her acute abilities.

She smiled back in endearment, but standing this close, he sensed a war wrestling inside of her. Part of her wanted to help him, part of her resisted.

"I thought you made everything at those labs of yours."

He snorted. "We have a lot of interesting products we produce, but most of the steady income is doing lab analysis on patient samples from doctors and hospitals. Guess Dad was right. I got too close to the *respectable* side of life."

"I'm proud of what you've accomplished, Eddie. Very proud. Don't listen to him. I would rather you and Damian not work for him at all. I sensed dark things the last time I was there. Darker than before."

Eddie turned away and pretended to look at a ten-year-old picture of the family she still kept in the foyer. A torn, desperate, younger self looked back at him, someone he no longer knew.

"So, come, have a seat," she offered.

He did wish he could stay, but time was running out. "I can't. I'm… maybe next time."

Eddie swallowed back regret at the disappointment that hung heavy in her face. "Um, when I left home there were… things I assumed I would never need."

"And now you do." Olivia's eyes did not move.

"Do you still have the books?" Eddie prompted. If he stayed much longer, her mere presence would convince him not to move forward with his plan. There *was* a difference in her. She had apparently been hanging around a lot of good people, absorbing the light.

Olivia took a deep breath. "I may have forsaken the dark ways, but I keep my books. Locked up, of course." Her eyes flicked in Clare's direction and returned to Eddie.

Clare could not hide her interest in the books. The slight widening of her eyes gave her away. As teenagers, he and Damian often conspired to get access to their mother's books, succeeding only once, after which she hid them again.

"Does your father know about this?" Olivia asked.

"This isn't about Dad." Eddie knew his reply sounded harsh, but he didn't care. "He doesn't understand love anyway. Obviously."

"Love was never our problem, Eddie. It was morality that got in the way. Your father buries love deep. He thinks it has no power over him. He is wrong, of course."

Eddie averted his eyes to the beige carpet and focused his mind on his need for love in order to insure that was what she read.

"Why am I getting a bad feeling about this, Eddie?"

Eddie shrugged. "Because you were always a worry-wort?"

Olivia responded with a gentle smile. After two steps toward the den, she slowed. Every muscle in her face fell as she turned. "No. Something's definitely wrong. What are you into, Eddie? What are you planning?"

Eddie stiffened. The gig was up. She was still too sensitive for him to fool her. He had hoped to play on a mother's love for her son. But, again, Olympian blood was in his way.

"Nothing, Mom. I just fell in love." Allowing her to feel his true disappointment, he pulled his car keys from his pocket. "I would have thought you'd at least care about that."

"I care more than you know, son." Olivia's eyes were misting when she said, "Clare?"

"I'm not touchin' him." Clare folded her arms, raised her blackened brows, and pressed her lips together in sarcastic defiance.

Eddie swallowed in spite of his composure. Clare had always been incredible at psychometry, even as a small child. Not only could she read the energy off objects, she could touch people and know way more than she should, usually more than she wanted.

Their father had tempted her with extravagant gifts in recent years, hoping to entice her to move in with him when she turned sixteen. In anger and bitterness, she had rejected his offer, knowing he simply wanted use of her talents. Eddie felt sorry for her and was thrilled she was still standing her ground, even two months after turning sixteen.

Her reaction now appeared to be more than a mere teenaged protest. Was she afraid of what she would see in Eddie if she touched him? Something dark and sinister? The idea caused a stab in Eddie's heart. Maybe she was just being loyal to him and did not want to reveal his intentions to their mother. Either way, she should have wanted to know. He would have.

A longer visit would be nice, but he had work to do. Tomorrow was Saturday, the moon would be full, and it was Halloween. He needed the combined power.

"Sorry I can't stay longer. I've got a lot of work to do helping Damian prepare for the big night. It was good to see you both."

~~◊~~

Eddie closed the car door and shivered against the chilly air. Maybe it was his nerves. He stared at the house, his emotions whirling. Everything he felt—insult, anger, desire—was stronger than he remembered. More than likely it was the blood heat, which he had been warned could magnify every thought and feeling. If he was not successful, it might be a blood heat that never resulted in a consummation. *No.* He would win. He always won. He was smart, and he had connections. Now was the time to use them.

Vengeance toward the Appalachians filled his thoughts, which strengthened his resolve. Clenching his jaw, he started the car, then noticed movement.

A silhouette cast a shadow against the rust-colored bricks of his mother's home. It was Clare, standing by the side of the house. She had something in her hands. Eddie's heart leapt. He exited the car and strode across the grass.

"Clare?" he whispered.

With a guilty look, she raised her hand. "I made them a couple days ago, but changed my mind."

She was holding a red sachet, a red velvet scroll tied with a red ribbon, and a dark brown bottle.

Eddie raised his eyes as he took them from her. How could his sixteen-year-old sister be so in love she would risk their mother's fury by using the forbidden spells? The small brown bottle probably contained at least three hard-to-find ingredients.

"So, who's the guy, Clare?"

"Nobody."

"Yeah, right."

Clare shrugged. "I talked to a mage yesterday. She said I would meet somebody better. It's going to be a while, but... anyway, I didn't use them."

Eddie's fingers curled around the sachet meant to draw love to its wearer. How would he feel if he had received such a prophecy? Would it calm the tormented beast inside him?

He slid his thumb over the smooth, glass bottle and smiled. "You got in."

Clare smirked. "It wasn't hard. She keeps the key in the corner of her jewelry box disguised inside an old brooch. You just slide the pin off. Seriously lame."

She crossed her arms and shuffled her feet. "You have to reaffirm the chants for the sachet, you know. And you need some of her hair, and yours. I took mine and his out of the placket. Clothing's good for that, too, but you have to roll them into it." Her burgundy eyes squinted. "Don't do anything bad, Eddie."

Breath caught in Eddie's throat. He did not want to disappoint his sister. But then, she was young and had a lot to learn. Desperate people tended to do desperate things. And he was bordering on desperate.

No one else was going to have Aislinn if he couldn't have her. Someday, Clare would have to understand.

~~◊~~

"What's up, bro?" Damian Hawthorne answered the call in a cheery voice.

Eddie took a deep breath. "Damian? I need Logan and Raven."

"What?" There was a pause and a chuckle. "Wanting to jack up a party on Halloween?"

Eddie tightened his grip on the phone. "Not exactly what I had in mind."

"Okay. So, what *do* you have in mind? You know it's Halloween and I need them. I'm booked to the max. Helmer's got a sale going on, too."

"I might need a Red Sabbath, too."

"Whoa! Didn't see that coming. You've definitely slid over to the dark side, bro. Who's got you all fired up?"

"A few Appalachians. Like, maybe, all of them."

"All of them?" Damian chuckled with outrageous delight. "It'd be nice to put them in their place. I assume we're talking about something *without* Dad?"

"We don't need Dad."

"Maybe not. But if you're talking about a Red Sabbath, we might if we want to live. You need a sacrifice for that. *And* calling up a big nasty demon. Both Pentagram rooms are booked all night. No way I can fit that in. What's going on Eddie?"

"They've just crossed me for the last time."

"What'd they do?"

Eddie hesitated, then blurted, "They stole a woman from me."

"Ha! That must be one hell of a woman if you're wanting to take them all on."

"She is. Dad told me to kill her."

Seconds ticked by before Damian responded. "That one? That was like, a year ago, Eddie."

"I know. I tried to kill the bitch four times. Each time she survived. There's a lot of power around her."

Damian whistled. "I can't believe Dad didn't tell me that part. He usually tells me everything, especially when you screw up."

Eddie cringed at the reminder. "Nice. I told him she was taken care of. She was in a coma at the time. Her family *did* die."

"Yeah, I remember. I thought she wasn't expected to live."

"She wasn't, then." Eddie sighed. "I tried to arrange something at the hospital but it fell through. I kept trying every few months. She just kept living."

"Damn, Eddie. Does Dad know?"

"Yep. He checked up on her. Me, too, as usual. I should've known."

"So, what shape is she in? Why is she a danger?"

"Because that wacked mage—you know the old bat with the scraggly gray hair that lives in that old cabin—she said a fair-haired woman would come to me, and would change the family forever. 'Beware the consequences,' she said. Or something like that. Stupid old bat."

"Eddie, all your girlfriends are blondes."

"Yeah, but Dad believed *she* was the one the mage meant. She's fine now. Walks and everything. She met an Olympian in Romania and he formed a blood bond with her."

"She's an Olympian?"

"I didn't know for sure. I suspected she could be. She's got abilities."

"What line is she?"

"Nobody knows. But... anyway, I went to Romania and brought her back here. Then I formed my own blood bond."

Several four-letter words erupted through the phone, ending with Damian laughing. "You got balls, man. I cannot believe this. A girl with two blood bonds? What line's the other dude?"

"Heracleidae."

More colorful expletives blasted through the connection. "Seriously, bro, I'm impressed. Either that, or you've gone off the deep end. How 'bout that, my little brother besting a Heraclid."

"Well, almost. His people separated us. I almost had her back again. I was this close, man. But... right now, he's got her at The Appalachian's compound."

"*Oooo.* Yeah, that sucks big time. Quite a few warriors are always in and out of there. I'm sure they're building their defenses for Halloween. Hey, but if you've got a blood bond, you can still reach her, right? Wait, did you cut her neck or did you...?"

"I have fangs, Damian." Eddie smiled with satisfaction. "I did it myself."

The shocked silence on the other end of the connection made Eddie's smile widen to a satisfied grin.

# CHAPTER 26

"You know, this is really weird being up all hours of the day and night, back and forth." Aislinn fished a lilac T-shirt out of her suitcase and shook out the wrinkles before slipping it over her head. "Between jet lag, spells, and you all-day-sleeping vampires, my time clock is so messed up."

"Aislinn, we are not...."

"Yeah, yeah. I know."

Bastian glowered. He was combing his hair with Aislinn's wide-tooth comb while sitting on the bed, completely naked. Which made getting dressed very difficult for Aislinn. She could not resist stealing glances at all of his Olympian glory. Every glimpse made her blood start pounding in her veins. She thought he rather resembled muscle-bound statues of *The Thinker*, except combing his hair instead of balancing his chin in thought. Bastian *was* thinking, however, since his gaze had been locked on her body as she dressed. Aislinn was beginning to think she would never see his manhood in a limp state.

"*Whoo*, feels like the house is full of people." Aislinn made a face. Besides the emotions vibrating through the walls, she heard a door close nearby and voices carrying through the window by the bed, which meant some of them must be outside in the courtyard.

She attempted to brush the tangles out of her hair in front of a large, square mirror, and paused. "I'm picking up lots of serious emotions, and lots more people. Wonder what's going on?" She was still basking in the fantastic sensations she had experienced in the shower with Bastian, and their continued snuggling in her room, and knew he was too. His contentment shifted to hard lines of concern, so he was probably having telepathic communication with Marius.

"Many have come," he stated.

"Why?"

He dropped the comb to the bed. "All Hallows Eve."

"All Hallows…You mean Halloween? Wow, I completely forgot it was Halloween." She waved the brush at him. "See what you do to me, Mr. Vampire?"

His short smile fell to a frown as he stepped toward her. "Aislinn, I am not a…."

"Except, of course…" she ticked off on her fingers, "the biting, drinking blood, sleeping in dirt, getting burnt by the sun, having supernatural powers, and… let's see, mesmerizing women."

"Hmm, so, you are mesmerized?" He reached for her. She sidestepped to evade his eager grasp.

"Not so mesmerized that I'm going to let you undress me again." Although, if she were honest with herself, that was not a bad idea.

"I am rested," he teased, slowly following her. "Though it is daylight, I could use energy to whisk your clothes right off of you."

She blinked and considered how fun that would be, and eyed his rising erection. Her breasts and groin warmed at the tempting prospect. The blood heat made it more than tempting.

"Okay, another time and that might actually be fun," she said. "But, knowing there are even more people in the house, all probably with super-hearing, I'm just a little self-conscious of any rhythmic banging of the bed."

"Who needs a bed? Besides, they are readying for battle. They will never hear us." He reached a long, firm arm toward her.

She sidestepped again, but dropped her teasing smile. "Why are they readying for battle?"

"All Hallows Eve," he answered as if this should be obvious. Reacting to her scan of his tattooed arms and chest, he added, "I am not concerned with battle when a beautiful woman is in front of me."

"*Oooo.*" She raised both brows, feeling her body warming again. "You know, this blood heat thing is dangerous. It's a good thing I'm not registered for classes this semester—I'd flunk them all."

A knock at the door arrested their attention. Before either could answer, the door swung open and Dimitri stepped in, holding folded clothes in one arm and wearing a mischievous glint in his aqua-blue eyes.

"Darn." He smirked. "I've seen *him* naked. Nothing special, there. Now if *you* were naked…."

Bastian let out a roar and stomped toward him. Dimitri was ready for him. He threw the clothes at Bastian, turned the lock on the door, and leapt out into the hall in a blur, slamming the door behind him.

Bastian yanked open the door, splitting the wood of the door frame and pulling the door off one of its hinges.

"Bastian, stop, stop, stop!" Aislinn managed to get ahold of his arms just before his foot touched the hallway. "You are naked. Get back in here!"

He pivoted with one foot still in the hallway. She pulled harder on his arm, which did not move him. She ran her palm up his stomach to the scars that had nearly solidified across his chest, succeeding in distracting him.

Bastian caught his breath at her touch. "He tried to see you naked."

Aislinn shook her head. "No, he didn't. He knew I was dressed. I could see it in his eyes. He just wanted to get you upset—like always."

"Well, he succeeded. I will show him what it means to compromise my woman."

"No, you won't. You are not going down there all angry and naked. Especially not with Miss Spider Legs down there." Aislinn let her own anger rise, reaching for his mind so he would feel it.

Some of the fury left Bastian's face.

"Besides," she added, "Dimitri knows you're all riled up with the blood heat. He's just yanking your chain."

"Yanking my what?"

She wagged a finger. "I need to educate you in our American sayings. Come on, shut the door and put some clothes on."

Heaving a sigh as though regretting the chase, Bastian positioned the door carefully against the splintered frame and scowled at the scattered clothes.

Aislinn picked some of them up. "How'd he know to bring you clothes?"

"I asked him."

"When?"

"A little while ago."

"Oh, the mind thing. You know, that can come in really handy. Not that I want to bite everyone's neck to get instant texting."

A frown of disapproval creased Bastian's forehead and he took the clothes from her, which was not the reaction she was expecting. As he dressed, Aislinn regretting watching parts of him get covered up. When he buttoned his new blue jeans, she caught herself actually licking her lips. Then rolled her eyes at herself.

"So…." She swallowed and handed him the white polo shirt. "What's this battle everyone is preparing for?"

"All Hallows Eve is always a battle."

"Seriously?" She chuckled with disbelief. "Why?"

"Because we can see the demons everyone calls up."

Aislinn blinked. "What do you mean? Who goes around calling them up?"

"Devil worship groups, some. Dark covens. But mostly demons are attracted to the celebration of evil acts against humans."

"Celebration–of–evil–acts–against–humans," she repeated slowly. "What country did *you* celebrate Halloween in?"

"It is different in every country. Here, the demons are attracted to the…" he seemed to be searching for the right words, "fear and horror."

Aislinn stared at him, aghast. "Bastian, I don't think I'm following this. I mean, it's just a fun night."

"Not for us."

Aislinn crossed her arms. "Show me what you mean. In my mind. Can you do that?"

He nodded, placed hands on either side of her head, and closed his eyes. A menagerie of costumes and gruesome masks, many with fake injuries, blood, or weapons floated across her vision. Teenagers were smashing pumpkins, stealing candy from small children, and vandalizing. Adults were enjoying scaring children, and scaring themselves. Children screamed at moving shadows, barking dogs, and costumed people at front doors. People huddled in front of televisions, recoiling from chain saws, axes and other weapons used to graphically assault victims. In the night above, shadowy creatures basked in the mischief and swarmed like black sharks in a vast sea of smoke. Hideous demons wafted down streets drinking in the fear that filled the air, floating in and out of houses and people, laughing with eerie, twisted joy.

Aislinn's eyes popped open. "Oh no. For real?" She placed a hand to her chest. "You mean that's really what's going on when people are…?" She gestured with open hands, at a loss for words.

"Yes."

"But… Halloween parties? Those are harmless, Bastian. People are just having fun. And dressing in costumes is…."

"It depends on everyone's intent. Humans do not fully understand the spirit world. What you emulate is attracted to you. Good or bad. I have lived in many lands. Olympians know where the dark arts are used and what they cause. The air will be full of demons tonight, swarms of them."

Aislinn plopped into an old wooden chair near the dresser. "Is this going to ruin the rest of my Halloweens?"

Bastian laced up the brown leather loafers Dimitri had brought him, and did not answer.

Aislinn scowled. "Can we just make a list of the bad things, and the good things, about this whole Olympian life, so I can kinda weigh everything and decide whether I want it or not?"

Bastian's tawny brows rose, a hint of mischief in his eyes. "I think, my lady…."

"Don't even say it." She raised a hand. "Don't tell me it's too late. I am in complete control of my destiny."

He raised his brows even further and a slow, dangerously handsome smile spread wide across his firm jaw, which made Aislinn's heart beat faster. When his smile dropped and his head turned toward the door, Aislinn was certain she was hearing wisps of telepathic communication.

"What's going on?" she asked.

"Bad things are happening already, and it is only morning."

"What bad things?"

"One of Cirillo's martial arts centers has been set on fire. Also a church. Good places are being attacked, vandalized. More warriors are getting signs of impending battle. Cirillo is organizing his generals and sending them out. All Olympians are being called in. Even the old ones." He turned toward her, lines forming around his eyes. "Today will be a very busy day."

"Hey, I have to pick up Gramma today." Aislinn stood up, concerned that the rising tide of events could affect her family, and her ability to reach them.

"You must stay close to me, Aislinn."

"Then you'll have to come with me to get Gramma." She placed her hands on her hips. "In fact, we should stay at Gramma's."

"I am needed here."

"I am needed by my family. Aunt Julia can't be stuck doing everything. She has arthritis. What if Gramma needs help getting out of the wheelchair?"

"I will speak to Marius concerning it. Come, let us join the battle plans for now." He held out a hand. "I will take you to your grandmother after that."

Bastian froze with his arm outstretched, his eyes becoming unfocused. Aislinn reached for his mind, and heard more whispers. A mental wall of hesitation and secrecy met her, which was not like Bastian. She slid her hand into his and took a step forward to press her pelvis against his and rub. As soon as his eyes were diverted to her body, she slipped tighter into his mind.

....*cannot take the risk, Bastian. Cirillo does not want her to know all the plans. Edward may still have some hold on her.*

*No. She is mine now!* Bastian insisted with such force Aislinn flinched against him.

*Aislinn, stop.* Bastian's mental wall solidified and blocked her from the conversation.

Aislinn's mouth fell open. "Is that about me?"

"Do not spy on others' conversations."

"*Don't* tell me what to do." She let go of him, and splayed both hands. "If I'm being discussed, I have a right to know about it."

"They are merely discussing strategies."

"Not a dumb blonde, Bastian, remember? They think I'm going to give something away, don't they? Like I'm a snitch or something."

He grasped her shoulders, his face inches from hers. "I know that your heart belongs to me. It does not matter what the others think."

"I'm going down there right now and give them a piece of my mind." She struggled to escape his grasp.

"Aislinn, listen to me. Your emotions are high."

"Yeah, and they're gonna get higher."

"Stop. Remember what I was about to do a minute ago? To Dimitri?" She paused, glaring at him.

"Going down there right now is no different than me running down the stairs naked."

The sting of embarrassment traveled up her neck to her cheeks. These people were downstairs discussing her, wanting her ignorant of their plans, considering her compromised. She fought back tears, then swallowed, mortified at her violent emotions. "It's not fair! Eddie did those things, not me."

"I know. I know. And I would prefer to make certain Edward can never do those things again. But... Aislinn, we may have to do battle today, we do not need to be fighting each other."

She took a deep breath and let her shoulders relax a little, but every notion that these people were becoming family evaporated.

"Let's get something to eat," Bastian suggested. "Frau Beatie has left food warming in the kitchen. I am hungry."

"I don't feel like walking past the library."

"I know another way."

~~◊~~

"Wow, is this a narrow staircase or what?" Aislinn hunched her shoulders, afraid of spider webs in the dark channel. "Must have had skinny people living here when it was built."

"I heard the others speak of this." Bastian descended each step with care, taking the lead and holding onto Aislinn's hand. "Cirillo built it as a fire escape after his oldest son became a fireman and suggested another escape route was needed on this side of the house. The children used it to sneak out at night.

"It needs a window. It's kinda creepy in here. I think I just touched a spider web. Probably left by Miss Spider Legs."

"Aislinn."

"I'm trying."

"You are not."

"No, I'm not. And don't expect me to smile and be chatty if I see her."

Bastian sighed in the darkness. His shoulders were so broad he had to take the stairs sideways.

"And don't expect me to be chatty with anyone else either, since I'm now the outcast."

"Aislinn, please, let's keep our emotions in check and have something to eat. I assure you if anyone insults you, I will kill them for you."

She snorted and smiled. "Okay."

Bastian turned a lever and pushed open a narrow panel. As they stepped into the green grass and looked back, they discovered the panel blended back in with the siding on the house.

"Wow, wish I had one of those growing up." Aislinn smirked. "Me and Anya would have gotten into so much trouble. Hey, look, we're outside of the courtyard walls."

In the bright sun, she could see cows and horses grazing in acres of green beyond the diamond-shaped courtyard of houses. Rolling pastures were broken up by maroon, orange and gold-leafed woodland fading into a backdrop of bluish mountains. A cool breeze full of earthy farm smells was blowing.

"Um, that brick wall is kinda high."

"Not a problem, my lady. Bastian encircled her waist with his hands and sat her on top of the wall. Pivoting with one hand, he vaulted the wall in a continuous movement, landing like a cat on the other side. Smiling, he retrieved her and pulled her close before lacing her hand into his."

"You know, it'd be nice to walk around this property," she said. "I'd like to see it all."

"Another time. I need to get out of the sun."

"Oh. Sorry. Forgot. Mr. Vamp—"

"Don't."

She was still giggling when they entered through a screen door to the large porch crowded with picnic tables.

Several people called out greetings. Andromeda was just withdrawing a long, bare leg from one of the benches and froze when she spotted them.

Aislinn was shocked at the lightning bolt of fury that seared through her body. Her arms tightened, ready to strike. A growl vibrated deep in her throat. She no longer cared that it was an inhuman response. She wanted to call on the dark emotions emerging inside her, and allow them to explode.

Longing and betrayal glowed in the woman's eyes as they landed on Bastian, changing to an angry scowl when they shifted to Aislinn. She was asking for her neck to be ripped open. Bastian's arm slid around Aislinn's waist so completely that his hand was resting on her stomach, holding her tight.

Like bees, all the bodies in the room swarmed around Andromeda and swept her out of the room before Aislinn could take a step forward. All the energy in the air exited with the people. Even the bug zapper was silent.

Aislinn blinked at the empty tables. "I don't want to stay here anymore."

"This is the safest place for us."

"We can go to Gramma's, or we can go to my apartment in Brevard. But not here. I am not staying."

Ma Beatie stepped through the far kitchen entrance to the porch. "Well, star-crossed lovers, we've still got fixins in here. Get 'em while the gettin's good."

~~◊~~

Aislinn tapped the display of her phone with anticipation, exhaling as it rang. "Aunt Julia? How's Gramma doing?"

"Oh, she's happier than a June bug and makin' about as much noise."

Aislinn laughed and let her shoulders relax. "What is she doing?"

"Fussing to go home. The doctor won't give her the okay until he examines her. He had an emergency this morning, but he's comin' by as soon as that's over. Might not be 'till after noon, the nurse said."

"Oh, good, I still have plenty of time to get there. I've... had a few delays this morning. Did you just get there?"

"No, I got to worrin' last night and thought I'd do better if I just slept in this easy chair through the night and made sure Mama was okay."

Aislinn smiled and felt a stab of guilt. "You're a good nurse, Aunt Julia."

"Oh, go on with you. See if I'm such a good nurse a week from now after trying to keep Mama in a wheelchair."

Aislinn could hear Gramma protesting loudly in the background. "I don't need no bloomin' wheelchair!"

"See what I mean?" said Aunt Julia.

Aislinn chuckled with relief. "Well, I'm going to get a ride there. I'll bring... a friend."

"Who, Eddie?"

"Uh, no. Not Eddie."

"Oh, okay. Might could use a couple people to sit on Mama, so bring more. Oh, guess what?" Aunt Julia's voice lowered. "All the nurses here are abuzz. That real sweet night nurse, Norma, she was found dead as a doornail this mornin.' They're all a'cryin' over here. They're sayin' she was fit as a fiddle night before last. The police are sayin' it looks suspicious even though they can't figure what killed her. Ain't that the strangest thing? And here she was a'takin' care of Mama."

It was just the sort of gossip Aunt Julia loved, but Aislinn felt a chill run up her spine. She did not know why, since she had not met the woman, but it was just too close to Gramma for comfort.

"I got to know her real good," Aunt Julia added. "We got to talkin' about gettin' old and wrinkled. She was all excited about this new life she was getting into and products to get rid of wrinkles. And you should'a heard her talkin' about this handsome young man she met. Why, it was a tale you wouldn't believe…."

"Uh, listen, Aunt Julia, I don't mean to interrupt, but let me run and make some arrangements. I'm gonna get there as soon as I can. Love you."

"Love you too, sweetie."

# CHAPTER 27

Aislinn ran upstairs to splash water on her face and brush her teeth. Looking into the mirror, she wondered if she could sneak her suitcase into the car before they left to pick up Gramma. That way she wouldn't have to come back. Something told her a fight with Bastian over permanently leaving the compound would be a big one. Marius might order Bastian to stay. But he couldn't order her.

Gramma's would only be an hour away, so maybe the blood bond wouldn't bother them too badly if Bastian was forced to return to Cirillo's house. Missing his body would definitely bother her. Plus, she had to admit her feelings were growing stronger for him. Already, she could not imagine life without him. He was her protector, her lover, her friend, but also someone who adored her and had no problem declaring that he planned to do so for the rest of his life.

There was no denying that Olympian life with him would be exciting, though all the trouble she had encountered the past few days was more excitement than she cared for. In retrospect, one of her fears that had kept her from settling down with anyone was the fear of being bored. She did not know why she had felt that way in the past, but Bastian would certainly keep her on her toes. Having him by her side would be the ride of a life time. In many delicious ways.

Even if, at the moment, she didn't actually have him by her side. She had finally talked Bastian into taking her to pick up Gramma. Duncan had agreed to accompany them for the rest of the evening so they would have added protection. Aislinn wanted Dimitri to accompany them as well, but Bastian did argue over that, and added that Dimitri had been up all night assisting Cirillo and was still resting.

Aislinn had every intention of staying the night in Brevard to be certain Gramma was being taken care of.

Everyone was ready to go, except that Cirillo had asked Bastian to assist Ma Beatie in healing a wounded man that had just been brought in. Bastian had accommodated him as if he were Marius. Aislinn huffed and rolled her eyes.

Marius would always be telling him what to do. Probably telling her what to do as well. Could she deal with that? Could she commit to a life as part of a tribe? He might even insist on her living in Romania, or somewhere in the Balkans, although she had always wanted to visit Greece.

What if she chose to be part of Cirillo's tribe instead? Aislinn seethed, remembering her outcast state. She wasn't actually part of anybody, since no one trusted her at the moment.

If Bastian wanted to stay at the compound, that was his choice, but she would not stay here where she was not wanted. Bastian could actually help with Gramma, as strong as he was, which would be a great help to Aunt Julia.

She went back to the bedroom and stuck her toothbrush into her suitcase.

Her phone rang. It was Aunt Julia.

"Hi, Aunt Julia, how's it going?"

"Hello, Aisy-girl, how are you doing this morning?" Aislinn froze at the sound of Eddie's voice.

"Eddie?"

*Aisy, if you want to see Gramma again, I suggest you listen. And don't make the mistake of talking to the Heraclid. I have a link to your mind as well as the phone line.*

Aislinn inhaled sharply. She was hearing Eddie's voice through the phone *and* his mental voice at the same time.

"Eddie, what's going on? Why are you answering Aunt Julia's phone? Where's Gramma?"

"Oh, yeah, she's doing great," Eddie said out loud. "They released her a few minutes ago." *There's a bridge down by the creek on the other side of the pastures. Follow the brown fence. Meet the car that's parked there now. They'll bring you to me. I just want to talk, that's all.*

Aislinn reeled from the dual conversations. "Eddie, whatever you're trying to pull…."

"Uh, huh. Sure we'd love to have you come join us. I told Aunt Julia you had gotten delayed anyway." *I've got Gramma and Julia in the car, Aisy. I just need to sort things out. I'm suffering from a blood heat, too, you know. Come of your own accord and nothing will happen to anybody. Blood heats can make you a little crazy. Right now I'm feeling a lot crazy.*

Fear crawled up Aislinn's spine and stung her entire body like sleet. "Eddie, how could you even think of doing something to Gramma and Aunt Julia? Aunt Julia loves you!"

"Yeah, we're headed up to Ned's Main Street Café," he replied, mimicking a jovial conversation with her. "Aunt Julia's crazy about this place. Their biscuits are home made. And Gramma says she's sick of hospital food." *I fell in love, too, Aisy-girl. It's pretty rough when it's one way. Just come talk to me. Gramma and Julia are with me. Maybe they can talk some sense into me. Who knows? They're safe right now, but....*

"What do you mean, right now?" Something sharp pierced Aislinn's heart. Not Gramma. Not Aunt Julia. They were all she had left.

She reached for Bastian. His mind felt strange, distant, absorbed. He must be deep in the trance of healing. Could she wake him out of it? Would it mess him up? Could she do it without Eddie hearing?

*I know the Heraclid is in the house, Aisy. If you tip him off, Gramma and Aunt Julia die in a car wreck. 'Cause I've got 'em in a car right now, and I don't care if I die.* Like a tunnel through his skull and into his eyes and ears, he shot her a mental picture to convince her. Aunt Julia was rambling away about the fantastic biscuits and sausage gravy at the café. Eddie glanced up so Aislinn would see into the rear view mirror. Gramma was in the back looking pale, grumpy, and distrustful, but unharmed.

Panic clenched at Aislinn's chest so tight she could not breathe. "Not another car wreck. Eddie, no. Don't hurt anybody. Please. They're all I've got."

"Oh, really? That busy, huh?" *Do what I ask, Aisy. I've sent the car. Just get in. It will be across a creek on a dirt road back there on the other side of the compound. Walk away from the back of the house toward the pastures. Follow the brown fence. If my people see anybody else coming, they'll leave.*

"Wait, what? I thought you were near Ned's Café."

"Well, we'll see you when you get here. Drive safe, okay?" *A friend of mine will bring you to me. He just thinks you need a ride. He doesn't know anything. He's okay. Go with him.*

The line went dead.

*Eddie! I'm not going with a stranger. You come and get me! And bring Gramma!*

*Aisy, don't push me. You don't show, and I guarantee you will have to identify some bodies at the morgue.*

Aislinn gasped, her throat convulsing. Her body began to shake. *No. Eddie, listen to me, you hurt Gramma and Aunt Julia and I will kill you. I promise you that.*

Mental laughter was his response. *Aisy, you couldn't hurt a fly.*

*I've changed.*

*Oh, really. So have I. I have nothing to lose now. And by the way, Julia gave me her cell 'cause mine is dead. At least that's what she thinks. So it's me or nothing.*

*You son of a bitch.* Tears burned Aislinn's eyes. How had he picked them up from the hospital so early? It was only 10:30AM. The doctor wasn't supposed to arrive until after noon.

*I have persuasion too, Aisy. One thing I was always good at. You just never suspected. The doctor was planning to release her, so it didn't take much to convince the nurses. I always win, Aisy. You have ten minutes to show. Otherwise, my friend calls me, and it's the end of your family.*

*Eddie, wait. Eddie? Eddie, you answer me right now or I'll scream in your head!*

*Yeah, that hurt last time. Your abilities are growing. Make me even crazier and I'll forget I even want to talk to you.*

Aislinn tried to see through his eyes again. The blood bond kept the connection soft. She broke through his wall. He was driving. She could see a blurry image of a road through the windshield. Aunt Julia was still chattering.

*Don't push me, Aisy. Not kidding. There's a dump truck coming towards us up ahead. Just one swerve of the car and the right side where they are sitting will be what gets smashed in.* He swerved the car to the left and back, causing Aunt Julia to squeal.

*Eddie, I swear if you do something to them…* Aislinn could not stop the flow of tears running down her cheeks. She pulled out her phone and dialed Gramma's cell phone feverishly. She was choking with panic. A default voicemail message played. Gramma always answered if she could. Then Aislinn remembered. Gramma was taken to the hospital in an ambulance. Her phone might not be with her.

After the beep, Aislinn said in a rush, "Gramma, this is Aisy. Stay away from Eddie. He wants to harm you. I will find you." Aislinn's chin began to shake so that she could not continue the message. She hung up.

Could he detect her calling out to Bastian? Possibilities raced through Aislinn's mind. Fine tuning the art of telepathy was a skill she had not mastered. She needed to know how to block one person, and contact another. She could dial the police on her phone and possibly hide it from Eddie's mind. Could she keep him busy enough in a conversation? Would he know she had warned the Olympians in the house?

Her hand shook as her mind raced through options.

*Oh, and just so you know, if I see Olympians coming, it's over Aisy. That goes for the cops, too. I can tell you're trying to block me. You don't have enough practice with that. Sadly, that will come later.*

Aislinn cursed at him, sobs tearing at her. *Eddie, I cannot believe you would actually do this. How can you blame me for breaking up with you, now? Look at what you are. Is this the kind of person you think I want to be with?*

*You have eight minutes left.*

Aislinn rushed from the bedroom and halted at the top of the spiral staircase, stuffing the phone in her pocket. She would have to explain if she was seen going out the front door. There was the narrow hall off the foyer that led to the house where Marius and Gabriella slept, but she would have to cross the grass courtyard and find a way over the farthest brick wall between the houses. The kitchen and back porch always had activity going on. Her gaze found its way to the dark corner across the landing. She headed for the narrow escape staircase.

Though the sun was out, a cool breeze made her shiver as she stepped into the grass and stared across the fields beyond the courtyard. Would the cows consider her an intruder if she took a shortcut across their manure-strewn pasture? She didn't know much about cows. But animals had an odd way of tolerating her presence, and even seemed to be drawn to her. She headed for the pasture.

*You have seven minutes, Aisy. Follow the fence surrounding....*

*Just shut up, Eddie! I'm on my way.*

*Okay. That's good. If everything goes well I'll drop Gramma and Julia off at the house after we eat. Then you and I can meet up. I promise. I'll give you a visual to prove it.*

*I don't trust you to do anything, Eddie. I don't know what to believe any more.*

*Believe that I love you. That won't change.*

*Eddie, you have no clue what love is, or you could not do this. Love does not do this.*

Aislinn glanced in all directions to insure she was not being observed as she hurried along the fence. Golden rays of sun warmed the beautiful green and tan pastures. The sight did not fit the state of her heart.

*Look, Eddie, don't hurt anybody. Please? You and I can work this out. Just you and me.* Aislinn headed for the trees at a walk-run, her legs already feeling the strain.

*Eddie, talk to me.* She felt sure if she kept him talking, he would soften.

Gabriella opened her eyes. Alarm pressed in on her from all sides. She sat up in bed. Vivid battle scenes in strange buildings full of costumed people had plagued her dreams since they arrived in North Carolina. This time there were scenes of Aislinn looking dazed, ashen-faced, wearing a red slip with lace at the bodice. Gabriella breathed in and out to make sense of the scattered images.

The alarm did not dissipate. Something was not right. Reaching outward, Gabriella detected life and activity, concern and worry. It was always in this quiet state, drifting from dreaming to awake, that her abilities were enhanced. After so many reinforced blood bonds, her psychic abilities were nearly as strong as Marius, but in unique and different ways.

Tapping at the window caught her attention. A crow turned its head sideways at her, tapped on the glass again, and flapped its wings. Gabriella wondered if it was puzzled by its own reflection.

Aislinn's face drifted across Gabriella's mind. Something wasn't right about Aislinn. Running. Scared. Distorted energy surrounded her. Gabriella pushed to focus, but it was no use. The clarity would not come. The bird flapped its black wings again, and flew away.

Marius was still sleeping. Gabriella watched him breathe. This was the only time his face was relaxed, devoid of so many responsibilities. She loved examining his handsome features, the dark eyebrows, straight nose and strong, determined jaw when he was not aware. It was hard to resist the urge to run her fingers through the black hair on his chest.

But, dreams came to her for a reason. She grabbed her favorite jeans and donned a green shirt. Marius always gave her that special 'you look great' smile when she wore green. She tied her athletic shoes and took one last look at Marius. His right arm twitched as though sensing she was no longer beside him. Either that, or it was the battle sign throbbing. A battle that seemed to hang heavy in the air, looming on the horizon.

Disturbing energy intensified as Gabriella paused on the walkway outside the guest house. She turned to gaze across the grass courtyard to the quiet fields of cows beyond, just in time to see a figure that looked like Aislinn, a tiny dot of lilac shirt and blonde hair, disappearing into the woods. Ma Beatie, her sister, Shirley, and her granddaughter, Calista, were the only other women at the house with blonde hair.

"Aislinn, what are you up to girl?" Gabriella whispered. Could Aislinn have changed her mind about Bastian? That did not seem likely. The resonance between Bastian and Aislinn was more electrifying and all-consuming that anything Gabriella had detected between Edward and Aislinn. Edward might have found a way to place another spell on her. Something they might have missed.

Gabriella started to yell, but hurried over the brick wall instead. Thankfully, intermittent absent bricks were part of the design and made it easy to scale. Her Olympian strength did the rest.

Red hair rose on Gabriella's arms and the back of her neck as she landed in the grass. She began to run. Alarm was growing stronger. She reached for Marius' mind as she followed the fence line. He was still asleep. She knew he needed rest before the coming battle. She bit her lip wondering if she should wake him with a strong mental yell.

Bastian's mind felt distant, preoccupied. Though she was not allowed to have his blood, being near him for the last ten years and joining in on Marius' telepathic conversations had created a connection of sorts. Dimitri as well. Marius grumbled over that ability, but admitted it presented advantages.

A foggy place of bright light and concentration was all Gabriella perceived when she pressed for Bastian. *He must be healing someone.*

Her legs pumped faster as she followed the fencing all the way to the trees. Dodging low branches, she threw a mental call to Dimitri to see if he was awake. He was not.

She cleared the thick woods and stepped onto a sloping pasture with an old wooden bridge across a wide stream. A cluster of oak trees close to the bridge nearly obscured the view, but Gabriella's sharp vision detected a white car on the other side.

Aislinn's lilac shirt disappeared into the car.

A sense of warning pierced Gabriella's spine. She ran across the field toward the bridge. Her feet sounded loud as she pounded across the wooden slats.

A man with brown hair in a ponytail and the hard features of someone who had experienced a rough, dangerous life, exited the driver's side. He shut the door and walked toward her. The token smile he offered did not reach his eyes.

Gabriella stopped, glancing from him to the car, deciding on a course of action. The windows were tinted too dark to see through. Still, she could make out Aislinn's lilac shirt in the front seat, very still.

"Hey, there," the man said. "The lady called for a ride. She's going to see a friend. Were you coming, too?"

A crow swooped low over the man's head. He ducked and waved the bird away.

"I want to talk to her," Gabriella demanded. "Right now. Ask her to exit the car, please."

The man's smile faltered. "Well," he drawled. "I guess that's up to her. Come on, then. You're welcome to ask her." He raised both hands as if in surrender and leaned against the car, his eyes rolling upward as if looking out for the black bird.

Gabriella advanced with slow steps. As she gripped the handle of the passenger side door, the sense of warning intensified to a firestorm. She let go of the handle just as the back door flew open. A man with red eyes and fangs was in her face with lightning speed, his arms pinning hers.

*Marius!* she screamed.

She kicked and twisted against the vampire with all her might, but the first man had fisted her hair and yanked her head backward. A cloth was pressed hard against her nose and mouth. She tried to hold her breath, but as she struggled, a needle was slapped into her arm, the contents burning.

"Let me take her blood first." The gray-skinned vampire hissed. "It will make her weak."

*Marius! Dimitri!* Gabriella threw as much psychic power into the call as she could. *Mariuuuus!*

~~◊~~

Marius sat straight up, shocked out of a deep sleep. Gabriella was not in the room but he was certain he had heard her. He called out to her mind, reaching beyond the walls with all of his senses.

Silence. Emptiness. That had not happened in ten years.

Instinctively, Marius knew she was not merely sleeping. Her sleeping mind had a different feel to it, a whisper of dreamy images. He flew out of the bed and pulled on clothes. When he wrenched open the door he nearly collided with Bastian.

"I can't hear Aislinn." Bastian looked pale with panic.

"I can't hear Gabriella."

*Dimitri, have you seen Gabriella?* Marius sent to Dimitri's mind.

*No, sir.* Dimitri's mind sounded groggy. *But, someone called my name and woke me. It sounded like her. What's wrong?*

Marius stepped toward Dimitri's room and flung the door open. Dimitri was sitting up in bed.

"Get dressed. Gabriella and Aislinn are missing. We can't hear them."

"Who's missing?" Cirillo's eyes widened and brows furrowed in alarm. "Chief, let me call you back." Cirillo lowered his cell phone.

Marius' heart was slamming in his chest despite his efforts to remain calm. "Gabriella would never leave without telling me or leaving a message. Her mind is closed as if she were... unconscious." Fury welled inside him at the thought. Who would dare violate his woman? No Olympian in his right mind would dare touch the wife of the Prince of the Balkans.

"It is the same with Aislinn," Bastian added beside him. "I cannot hear her. At all."

"Well, now, Bastian," Cirillo remarked, his expression firm. "You and Edward were on orders not to contact her unless she chose one of you."

"I tell you, she chose me. She came to me. We are mated. We exchanged blood...." Bastian threw a guilty glance at Marius, "only three hours ago."

Cirillo's brows rose higher.

"It is true." Marius turned to Cirillo. "She came to him yesterday, of her own free will, before she left to see her grandmother and Edward spelled her with the bracelet. They also spent most of this morning together, until Bastian assisted with healing."

"Before the fiasco with the spelled bracelet," said Cirillo, "Edward told me Aislinn agreed to meet him to talk things out. Are we certain she did not agree to the bracelet? Are we certain she has not simply followed through with meeting Edward?"

A small voice piped up. "She told Edward to take a hike."

Everyone turned. Cirillo's grandson, Ethan, stuck his head out from behind one of the high-backed chairs in the library.

"When did you hear that, Ethan?" asked Cirillo.

The boy cringed at the sharpness in Cirillo's voice. "I was… um… just sittin' at the top of the stairs."

"Were you sneaking through the back staircase again?" Cirillo's eyes narrowed.

Ethan ducked his head.

Marius knelt beside Ethan, willing his heart to stop pounding. The boy's eyes went wide in awe.

"Ethan, this is important. What exactly did Miss Aislinn say to Edward?"

"Uh…." The boy looked scared.

"It is okay," Marius assured him, adding a touch of persuasion. "You can tell me. Even if they are swear words, that's okay. Tell me, Ethan."

"Um…." Ethan's eyes shifted toward Cirillo and back to Marius.

"Tell me, Ethan," Marius crooned, increasing the persuasion.

"They argued a lot. And then she said, 'I don't want you in my head. I don't want you in my bed. And I don't want you in my life.' Edward got real mad. He slammed the front door."

Marius read the boy's emotions and intent. He was open and honest. "Did you see Miss Aislinn and Miss Gabriella leave, Ethan?"

Again, Ethan's eyes darted to Cirillo.

"Tell the truth, Ethan," Cirillo urged. "Even if you think you're going to get into trouble. This is very important."

Ethan's eyes locked on Marius. "I was down by the frog pond. But I didn't get any ticks on me, I swear," he added in a rush.

*Cirillo, is this pond restricted to him?*

*Yes,* Cirillo confirmed for Marius. *He gets ticks on him and snakes show up sometimes.*

"Ethan," Marius continued to hold the boy's gaze, "what did you see at the pond?"

In a small voice, Ethan answered. "I saw Miss Aislinn go through the woods. The rabbits were following her. And a crow. The animals like her. She had a purple shirt. It was kinda bright."

"Was she just walking? What did her face look like?"

"I couldn't see real good. But she was kinda scared, and she was hurryin'."

"Go on."

"Well, she went to the troll bridge. I thought about going to see what she was doing, but I was afraid I'd get in trouble."

"And?"

"Um, Miss Gabriella came by right after that. She was in a hurry, too. I think she was chasin' Miss Aislinn."

"What makes you say that?" Marius was careful to keep his voice neutral so as not to alarm Ethan.

"I felt her worryin'."

*Cirillo?*

*Yes, Ethan shows empathic abilities already. He's quite the snoop.*

"What did Miss Gabriella do then, Ethan?" Marius asked, fearful of the answer.

"She followed Miss Aislinn."

"Did you follow them?"

"No. I got a bad feeling about the car."

"What car?"

"Just a white car. I didn't like it."

"Did you see what happened at the car?"

"No. But I heard it."

"What do you mean?" Marius' heart constricted.

"Miss Gabriella was upset. She wanted to see Miss Aislinn. Then she was making funny noises. Then the car drove off real fast."

Marius swallowed, but managed to nod at Ethan. "Thank you Ethan. You have done well."

Ethan looked down, embarrassed but wide-eyed at the complement.

Marius forced himself to breathe steady. "The sun is still high. I cannot take a flying form. What have you got, Cirillo?"

"I've got drones." Cirillo lifted his eyes, unfocused, and Marius knew he was contacting his warriors.

"Why did you prevent me from killing him?" Bastian's voice was nearly a growl beside him. "If I get the chance again, I will not stop, my lord."

Marius held up a hand, though he could barely contain his own desire to throttle Edward. "He has to be judged first. This feels wrong. My Gabriella would never do something like this willingly. She would have had a strong reason for following Aislinn."

Gabriella's fateful words rang in his head: *"I feel her in my future, Marius. Something she and I will do together."* Marius closed his eyes. He should have pressed her for a clearer vision.

"Bastian," said Marius, "do you know of anything Edward could hold over Aislinn?"

Bastian's eyes widened. "She was supposed to pick up her grandmother today from the hospital. She said her aunt would need help. Duncan and I were ready to go, but Cirillo asked for my assistance with a healing."

"That's got to be it," said Marius. "If he was going to threaten her, he would use her loved ones. Cirillo, can you have Earl contact the hospital and find out if her grandmother was released, and if Edward was there?"

Cirillo nodded, his eyes still unfocused with telepathic conversations.

"Ethan." Marius forced his voice to stay calm so the boy would not see the fear that was threatening to strangle him. "Can you take us to the woods where you saw the women?"

Bastian scented the wooden plats of the bridge and kept going until he was forced to stop at a dirt road. His fear of losing Aislinn was nearly choking him.

*Not again. Please, not again.*

For years he had perfected the art of pushing his emotions aside and focusing with precision to obtain his quarry. This time, terror gripped his heart with such ferocity that he could not gain control. Visions of Cecilia lying on the floor in a pool of blood, her head severed, replayed across his brain. He placed both hands to his temples. *Focus. You can do this.*

"Gabriella did not get in that car willingly," Marius said as he neared the graveled road. "I smell it. I sense a fight happened here."

"I smell a vampire." Bastian practically spat the words. There was no mistaking the foul odor. He knew it well. They always smelled like raw meat and old blood. His muscles tensed at the thought of a vampire touching Aislinn, or Gabriella. Oh, how he was going to rip the vampire's body to shreds when he caught up with him.

Cirillo turned toward the direction of the compound. "Beatie is sending Hera."

"Hera?" Bastian questioned. Andromeda had mentioned her younger sister was developing mage-like abilities, but would she be of use here? She was devoted to her older sister and might take up the offense of Aislinn being the one he chose instead of Andromeda.

"She's only been with us for a short while," Cirillo explained, "but she's been learning fast. I have also put a call in to our family's mage, but have not heard back yet."

Bastian continued to focus his senses on the direction the car may have headed. The fear experienced by the two women was the strongest thing in the air, but his years of ascertaining directional intent was kicking in.

*Northeast.*

# CHAPTER 28

A cloud of red and black wafted before Aislinn's blurred vision. She was lying on something soft and luxurious. Unnatural tingles cascaded over her skin as she breathed. The blaring red color was so dominant, unlike the gentle country patterns of rooms at the compound. She forced her eyelids open and blinked several times. The red color did not go away.

Five red walls surrounded her, draped in several places with red and black glossy curtains. Most of them were pulled back and tied with red ribbons. Red curtains also hung from the bed on which she lay, tied to the tall posts. Candles encased in glass sconces were flickering in each of the five corners of the room, providing the only light.

Whips, chains and metallic devices hung on every wall. Shelves held bottles and undecipherable objects. Red and black robes and negligées hung from hooks.

Above her, a long chain attached to a bar with handcuffs swayed. On the red ceiling a black pentagram had been painted, the points matching the corners of the room. Aislinn followed the chain to a series of metal rings and then to a round device with a lever like the one her parents had used to hoist up their garden hose.

She started to rise and heard the chink of metal. All of her limbs were chained to the posts on the bed. Aislinn exploded into wild, gut-wrenching, primal movement, crying and gasping. Her ankles and wrists burned as she gyrated and thrashed like an animal, until she thought her wrists and ankle bones would break. No matter how much she pulled, a few inches in any direction was all she could move. The metal cuffs burned as if made of glass shards and acid. She could smell her own skin burning.

Her breath came in rapid, harsh rasps as she ceased struggling and looked over her prison. Terror was stabbing through her entire body with such force the bed shook. Aside from the pentagram shape, there was no mistaking the purpose of this room. She had heard of such things but never desired to explore them. This was a room designed for torture and sex. The crushing energy of humiliation and despair hung thick like a pressurized cloud of doom. Whatever happened in this room was not play, but something evil, so heavy that the residual energy clung to everything.

Aislinn fought to push the horrid energy away, but the foul vibrations were now part of this room like trapped ghosts. The weight of hopelessness pulled her down a dark abyss in the earth, leaving her helpless and alone. A plaything. An object.

Something moved. Aislinn's eyes fell on what appeared to be a woman wearing a sleeveless black nightgown chained to a wall to her left, partially hidden by a curtain. A mass of burgundy-red hair hung limp around a barely discernible pale face.

"Hello?" Aislinn called out. The woman stirred, her head wobbling as if trying to rise. There was no mistaking the pale, heart-shaped face. Aislinn gasped.

It was Gabriella, but how? Gabriella's head fell back into the limp position.

Aislinn opened her mouth to call out again when a man entered from a door she could not see, causing layers of curtains to fly out from his movement. Aside from blue jeans and a gray T-shirt, he was wearing a creepy clown mask which covered most of his face except his eyes and mouth. A small cut-out under the red plastic nose allowed him to breathe.

"Oh, good, the sweet things are wakin' up. Time to party." He rubbed his hands together.

"Who are you?" Aislinn asked, afraid of the answer.

The tall frame and brown hair was a blueprint for Eddie. Even his voice was similar, but harsher, and older. What was not similar was the strange burgundy eyes, brown-rimmed with inner hues of red. They gleamed as he stopped at the side of the bed. He leaned over and ran fingers up her bare leg. She jerked her leg away, though the chain on her ankle halted the movement.

"I'm gonna be the answer to your prayers, if you're real nice."

Aislinn caught her breath and looked down at his hand resting on her thigh and realized she was dressed in a red satin and lace slip that was slit up the middle to reveal red lace panties. Someone had dressed her in it. Which meant someone had seen her naked. For the second time in a week, she had woken up in someone else's clothes.

The man squeezed Aislinn's thigh. Sensing evil, most certainly in his touch, Aislinn was horrified at the thought that he might have dressed her. She could smell alcohol and a strong male musky scent as if he had been moving around a lot. For some reason, Aislinn felt that a woman had dressed her, not this man. How she knew that, she could not fathom. Her psychic abilities were growing in strange ways.

"Please," she implored. "I need to get out of here. I think there's been a mistake." Every part of her wanted to yell demands at the man. She decided a sober tone might be better.

"Oh, there's definitely no mistaking you, sweet thing. Like I said, if you're real nice, we'll see what happens." A gleaming smile spread across the open mouthpiece of the mask, a smile similar to Eddie's but without the charm. "By the way, this room is soundproof. Some people like to scream. I like screaming. It's also cloaked in spells that suppress psychic abilities and telepathic communication from reaching beyond it. So, no one can hear you either way."

*Bastian, help me!* As soon as the call left her mind, Aislinn cried out in pain from the sensation of a long metal nail being stabbed into her brain.

*Aislinn!* Bastian's mental tone was frantic. Aislinn winced.

"See. I told you. Couldn't wait to try it, could you. You'll burn out your brain before you can get two sentences out. Oh, and don't try that psychic flash thing I've heard about. Because, *that* will really backfire." He sat on the bed and Aislinn flinched at his proximity, curving her torso to get as far away as possible.

She gritted her teeth and concentrated. *Bastian, hear me, please! Hear me!* The searing pain that followed made her head and shoulders shake and her eyeballs pound. Still, she was certain she felt his presence brush across her mind.

*Where are you, Aislinn!* Though Bastian was mentally shouting, his soul bursting with desperation, she could barely make out his words.

*I don't know!* Aislinn gritted her teeth at the pain. *I'm locked in a red room.*

"Usually I work on behalf of our customers, getting you sweet things ready for them." The man's fingers dug into the top of her thigh and under the strap of the panties. His red eyes glistened with desire. "Much as I'd like to have you for myself, you're a present for someone else."

Bastian felt Hera before he saw her. Her anger blew across him like hot smoke. He turned to find her glaring at him, her body stiff, amber eyes intense.

Cirillo put his hands on Hera's shoulders. "Hera, put your emotions aside. They have no place here. You are coming to the aid of your people. Fulfill your mission. We need you to read what happened here. Can you do that for us?"

Hera nodded, then threw a side glance at Bastian.

"Hera." Cirillo's voice was firm. "Even your sister knows she is useless in a battle if her emotions cannot be controlled. Regardless of what was going on in her heart, she would put it all aside and focus on her job. Will you do the same?"

Hera swallowed, embarrassment widening her eyes. "I will, sir." In silence she walked forward, taking deep breaths in through her nose and out through her mouth in the soft manner Bastian had used when focusing on a vampire's scent.

Hera stopped in the area between the bridge and the graveled road. She knelt and lowered her head, palming the air around her. Everyone remained silent, and waited.

"Miss Gabriella was just here. She doesn't like the man she sees, but is afraid for Miss Aislinn. She's demanding something."

Hera stood, her eyes glassy. In slow steps she walked across the grass and stopped as her feet crunched on the gravel. "Miss Aislinn was first. She gets in. She's upset about something. Great fear. Sacrifice."

Hera fell silent for a moment. Bastian could hardly breathe, willing her to see everything. He had to find Aislinn. He could sense her direction, but would he be in time on foot? If he lost her, his life would be over. No amount of angelic visions would persuade him to fight demons again. He would waste away and allow himself to die. But first, he would kill the Olympian responsible—and the vampire who served him.

"Struggle in the car." Hera's voice was soft. "Icky smell. Some... chemical." She paused and breathed. "I'm fighting but they are so strong. I send a psychic blast. It's not enough. I'm so heavy. It's dark now."

She took two steps back and let out a sob. "Miss Gabriella is... a vampire grabs her. He is fast. Same chemical. A sting in her arm. The men are happy. They got something good. They are laughing. They have done this before. They do this often. They want to touch the women. But... they're afraid someone will smell them. An Olympian. He will know if they touched them. They are going... going... *ugh*."

She made a disgusted sound in her throat. "Creatures. Noise. No. Masks. Costumes. Parties. Fun and... and fear. Lots of fear. Screaming. There's a secret way in." Her face wrinkled with the weight of the vision. "They have... power over... over... women. Girls. So many girls."

Bastian cursed vehemently, his fingers curling into fists.

*Contain it, Bastian,* said Marius. *Don't distract her. I know what you're feeling, believe me.*

Bastian forced himself to breathe steady. He tried to swallow the emotions, but could not. Aislinn had opened his soul, and emotions kept spilling out. Now his soul was being ripped in half.

Hera began breathing in gasps, her voice cracking. "Who am I? I'm so confused. They have me. They hurt me. They do what they want. My soul is far away… falling… falling… I hide it from them. I just pretend. I have to survive. I don't know who I am."

Tears fell down Hera's cheeks. She was shaking, staring forward in shock.

Cirillo gently grasped her shoulders. "Come out of it, honey. Hera, break it off. Come out. Now!" His shout seemed to stun her. She was blinking and looking at him, tears streaming down her face.

"Oh, my god," she sobbed, and wrapped her arms around Cirillo. He did his best to comfort her.

Bastian was frozen. What kind of horror had Aislinn been taken into? Why would she choose to go? Had Edward truly threatened her? Nothing was making sense. Edward's spells were powerful. Everyone spoke of the rumors concerning his family. But Bastian and Aislinn's bond was also strong. Why was their bond not strong enough to keep her beside him?

Fear clawed at Bastian's heart with taunting fingers. Regardless of what Aislinn felt, he was certain of what he felt. He did not need the blood bond to remind him. He would not live life without her. He would find her, whether she was willing or not. Then he would relish killing Edward. *Slowly.*

*Bastian, help me!*

*Aislinn!* Bastian cried out through their connection, all of his fear bolstering the frantic response.

"Bastian, what is it?" Marius was asking.

*Bastian, hear me, please! Hear me!* Aislinn called again.

Pain filled Bastian's mind. She was in horrible, knife-rendering pain.

*Where are you, Aislinn!*

*I don't know! I'm locked in a red room.*

# CHAPTER 29

"By the way, there's a few rules," the clown-faced man instructed as if he were teaching her a card game. "You call me Master. Nothing else. If you call me something else, there'll be a little punishment. I won't be asking for much. You're going to say a few things, repeat them to me, and then you're going to swallow something. That's all."

He sighed. "A little lame for me, personally. I like the whips and chains. You'll learn to like them. The hoist, too. But… like I said, you're a present. I can't damage you. Unfortunately, if you don't do what I ask…" he pointed to Gabriella, "she gets punished. Feisty one, too. Had to give her another dose to keep her down. You? You slept like a baby."

His hand slid up and down Aislinn's thigh as if he was working hard to control himself. "So soft. And your blood smells so good. No wonder he likes you. Okay, sweet thing, what is my name?"

Aislinn glanced toward Gabriella still hanging limp from chains around her wrists. Fear and fury battled for space inside Aislinn's brain. Everything in her wanted to defy this man. But, she was not willing to take chances with Gabriella.

"Master." She averted her eyes, disgusted to say the name.

"Good. Good. You're doing well. See, it's so easy. Now, repeat after me, three times, 'Master, your will is mine today. Master, your orders I freely obey.'"

"What?"

The clown mask tilted to the side. "Not the response I was looking for. You're not being a very good girl." He stood, pulled something out of his pocket and turned toward Gabriella. Aislinn realized he was holding a feathered dart, one with a two-inch, needle-like tip. He pumped the air and aimed.

In disbelief, she watched the dart soar through the air and sink into Gabriella's shoulder with a muffled *thud*. Gabriella cried out in shock, jerked her head up, and blinked furiously to understand what had happened to her.

"Oh, my god! Stop it! Stop it!" Aislinn pulled against her chains. The thick, bracelet-like cuffs burned like ice on her wrists. "Don't hurt her, please. Please."

The man returned his gaze to Aislinn, his head tilting again. "Well, you're sounding a little nicer. It's all up to you, sweet thing. All you have to do is what I ask."

He hovered over her and spoke with a mesmerizing voice, the deep tones resembling persuasion. "Look into my eyes and repeat after me, three times, 'Master, your will is mine today. Master, your orders I freely obey.'"

Aislinn repeated the phrase, nearly choking on the third rendition.

"Good. That was very good." From a small table beside the bed, he picked up a small box, and struck a match. Aislinn gasped in fear as he lit a red candle on the table. "Now, let's test you to see if you're sincere." In a deep, musical tone, clearly ripe with persuasion, he ordered, "Say three times, 'Only Eddie's voice can I find. Only Eddie's voice in my mind.'"

Confusion wrinkled Aislinn's brow and she could not help staring at him, wide-eyed. Eddie? What did Eddie have to do with this? Was this man related to Eddie and doing this for him? Where was Eddie?

Slipping into the passenger seat of a car and hands slapping a chemical-smelling cloth over her face came back to her. Strong arms and legs had held her in place as a syringe was stabbed into her arm. Panic had pumped adrenalin into her veins and she fought hard, but the drugs had kept her from formulating any strategy for psychic energy. She had made one attempt at a psychic blast, hearing her attackers yell, before her world went gray and silent. This man did not appear to be one of the two who had been in the car.

"Hmm, not hearing an answer. All right, have it your way."

"No! No!" Aislinn cried out as the man whipped out another dart and threw it with unbelievable precision into Gabriella's chest just above her right breast. Gabriella screeched through gritted teeth.

"Stop it! Don't. Please, please, I'll do anything you say." Tears stung Aislinn's eyes.

Gabriella spoke up. "Is that all you got, *big man*? What a coward you are, tying up women for kicks. Can't get them to come on their own? Poor little boy."

"*Oooo*, see? She's feisty isn't she?" he said to Aislinn, resting again on the bed and not looking back at Gabriella, which surprised Aislinn.

"Please don't hurt her," she begged. "What do you want me to say?"

"Ah, that's more like it," he crooned. "By the way, these blue darts are the silver-tipped ones. Made them myself. Just for the girls with Olympian blood. The ones who don't know it."

His intense stare indicated he was waiting for her to react to his confession. Her eyes widened but she could not fathom the significance of silver.

"Now, say it for me, sweet thing, 'Only Eddie's voice can I find. Only Eddie's voice in my mind.' Three times." He held up three fingers.

"Only Eddie's voice can I find, only Eddie's voice in my mind," she repeated over and over.

"Now, open your mouth."

"W-what?"

He stood. "Do we need another lesson?"

"No, no, no." She shook her head violently. "I-I just didn't understand."

"Hmm, I'll let that one slide. See, I can be reasonable." He sat and leaned toward her. "I'm always reasonable if you obey. It's so simple. Open your mouth."

Terrified of what he would do, and fearful that he was another Olympian wanting to give her his blood, Aislinn managed to part her lips. From his jeans pocket the man produced a small brown bottle. He twisted the lid which contained an eye dropper, and whispered something in Latin.

"Open wider," he insisted, coming toward her with the dropper.

She obeyed. He squeezed the rubber top and three drops of something disgusting stung her tongue.

"Swallow."

She did so, wincing.

"Now, be a good girl and say, three times, 'This potion I freely accept for Eddie and me, this spell I freely cast, so mote it be.'"

Aislinn dutifully repeated the phrase.

"Open again," the man ordered.

Trying not to look disgusted, Aislinn opened her mouth and closed her eyes as the drops of liquid burned. Her ears began ringing. Like venom, the poisonous concoction coursed through her limbs and into her brain.

Gabriella's words came back to her. *"Did he utter any rhymes or poems? Did he ask you anything that you consented to?"* Aislinn knew then she was being put under a spell. One powered with persuasion. And she was probably being drugged as well.

In the absolute horror of that moment, there was nothing she could do about it, not without risking Gabriella. She was chained and completely at this man's mercy. She realized this fear had been with her always, from reading about women, and men, being held as captives or slaves, and having no recourse but to obey their captor's wishes and pray they did not suffer physical pain. Her fear was primal, raw. He could hurt her. He could rape her. He could flay open her skin if he wanted, and no one would know, no one would hear her screams, except Gabriella.

A memory from the hospital after one of her surgeries surfaced. While most of the hospital staff had been kind and attentive, she had awoken from surgery to two young nurses telling her to lift herself from one bed to another. Residual anesthesia, medication, and throbbing pain had such a hold on her limbs, she could not move them. She could not even open her eyes. One of the sharp-tongued nurses declared that she had better move, or they would have to move her, and it would hurt much worse. Their threat, utter distain, and total lack of empathy was frightening beyond anything she had ever encountered at the hands of people she would normally have trusted.

Afterward, she had told her doctor she would not be treated at that hospital again. She would go to the one across town. The smaller one. Her doctor had reported the two nurses, and they were reprimanded.

Would this man ever be reprimanded? Would there be anyone to make him pay some recompense for crimes that would go completely unwitnessed, except by her? Would there be some tape recording to prove his heinous actions? The thought brightened her and then horrified her. She determined in that moment that if such evidence were available, she would welcome it, and not fear the horror of her torture or demise being solidified in a recording. Except for Grams and Aunt Julia. They could never be allowed to watch such a thing.

Somewhere inside her shaking body came a voice, a notion, a light, that no matter what happened, she would grab at any opportunity to survive. She would fight, or she would acquiesce, whatever worked. But this man would only think he controlled her soul. Her soul would be free, merely going through the motions of whatever it took to survive. She would persevere.

"You're doing so much better," the man reassured her as if she were a child. "Now, say, 'My blood flows only for Eddie's demands. My body responds only to Eddie's hands.'"

"Don't say it, Aislinn," Gabriella spoke up.

The man stood, his limbs stiff with irritation. "Don't interfere, bitch. This isn't about you." His toothy snarl was vile and threatening. "Of course, we can *make* it about you."

Gabriella glared at him in defiance. "This isn't about any of us. It's about Edward."

For some reason, the man ignored Gabriella and affixed his reddish eyes on Aislinn. "But she knows what to do, don't you sweet thing?" He leaned over and slipped cold fingers over her breast.

At his touch, Aislinn felt a shiver of disgust come over her before she could stop it.

Gabriella raised her chin. "Don't listen to him, Aislinn. He's just a pitiful excuse for a man, having to control women in order to get it up. What's the matter, coward, can't afford a hooker for your kinky fun?"

"Oh, you do have a saucy mouth. I can fix that." With swift strides the man strode toward Gabriella, grabbed a roll of black tape off the wall, and tore off a piece.

Aislinn screamed, "No, no, no! Come back!"

When the man aimed for Gabriella's face, she squinted. The piece of tape flew upward and stuck to the man's face. He ripped it off with a growl, then had to unstick it from his hand.

"You little witch. Got past the pain to use a little TK, eh?" With lightning speed he grabbed Gabriella's chin and slapped the thick piece of tape over her mouth despite her jabbing with her elbows to ward him off.

"You're going to be fun later. Just me and you, babe."

"Don't hurt her," Aislinn cried out. "Please, come back to me," she added to entice him away from Gabriella. "I'll do what you want. Come back. Ignore her."

Aislinn heard a tiny hiss of whispers in her mind and noticed Gabriella wincing in pain. She hoped in desperation that Gabriella was getting through to Marius.

*Bastian!* Aislinn tried again to reach him. *I'm in a red room. Gabriella is being hurt.* Aislinn gritted her teeth at the needles stabbing into her forehead. Nausea rose in her chest and throat.

The clown face turned toward Aislinn, red eyes menacing through the cut holes. "You *were* being good, weren't you?" With a swagger, he returned to the side of the bed and leaned over, his hand rubbing the red material over her stomach and breasts.

To Aislinn's complete shock, the touch sent sexual heat racing through her body. Her skin tingled and breasts throbbed underneath the material. Aislinn blinked in confusion, unable to understand how her body could react to this monster.

Had he added his blood to the potion and created a blond bond? The smile she could see through the mouth area of the mask made it clear he knew exactly what she was feeling. There was sinister delight in that smile.

"You feel it, don't you? This is a house favorite." He spread a hand between her breasts, pushing the material into her skin. She tried hard to force her body not to react, but it was on fire.

*Aislinn! Who is he!*

*I don't know,* she screamed back. *He looks like Eddie. Red eyes.* After an explosion of pain like a wooden bat being whacked into her head, and a heave of her stomach, Aislinn knew she could not try to contact Bastian again. She was going to throw up or pass out.

~~◊~~

Marius shook. He had fallen to his knees. His beautiful Gabriella was being tortured, and he had no idea where she was. Again and again he tried to reach her, but only a few words came through before searing, horrific pain snatched her voice away. It was unnatural, this pain. Power was behind it. Demonic power.

He inhaled slowly and concentrated to think it through. Clearly Gabriella's body was being hurt. But the spikes in her mind—*that* pain held the signature of evil. Perhaps spells. Perhaps a demonic presence offering protection in return for... what?

"Cirillo, they are held in a red room protected by evil," said Marius, his eyes still closed in concentration. "Do you know of such a place?"

"Not specifically," Cirillo answered. "But if we have to, we'll focus on the greatest concentration of demonic energy we can. And magic. It would take a lot to block you. A level that high has to stick out."

"It would take my people hours to cross the ocean. This is your kingdom, Cirillo. Who can we call on to help?"

"Everybody," Cirillo answered with resolve. "I'm organizing everyone as we speak."

Marius opened his eyes, surprised to find them wet. He had not shed a tear in decades. Bastian remained on his feet beside him, holding the sides of his head with both hands. He was breathing in the strange gasps of a man in shock.

Thunder rumbled above their heads and lightning slashed the sky in response to the level of energy both men were putting off.

Marius knew Bastian was trying to communicate with Aislinn and was experiencing the same excruciating throbbing in his head. Yet, neither man could let go of their tenuous connection. Marius had never lost his woman before. Ever. He had never experienced a moment when he could not touch her mind or sense her presence.

But Bastian had.

And he had stopped Bastian from killing Edward. If he found the man that had injured Gabriella, would he be able to stop himself from pummeling him without mercy? Probably not. He would take pleasure in tearing him limb from limb. His patron saints and angel had better be stronger than his desire to hurt the man that was hurting Gabriella.

~~◊~~

Aislinn repeated the last phrase, and felt the dreamy compliance of persuasion relax her. The man's persuasion was so strong that for a moment, the only thing that existed in her awareness was his red eyes.

Again she was ordered to open her mouth and accept the drops of liquid as he chanted strange words.

Revolted at the bitter taste, Aislinn let him see her swallow, knowing he was watching for the throat movement. With sheer force of will, she tore away from his gaze and glanced at Gabriella, unable to discern whether she was wincing in pain from the darts or from an attempt to contact Marius. Tears were running down her reddened face. Her eyelids were pressed tight.

"Now, say three times, 'From Olympian life I will abstain. By Eddie's side I will remain.'" The fateful chant threatened to swallow her as if the walls were closing in.

Gabriella squealed in protest, pulling hard on the shackles. Aislinn saw a small piece of the wall give way. Wood splintered around the bolt connecting her chain to the wall. *Of course*. Gabriella was an Olympian. She would have more strength than the other women usually brought here. And there was no question in Aislinn's mind that other women *were* brought here. Lots of them.

To Aislinn's horror, the man straightened, took out another dart, and threw it.

Aislinn screamed, "No! I did what you asked!"

The dart hit with a thud below Gabriella's right breast.

Garbled grunts of pain escaped Gabriella, and she coughed up blood.

Aislinn shook her head violently. "No. Stop, please. Ignore her and focus on me. I'll do whatever you want. Just me and you, Master." Aislinn choked on a sob.

Rushing through the requested words in order to keep his attention on her, Aislinn opened her mouth to accept the potion. A loud buzz like a giant insect reverberated in her ears as the thick drops fell onto her tongue. Her head throbbed mercilessly even as her mind acceded to his persuasion. She could hear faint, creepy laughter echo around her. Black smoke-like entities began to materialize.

The man looked up suddenly as if he had heard their laughter, too. He glanced around and a slight, evil smile curved his lips as if he were unbothered by it.

Faces began to form in more places in the room, and Aislinn blinked furiously to dispel the images. In the curtains, in the air, in the man's shirt. If there was a defense against this torturous mixture of persuasion and spells, she wished someone had taught her. She knew nothing of the strange world of potions and spells other than what she had experienced the day before. Wait, wasn't there something Gabriella had tried to teach her?

"Now, this one's important." He leaned closer, his eyes unblinking. "Say, 'No other lover exists for me. Only Eddie my eyes will see. Should I depart from Master's command, my body will know pain I cannot withstand.'"

A grunt escaped Gabriella. Her chains were rattling as she struggled and banged against the wall.

That one made sense to Aislinn. Eddie wanted her to forget Bastian and be his alone. Regardless of who this man was, this *was* orchestrated by Eddie. What had Gabriella said about claiming that she was free? Aislinn's mind grew fuzzy. If only she could remember what to say.

With his eyes locked on Aislinn's, the man reached for his pocket and whispered low. "The next one goes between her ribs, just inside the left breast. This silver tip is long enough to reach the apex of her heart."

"I'll do anything you say, Master. Just let me do this. Ignore her." Aislinn repeated the words he demanded, opening her mouth again for the stinging droplets. Tears were falling from the corners of her eyes into her hair. But she could no longer remember why.

"And last," the man purred, "maybe I'll just insure that there's a little piece of you left for me." He winced as he pricked his finger with the dart. He held the pooling blood over Aislinn's lips, eyes brightening. With a slow turn of his finger, the crimson fluid dribbled into her mouth and onto her tongue. "Now, sweet thing, keep your eyes on me." She turned toward him as he lifted her chained hand and pricked her finger with the dart. She barely felt it, which was odd.

"Repeat for me." His fiery-red eyes pulsed with eager excitement. "'A secret we hold, Master, between us two, a part of me will always belong to you.'"

Gabriella was stamping her feet on the wall. More plaster fell. Aislinn acted as if no other sound was in the room dare he focus on Gabriella. Locked in the man's intense gaze she recited the grave words. She watched his mouth open and form a demented smile. Slowly, he leaned toward her blood-stained finger, his tongue sticking out of the opening in the mask.

She felt a strange pressure between her finger and his tongue, like an invisible balloon had appeared, causing resistance. He hesitated, and frowned for a moment.

"Hmm, never encountered that before. Another Olympian's claim. Won't stop me, though." He gleefully lapped her finger.

An unseen door flew open, blowing the red curtains, and Eddie stepped into the room, his face livid.

# CHAPTER 30

"Report Ken," Cirillo commanded into his cell phone. "I'm putting you on speaker so everyone can hear. Marius Brancusi is here with the other Balkans, Bastian and Dimitri. Ken is my private investigator," Cirillo explained to Marius. "Had him start checking out Edward when you contacted me before you arrived. Beattie said she had a bad feeling about Edward, so I decided to act. She's usually right about people."

"Good to have you with us, sirs," said Ken through the speaker.

"It was until someone stole my wife," Marius replied curtly.

"What?"

Cirillo leaned toward the phone. "Ken, two women are missing. Aislinn Thomas is believed to have entered a car at the back of our property where it meets our neighbor's land. Gabriella, Marius' wife, apparently followed. We believe they were both taken by force."

Ken whistled. "Olympian involvement or human?"

"Mostly Olympian, but rogue. Edward Hawthorne is involved. Possibly his father. What have you found out about them?"

"Horace Hawthorne is a master of disguise," Ken began. "He has companies that own companies that own companies. Edward tries to be just as elusive as his father and lives in several locations, including a town house in Asheville. He's believed to own three labs and two downtown bars, under hidden corporations, but also assists his brother with The Haunted Hawthorne Hall complex every year. Turns out he did temporarily live with Aislinn Thomas over a year ago, for about a week, right before her family got killed in an auto accident. But get this. The truck that hit her was driven by a guy who worked for West Carolina Construction. Guess whose parent company owns the construction company?"

"Edward's?" Cirillo knitted his brows.

"Ultimately Horace Hawthorne, but Edward is on the payroll. For no apparent reason the driver took one of the company trucks around six o'clock and was headed down the same road as the Thomas family, from the other direction. Witnesses say he just swerved right into them. The driver couldn't remember anything, even driving the truck. He died after being released on bond. It appeared to be a suicide, but law enforcement was suspicious."

Marius exchanged looks with Cirillo. "So, the murder of her family was planned."

"Aislinn's grandmother sued and got a quick settlement," Ken added. "Apparently the company was anxious to keep the publicity down. The family agreed not to talk further about the incident."

Bastian, who had been pacing, froze. "Why *her* family?"

"Ken, do you know why the family was hit?" Cirillo asked. "Could Aislinn have been the target?"

"According to the brother of the Hawthorne family chauffer, who we conveniently got drunk yesterday, Aislinn Thomas was the real target. Something about a mage predicting Eddie's blonde girlfriend would change the family forever."

Bastian was speechless, staring at Cirillo in disbelief.

"No wonder attempts on her life continued," said Marius. "Yet, they were unsuccessful. Someone protects her." Gabriella had told him there was more than meets the eye when it came to Aislinn. Now, Marius was beginning to believe.

Cirillo rubbed his chin. "Ken, any more specifics about the Thomas girl being the target?"

"No. I couldn't get any more than that. She's got loyal friends, mostly from the therapy center where she's spent the last year as a patient. She lived with her grandmother and aunt while recuperating. Then moved into an apartment close to Brevard College a few weeks ago. Her bloodline is a fragmented, confusing story."

"We can get into that later. What about Edward. Did you find him?"

Ken chuckled. "You can run, but you can't hide… from me."

Cirillo smirked. "That's because you have the best danged persuasion in the whole eastern U.S."

Ken's chuckle turned mischievous. "And, the fact that my brother's got the best psychometry in the entire U.S. However, the Hawthorne family's got dark power all over them. Spells on top of spells, Cirillo. Lots of guards at every single location. Whispers from staff are that they make deals with demons. You go after them, it better be with spiritual strength as well as physical. People who cross them either die or disappear."

Cirillo nodded. "Earl found out Edward picked up Aislinn's grandmother and aunt from the hospital this morning. The doctor had not given his consent, but the nurses were convinced he had. Sounds like persuasion was used. I sent someone to the grandmother's house. The grandmother and aunt can be seen through the windows. But no Edward or Aislinn. They're standing guard."

"Well, we've had our sites on the Haunted Hawthorne Hall complex since you had us checking all the locations connected to the family," said Ken. "The place is huge. Four buildings. Two roads lead in. One is the main entrance to the original Haunted Hall. Splits off to the left for The Party House, the delivery area, barn and employee parking. Other side goes to the right, to The Devil's Tower, but you have to have special permission to park there. Halloween is biker night at the tower. There's a hidden back entrance that the public knows nothing about. No gravel, just grass. Three cars drove in this morning. Then two cars went in a while ago, a white older model sedan, and later Edward's black Corvette."

Marius felt his heart skip a beat. "Our women were taken in a white car."

"Well sir," said Ken. "That could be the vehicle then. Windows were blacked-out. The road winds through the forest in back of the complex. Looks benign to the observer, but some teenagers tried to bust through the metal barrier across the road in order to sneak in while we had it under surveillance. Guards came out of the woodwork, visibly armed, too. Scared those teenagers to death. They'd better be glad they're still living."

Cirillo flicked his eyes toward Barry Parker. Barry walked over to the map on the wall and rested his finger on a spot. Everyone gathered to observe the location of the complex in relation to where they were.

"Ken, any advice on the best way to go in?" asked Cirillo. He brought up the terrain on his computer.

"First, from the air," Ken replied. "If you have any shifters, I'd have 'em coming from several directions. We've seen two drones of theirs. Security is everywhere, and tight. We could use persuasion and take over deliver trucks of food, or pose as employees or patrons. Most of the party rooms are booked way ahead of time, and today's their biggest day of the year. But keep in mind, though the Hawthornes are up to their usual Halloween antics, Horace and Damian Hawthorne have been going overboard with the charity giving. They're touting their work hiring ex-cons, but also made a special day this year for handicapped and special needs kids to do the Hayride for free. Tread carefully, Cirillo. They can do no wrong as far people are concerned right now. They've positioned themselves well."

"So, Edward is somewhere in this place?" Bastian had moved to Cirillo's computer for a topical view.

"Looks like it," Ken affirmed through the phone. "Do either of you have the women's cellphones? I can get my connections at the police department to trace their locations."

"Gabriella wrote down Aislinn's cellphone number," said Marius. "But her phone is still in our room. I can retrieve it and at least get Aislinn's number."

"Barry, would you get that?" Cirillo glanced at Barry.

Marius nodded to him in appreciation.

"I've got eyes on the place," said Ken, "but night will be falling in a few hours and the customer lines have been steadily two hours long since 2:00 when they opened."

"Great place to hide somebody," Cirillo remarked as he zoomed in on his computer. "Hera said she saw costumes. Being Halloween, we didn't know where to start. If the two women are there, her vision would make perfect sense."

"Hera?" questioned Ken.

"Andromeda's younger sister, remember?" Cirillo clarified. "From Italy."

"Oh yeah, I remember. I heard Andromeda's there, too." Ken's voice sounded appreciative.

"Her sister's turning out to be a gifted mage. She has been staying with us. Family difficulties were causing her to lean toward the dark side. You know how teenagers *looove* the dark side."

"Yep. I was one of those once."

"If you've tracked Edward to the H3, that's where Aislinn'll be. And I'm guessing Lady Gabriella as well."

"Gabriella dreamed of bizarre costumes," said Marius, more to himself than anyone else. He should have taken the time to question her further concerning her recent dreams.

"What's that?" asked Ken.

"Nothing," said Marius. "How far a drive is this H3?"

"From Cirillo's, it's about forty-five minutes. If it were dark, you could fly there in fifteen."

"Sun's still up, Marius," said Cirillo.

"I do not wish to wait," Marius responded. His inability to speak with Gabriella was gnawing away at his stomach. No amount of security or walls was going to keep him from ransacking the place until he found her.

Cirillo faced the phone. "Ken, is it worth sending men to any other location?"

"We could, but... with it being Halloween and all the unusual demonic activity cropping up, I'd hate to waste anyone. Edward's got a mother and sister at a fairly big place, but his mother has been separated from Horace for several years."

"Any chance either of the women could be hidden at Edward's mother's place? Or Horace's compound? What about Edward's lab or bars?"

"Hmm, I would say no to the mother. As for Horace's compound, if your son was trying to hide a woman that you believe will bring down your family, would you keep her at your place?"

Cirillo snorted. "Good point."

"One lab has a night shift and a truck bay for deliveries. But, Cirillo… lots of whispers of demonic activity from the people who work at the H3. Some claim remembering being brainwashed to stay loyal and not speak of anything they're told not to, and from people wearing masks to hide their identity. Sounds like persuasion to me. I would expect anything to happen there, not to mention the road leading in is a total parking lot on Halloween. You can use flyers, but you might even need a chopper. You'll have to be lean and mean. My brother and I are ready if you need us. We have access to a news chopper. The H3 would love the publicity and probably not stop us."

"Let us go, now," Bastian begged. "I can follow the scent of the vampire."

"I agree, Bastian." Marius answered, though it was difficult for him to think strategically with fear and fury threatening to choke him. "I know Gabriella is still alive. But we need blood for strength, and we need the night."

"You've got the run of the place," Cirillo offered. "All the cow's blood we collected from the last one butchered is gone. I'll put one in the barn. Make it fast and easy. I've already got teams organizing and waiting for instructions. Some can handle the sun just fine. They may not be as gifted, but they're fantastic warriors. And… I'm thinking we pay a little visit to Horace Hawthorne. He may not have the women at his compound, but he'll be mighty pissed to have Olympians on his front lawn. In fact, why don't I just send two people over to the wife's place? Let's go shake him up."

Marius nodded and placed a hand of gratitude on Cirillo's forearm. "We will take blood for strength. Then, we will go hunting. For Olympian blood." Marius turned on his heel, and then doubled over in pain.

In his chest he felt the acidic sting of silver-coated metal. Gabriella was in pain. She was having trouble breathing. Marius slapped his hands to his head and roared in agony. Power detonated from him in an explosion of energy.

The glass window behind Cirillo's desk shattered outward. Shards blew into the yard and rained over the grass. The tremendous force threw some of Cirillo's warriors into bookcases.

Marius gasped for air. His canines burned with desire to sink into a man's neck. Gabriella's torturer would not live through the night if he could help it.

"Marius?" Cirillo spoke softly.

Gulping breaths with effort, Marius lowered his hands and lifted his eyes. From the alarmed look on Cirillo's face, the whites of his eyes were probably pulsing red.

"He is injuring her with silver," Marius explained, his voice sounded like the growl of a werewolf.

"All right, Marius." Cirillo rounded the desk. "We go in. We get the women. We get out."

"I want Edward," Bastian stated through clenched teeth.

"I want the man who tortures my wife," Marius added.

"I mean it." Cirillo's tone hardened. "I will call on our blood bond, so help me God, if I have to. We'll apprehend Edward. And we'll apprehend the other guy. We try them in Olympian court. I've called The Plymouth and The Augustine. I'll be the third. And don't give me that look, Marius. You're compromised now. You *cannot* be the third judge."

Marius seethed with a rage that emanated from his very soul. Power billowed and rose inside him, making his arms and torso shake with the effort to contain it. Books fell off of shelves on either side of the room.

He knew Cirillo had the right of it. He could not judge this man without prejudice. But he might just reach him before Cirillo could stop him.

Like all tribal leaders, he and Cirillo could use their blood connections with their own warriors to stop them from doing something that could endanger themselves or the tribe. But only if that connection was open and they sensed what was happening. As leaders, their minds tended to expand with each blood bond, growing into a coliseum of whispering voices waiting for their Prince or Commander to single them out. Marius had exchanged blood with Cirillo years ago, out of trust. If Cirillo thought he could stop Marius by calling on his blood, he would have a fight on his hands.

The narrowing of Cirillo's vivid brown eyes showed he knew it. "Ken will keep his surveillance on the place," Cirillo assured him. "Edward won't escape. This is a rescue mission. Not war with the Hawthorne family."

Marius could not respond. He did not want to be at war with Cirillo, but the Hawthorne family had crossed the line.

Cirillo's glare shifted to Bastian. "Bastian?" he queried, looking for compliance.

Bastian turned and walked out of the library, refusing to answer Cirillo.

# CHAPTER 31

"What do you think you're doing?" Eddie demanded of the man wearing the mask.

"Just looking out for you... *friend*. Remember?"

Eddie's gaze shifted to Aislinn. *Yes!* Her heart leaped at his look of alarm, until it shifted, very slowly, to a calm expectant hunger.

"Are you okay?" Eddie asked her.

"Eddie," she sobbed, and froze. What if the man in the mask got angry because she spoke? "Eddie, can we get out of here? Please." Her body began to tremble at the thought of rescue.

Without reacting to her plea, he scanned the room until he spotted Gabriella chained to the wall on his right. "Get *her* out of here." He squinted, finally looking angry. "That's not what I think it is... you played target practice on her?"

The man in the mask raised both palms upward and shrugged in mock apology.

Eddie muttered curse words under his breath. "Have somebody dress her wounds. We'll both be sorry if she dies. Stupid Raven. And keep her in the Dungeon until we can take her somewhere else. Otherwise, her mate will sense her. You need to move fast in the hall. Get her asleep so he can't touch her mind."

"Sure." The man shrugged again, but with a smirk of rebellion, as if Eddie was spoiling all his fun. "Have it your way."

From the menagerie of objects on a shelf, the man selected a cloth and bottle. In silence he poured some liquid onto the cloth. He stepped toward Gabriella and fisted her hair with one hand while forcing the cloth over her nose with the other. Gabriella squirmed but Aislinn knew the drug would win. Gabriella was wounded and her mouth was taped. She would have to breathe.

"Eddie," Aislinn begged softly, "do something. *Please.*" There had to be some part of him that would respond to her pleas, if he truly cared.

Eddie stepped to her side, cupping her face in his hands, his voice a whisper.

"I can't. No one's allowed to see this place. He's moving Gabriella from this room. But, she'll be okay."

"What is this horrible place? Where are we?"

"That's a secret, I'm afraid." His eyes were sympathetic pools of green and gold, pulsing with a lustful glow. A glow she had learned to associate with winning. Aislinn felt lost for a moment in his confident gaze and tried to deduce what it was he had won. The clown man's words were repeating themselves in her brain. ...*only Eddie.* ...*only Eddie.*

"Eddie, I...." Aislinn felt a rush of nausea and could not remember what she was going to say.

"It's okay, sweetie-girl. Just you and me now. Don't worry about anything." He brushed the back of his fingers against her cheek, his eyes twinkling with anticipation.

Aislinn flinched as a door closed. Fearing someone else had entered, she lifted her head and realized Gabriella and the man were gone.

"Eddie, get me out of here."

With tenderness he pushed back hair from her face and planted soft kisses on her cheeks and temples. Aislinn felt his hand glide across the silky red satin to where it opened over her stomach. She gasped and closed her eyes as desire for his touch flashed across her tingling skin. The bed began to feel hot.

"Mmm, I love these things, don't you?" His fingers gripped the slick material at her sternum and massaged in circles, causing it to travel over her breasts, stomach and thighs. Each brush against her skin sent her into shivers of desire. The buzzing in her head was still loud, but began to lose importance. Only Eddie mattered, and how he was making her feel.

"Mmm, what is this Eddie, magic?"

"Oh, yes. A special material." Eddie murmured between scattered kisses on her face. "Only we make them. Sorry I couldn't get here sooner." His voice became dreamy and sensual. "I'll take care of you. I don't have the keys to these cuffs right now, but I can get them. These are silver, so I can't touch them."

"What do you mean?" Aislinn was trying to think straight, to demand things from him, something about her family she needed to know. But each slide of the red slip guided by his hand interrupted her thoughts, replacing them with carnal images. ...*only Eddie.* ...*only Eddie.*

"We're Olympians, love," he said between nips on her neck. "We're allergic to silver."

Aislinn turned her head to view the shiny cuffs, the motion making her feel sick. Her wrists were red, swollen and burnt.

"For real? It hurts, Eddie."

"Don't worry." Eddie positioned his body closer. "I'll have you out in no time. I just can't pull them off right now."

Aislinn's eyes crinkled in confusion. "Just like... vampires."

"It's where the legend comes from. Did you ever wear silver?"

"Wh–... uh–..." Aislinn stammered. "No." Her voice softened in disbelief. "But, that's just because I liked gold better. Silver made me...." The word *uncomfortable* formed in her mind.

"Mmm, hmm." He nuzzled her ear. "My blood flows through you, now. The chains will keep you weak. But it's okay. You're safe with me." He turned her chin toward him, gazing into her eyes. "I won't let anyone touch you. Never again. You are safe as long as you are with me. Only me."

"Yes, Eddie," she replied. "Only you."

"I love you, Aisy." Eddie let out soft moans of pleasure and brushed his lips over hers, teasing, tempting. She could not resist the lure of his voice and his mouth.

Her body acted of its own accord and she raised her head to solidify their kiss. He growled softly and began kissing her thoroughly and deeply, over and over, until they were both out of breath.

"I love you so much, Aisy," he cooed as he released her mouth. "So much." He pulled off his shirt and stretched out beside her, snuggling his cheek against hers. He slid one side of the delectable material off her tingling shoulder. "You love me too, don't you?" He paused to read her eyes.

"Yes," she replied, unable to look away from him. Of course she loved him. *No other lover exists for me, only Eddie my eyes will see.*

Eddie pulled the other sleeve off her shoulder and kissed her skin. The swish of material caused Aislinn's breasts to swell with yearning. She began squirming like a silky cat, allowing the sensual, amazing material to ignite her torso.

"I'm the only man for you, aren't I?" His hand slid over her breast and squeezed.

She sighed with pleasure and closed her eyes.

"No, keep your eyes on me," he whispered, his voice a velvet caress.

She obeyed.

"You hear only me, don't you, Aisy?"

Her mouth opened to answer, but she hesitated. Perhaps it was the strange whispers that kept brushing her mind, a voice desperate and pleading. Her brain was having trouble remembering. *Only Eddie's voice can I find, only Eddie's voice in my mind.*

"I hear only you, Eddie."

The voice was screaming, demanding something, but she ignored it. The voice made her head hurt.

Eddie cupped both of her breasts. "You choose only me, don't you, love?"

"Yes, Eddie." Aislinn gasped as he began kneading her breasts, eliciting delectable sensations. "Always."

"Good. Let me make you feel good. You want me to, don't you?" She felt his tongue lapping at her neck. He let out a long, moaning, "Mmm."

"Yes. Yes." Heartbeats were throbbing in her skull. Nothing existed but her and Eddie and how much she wanted to please him.

"That's my Aisy-girl." Gently, he untied the ribbon holding the front of the slip together, and pushed the material aside. He unzipped his jeans.

The door to the room swung open. The man looked like Eddie's twin wearing a dress shirt and suit jacket, except for a burgundy shade to his eyes.

"Hey, bro, Dad's here. Better move it."

~~◊~~

Eddie unlocked Aislinn's handcuffs with the key the man tossed him. Aislinn rubbed her body against him in an attempt to continue their lovemaking, but he pulled her from the bed and hastily retied the gown. His face looked panicked as he grabbed her hand and ran out the door jerking her in tow.

"Eddie," she pleaded, thinking she had displeased him, "what's wrong?"

Aislinn stopped talking at the sight before her. They had stepped into a dark room with spotlights aimed at a raised platform. A young woman with long, curly brown hair, wearing a white, fringed teddy and white high heels, stood a little unsteady on the platform. Her eyes appeared unfocused, almost dead, and her head wobbled slightly as though she were drugged.

Several men were seated in the dark. In far corners, Aislinn could make out the outline of security guards in red jackets, standing at attention. Eddie's footfalls were soft as if trying to avoid their attention. They all turned to stare, and Eddie froze.

"Ten thousand for that one," said one of the seated men.

Terror swept through Aislinn when she realized the man's finger was pointing at her, not the girl on the platform.

"My apologies gentlemen." Eddie nodded, adding a polite smile. "This one is already taken."

The man's eyes narrowed. "I *like* her." His tone inferred he was used to getting his way and expected Eddie to acquiesce.

"Yes, gentlemen," said one of the men, getting to his feet and slapping his hands together, "that particular girl *is* paid for." Aislinn found herself unable to move save for the knocking of her bare knees. In a game-show-host voice, the man continued, a faint reflective glow discernable in his eyes. "However, if blondes are your thing, we have another one available today. She's up next."

He pointed a hand toward the girl on the platform. "In the meantime, Jeanie here is a great buy. Look at that voluptuous body. Those plump tits are real, too, gentlemen. Skin so soft it's begging to be touched. *Ooof*, I can barely stand it, so close. And it's all for *your* pleasure. Your wildest desires. And she can deliver. She'll make you *lots* of money." He sauntered toward the platform and slipped his fingers under the girl's chin, causing her a slight shiver. Her eyes widened in fear but she managed a practiced smile.

"She's got the face of an angel but is a demon in the dark, trained to fulfill your exotic deviancies, and those of your customers. She's disease-free and a tight box. Mr. J, just for you I will lower the price. At a bargain, bidding starts at seven thousand. Now, what am I bid, gentlemen?"

"Aisy, move," Eddie hissed. He was dragging her toward a metallic door. He pressed his thumb to a keypad and a bolt slid.

Unable to control her shock and revulsion, Aislinn turned and out of habit attempted to launch her sluggish empathic senses toward the woman on the platform. Behind the young woman's glazed eyes, she was intent on standing without falling, fearful of getting punished if she fell or fainted. The woman's terror and humiliation was palpable, along with despair so profound, hope's flame had nearly gone out. She was a slave. There was no escape. There was only survival.

Aislinn practically fell over Eddie in her need to exit the room. Her fingers tore at the door frame. Her breath came in shuddering gasps, even after Eddie closed the door.

Eddie grabbed her shoulder and shook her. "Hey, hey… calm down."

"Eddie," her voice came out in a rasp, "that's… that's…."

"Shhh." Eddie cradled her face in his hands. "Listen to me Aisy. Ignore what you see. What you see can get you killed. My father is here, and he wants you dead. If he knows what you've seen, he won't hesitate. Follow me and do what I say. Smile at anyone who sees you. Look happy. Got that?"

# CHAPTER 32

Aislinn managed to stay upright as Eddie pulled her down so many winding stairways and corridors she lost all sense of direction. At one point they were running along a covered walkway that was two stories above ground and swayed from the movement of its occasional passengers. Rows of windows on the right side revealed a massive courtyard below, full of trees, lights and several hundred people partying and dancing to pounding music.

Red-vested waiters passed her and Eddie in both directions on the covered bridge with trays of food or dirty dishes. When Eddie paused to let three servers go by, Aislinn looked back through the window and saw the walls of a four-story, stone tower with battlements at the top. Had that been where they came from? Something about it was familiar.

Eddie urged her to go faster, one hand locked on hers and one hand pressing against the small of her back. A glimpse beyond the courtyard revealed a giant barn with an orange glowing sign advertising Hair-Raising Hayrides.

The barn looked familiar, too, though the neon sign did not.

Eddie burst through a door and leapt up a wooden staircase. Aislinn could hear and feel incredible numbers of people screaming and yelling somewhere in the building. Their continued blood-curdling screams made the hair on her arms stand on end. Combined fear from so many minds, mixed with hers, coupled with hysterical laughter, was building an overload, a blast of white expanse into her muddied senses.

Eddie ran down a long, enclosed balcony on the side of a building with windows and screens, giving a better view of the ever-moving courtyard of people below.

Eddie placed a phone to his ear. "Damian, where is he?"

"He's going through the tower with some security guys," said a voice. Aislinn recognized the voice of the young man who had called Eddie "bro." Though he had burgundy eyes, he was not the man in the mask.

"Whew, we got away in time."

"Wait a minute," said Damian. "Hang on, I've got some chatter. Aw, crap, I think somebody must have reported seeing you. He's talkin' about going for the Mansion now. One of my security guards just told me."

"All right, we're going over to The Party House," said Eddie. "I can't keep her exposed like this. He'll be able to sense her location out in the open."

"Who, Dad?"

"No, the Heraclid."

"Oh. Well, Dad's claiming his mage says Olympians are headed here. Boy is he pissed. Those Appalachians are going all out for the girl."

Eddie cursed. "It's not just mine. Stupid Raven took Gabriella, too. She's Prince Marius' wife, Damian. What do you *think* he's going to do? He'll leave this place in pieces trying to find her." Eddie heaved a sigh. "They shouldn't have known she was here. Somebody's ratted us out."

"Not my staff. I'll fire their ass, or worse."

Eddie pulled harder on Aislinn's arm and she cried out. He made no effort to slow down.

"Only the Appalachians know who these two girls are," he said. "Maybe we have a mole. I gotta get her under cover. Is anybody in the Loud and Luscious Room?"

"Nope. Last minute cancel. It's all yours."

"It's spelled and warded, isn't it?"

"Yeah, but not strong like the Red Room or the Dungeon."

"Can I get in it?" asked Eddie.

"Your thumbprint will open all of them."

"All right. Keep this line open." Eddie banged through swinging doors marked STAFF ONLY, nearly dragging Aislinn.

"Eddie, slow down," she begged. "My legs are killing me."

"Aisy, if we don't hurry, we'll both be dead."

Faces swooped at Aislinn and she squealed and ducked. Hideous laughter erupted in the air.

"Eddie, what are they?"

"The mansion's haunted. Hurry, we're almost out."

A gray figure materialized beside the door they were approaching. His scowling face looked comprised of anger and evil amidst wrinkles. Aislinn closed her eyes and curled against Eddie as he punched in a code beside the door, ignoring the opaque figure nearly touching them.

The door did not respond.

"Go on, grandfather!" Eddie yelled. "I need to get out of here."

Aislinn opened her eyes to see Eddie wave an arm at the floating specter. The figure dissipated into whirl of gray. Eddie punched in another code and the door opened.

They mounted a walkway suspended between two buildings, again with windows along both sides. Busy waiters and waitresses increased in number, and they had to artfully dodge them. Several greeted Eddie which he did not look happy about.

Through the windows to the left, Aislinn could see clumps of tall oak trees and hundreds of cars in parking lots, rows of orange and white lights outlining everything. Long lines of people were snaking around the front buildings, waiting to get in. Aislinn no longer heard so many screams but a general pressure of terror and delight whirled like a tornado of hot and cold air in her battered senses.

Through the windows on the right was the busy courtyard below. Looking across to the barn, Aislinn realized there was a two-story high, covered walkway on either side of the massive barn as well. Each of the four buildings was apparently connected to the others by staff walkways above the grounds.

Glancing back toward the looming tower, certain that's where she had been chained up, a red neon sign made to look like dripping blood rested above a dark archway at the bottom of the tower. It read: The Devil's Tower.

Aislinn gasped. She *knew* this place. Why didn't she realize it before? This was Haunted Hawthorne Hall, known as H3—the scariest and best place to be on Halloween. Every teenager dreamed about it, waiting desperately to turn sixteen to meet the minimum age limit.

Five friends had talked her into going when she was sixteen, three boys and a girl. She had screamed so much she was hoarse the next day. She had been terrified by the tall, slow-moving, costumed men that preyed upon patrons standing in line attempting to unnerve them before they entered the Mansion. By the time she had made it to the creaky front doors, she was desperate to run all the way through, wanting only to get out. At the time, she did not realize she was absorbing the emotions of all the terrified people in the building. She had just begun to understand her empathic abilities. It took several more years to learn to block the assaulting emotions.

The three boys in their group had alternated between yelling in shock and laughing in nervous hysteria, trying to look macho while walls periodically closed in on them and skeletal hands or zombies popped out to grab and screech at them. She and her friend, Tamara, had found nothing to laugh at, except when they finally made it out the back, only to run into a man with a hockey mask and a chain saw. Poor Tamara actually threw up in the parking lot.

Why would Eddie bring her here of all places? And then it hit her. Eddie's last name was Hawthorne. He had claimed he was a distant relation to the Hawthornes who owned H3. But if Damian was his brother, then his connection was not distant at all. He was Mr. Hawthorne Sr.'s son!

Dark, looming shadows rose in Aislinn's mind as she questioned where Eddie was taking her. This time, she retained the knowledge that she was under a spell. She had consented, but with full knowledge, and though the spell made her feel absolute devotion toward Eddie, a part of her knew she was feeling what she was supposed to feel. What she had agreed to feel.

Heading through another STAFF ONLY door, and down a staircase, the three-story building was packed with stifling throngs of costumed people in endless corridors and banquet areas, all drinking and partying. Music pounded in Aislinn's sensitive ears from every direction.

"Hurry," Eddie commanded, all the while pulling Aislinn, making her arms, spine and legs throb. She was wearing nothing but the stimulating red satin slip and panties, and running in bare feet. Thankfully, she did not look completely out of place since one group of women were more scantily clad than her, and covered in glitter and paint. Other people they passed were dressed in a menagerie of masks, robes, and multicolored wigs.

Aislinn's nerves and muscles, even her bones, vibrated from the music and excitement of the people in the building. Heightened emotions battered her like a roaring ocean in a relentless storm. The red negligée added to her misery with its strange ability to stimulate sexual responses, which had become a perverted irritant. She wanted to rip it off but had nothing else to put on. She prayed for some way to get off of the property and its massive prison of unwanted sensory overload.

They passed room after room, each with their own party going on and different themes of decorations and costumes.

"Eddie," a voice called through the phone.

"What?"

"Dad's bullying everybody, and comin' in large and in charge. He's going to look in every place we've shielded is my guess. We need to think of some place he doesn't know about."

Eddie sighed and bent over, breathing heavy. "Just great. Here he is, ruining my life again. All right, I'm going upstairs to the costume room before heading over to the Barn. Maybe I can disguise both of us."

Relieved at the thought of being able to put something else on, Aislinn trudged up another staircase without Eddie having to prompt her. She slipped twice and feared her legs were growing numb and useless. Eddie had to lift her with both arms.

"Hey Eddie," came Damian's voice again. "You'd better do more than that. Security has spotted several people in staff uniforms that they don't remember. I think Olympians are here already."

~~◊~~

Eddie stopped to press his thumb into a tiny screen next to a door marked: COSTUMES, STAFF ONLY. He swung it open and froze. A beefy man stood in the room, his hands folded in front of him. Eddie recognized him. His name was Butch and he looked it.

"Mr. Hawthorne would like a word with you, Edward," said Butch.

"Tell him to go f–..." Eddie's phone rang. He looked at the display, rolled his eyes at the word "Dad," and placed the phone to his ear.

"Give up the girl, Edward." Horace Hawthorne spoke.

"No," Eddie declared. "She's mine."

Horace cursed with vehemence. "I appreciate that kind of tenacity, son, but you can always get another blonde. There are millions of pretty women in this world."

Eddie turned as a door at the end of the hallway opened. Horace and a personal guard stepped through. Eddie stuck his phone in his pocket and faced them, resolute. Something tingled at the back of Eddie's neck and he whirled to see more of his father's guards coming up the other end of the hall, chewing gum and trying to look as if they just happened to show up there.

Eddie reached for his earpiece, but remembered something. He and Damian had cut each other and drank each other's blood when they were younger, curious to see if the stories of blood bonds were true. It had only taken a few hours to start working. They had not kept in touch over the last three years, and Eddie, after a few fallouts with Damian, had nearly forgotten they had the connection between them.

*Damian. Damian, hear me. I need some help. Find me some guards to balance this out. Dad's got four.*

*Whoa, bro on call. How long has it been? Years? I forgot we could do it. Okay, I'm on it. I'm sending The Party House security staff up there. Give me a minute.*

Horace Hawthorn's reddish-brown eyes squinted as he stopped at least twelve feet from his son. It was the first time Horace looked hesitant before a confrontation, and Eddie felt buoyed by that hesitancy. Anger and fear hung heavy in the air as Horace glanced from Eddie to Aislinn. The bodyguards waited and watched.

"I want her, Dad." Eddie stated. "Just like you wanted Mom. Remember all the old stories about how you defied everybody to get her?"

"Yeah, and look where that got me. You see her by my side?"

"That was because of *you.*" Eddie let all his hatred burn into the statement. "And we both know it."

"No, *she* grew too much of a conscience. Women do that. A very dangerous thing in our line of work. You think it won't happen to you, boy? She'll leave you some day for exactly the same reason."

With his focus still on his father, Eddie spoke to Aislinn. "Who's the only man for you, Aisy-girl?"

Aislinn answered without hesitation. "Only you, Eddie."

Horace snorted. "You think spells will keep her loyal for years?"

"It's more than spells with us," Eddie retorted. "I love her, and she loves me."

"Love isn't going to take care of the Olympians you let loose in my front yard." Horace's voice had become a growl. "Olympians showed up at *my* compound. And at your mother's. That hasn't happened in twenty-five years. And it's not my blood they're after."

"Actually, it is your blood... *Dad.*" Eddie sneered. "And I can promise you one thing. Someday when she and I have a son, I'm going to treat him a damn site better than you did me."

Horace's face stiffened. "I gave you everything you needed, son. Or wanted."

"Sure. Lots of *stuff.* Birthday presents the guards had to put together because you weren't there. A brand new car Enrique had to teach me how to drive because you were too busy. Christmases we had to make appointments for. Oh, there was lots of *stuff* under the tree. Just no family."

"People would kill for what you have."

"People *have* killed for what we have. I've known for years what goes on here. And I know how much money it makes you."

Horace's jaw jutted forward. "You benefited from that money. From my hard work. We're Alcmaeonidae, son. We're smart and we use our brains, not brawn. Every business has to make tough decisions in order to make decent money."

"Not quite like yours."

"You enjoyed it well enough," Horace accused.

"Yeah, well, I grew up. *And* decided on a real woman. Not some pretty face that's had the will beaten out of her."

"Ha! And spells don't do the same thing? I understand you have a few lucrative underground businesses of your own. A little too far on the dark side for making accusations, aren't you?"

"I know you check up on me. But I have security teams at my buildings as well. Besides, isn't this Damian's now? Isn't that what you've been saying for the last two years? 'It's all yours, Damian, I know you'll run it right.'"

"That's right. Damian knows how to run a business on and off paper. That's why I made him the CEO."

Eddie clenched his teeth. Another stab to infer Damian was better than he was. He should have defied them all and joined the Appalachians like he wanted when he was twenty. The fear that his father would rather have him killed than risk his dark business deals still loomed over him. Then again, there was that small part of Eddie that wanted to prove his father wrong, to show him he was just as brilliant as Damian. What an idiot he had been. All those wasted years.

Orthon chose that moment to rise inside of Eddie. He shouldn't have been surprised. Orthon loved anger and conflict. Eddie swallowed and concentrated on subduing Orthon. Then he changed his mind and let Orthon's energy strengthen him.

"Don't forget, Dad, half of what Damian has here came from *my* ideas. I made this place great. He just runs it."

"You're my son. Of course you have brilliant ideas."

Eddie snorted at his father's quick flip of attitude. "I'm half Mom's son, too. The better half."

"This is pointless. Just wait 'till you're a parent and all your hard work is thrown back in *your* face. I'll be around to see that day, too. Unless, you're still in hiding."

"Hiding?"

"They're saying one of the Heraclids has a blood bond with her. Of all people, why'd you have to pick a fight with The Balkan's right hand man over a *girl*? You know how long he's been around? What the hell were you thinking? Olympians are going to be sniffing all over this place soon like a pack of wolves."

"He'll never find me, or her. My blood bond overrides his, anyway."

"He's got the fangs, son."

"So have I, *Dad*. Remember?"

Horace's brows rose. "I thought you were lying about that."

Eddie felt satisfaction burn in his veins. He allowed all the hatred he was feeling to well into his jaws, making his canines sting as they lowered. Then he smiled. "Yeah, Dad, I can actually do something Damian can't. And something *you* can't. How 'bout that?" Disgust and sarcasm laced Eddie's voice, but he did not care, not any more.

"Watch your mouth, boy. I've got skills you'll never have." There was no disguising the reluctant pride and jealousy in his father's voice.

Eddie's heart lurched. Finally, when he no longer cared about his father's approval, he received it.

Horace scowled. "That's not going to help you now, is it? You'll never stop them from sniffing her out. That Sebastian's been a hunter longer than I've been alive. You think all of our wards can keep someone like him out?"

"We've done it before. That's one thing Damian *is* good at."

"So he is. And if he's willing to help you, it's his neck. But..." Horace pointed a finger at him, "you bring down this business and I'll take her out myself, even if you're in the way. I told you to take care of this."

"I did take care of it," Eddie declared. "And I'm still winning."

*They're up there now, bro,* Damian said.

Eddie watched the hall entrance door open behind his father. Burly security men stepped through, their eyes darting everywhere to assess the situation. Eddie heard the door behind him open as well, and knew Damian was smart enough to send his guards to both ends of the hallway. All of Damian's guards were ex-cons and absolutely loyal to him for giving them a decent job.

*Thanks, Damian.*

"Get her off my property." Horace pointed at Aislinn. "You want to fight The Appalachians, you do it at your own place."

"Fine. Then get outta my way."

With a flick of Horace's head, his bodyguards backed off and lined up against the wall.

# CHAPTER 33

Frigid air chilled Bastian's wings as he and Marius circled the sprawling amusement park. Unlike the vulture forms they had chosen, they weren't looking for something dead. They were looking for something to kill.

Bastian felt buoyed by Marius' rage which had grown a sentience of its own. If Bastian had possessed more than a beak at that moment, he would have smiled. Marius was going to have difficulty restraining from killing the man who had harmed Gabriella. Bastian was counting on it. He yearned to crush Edward's throat, just as he had crushed vampires before. Followed by lopping off their heads.

But first, Aislinn was somewhere below. Her mind might not be open to him, but their blood bond gave him a keen awareness that transcended spatial dimensions. Even though his senses were restricted in the animal form, Bastian knew Aislinn was in the red-roofed building full of costumed people, many of them on two rows of balconies. The pull was unmistakable. Marius confirmed Gabriella was somewhere in the complex as well, but was having trouble choosing the building. As they thought back and forth to each other, a dark mass appeared, swirling above them.

Bastian and Marius dove. Orange eyes and bat-like wings gave chase. Bastian allowed Marius to glide under him, then somersaulted in the air in order to strike with talons and beak. It held the imps at bay, but he and Marius knew they needed their weapons.

*Bastian, the balcony,* Marius ordered, then banked to the right, toward a balcony filled to capacity. Women and men cried out and ducked at sight of two massive birds with ten-foot wing spans diving at them.

The two Olympians landed in the open spot amidst more cries. Forming black, smoke-like energy around them helped mask their change into men. They uncoiled to their full height, surprising everyone. Women switched from squealing to eliciting *"oooo's."*

"That was totally cool!" yelled a young woman in a black, fairy-like costume who had hidden at the edge of open glass doors.

Another girl in a red and black vampire costume waved her friends forward. "You gotta see this. It's a show."

The swarm of imps dived and circled, which captured the attention of the partiers. Bastian and Marius took the opportunity to push into the expanded room of costumed bodies dancing under a disco globe, the colorful flashing lights the only illumination in the dark.

*Marius, Aislinn's near but I'm sensing fear and fast movement again.*

*I see two doors leading to the hallway,"* said Marius. *Let's get out of here.*

Shrill screams alerted them to two imps flying through the open glass doors, zipping like black arrows.

"Look, real bats!" A girl shouted.

"Nah, they gotta be fake," said a guy, sloshing his drink. "It's some projection or something."

Girls squealed and scrambled out of the way, half of them laughing. Bastian looked at Marius in alarm. The people should not be able to see the creatures.

Marius raised his eyebrows into a frown. *The Hawthorne's probably called them forth and requested they give people a scare. That's what they're all here for anyway.*

Bastian followed Marius as he dodged gyrating bodies, heading toward the hall. Then he breathed in a familiar stench. Raw meat and blood. Only one thing smelled like that to him.

*My lord, a real vampire is in here!*

*I smell him,* Marius answered, then twisted to avoid an imp that swooped at him.

Bastian punched the imp so hard it splatted into the ceiling. He had no time to waste on demons. Something struck him about the scent of the vampire. *Marius, it's him. The one who took Aislinn and Gabriella.*

*Don't lose him,* ordered Marius. *And don't kill him... yet.*

From their pockets, they each pulled out a hilt. The swords sprang to life, their high-pitched song noticeable only to the imps and the vampire over the pounding music in the room. Women *"ooo'd"* and *"ahhh'd"* at sight of the swords, convinced they were part of a show.

Marius scented the room and noticed a thin, pale, brown-haired man sitting on a loveseat at the far wall with his mouth covering the neck of a moaning woman. Marius could smell the blood and knew it was real. The man straightened suddenly, red drops dripping from his fangs, and frantically scanned the crowd as if having sensed Marius' power. He fixed widened red eyes on Marius, and dashed for the door.

Bastian was after him, pivoting gracefully between tightly-packed dancers, and leaping over a row of chairs. The crowd of partiers, most of whom were dressed as vampires, and quite drunk, exclaimed and pointed at Marius and Bastian, still expecting a performance.

"What are they going to do?" asked a girl in a purple vampire costume that Marius passed. "Is this a new act?"

"I don't know," said the one next to her, garbed in black and silver glitter. "They always come up with new stuff every year."

*Marius,* Cirillo spoke into his mind, *I have men infiltrating each building, several in H3 uniforms. They're using lots of persuasion and getting mixed stories of seeing Aislinn in a red negligée being pulled by Edward through the upper walkway connecting the Haunted Hall and The Party House.*

Marius watched Bastian shatter the sheetrock in the hallway with his body from sheer momentum. Quick on his feet, he dashed after the vampire.

Marius cleared the doorway as costumed patrons made way for him. *Cirillo, we've engaged a vampire at The Party House. Bastian says he's the one that took our women. If Aislinn is in this building, Bastian and I may need to split up. I feel like Gabby is close, but the direction is confusing. She might be closer to the barn or the tower. I've positioned Dimitri at the tower with Duncan. Can you send me help to capture the vampire?*

*I'll send two flyers, Thomas and Chang. Where do you want them to land?*

*On the balcony near the northwest side of The Party House. The people will think it is entertainment. Tell them to disguise their shift but engage weapons immediately. Imps are everywhere, and corporeal.*

*Roger that.*

*Bastian,* said Marius, *I'll take the vampire if you want to stay on Aislinn. Cirillo is sending help.*

Up ahead, Marius could see the vampire slamming through a doorway marked STAFF ONLY seconds before Bastian did. Several waiters and trays went flying as the vampire tossed them in his wake. Bastian was nearly on the vampire's heels.

*Cirillo, we're in the walkway bridge leading to the barn! Send your flyers there.*

Bastian jumped over a waiter on the enclosed walkway, and then froze. Marius nearly collided with him.

"What?" he asked, irritated.

"Aislinn's moving different," said Bastian. With panic and desperation on his face, he lowered his gaze and scanned the throng of bodies in the courtyard below through one of the windows.

*Marius, update,* came Cirillo's voice. *Horace and Edward just had a confrontation at The Party House. I've got eyes on Horace, but no sign of Edward. A staff member says there are hidden staircases and tunnels all over the complex, and only Edward and his brother Damian know them all.*

*Acknowledged,* Marius responded. *Bastian thinks Aislinn's somewhere in the courtyard. We're going to head down there. Through the barn. We can go after the vampire another day.*

*I've got Nathan and Darius in the courtyard,* Cirillo added. *Wait ... Renaldo is trying to fly above it but he says imps are dive-bombing him.*

*We encountered them as well. I think they've been called up to thwart flyers. Renaldo will get stuck having to fight them. Let him be our eyes on the ground.*

*All right, will do.*

*Marius.* A faint sweet voice broke through Marius' mind, and his heart nearly stopped.

*Gabby?* Marius stood frozen next to Bastian. The waiters were scrambling to their feet and staring at them. He and Bastian still had their swords out. *Where are you?*

Gabriella's thought patterns were erratic and blurred. He could tell she was trying to send words but they would not form. Pain filled her mind.

*Keep thinking of me,* Marius pleaded. *Try.* She did not answer him, but he felt a pull. Clearing his mind and ignoring everything around him, he allowed all of his senses to soar over the endless wave of bodies, walkways and buildings.

A tiny spark of her energy flashed in one direction—The Devil's Tower.

~~◊~~

In a narrow, dank tunnel, the uneven stone and dirt flooring caused Aislinn's throbbing ankles to twist and turn. She wrenched free of Eddie's hold on her arm.

"Eddie, you have to let me catch my breath." She leaned against the root-covered wall for support, hoping he would stand still. Her bare feet were bleeding and burning. Her heels were already numb. Her legs would not last much longer.

"Okay, but only for a second." He agreed. "We have to hurry to outrun my Dad. He thinks we're leaving."

"Eddie, why does your Dad hate me? I mean, I've never met the man."

The shadow that crossed Eddie's features unnerved Aislinn. "Because a mage said a blonde girl I met would hurt the family. Well, actually she said you would change the family forever. My Dad took it serious."

Unable to fathom how she could have any impact on Eddie's family, Aislinn shook her head in disbelief. "Eddie, that makes no sense."

"I know, I know. But he believes the mage. He thinks you'll destroy everything he's built."

"But... wh–... Eddie, every girl I've seen you with has been a blonde."

Eddie pursed his lips and averted his eyes. "She said it would be a blonde that captures my heart. I never told my father that part."

~~◊~~

Eddie ran up the rickety, unused staircase leading into The Devil's Tower, his hand tight around Aislinn's wrist. If he could make it through the first floor with three bars full of patrons to the secret stairwell on the other side, he could lock Aislinn in the Dungeon, which his father had already checked. The room was shielded, but he needed to render Aislinn unconscious, and cast heavy spells to cloak her. Then he could arrange for a car, and their escape.

He pushed up the trap door and stepped into darkness. A wall had been built to cover the access and only he and Damian knew how to open it. He felt behind an old piece of wood for the rusted bolt, and slid two panels open. It took all his strength to move a stacked shelf unit out of the way. Damian would not appreciate him exposing the old tunnel they expanded, so he dutifully re-slid the shelf into place.

"Is this a closet?" Aislinn asked.

"Yes," Eddie replied. "Hold on, let me find the access box. Here we go." A door opened. He led Aislinn into a narrow corridor with rest rooms. Two men in biker garb were shuffling through. They leered as they laid eyes on Aislinn in her negligée. Live music blared from the three bars.

"Hey, did y'all see the show?" said one woman to another as the two rounded the entrance to the corridor, heading for the Ladies room.

"What show?" asked the second woman. Eddie passed by them, his arm tight around Aislinn.

"Some guys in the bar were fighting the realest-looking demon and vampire I ever saw. With swords. This place is so cool. They really know how to do it up right."

A chill swept across Eddie's arms. He and Damian planned many shows for the H3, but he did not recall a demon and vampire fight with swords.

He wove through happy bikers, and spotted a crowd cheering for a fight in an adjoining hallway. Eddie's jaw dropped as he realized it was Dimitri, and he was fighting one of the three real vampires they employed. The creature was incredibly fast. But, so was Dimitri.

Eddie did not expect to feel regret, but he did. He wanted to fight with Dimitri. He had chosen sides, and was now on the wrong one.

Duncan ran into the hall, his bronze skin glistening with sweat, evidence that he had been fighting as well, probably the demon. He hovered beside Dimitri, waiting for an opportunity. The vampire hissed and crouched, ready to spring.

Eddie needed to find a way around the room. He could not risk being seen.

"Dimitri!" Aislinn called out. "Duncan!"

"Shhh!" Eddie tried to shush her, and grabbed her arms. But Duncan and Dimitri had both turned their heads, hearing her over the cheers and music.

"Aislinn!" Dimitri yelled.

Eddie cursed under his breath as Aislinn pulled toward Dimitri, hindered by Eddie's hold on her.

"Go!" Duncan slapped Dimitri's arm. "I got this."

Eddie squeezed Aislinn's wrist hard and yanked her toward the U-shaped bar. Cheering rose. Eddie looked back and realized Duncan was now challenging the snarling vampire on his own.

Dimitri, however, was dodging bodies to get to Aislinn.

Dimitri would hunt him down, of that Eddie was certain. He had seen the way he looked at Aislinn. Probably wanted her like everyone else.

*Damian,* Eddie called out with his mind. *I got a Heraclid on my tail. Is the panel behind the Laughing Skull bar still accessible?*

*Yes, go for it. Press the wall behind the frig. You'll have to go up and then crawl over to the back staircase that leads to the second and third floor access. I'll have some guys waiting on the third floor. We'll corner him there.*

~~◊~~

*Sir, I've got eyes on Aislinn!* Dimitri shouted to Marius telepathically. He skirted around drunken bikers with such speed they did not have time to take offense.

*Are you still at the tower?* Marius asked.

*Yes. The Laughing Skull bar.*

*We're on our way across the courtyard. Have you seen Gabriella?*

*No. Just Aislinn and Edward.* Dimitri pushed off a vacated chair and landed on the other side of the bar. The bartender back-stepped in shock.

*She is moving up,* declared Bastian into the connection. *She still can't hear me.*

*Dimitri, do you have back up?* Marius asked.

*Duncan is fighting a vampire. Duke and Barry are in The Pirate's Code bar using persuasion on some security guards.*

*We're headed across the courtyard,"* Marius informed him. *We'll fly if we can.*

*Use persuasion on the guards at the entrance,* Dimitri warned.

He noticed an employee was staring, wide-eyed, at a wall, obviously because Edward had just disappeared into it. Normal eyes may not have noticed the outline of a panel slightly ajar. Dimitri rushed forward and grabbed hold of the edges with his nails. The unlit, narrow stairs were dangerously vertical. He sent a visual to Marius. *They've gone up this hidden staircase. I'm on the first floor now, with all the bars, but climbing up. Don't know where it goes. Second floor probably.*

*Keep me apprised, Dimitri. Stay on them.*

~~◊~~

*My lord, let's fly to that window,* Bastian urged Marius, pointing to a second story, medieval-designed window with purple and red glass. *We could lose her.*

*Agreed,* Marius responded.

In unison, they pulled a black cloud of elusion around them to disguise the moment when they transformed their bodies into condors. Beating the air with immense wings took energy but in only seconds they had lifted high above the cheering crowd who were praising what they assumed was a stunt.

Screeches from demonic imps filled the air and closed in on them. Bastian swerved to the left and right, avoiding their talons. To his surprise, two large American bald eagles appeared and began diving at the imps.

*They are Cirillo's warriors,* Marius informed him. *Change and throw all your power with me into the window.*

Bastian knew the timing had to be precise. His mind stayed linked to Marius as they rose nearly to the top of the tower. They morphed in sync, allowing their bodies to freefall in a moment of weightless, primordial soup. Solidifying mid-air into humans, they aimed all of their rage and will ahead of a perfect dive at the pre-chosen window.

The energy blasted into the tower before their bodies hit, hurling glass, wood, and stone into the opening.

Bastian tumbled in a tucked roll across a purple carpet. Jumping to his feet, he was surprised to find naked people screaming and scrambling to get on the other side of furniture. Several men ran for a door on the far side of the lushly decorated room full of silks and satins and loud music.

None of the women were Aislinn. He knew it before he scanned them but he scanned in desperation anyway. Ignoring their screams, he strode through the door into an L-shaped hallway. A cacophony of seductive and heavy metal music vibrated from two other rooms. Men in red jackets sporting H3 on the pocket opened the two nearest doors and eyed Bastian as if trying to discern whether he was the cause of the noise and screaming. They started talking into ear microphones.

Surprisingly, instead of coming after him and Marius, they each looked alarmed and closed their respective doors. Bastian heard locks click. The same happened in the room they had just exited as patrons were pulled back in and the door was slammed shut.

"Not the fight I was expecting," said Marius.

"Nor I," Bastian agreed, still confused at the absence of security guards.

"What do you feel, Bastian?"

"She is near, but still moving." He tried to focus beyond the walls, floor and ceiling. The pull was bewildering. He headed down the hallway toward elevators, and stopped, turning his body in all directions. "I can't pinpoint her."

"Dimitri as well," Marius confirmed. "I feel him close. Gabriella is stronger here. There is demonic power in this building. I think it is interfering. Purposely."

As they took a step toward the elevator, metallic gates with spikes at the bottom rolled out of the ceiling above and fell with a *thud* in front of them, blocking access to two elevator doors and a wooden door marked EXIT. They backed up in surprise, then turned to hear another set of bars falling in place behind them, shaking the floor under their feet.

"What in God's name do they trap in here?" Marius asked.

"Us, at the moment," Bastian replied.

~~◊~~

"Bastian, swords," Marius whispered as his nerve endings prickled in alarm. Bastian synced minds with him, as they had done for a century, and retrieved his sword hilt, mirroring Marius' movements.

No will was needed to call on the power of the swords. They sprang into existence as if waiting. The ringing sound Marius expected sounded different. The notes warped and curled as if altered by a finger on a violin string.

He did not know what that meant, but the air between the two sets of bars thickened and charged with pressurized intensity. From the ceiling, dark shapes seeped into the air and nearly solidified into human-looking men. Four of them. Their radiance was of handsome, benign beings dressed in earthy, flowing garments.

The most handsome of the four floated forward. "You seemed destressed, tired. How can we help?"

*Cirillo, I need back-up. Second floor. The tower.*

The man's image warbled and darkened in color as if he had overheard Marius' call.

*I can send Duke and Barry now,* Cirillo answered. *More in a moment. What have you got?*

"Now really, and we haven't even talked," said the shimmering man. He looked around the wide hall, seemingly surprised by the location. "I do not find many portals in America. This one seems to be open all the time. Such dabblers these mortals are."

*Don't know yet*, Marius replied. *Could be demon or Fae.* He knew not to be fooled by the gentle, soothing voice, and kept his mind focused on all four figures, waiting for the slightest move to indicate attack.

He readied his sword. "If you are of the Fae and truly desire to help, then retract the cages for us. Otherwise, we wish you well and bid you a good night."

The man tilted his head, watching Marius with a mischievous curiosity. "But I just arrived here. I have been summoned to speak with you. Though my benevolence can go either way." He flashed an irreverent, playful grin.

"Seelie or Unseelie?"

"Now, is there *really* a difference?" The man's voice was taunting and melodious.

"Always is," said Marius, knowing the Seelie were fickle at best, and the Unseelie were not to be trusted at all. "If you have been summoned to speak with me, then your presence here serves only to distract me. And that I cannot allow."

Machiavellian delight sparkled in the man's eyes. "You seek a woman." He glanced at Bastian. "Or two. You will go down, and then you will go up before you find her."

"My lord, they waste our time." Bastian's impatience was palpable in the pressurized space.

As if affronted, the man's brows raised. "And *you*, well, the Unseelie Court are not very happy with you."

"Oh? And why is that?" asked Bastian.

"You were so much fun there for a while. Grunting about like an animal. Sniffing the shadows for vampires. We have not seen so many beheadings since the French Revolution. But now, alas, the love of a woman… well, it seems to have taken the wind out of your sails. Or wings, perhaps?"

"Be gone with you," Bastian ordered.

"Before we have had any fun?" The man gestured with open hands. "I do not think so. Your lady love was ready to give herself to your rival a short while ago. How she moaned for him. You should have heard the sound."

Marius sidestepped in front of Bastian. *No. Don't lose it.*

A malicious chuckle echoed in the air from the man, and the other three men mocked the echoes. Marius felt his blood begin to boil. These beings acted more like impudent teenagers out past midnight than actual men. Even for Fae men.

"We could always call her back into *our* world, you know," the man teased. "She had a little of our magical blood. One only needs a little to see beyond the veil between worlds. And *oooo*, such passion to be wasted in this mortal land."

*Fae blood,* Marius thought. Their blood was unpredictable. It made sense that an unseen guardian would have blocked his scan of Aislinn. He would never have allowed Bastian to exchange blood with her had he known. It was an old rule, but a firm one. Stay clear of the Fae, and any human possessing their blood.

The floating man frowned, flexed his shoulders, and rolled his eyes as if disgusted by the stone walls surrounding him. "But then, so many of you Olympian aliens have given the lass your tainted blood now, the spark of Fae in her is getting quite lost in all that jabber. We are quite losing count."

Marius felt Bastian's mind whirling with fear and revulsion. He could not help having a similar reaction as well. Clearly, this demon, or Fae, was insinuating more Olympians than just Bastian and Edward had exchanged blood with Aislinn. He prayed it was a lie. Deceit was not beneath an Unseelie Fae. Not while he was toying with a mortal.

"Still," the man continued, "I *could* lure the lustful little wench to my own bed. She's been in two already, here. One red. One black. But will know four lips."

*Bastian, don't fall for it,* Marius warned. He wove his power around Bastian to keep him from rushing the glistening figures, knowing it was what they wanted. Bastian was nearly shaking with the desire to lunge. *Listen to me Bastian. We pull out crucifixes. Then we laugh. That's an order.*

Nothing angered a demon more than being laughed at, and the Fae did not appreciate the presence of crucifixes, so Marius was counting on either a real fight, or a retreat.

He pulled his golden crucifix out of his shirt, as did Bastian.

The four men's expressions fell. The taunting one lost his sarcastic smile. "Now that just isn't even nice. And here I thought this was going to be fun. See if I help you at all now."

Marius imagined the men in pink bunny outfits and slippers, sent the image to Bastian, and then roared with laughter.

Bastian followed suit, even imagining other absurd clothing and hair decorations, based on the varied costumes they had observed during their chase.

The four surprised faces turned hideous and surged toward them.

Just before hitting their shining blades, the jeering man's image swirled like a man-sized tornado and disappeared into the ceiling, obviously done with the game.

A second man did the same. The two remaining, however, let loose an ungodly, eardrum-pounding roar. As Marius and Bastian recoiled form the pain in their ears, the two figures aimed clawed hands at the Olympians' faces.

*Swing at the arms!* Marius ordered. The supernatural roars were forcing him and Bastian to squint, but demon claws often contained poison, and Marius was taking no chances.

They sliced at the two demons in blurred strikes, anticipating their gyrating bodies to soar above and below them.

In a matter of moments, ash was raining down onto the stone floor.

Bastian retracted his sword, pocketed the hilt, and grabbed the bars of the gate in front of him. Marius joined him. They grunted and pulled, fighting against an electric motor. When they had raised the gate nearly two feet, Bastian told Marius, *Go under!*

Marius dropped and rolled. As soon as he cleared the spikes, he knelt and bore the weight of the gate. Bastian rolled underneath. Marius let the gate drop.

"She's closer!" Bastian yelled, slamming a hand against the elevator button.

# CHAPTER 34

Formless arms of evil, debaucherous and cruel closed around Aislinn like a living, breathing monster the moment Eddie pulled her through a section of wall. She stiffened in recognition of the darkened auction area. So much evil happened in this room, it pulsed with a dimension of its own.

Eddie looped an arm around her and said, "Run!"

She bolted, wanting desperately to get away from the horrible energy. An elevator at the opposite end of the hallway opened and men wearing red jackets with H3 emblems on their pockets spilled out of it. At first, Aislinn thought they were after her and Eddie, until Eddie pointed a thumb behind him and called to them. "He's right behind us!"

The men parted as Eddie and Aislinn rushed through their towering ranks. Three of them had guns out. Aislinn slid to a stop, horrified, and whirled in time to see Dimitri scramble out of the same hidden entrance they had just vacated.

Dimitri pulled out his hilt in a blur. The blade sprang to life, sending a clear note into the air. The gorilla-like men continued their charge down the hallway toward him.

Several bangs from guns drove the breath out of Aislinn's lungs. In disbelief she watched Dimitri time the flat of his blade in such perfect strokes that bullets clanked loudly against the metal and ricocheted into the walls.

Except for three small metallic darts of some kind, lodged in his neck. Dimitri tore the darts out and threw them to the floor, but it was too late. The men rushed him and knocked him over by sheer force, punching him everywhere. Aislinn gasped as a cloth was slapped onto his face. She knew the panic and helplessness of being robbed of air, knowing the horrid chemical was going to strip you of all your strength. Dimitri twisted and struggled, causing the men to fall out of the heap and have to jump back on. Suddenly, he went still.

"Chain him in the Dungeon," Eddie called out to the men. "Don't be seen. Hurry." He tapped 3339 into a keypad on the wall beside the open elevator. To her surprise, a panel slid open revealing a second elevator. This had padded walls of gold and red satin material. Eddie pulled Aislinn into it. The men squeezed in after them, bearing Dimitri's limp body. Eddie tapped 666 into a golden keypad on the inside panel.

Aislinn leaned against Eddie, breathing in short, clipped breaths. Her knees wobbled so much, only Eddie's arm around her waist kept her upright. Watching Dimitri get brutally beaten and subdued had injured her own heart, leaving unseen bruises. He had come to rescue her, and now he was their prisoner as well.

So many hands were around Dimitri's neck, while others were locking cuffs around his wrists and ankles, she could not tell one body from another. They kept falling and getting back up as Dimitri fought them off. He was covered in blood.

Once Dimitri was contained, the largest man kicked Dimitri in the head. His body went limp. Aislinn steeled her nerves and pretended he was nothing more than a mannequin. She succeeded in showing no reaction.

The men were heaving, out of breath. As one they turned toward the man with the blood-red eyes. One of them had called him Helmer. But Eddie had called him Hel. Aislinn thought Eddie had the right of it.

She wondered how he could look so much like Eddie and the man who had entered the Red Room to warn Eddie his father was on the premises. Eddie had often complained of a brother his father preferred. Was there a third? Either way, neither was the auctioneer. Helmer's creepy voice caused her insides to quiver in fear. Though his mask was absent, there was no disguising that taunting malicious intonation.

"We should chain her, too," suggested Helmer.

Aislinn looked up at Eddie and gave a small shrug. "It's up to you, Eddie. I won't disobey you. I will stay here if that's what you want. I need to rest my feet." Aislinn focused on the pull of their blood bond and allowed her body to react with desire for him. His own desire for her reflected in his green-gold eyes.

"Don't believe her, Eddie," Helmer said. "She was fighting you earlier in the bar. I saw it on the security camera."

Aislinn forced herself to look into Helmer's hideous eyes, her readable thoughts calm and contained. "Master, you did not order me to forget Dimitri and Duncan. Only someone I loved. So, I remembered them."

Helmer sauntered toward her, a smirk forming in his face. He gripped her jaw and tilted her head to expose her neck. "Let me bite you."

"Hel." Eddie's tone was a warning.

With Helmer's hand squeezing her windpipe, Aislinn spoke with difficulty. "You ordered me to give my blood only to Eddie. Do you wish me to disobey?"

Helmer's hand relaxed.

Aislinn coughed but kept her gaze zombie-like and compliant. She allowed nothing else into her mind but Helmer's orders, repeating them to herself in case he was able to read her.

"Just testing her," Helmer said, glancing with satisfaction at Eddie.

"It's okay, Aisy-girl," Eddie crooned softly, rubbing her shoulder as if to make up for Helmer's rough handling. "You don't have to think about his orders right now."

Aislinn gave Eddie a weak smile. Helmer might not be able to read her thoughts, but Eddie must have detected the repeating phrases.

"I'm going to get us a ride, then we can get out of here," Eddie explained. "I want you to sit on the bed and do nothing else. Can you do that for me, sweetie-girl?"

"Of course, Eddie." Her body was screaming in agony and deprivation. She had not eaten since breakfast. Her feet were bloody and throbbing. But a strength was growing inside her. A sense of something, or someone, ominous and close. Aislinn simply let go of all personal needs and wants, and filled her mind with the sight of Eddie. *Only Eddie.*

"All right," Eddie spoke to Helmer. "Let's leave them in here. She can't help Dimitri anyway. If he wakes up, he can't call anyone, and no one can hear either of them. Dad's already looked in here, so he won't come back."

Helmer frowned. "You never know about Uncle Horace."

"What about these guys?" Eddie's question was so soft, Aislinn was certain the other men could not hear.

"They're sworn to me," Helmer replied in an equally hushed voice.

Eddie exhaled with obvious relief.

Helmer pressed an earpiece against his ear in a listening pose. "Uncle Horace is headed out in his limo."

"I need her unconscious." Eddie flicked his eyes to indicate Aislinn.

"Okay, but...." Helmer's eyes widened. "The Balkans just busted into the second floor window. Son of a... all right, look, I gotta send some guys up there. Eddie, go get Jerod. I'll tell him to loan you his car. We've spelled it before. He can reinforce it."

The men exited the room. Aislinn dutifully sat on the bed, expressionless.

Eddie looked back and gave her what she supposed was meant to be an encouraging thumbs-up. Wisps of dark gray shapes whirled around his head as if giant dragonflies were flying and casting shadows on him. He slammed the heavy door.

Aislinn did not move.

She was not certain whether the room was designed to look like a dungeon, or whether it actually was. It was certainly cold enough. The stone floor was rough.

Many of the same accoutrements as the Red Room were suspended from walls and ceiling in this room. Black curtains hung in various places. Candles flickered in sconces attached to the stone walls. Aislinn had noticed two chaise lounges and the circular bed, all bedecked in red and black satin when she entered the dismal room. She did not turn to survey it in detail.

She waited.

As she feared, after a lonely fifteen seconds or so in which Dimitri tried to get her attention, clearly not unconscious as the men had assumed, Helmer swung open the door. He leered at her, grinning with satisfaction. Then re-closed the door.

Aislinn shivered in the red negligée and listened for the clicking of bolts. Footsteps moved away, but Aislinn had the oddest feeling that she was being watched.

For another few seconds, she did not move.

"Aislinn," Dimitri's voice was weak. "Are you okay?"

She ignored him.

"Aislinn, listen to me. You do not have to stay under a spell. You can break through this. Remember what Gabriella said? Repeat it. 'By the power of God, I choose to be free from any spell. I am now free to choose my destiny. I am free. I am free. I am free.' Say it in your mind, Aislinn."

She remained frozen, but her mind was mulling over the affirmation. Like a broken recording, the words, *I am free,* repeated on a loop. The feeling of being watched began to dissipate. Finally, it lifted. She did not know why she had felt it, but was certain if there were security cameras in the room, the person who was supposed to be watching was busy attending to something else. Or perhaps the entity listening was her own fear. She was not sure. But she no longer felt eyes.

She stood, and blinked in surprise. Three women were chained to the wall beyond Dimitri, somewhat hidden by one of the black curtains. Two of the women wore clothing as sparse as hers and were slumped on the floor, lifeless and pale. Their eyes appeared half-open and glassy. They did not speak.

The third woman was wearing a blood-streaked black, silky gown and hung limp from chains attached to the stone floor. The mass of tangled red hair was unmistakable.

"*Aaarrgg!*" Dimitri cried out. He grimaced at unseen pain.

"You can't contact anyone from here, Dimitri."

"How is that possible?"

"I don't know. But Eddie said this room is shielded, just like the Red Room I was in."

Dimitri let his head fall back against the wall, his eyes crinkled in pain.

Aislinn stood before Dimitri, waiting for a possible reaction. Nothing happened and no one entered.

Dimitri continued to rest his aching head against the bricks, and watched her. She looked over at the women chained to the wall. No movement other than their half-lidded, opaque eyes, as if they were drugged.

On either side of Dimitri, black curtains had been tied back. Aislinn loosened the cords, and sheets of black satin billowed around her. She knelt before him and leaned in close.

"I don't know if there is surveillance," she whispered. "If you bite me and take my blood, will it give you the strength to break free?"

Dimitri swallowed as if it were painful, a frown forming between his brows. His lips barely moved. "Yes, but I can't...."

"Will I be able to talk to you telepathically?"

"Maybe, if I reach out to you. But Aislinn...."

"What if I drink your blood as well? Will that make the connection stronger?"

"Yes, but..." he coughed. "I will be dead, because Bastian will have killed me."

Aislinn's eyes widened. "Why? Oh... blood bond thing."

"Mmm, hmm."

She gave him a soft smile, amazed that his sense of humor was still intact. "You look half dead already, Dimitri."

He snorted. "Thanks."

"Look. You're injured and bleeding. You need my blood to escape. And if something happens, I've got to be able to reach... somebody. Eddie's spell is still strong. Well, Helmer did it. I consented to it to save Gabriella. I cannot hear Bastian. My mind is still a little... wacked. Could you be affected by the spell, I mean the potion I drank?"

"Depends upon what they put in it. Do you feel drugged?"

"Yes. But it's more like... like being relaxed and compliant, like I allowed a noose to be put around my neck. I just gave in to the guy."

"What guy?"

"Helmer. The one with the reddish eyes. Like Damian, Eddie's brother, but redder."

"I think Helmer is Edward's cousin then. The family's known for reddish-brown eyes."

"Oh, he did say Uncle Horace just now, didn't he? Then Eddie's cousin is..." Aislinn fought to think for herself, feeling pain forming in the center of her head, "a sick master. Oh, my gosh. I just felt like someone hit me in the head for saying that. I guess the spell still has power." She shook her head and gulped breaths. "Either way, Gabriella's unconscious over there."

"What?" Dimitri whipped his head around and pushed away from the wall.

"You can't see because of the curtains."

"Thank God I at least know where she is."

"Dimitri, Eddie is coming back here to take me away. His father ordered us to leave. I need to be able to communicate with you. I am trying to get past the spell by telling myself 'I am free,' like you said. I don't know if that will work, but...."

Dimitri shook his head. "There has to be another way."

"Dimitri, please. I need to be able to reach you without feeling like someone's bashing my head in. And you need strength." She brushed her hair back. "Come on. Quick." She arched her neck and took hold of his face.

"Oh, hell no. Definitely not your neck. Bastian will pulverize me."

Aislinn frowned and stuck her arm in front of him. Dimitri lowered his head, then glanced at her as if to be sure. He had the look of man walking to the gallows.

"Hurry Dimitri," she hissed. "I need you to break out of here."

After a deep breath and a murmur of, "God forgive me," he pressed his lips against her pulsing veins and closed his eyes. For a second, he did nothing.

"What's wrong?"

With his eyes closed, he whispered against her arm. "Waiting for my canines to descend."

"I thought that was instantaneous."

"If I thought of you as more than a sister, they probably would. But now, everything's different."

Aislinn felt a flutter in her stomach, but also a warm rush of affection for Dimitri.

"And," he added, "I can feel Bastian in your blood. More than Bastian. Wait, Aislinn, there's something you must know. If we speak telepathically, call out my name first. We never just say 'hi.' *Always* say my name and visualize it as separate. Or visualize me. Otherwise we can't isolate the conversation from anyone else. A name is an address. Okay?"

Before she could nod, he opened his mouth and bit down. She grimaced at the sting. But it was nothing to the pain searing through her body for disobeying Helmer's orders. She shook with the effort to fight against his words ordering her to remove her arm, and her soul screaming to keep it there.

*Should I depart from Master's command, my body will know pain I cannot withstand.* She gritted her teeth. *No! I am now free!*

Mere seconds after Dimitri started drinking her blood, she felt the pain ease and the familiar sense of euphoria wash over her. She closed her eyes, concentrating on letting the intense thrall win over the pain. The heady sensations did not rise to the level of Bastian's, but helped to counteract the spell's power over her body.

She nearly sighed, but managed to suppress it. The endorphins released by the Olympians' canines were amazing. She could imagine women craving it. The lure of vampirism would be unbelievably tempting to an Olympian. Women would always remember the fantastic sensations they produced. This race of beings could have their way with women, erase any thought of pain, and leave them with a vivid, unforgettable memory of bliss, one they would willingly repeat. Suddenly, Marius' strict rules made sense. The code of honor they lived by was a necessity. Not just for them, but for all of humanity.

After a full minute, Aislinn began to feel a touch woozy from blood loss. Dimitri tilted back his head, his face relaxing as if dealing with a rapturous high. He seemed to gain control and opened his eyes.

"More?" she urged.

He shook his head and focused on the puncture wounds he created. He leaned down and lapped with his tongue. Aislinn watched with amazement as the bleeding stopped. His tongue caused tingles to run all over her skin, and sent warmth through her stomach, all the way to her thighs. *He's a brother. He's a brother. He's a brother,* she chanted in her mind.

She glanced at the streams and smears of blood in various places on his body. Two were still bleeding. As he let his head fall back against the bricks, she grabbed his forearm and licked blood still flowing from what appeared to be a nasty knife wound. His blood had a sweet, coppery taste, similar to Bastian's, but different. If she could just stop all of this bleeding....

"No, Aislinn! Stop!" Dimitri jerked his arm away, his eyes widening. He watched her lick the blood from her bottom lip. "You're ingesting my blood. You can't *do* that! Spit it out right now!"

"But, my saliva can seal your wounds, right?" She glared at him in consternation. "Hey, look, I think it's working."

Dimitri examined the slash on his arm. "Well I'll be...."

Aislinn spied another gash on his hand and stuck out her tongue, but Dimitri brutally shoved her away, knocking her to the hard stone floor.

"No!" he yelled through clenched teeth, the candlelight glinting off his fangs. "You are *female*. You could create a blood heat. Do you want that between us?"

"But… I'm… I'm sorry." Aislinn swallowed and averted her eyes. "I didn't think about that. My mind's a little fuzzy. I just want to stop your bleeding. Make you better."

"It's okay." He took a deep breath. "You've given me enough blood to heal on my own. I think we'll be all right." The frown wrinkles around his eyes contradicted his belief in those words.

She bit her lip, contrite. "I'm holding you to your promise to be my brother, though."

He gave her a small smile. "Best promise I ever made. And we can't change that now anyway."

"What do you mean?"

"There are… things we Olympians can agree to, that bind us with a kind of power, a connection. By offering to be your brother, as far as the supernatural world is concerned, I really am."

Aislinn's mouth fell slowly open. "Really?" She felt a surge of elation. *A new family member.* "Can I ask Duncan to be my brother, too?"

"He has to offer first." Noting her look of dismay, he added, "It's the way the rule works."

"Rules. Always rules with you people." Considering the presence of the other women in the room, Aislinn whispered, "The blood thing'll be our secret. Deal? Neither one of us tells Bastian or Marius."

"Deal. Absolute deal. I want to live."

She chuckled. "Okay, let's try this thing." She focused on Dimitri's aqua-blue eyes. *How old are you?*

"You have to give it a few minutes, Aislinn. Sometimes hours."

*How old are you?*

Dimitri blinked. "Oh my god, I hear you." *I'm forty.*

Aislinn's jaw dropped. "Still can't believe you're forty."

He frowned, puzzled. "But, that's too fast. Your abilities must already be enhanced because of the blood exchanges with Bastian."

"Don't forget Eddie."

"Oh, that's right. You had another Olympian bloodline. That must be it."

Aislinn considered the blood drops she received from Helmer. Dare she inform Dimitri? Pain splashed into her body like glowing pieces of coal spraying from a fire. *A secret we hold, Master, between us two.*

"No. I can fight it. I am now free."

"Aislinn?"

"Um, Dimitri, since we already have one secret. Helmer, at least I think it was him, gave me his blood and took mine. Just a few drops, but…."

Dimitri's eyes widened as he let loose a string of expletives. "Oh, Aislinn, I am so sorry. It's not supposed to work like this. You're so new, and everybody's just…." He seemed unwilling to finish.

"Wait a minute." He sat up straighter. "Three blood bonds. And a taste of mine. Your emotions are going to be all over the place. But that's also more power. You should be able to override any spell or persuasion used on you."

"Really?"

"Yes. Fight it, Aislinn. Fight any suggestion they gave you the minute you think it. Call on your emotions and focus."

"Okay." The idea made her feel stronger, empowered. She *was* able to keep her cool once they had dragged Dimitri into the Dungeon. She *was* able to formulate a plan. She looked over the chains. "Eddie said these cuffs were made of silver. That's a problem for you? Uh, for us, right?"

"It is."

"Okay, let me find some material." Aislinn grabbed the nearest curtain but decided it would be too cumbersome. In the menagerie of sexual accoutrements hanging from spikes and shelves, she spied ties, stockings, and ropes. She went for the ties. Threading them under Dimitri's tightly bound wrist cuff was difficult. She winced and yelped as the cuff burned her.

She stepped back in relief. "Can you pull it off, now?"

Dimitri closed his eyes. After a deep breath, he growled and pulled with all his might. The left chain blasted out of the wall.

Aislinn ducked and pivoted as the chain swung forward. She realized she had moved amazingly fast.

"Give me another tie," Dimitri commanded.

Aislinn handed him the last two she had. Dimitri wrapped them around the cuff linking his right arm and yanked.

Again, Aislinn had to jump out of the way as the chain separated from the wall and flew forward. Dimitri grunted until he was able to break the cuffs off of his wrists, and finally, snap the cuffs off his legs.

He rushed to Gabriella's side and gently lifted her head. "Hey, Gabriella, you with me?"

A sob caught in Aislinn's throat at sight of purple and blue welts swelling around Gabriella eyes and cheeks. A cut on her lip was caked with blood. Aislinn wondered at that since she was Olympian. Why wasn't she healing? Crimson streams flowed over the silky black gown from the wounds the darts had inflicted.

Dimitri hissed several harsh words that sounded Greek.

Aislinn thought he was leaning forward to lick Gabriella's wounds until she heard him sniff. "Son of a bitch," he exclaimed. "They left silver in her."

"Oh," Aislinn remarked. "Helmer threw darts at her. He said they had silver tips."

"Monster's made sure she keeps bleeding. She's really weak now. Can't heal. I don't know if I can get them out. It's all swollen around the entry points."

Worm-like tentacles of gray snaked outward from each inflamed puncture like pulsing roots, as if a disease was growing.

"Aislinn, do not tell Marius of this, before I can. Understand?"

"I, uh…." She hesitated out of confusion, assuming she had no way of contacting Marius anyway.

"Do you understand!"

"Yes," she cried, recoiling from the fierce glow in his eyes.

Dimitri wrapped the ties around his hands and broke the silver cuffs from Gabriella's blistered wrists and ankles. Then he lifted her into his arms.

"Do you know a way out of here?"

"Sort of," Aislinn confessed. "Eddie used his thumbprint to open the door to this cellar. He's getting a car ready, so I don't know if we should go up that car ramp. If you can bust through this door, I remember the number he punched in to get on the elevator."

"Do you know if the elevators have the same kind of shielding?"

"I don't think so." Aislinn curled over in pain. Some etheric creature was eating at her insides. *From Olympian life I will abstain. By Eddie's side I will remain. No!* she screamed in her own mind. *I am free. I am free. I am free. I go where I want to go!*

"Are you okay?"

"Yes. It's just… the spell and persuasion are attacking me."

"Say it with me," Dimitri ordered in a gentle tone.

They repeated the affirmation together, looking into each other's eyes.

"We have to get where I can contact Marius," said Dimitri. "Let's go."

# CHAPTER 35

*Eddie, we got problems!* Damian's mental tone was ripe with panic. *Helmer trapped the Balkans in the lock out cages on the second floor, and sent demons after them. But....*

*Good!* Eddie responded. *The car's ready. Just keep them busy. I'm headed down to get Aislinn.*

*No, you don't understand. I'm looking at the security video. The demons kept them busy, but they're gone already. The Heraclids are breaking out of the cages. Oh... wait... hold on, Eddie.*

Since Damian was apparently listening to other communique, Eddie ran down the garage ramp that led to the Dungeon entrance and elevators. The area was carefully constructed to appear a haphazard storage area for wine and food supplies in order to hide the faux wooden panel that disguised a metal door to the shielded Dungeon where his father's goons took girls before they were ready for auction. Though neither Helmer nor Damian showed any consternation concerning the practice, Eddie still felt a nagging pang of guilt, which he took great pains to hide.

*Eddie,* said Damian, *security says Dimitri just got on the main elevator down there. Your girl's with him. And he's carrying The Balkan's wife.*

*What?* Eddie stopped near the racks of wine. He heard the clunk of the elevator doors, and his heart sank.

*Dammit, that Dimitri is using persuasion on my guard.* Damian fumed. *He's just following Dimitri's orders like an idiot. The elevator camera's going fuzzy too. Dimitri must be using a lot of power.*

Eddie ran behind the stacks of crates. Dread filled his chest at sight of the shattered remains of the Dungeon door.

"*Noooo!*" he yelled, partly bent over. He cursed and kicked the nearest crate, not caring how much it hurt. Helmer's wingman, Jerod, had a car waiting and ready for Eddie, engine running. The dark tinting would have disguised prying eyes so he could drive out of H3 unrecognized. Helmer and Jerod had placed several spells on the vehicle hoping to block scans. He was so close. So close.

*Damian, can you stop the elevator?*

*Yeah. Where you want it?* Damian asked. *Can't be the second floor. The Balkans just busted into the stairwell. They've met up with the Appalachians and are heading downward.*

*Do it. Just stop it now.*

*All right. It's stuck between the first and second floor.*

Eddie's shoulders fell. What to do? The weight of hiding and running from his father and the Olympians was bending him to the breaking point. Dimitri could have broken out of his chains, but Aislinn might also have helped him. In which case, Helmer's persuasion and spells were not holding her. His *love* was not holding her. He gritted his teeth and considered his options. One way or another, he was not going to lose.

*Damian, Marius will sense Gabriella. Bastian will sense Aislinn, too. They'll head for the first floor. The minute they get there, send Dimitri and the women straight to the third floor.*

Eddie jumped into the hidden elevator and punched the number 3 button.

*Okay*, said Damian, *but what are you going to do?*

*Hold them on 3 'till I get there. When I tell you, let Dimitri and Aislinn get out. You got security on three?*

*Yeah, two guys.*

*Have them ready by the door to restrain Dimitri. I'm going to grab Aislinn. Marius and Bastian will head up once they sense the change in direction. If I can get Aislinn back down to the garage in the secure elevator, it will confuse the heck out of Bastian. He won't understand where she is. I can go up the ramp and we're gone. Can you keep the Olympians busy while we escape?*

*I can try. We'll make 'em work for it.*

~~◊~~

*Marius, sir, can you hear me?*

*Dimitri!* Marius responded, relieved to hear Dimitri's mental tone. *Where are you?*

*I'm in the elevator. I hit the button for the first floor, but it's stuck.*

*We're on the first floor,* said Marius. *We can break into it.*

*Wait… wait… we're going up. I think someone's controlling it.*

*Dimitri?*

*Still going up. I think it's stopping on the third floor. It's finally opening. Oh crap. Security guards.*

"Everybody, upstairs!" Marius ordered. He had seen the vision Dimitri sent him of Gabriella in his arms. No walls or stairs were going to keep him from making it to the third level even if he had to blast straight through the ceilings and flooring.

A small army of Olympians pounded up the stairs behind him, their footsteps echoing like thunder in the stairwell.

*Cirillo!* Marius called out. *We're heading to the third floor. Dimitri is fighting with security guards. He's got Gabriella and Aislinn with him.*

*I'm entering the tower now with the rest of my men, Marius,* Cirillo answered. *I've recalled everybody to the tower. I'll have them guarding every entrance to every floor in seconds. No one is getting by us.*

One pull on the L-shaped handle leading to the third floor told Marius it was bolted, just like the second floor door they had busted open. He could feel the electric current in the frame and walls.

"Bastian, build power with me," he ordered, focusing on the door. It was not difficult to call up all the rage, indignation and strength of will he possessed. Nor, he suspected, did Bastian. Together they built a raging firestorm inside and outside of their bodies.

"Men, step back." He could hear the shuffling steps of Cirillo's warriors.

"Now!" Marius called to Bastian. The blast detonated splinters of wood around them. They held up their arms to deflect the shards. As the dust settled, the bent bolt holding the door simply fell to one side.

Bastian charged through the remaining slabs of wood with brute force, taking strips of wood with him.

"Aislinn!" Bastian yelled, slamming his hands against the elevator door.

"Where is she?" Marius asked, crawling through the tattered opening behind Bastian.

"She's in there." Bastian kicked the metal door with such force, his foot left a dent. Howling in fury, he grabbed the seam of the metal doors and pulled with his fingers.

"My lord?" Dimitri called out.

Marius whirled. He could not believe the site before him. Gabriella lay on the floor. Beside her lay the bodies of two unconscious security guards.

Marius leapt to Gabriella's side, fell to his knees and took her in his arms. "Oh my love," he whispered, "what have they done to you?"

"She needs blood, sir," said Dimitri. "They left silver in her so she would keep bleeding."

"Despicable cowards." Marius bit into his wrist and held it over Gabriella's mouth.

"Drink, my love, drink," he urged. Crimson drops oozed from his wrist onto Gabriella's lifeless lips.

"Dimitri?"

"I got it." In tune with Marius' mind, Dimitri gently opened Gabriella's mouth so the blood would land on her tongue.

Her eyelids fluttered. Marius' heart slowed its fierce pounding.

"Drink, Gabby. *Drinnnk*." He fueled the request with undeniable persuasion until her mouth had no choice but to latch onto his arm. As the blood flowed from him, he closed his eyes, the release a balm to his soul.

The creak and groan of metal he could hear going on behind him was probably Bastian forcing the outer elevator doors open.

Marius could also hear the tramping of many feet echoing in the stairwell. He felt Cirillo's presence beside him and opened his eyes.

"Good god," one of the warriors whispered behind Cirillo.

"Cirillo, sir," said Dimitri. "We have to get the silver out of her. Aislinn said they're dart tips."

"Darius, you got your tools?" asked Cirillo.

"Yes, sir," replied a dark-haired young man who stepped forward.

"Get this silver out."

"My lord," Bastian cried out. "Her direction has… changed."

Cirillo turned to him. "We've got every exit covered, Bastian. Stairs, elevators, even the whole building. We'll get her, and we'll get Edward."

Darius knelt and opened a leather pouch that was slung over his shoulder. From it he extracted bent needle-nosed plyers.

Gabriella moaned in pain, her face crinkling as Darius carefully dipped the plyers into her swollen tissue.

"It's okay, *agápi mou*," Marius crooned in Greek. "We're getting the silver out. Keep drinking so you can heal." He kissed her forehead.

"Marius," said Dimitri. "Aislinn said Helmer's the guy who did this to Gabriella. We think he's Edward's cousin."

Marius' scorching gaze rose slowly. Dimitri seemed to quail. From the burn in Marius' eyes, he had no doubt the whites of his eyes had turned to bloodthirsty orbs of fire.

"Where can I find him?"

"No idea," said Dimitri. "But he's got kinda unusual eyes. I mean, the irises. They're a dark red."

"Give me the visual."

Dimitri obeyed.

"Marius," said Cirillo. "I've got an ambulance on the way to take Gabriella. The EMTs are all loyal to me. Do you want to ride inside with her?"

"No, I have someone to find."

"Marius," Cirillo's tone hardened. "You will not be able to stop. You could lose your tribe. It's not the same world it was a hundred years ago."

"Cirillo, ten years ago my world changed forever. Today, an Alcmaeonidae almost took that from me."

Cirillo knelt in front of him. "You can apprehend Edward. He left the country and went after your warrior's mate. He wronged a female under your protection. But Helmer is part of my jurisdiction, and he's mine to arrest."

"He nearly killed my wife!" Marius shook with fury, a fury so strong it was colliding with Cirillo's power. He could feel Cirillo's warriors gathering close, adding their power to Cirillo's, as was their right. The pressure of it gathered in the hallway as if they had all been thrust under water.

Cirillo stood. "Dammit, Marius, you know if you get your hands on him, you'll *kill* him. Don't make me call your blood. Because I will."

"Marius," Gabriella barely whispered.

Marius gently cupped her bruised face with his hands. "What is it, *agápi mou.*"

"Don't fight Cirillo," she said with great effort, her voice raspy. "Go get Aislinn. She is in danger."

# CHAPTER 36

*Eddie, Olympians have blocked all exits from the Dungeon to the third floor.* Damian's mental voice sounded frantic and defeated. *They're stationed all over the forest road, and surrounding the tower. Half of my guards are down. I don't want to call the police. You know what that would risk. You're never going to make it out, bro. Not unless you let her go.*

Eddie roared in rage and punched the red and gold padding of the elevator, tearing the plush, silken fabric. So close. He was so close.

Gasping in fury, he hit the emergency stop button.

*Eddie, you know what they could do to you,* Damian implored. *Send Aislinn out and let me get you into hiding. They can't track you. If we give them the women, they'll leave.*

*"Noooo!"* Eddie yelled out loud, slamming his fist into the elevator again.

~~◊~~

"My lord," Bastian implored, feeling his insides turning over to the point of painful. "I sense her moving down. I'm going after her." He lunged through the shattered door and vaulted down the curved stairs five at a time, not waiting for Marius' permission. At the second flight of stairs he stopped. Something was wrong. The train of warriors following him nearly collided with his tall, rigid frame.

"Bastian, what is it?" asked Duke.

"Something's changing."

Aislinn's spirit washed over him. He felt a wind-like pressure, a dense expanse of her soul dressed in fear and exhaustion. It was everywhere. Her thoughts were a touch away, but remained mute. Her spirit was dissipating, moving upward, away from him.

"Up!" Bastian declared. "Up! Let me by."

Duke and the other warriors flattened against the stone stairwell to let him pass. "Bastian, are you sure this isn't some kind of trick?"

"No!"

He leapt stairs three at a time and slid to a stop at the solid wood door to the fourth floor. A sign on the stone wall read: Key Card Required.

"Not today," Bastian said through gritted teeth, and began pounding the door with his foot, ignoring the pain.

"Let us help," Duke suggested. Bastian acquiesced and allowed the warriors to focus their power and kick open the door. When three of them kicked at once, the door broke off its frame.

They all pushed it out of the way and spilled out into a foyer that appeared transported from a century long past, and smelled of evil.

Pillars stood on either side of two medieval-looking doors with antique signs reading: Sabbath Room One, and Sabbath Room Two. Candles flickered in sconces, their golden light reflecting off a black pentagram painted on the shiny, tile floor.

There was no sign of additional stairs. The direction "up" still felt right to Bastian. But before he could look for an access, shadows began to ooze from the walls.

"Incoming!" Duke called out to the men.

Weapons came out of pockets and jackets.

Screams and insults to the Olympians filled the air from hideous, non-human voices.

Swords began slashing and stabbing. Bastian drew his own sword as a shape solidified beside him. He pivoted and skewered a putrid-smelling demon, thrilled to find something to sink his sword into. The demon appeared shocked it had been dispatched so quickly and faded into a whirl of gray smoke and ash.

Duke was carefully fighting a demon whose body had little form but whose face and spirit embodied the essence of murder, the taking of life undeserved. Bastian had dealt with those before. To his surprise, the creature did not dissolve or explode from a stab of Duke's sword, but instead laughed with gleeful scorn and disappeared into the ceiling.

Duke had no time to puzzle over it because both Sabbath Room doors opened, and solid bodies stepped out. Whorls of orange and red in their eyes belied their human appearance, and revealed their bodies' possessions by unearthly spirits. Some of the people backed up, clearly not possessed, but unsure whether the bizarre scene of men holding swords could be a possible Halloween act of some kind.

Tension and dread filled the wide foyer; each warrior hated having to fight possessed humans, knowing they would have to inflict wounds with blessed weapons in order to dispose of the demonic presence. And unless the demon was very old, the human host would be left behind. Bodies to clean up.

Duke proved to be a resourceful and competent captain, directing the men with telepathic direction and blurred flicks of his eyes and fingers.

Earl struggled with one of the demons who was wielding a long knife, and slammed him into a wall. The demon whirled and headed for Bastian, who fought him sword to knife, surprised at the strength of the being.

Duke, Barry, and Thomas, whom Bastian recognized as one of Cirillo's flyers, each engaged a demon. Wide-eyed humans in robes gathered at the doorways to the Sabbath rooms, still confused as to whether the fight was real or not.

Earl stabbed the demon Bastian was fighting in the side. A hideous wail filled the room, and the entity dove for the shattered door to the stairs, stumbling downward.

Bastian and Earl looked at each other in surprise but had no time to wonder why the demon gave up so quickly. Clouds of solidifying creatures were diving at Bastian.

"Bastian!" Duke turned his head toward him after slicing into his opponent. "They're after *you*. We're just in the way. Step back. Focus on Aislinn. We'll cover you."

Earl immediately took over the fight with the airborne creatures.

Bastian did as Duke asked and backed between the demolished door to the stairs and the metal elevator doors. He feared closing his eyes to focus on Aislinn, but the warriors all responded to Duke's orders and kept the demons at bay, away from him. Before Bastian's eyelids could close, he knew Aislinn's direction was still up.

Sparkles of white, like snow in sunlight, wafted before his face. He turned toward the shattered door frame, trying to make sense of the phenomenon. Then he remembered.

The glittering specs danced as if excited by his awareness. A flicker of gray light caught his eye and he turned to his right. In front of a wall of stone stood a figure.

"Aislinn?" he whispered, hope causing his heart to skip a beat.

His brief spike of joy evaporated as he realized this Aislinn had translucent brown hair and green eyes. The girl's young image hovered a foot above the floor. She wasn't solid. The stone wall was visible through her.

Tiny, glittering speckles whirled around her like silent snow. An unseen breeze rustled the black lace on the sleeves and the hem of her dress.

"Who is that?" Marius asked, surprising him by stepping through the demolished door and into the chaos of the foyer. Cirillo appeared beside him.

"Anya." Bastian knew it in his bones. This was Aislinn's cherished sister.

The two leaders were immediately besieged by wailing demons.

"They're here to stop Bastian!" Duke yelled at Marius and Cirillo. They both raised swords to shield Bastian, whose gaze was fixed on the ghost before him.

A wan smile touched Anya's pale gray lips. She seemed pleased Bastian had read her spirit. Slowly she turned and disappeared into the wall.

"No, wait!" Bastian raced after her. He halted at the wall where she had vanished.

"Anya, help us!" Bastian called out to the girl, slapping his hands against the stone surface. "Please."

With an electronic click, a tall, rectangular section of the stone wall came ajar. It was four inches thick. The flat stones covering its surface were mere decoration. Beyond the cleverly disguised door rose a dark stairwell.

~~◊~~

"Come, Aisy," Eddie urged. "I've got an escape planned."

Eddie nearly pulled Aislinn's arm out of its socket as they trudged up a spiral staircase in the dark. The sounds of Dimitri fighting with two security guards vanished as soon as the door behind them closed with a deep thud. With it vanished Aislinn's hope of escape.

Her bare feet were numb. She was so cold, her body felt hypothermic. Her fingers and toes burned. Reality had begun to fade into hopeless compliance with Eddie's demands and threats.

"Dimitri and Gabriella will be fine as long as you comply," Eddie instructed.

Aislinn dared not speak. If Eddie believed her to be unaffected by Helmer's spells and persuasion, he might snap and do something drastic. Her mental awareness of the freedom phrase Dimitri had reminded her of could not be recited. Not unless she maintain her focus on the separate window of thought. One Eddie could not detect. Her soul felt split into several personalities.

She clung to the promise that Gabriella and Dimitri would be okay.

*Aislinn, can you hear me?* The hushed male voice touched her mind with such gentleness, Aislinn was not sure who it belonged to.

*Dimitri?*

*Yes.* As soon as she felt Dimitri's tentative reply Aislinn knew she had to keep Eddie's mind busy. Dimitri was trying to make sure he was not overheard.

"Eddie, how much further?"

"Not long, sweetie-girl. Just need to open this door." He tapped a code into a lighted box beside a rustic door frame, and pulled at several metal latches.

*Where has he taken you?* Dimitri's voice was a wisp in her cluttered mind. *I heard a door slam shut.*

*Dimitri, we're heading up some stairs.* She visualized Dimitri in a safe, distinct closet of her mind. Which made sense, because in another compartment of her mind, Aislinn had shut away her telepathic connection to Bastian. Eddie would react violently to him, so she dared not attempt to contact him. He would not expect her to be able to communicate with Dimitri.

She finally understood. This was how the Olympians did it. Connected to so many minds, a single conversation could be overheard. She had worked it out. Her brain was capable of separating conversations by sheer will, and by practice. She imagined a separate place for each conversation, rooms in an endless hallway. If she had not been so miserable in that moment, she would have *whooped* in celebration.

Eddie shouldered open a thick door. Then he pulled her out into the night air. She shook violently from the cold wind.

Air froze in her lungs at the site before her. Huge rectangular stone battlements surrounded the circular roof. They were outlined in tiny lights. In the center of the roof stood a pinnacle that housed the access door they had just stepped through. Square openings between the battlements stood only three feet high, revealing a dark, stormy sky full of strange, moving shapes far above the buildings.

Antennae and dishes of all shapes covered the pinnacle which was topped with a giant pole. A flag displaying a red H3 flapped fiercely in the angry wind. Two weathered wooden tables sat off to one side, along with a small menagerie of thick wooden chairs.

Aislinn's stomach flip-flopped as Eddie led her across rough, flat stones to an opening between two of the battlements which gave a spectacular view of the entire complex and the partiers dancing below. Music pounded from all directions, the loudest from the courtyard, and from The Party House.

Four stories high, wind whipped at Aislinn's hair and clawed at her sparsely-clothed body without mercy. The air smelled of electricity and crisp winter ice, along with a foul scent she recognized from somewhere.

*Oh no.* It was the forest in Romania, during the fight with demons. The night had been filled with a putrid scent and unearthly sounds of wicked, narcissistic glee as the demons had attempted to wreak havoc on Bastian, Dimitri, and Marius.

For once, a slow song began to play from the speakers, causing the swarms of people to begin to slow as well. Lights twinkled from the trees in the courtyard and on the balconies of the adjacent buildings. A tractor pulling a packed trailer of people throwing hay rumbled off into trees, away from the barn.

Odd shadows that she had noticed earlier around Eddie began to multiply. Some blinked into focus resembling creepy specters with eyes and teeth, and tiny, unpleasant faces.

"Eddie, is that... bats or something?"

Eddie wrapped an arm around her waist and looked out over the courtyard. "Not exactly."

Aislinn watched him, and found herself wanting to step back from the manic sadness creeping into his eyes. "What do you mean?"

"They're just demons, Aislinn. They come here a lot. They love Halloween, and... other stuff that goes on here. I suspect the ones around my head are whisper demons."

"Whisper demons?"

"You can see them fully now, can't you?" The fatalistic sorrow in his voice tugged at her heart, but chilled her already frozen body. She didn't want to talk about demons. Especially if they were circling Eddie's head.

"Eddie, we're too close to the edge. It makes me nervous. Did you say someone was coming? Is it a helicopter?"

His fingers tightened on her waist. "They whisper things, you know."

"Um, okay."

"As long as you keep listening, they keep whispering." His voice sounded strange. He lifted his eyes to watch the circling creatures, which were becoming more solid by the second. "They whisper all kinds of crazy thoughts. If you don't listen, they go away. But once you start listening, more keep coming. And more. Their whispers fill your head. Their thoughts become yours."

Before she realized what Eddie was doing, he had slapped a handcuff to her right wrist, and encircled his left.

"Eddie? What the...."

"I love you Aisy. We can stay together now. They can't separate us." He reached out to touch her face. His fingers were shaking. His mind opened to her. What she viewed there chilled her to the bone.

"Eddie, no!" Aislinn struggled. Tears stung her eyes. "You said you loved me. Eddie, no. No!"

"I do love you, Aisy. We will be together, one way or another." He wrapped his body around hers like a snake. She tried to push him away, but his right hand grasped her neck in a death grip, his nails extending and sinking in. She gasped for air, waiting for him to rip open her throat.

A roaring sound grew like an advancing tornado. The door to the stairs burst open with such force the hinges broke off, causing the door to fall over and slide to a stop.

Bastian stepped into the night air, his chest still heaving, his jaw set. Aislinn felt her heart leap with fear, then joy, then fear again. He was carrying his sword. His silver eyes looked cold and deadly, ready to attack and kill. Dressed in black, he looked magnificent.

Aislinn choked as Eddie's nails sunk further into the tender skin of her neck, drawing blood. She could feel it dripping down the sides of her neck.

"Eddie, no," she sobbed.

"You move, she dies," Eddie told Bastian.

The wind howled and gray clouds billowed toward the top of the tower. Lightening crackled above their heads. Thunder followed, shaking the stone roof under their feet.

Eerie screeches pierced the night. Winged shadows danced on the wailing wind and around Eddie and Aislinn's heads. Aislinn could do nothing to avoid the creatures' wings so close to her face.

Bastian's eyes lost all of their color, save the red seeping in from the sides. They began to glow as they took in every detail. Aislinn could see the fight going on inside him, the desperate desire to save her, the deadly wish to attack Eddie, and the fear that either could cause her greater harm.

Figures appeared behind Bastian. Cirillo, Marius, Duncan, Earl, and Dimitri quietly sidestepped onto the tower roof, each taking position but making no threatening moves. More faces spilled out behind them. Aislinn recognized them from Cirillo's compound. Each had picked up the stiff wariness of the other. They watched and waited.

"One step and she's dead," Eddie threatened. "Leave now and she lives. I mean it."

Aislinn could barely breathe. Her body was shaking so violently her own movement caused Eddie's nails to slice deeper grooves into her throat.

Cirillo raised his left hand. "This is not the way to settle this, Edward. If you truly care about Aislinn, let her go. Let no harm come to her. No harm will come to you."

Eddie laughed. "You can't guarantee that."

"Oh yes, I can." Cirillo's jaw jutted slightly forward with determination. "Remember our conversation, Edward? It's not too late."

"Eddie…" Aislinn pleaded, her voice distorted and high-pitched from the hold he had on her windpipe. "Please. We can send them away, and we'll talk. Just you and me."

Poised in the open space between two battlements, Eddie whispered, "It will always be you and me, Aisy-girl. I won't let them separate us."

Cirillo's raised hand moved slow and rested in front of Bastian's chest. Aislinn understood the warning for Bastian to stay where he was, to do nothing. Perhaps he hoped to reassure Eddie that he would prevent Bastian from lunging at him. But Aislinn could tell by the look on Bastian's face, he was all hunter, focused on his prey, calculating the moment when he could strike.

"Edward, you are an Olympian," said Cirillo. "It does not matter which tribe. You are better than this. You were *meant* for better than this."

Eddie swallowed. "Maybe at one time that was true, sir. But not now. I don't belong anywhere. Aislinn is all that matters to me."

"Then prove it. Let her be safe. Love means you protect the ones you love, even if you have to let them go for a time."

"I am protecting her. From my father. From all of you. And from *him*." He glanced at Bastian. "If I give myself up... *he* gets her."

"Eddie," Aislinn implored. "We have a blood bond. You and me. He can't take that away, remember?"

"Shut up, Aislinn."

Her lips clamped shut. She did not want to be silent, but she felt compelled to obey him, either from the spell or from fear of what he might do.

Duncan whispered, "She's under a spell, sir. I see it."

Aislinn focused on Duncan's golden eyes. Of course. He could see auras.

An invisible hand was squeezing her heart when she shifted her focus to Bastian. Her mind might not be able to think about what she felt for him, but something inexplicable was there, an enormous pressure rising to the boiling point and pushing to break free. If she dared allow herself to feel it, Eddie might crack and rip out her throat.

Bastian breathed slow and steady. His shimmering alien eyes, red with the centers turned white, stared, waiting for that one opening when he could act. Aislinn wondered why he did not speak into her mind. Perhaps he too feared Eddie would hear, since they were all so close.

Eddie's arms tightened. "You'll never have her."

An odd *thud* interrupted the silence and Eddie jerked. Everyone's eyes shifted to his body. Aislinn gave a small whimper as she realized something sharp had grazed her side with a razor-like burn.

Eddie looked down in disbelief. Aislinn gasped. An arrow was sticking out of Eddie's abdomen. Aislinn turned her head just enough to catch a glimpse of a female figure running toward the tower with perfect balance along the roof top of the covered walkway that led to The Devil's Tower. Andromeda's long black hair was flying, her crossbow held high as she stopped to aim again.

In that moment Eddie squeezed his arms tight around Aislinn, pushed off with his feet, and hurled them both off the tower.

# CHAPTER 37

Aislinn screamed as stars, lights and buildings scrolled upside down in her sight. Mortal terror burned through her torso like a thousand hot swords. Her forehead and arms hit with a bone-cracking bang against a wall of gray and brown bricks. A fireball flashed in her shoulder and arm, causing her to scream again, the sound ripping through her chest along with the ripping of her shoulder muscles.

Almost instantaneously, she heard an animal-like cry from Eddie and the jolt of his body slamming against the tower wall below her. The excruciating weight of his body dangling from her left wrist was tearing her body in two. Their free fall had snapped to a halt.

It took a moment for Aislinn's brain to register that someone had a vise-like grip on her ankle. Voices were yelling above. She tried to raise her head toward her chest; even that was excruciating. Many hands were grabbing at the pale arm that held her leg.

She began clawing with her left hand at the brick wall, desperate to find something to grasp. But her fingernails snapped and the tips of her fingers scraped the rough bricks and bled.

Eddie was yelling, "*Noooo!*"

Hundreds of screams erupted below as partiers in the courtyard saw what was happening. Some began to cheer, assuming it was a stunt.

Unintelligible words were coming from Aislinn's mouth as she cried out in unspeakable anguish and horror. Her hand was ripping away from her arm. Her arm was dislocating from her torso. She could feel strong hands making their way to her knees, then her thighs. Her nearly-naked body scraped up the rough bricks.

Thin bones in Aislinn's hand were compressing, burning, slipping from the handcuff. Eddie was going to plummet to his death before her rescuers got her to the top. Though part of her felt he deserved it for jeopardizing her life, her heart pounded at thoughts of him plunging through the air to his death, with her staring at the earth below ready to crush him. Whether it was because she cared about him as a human being, or because the spell made her care deeper, the thought was still horrifying.

Eddie was crying out, his voice miserable and desperate. "No! You can't have her!" He grappled for the metal link connecting their cuffs, his fingers slapping, then latching hold of Aislinn's wrist. How he found the strength to reach for, and hold onto her arm, she did not know.

She cried out as more bricks tore open her ribs on her upward climb. Her spine was stretched to the breaking point. Suddenly, the weight of Eddie's body became lighter. Aislinn gasped, fearing he had fallen.

Three enormous eagles, two American Bald Eagles and one Golden Eagle had dug talons into Eddie, one at his shoulder, the other two at his belt, causing him to yell in anguish and pain. The *whoosh* of their mighty wings blew Aislinn's hair like giant fans.

Hands continued pulling Aislinn, up to her hips, then her waist, and finally her shoulders.

The same arms were pulling at Eddie, depositing them both onto the stone roof. Applause and cheers rang out from the crowd in the courtyard below. But on the tower, the air was not one of celebration.

In the scramble of bodies and barked commands, someone had snapped the two handcuffs apart. Aislinn could not stop sobbing. The pain in her shoulder and wrist was blinding. She was grasping at people, not knowing who had ahold of her in the dark and not knowing why she grabbed for them. Only the feel of a solid body taking her away from the tower would make her feel safe.

"It's okay, Aislinn. I've got you, I've got you." Dimitri crooned. His strong arms curled around her and held her still. Shocked to see him, Aislinn pressed her face against his shoulder and wept, bloodied fingers latching onto his shirt.

The unmistakable sounds of heavy bodies scrambling, pulling, and grunting filled the top of the tower.

"No, Bastian! He has not been sentenced." Cirillo was yelling through gritted teeth.

"I have sentenced him," came Bastian's growling reply. "I am going to do vhat I should have done before."

"Marius, stop him!" It was Cirillo's voice.

For a brief second, Aislinn saw Eddie's body rise to the top of the pile of men and then get slammed to the surface of the stone tower with a horrific, bone-crunching splat that a normal human would not have survived.

A blur of blond hair told her Bastian was on top of Eddie again.

"Bastian!" Marius yelled. "I am giving you an order. Take your hands off his neck!"

The men wrestled and rolled. Lightning crackled over their heads. Thunder shook the tower with the force of an earthquake. Wind began to scrape at everyone's clothes and hair with a tornado's fury.

Dimitri's arms tightened around Aislinn as the two watched the frightening scene. Garbled choking sounded like it was coming from Eddie, though Aislinn lost sight of him under all the fighting bodies. Bastian's blonde hair was flying in the wind as he hurled men off of him, fangs glistening. How he was still so strong after fighting all of them, she could not fathom. With each growl that boomed from Bastian's throat, lightening crackled and splintered the sky above the pile of men.

Shock and exhaustion overrode any strength Aislinn might have had to call out to Bastian. Even if she tried, she feared he would believe her to be devoted to Eddie, merely trying to preserve him. She also feared the dark rage she was witnessing, and the animal-like desire to kill that now filled Bastian's mind. It was more appalling and predatory than she could have imagined, bordering on immoral. The spell could not block that level of emotion.

Marius was fighting hard to gain control of Bastian, bracing his boots against the thick bricks of the battlement wall. He grasped Bastian's throat and jaw, forcing him to look him in the eyes. "Bastian! Hear me!" Marius' voice echoed off the tower walls as if enhanced. Aislinn felt it pulse through her own body. "Cease, now! By your blood vow, I command you to stop. Now!" The last word was through gritted teeth and extended canines.

The throng of bodies seemed to freeze in place. The only sound was panting from the men and the rush of the ceaseless wind.

Dimitri pressed his lips to Aislinn's ear and whispered, "Works every time."

She did not understand how a simple statement from Marius could exact that level of response from the monster Bastian had become.

Eddie's choking grunts changed to weak coughing. The pile of men began to break apart, muscle by muscle, arms retracting, and then legs.

"Get Edward out of here," Cirillo was ordering someone. Two men lifted Eddie, his body limp. They hurried toward the open maw of the tower door.

The remaining men in the pile up uncoiled, including Marius.

"Your mate is safe." Marius' spoke through heavy breaths. "See to her."

"She is no longer mine," said Bastian, his voice full of bitterness and hatred. "She can't even hear me. Edward saw to that."

"Don't be ridiculous, Bastian," said Cirillo. "No spell can break a blood bond, only hide it. Edward would have had to reinforce his hold on her every day. It was a pitiful attempt."

Bastian got to his feet and the men retreated to allow him room, their movements still alert and hesitant as if worried what he would do. Standing proud and majestic, his black shirt hanging in rips and soaked with blood and sweat, Bastian stared at the dark clouds boiling around the tower, streaks of lightening still blinking through them.

Aislinn expected Bastian to turn to her with a look of love and relief. She expected him to reassure himself that she was alive and well. She expected him to take her in his arms.

He did none of those things.

Instead, Aislinn watched him do the most wondrous thing she had ever witnessed. He crouched low, one knee to the cold stone, arms rigid. He bowed his head and closed his eyes. His body pulsed with a grayish-black, fathomless energy, then reformed into a huge black bird. Massive wings spread ten feet wide as he launched himself from the tower and into the air. The *swoosh* of giant feathers was the only sound she heard as he glided ever away from her, into the night, the fierce silver-gray eyes never looking back.

# CHAPTER 38

"Aislinn, bite down on this." Dimitri held a leather belt between Aislinn's teeth. "Ready?"

Before Aislinn could nod, pain slammed into her shoulder and she screamed around the belt. Blackness washed over her and she slumped against Dimitri. Pain was pounding a sledgehammer into her shoulder, her ears and brain.

"It's okay," Dimitri was whispering. "It's okay. I got you." He held her tight, her back against his chest.

Her head was lulling. He guided her forehead into the crook of his neck. Duncan was wrapping her shoulder in some kind of a sling.

"We can give you something for the pain when we get to the compound," said Duncan, sounding guilty. "I need to wrap your arm tight against your chest, Aislinn. Don't try to use it, and don't try to unwrap this. It's got to stay put. You've got torn ligaments and muscle damage."

Aislinn opened her eyes with effort, trying to see what Duncan was doing that was causing her arm renewed pain.

"Any word from...?" Nathan broke mid-sentence, as he turned around in the front seat.

"No," Dimitri answered, his voice tight. "And I'm not calling out to him."

"Beatie is swamped," came Cirillo's voice from the front seat. "Tonight is way worse than usual. We're out of healers. I know an orthopedic surgeon. Let me call him."

Aislinn allowed her head to fall back against Dimitri's shoulder. The movement caused the silky red material she was still wearing to brush against her breasts causing uncomfortable tingles. Though someone had thrown a blanket over her, she possessed no other clothing but the accursed negligée.

Her head snapped to attention, pumped with adrenalin and determination. "Get this off me!" She threw off the blanket and grabbed at the tattered red material and ripped. The sling Duncan was trying to wrap around her hampered her attempt. "I can't get it off!" she yelled. "Undo this thing. I… I can't…."

"Wait, I'm not finished," Duncan complained.

She pushed him aside with her good arm and tore at the beige wrappings, unraveling them in record speed.

"Whoa! Aislinn, stop!" Dimitri attempted to hold her still.

"Get it off!" She screamed, not caring that she would be naked. "Get it off!" She was sobbing. Panic gripped her. She might as well be in a coffin, buried alive. One sliver of the material ripped free. She threw it to the floor of the SUV.

"Just wait 'till we get to Cirillo's," Dimitri pleaded, trying to grab her arms. "I can get you clothes."

"No, now!" Aislinn could not stop her flailing arms from ripping at the material, which caused searing pain in her shoulder. She didn't care about the pain, and didn't care what body parts they saw, as long as she could excise herself from the spelled negligée.

"Whoa!" Duncan had his hands up in self-defense and was trying to look away.

"Okay, okay," Dimitri acquiesced. "We'll get you a shirt. Just hang on. You're half naked." Aislinn pulled the remains of the red material over her head.

"This has got weird energy," Duncan stated in a confused voice. He held up the discarded scrap in fascination.

Dimitri re-wrapped the blanket around Aislinn to cover her breasts. "Cirillo, you got any shirts in here?"

"In the trunk. Here, give her mine. I've got a T-shirt on under this." He swerved to the side of the busy highway and skidded to a stop. In a flash, he had removed his black button-down shirt.

The men turned away as Aislinn wrapped herself in Cirillo's warm shirt.

"The panties. I gotta get them off too."

"What?" Dimitri asked in disbelief. "No, Aislinn, wait."

"They gotta come off. They gotta come off." She was crying again. "They gotta… I've got to…" She was sobbing so hard she couldn't speak, and reaching under the shirt.

"Aislinn, calm down." Dimitri took hold of her wrists to keep her still. She cried out in pain and frustration. She heard the trunk slam shut.

"I'm telling you, she's right," Duncan said. "The whole thing's been spelled or something. It's got this… weird energy. The colors I am seeing…."

The door flew open beside them and Cirillo shoved a pair of pants at her.

She pulled off the red panties and donned Cirillo's pants. They felt wonderful. Free of anything evil.

Finally nestled against Dimitri, wearing Cirillo's oversized camouflaged pants and black shirt, Aislinn attempted deep calming breaths.

The cry of an eagle pierced the night as Cirillo drove back onto the highway.

"Is that…?" Nathan leaned toward the windshield and peered sharply up at the sky.

"Yeah, probably," said Dimitri.

Aislinn eye's widened at their insinuation that Bastian was following the car in the rain and thunder. She considered calling to her mate telepathically.

*Her mate.*

She had not thought of him as such before. Her newfound safety gave her the freedom to feel it in her soul. Then a spike of anger shot through that feeling. Her *mate* should be in this car with her.

She leaned into Dimitri and sighed. Hungry specters of desire awoke in her body where she reclined against Dimitri. *Brother*, she instructed her body. *He's a brother.*

Her shoulder and wrist throbbed mercilessly, despite Duncan re-wrapping them. She closed her eyes against the pain. It was too many things. Always too many things.

In less than 24 hours, she had feared for her family's life, witnessed Gabriella getting tortured, allowed herself to be spelled and persuaded, and then yanked all over the H3 complex for what seemed eons of time. Escape and hope had been dashed when she was recaptured, and ultimately thrown off a four story tower. Death had lost its chance with the single, determined hand on her ankle. She would never forget the glimpse of Bastian's pale face grunting to hold on and not lose her along with Eddie's added weight, while other arms strained to hold on to him.

She still could not believe the same man left her on the tower, convinced she was lost to him. Or was he just consumed by rage? Surely that rage was focused at Eddie, but she suspected he was incensed that everyone had stopped him from getting his revenge.

Revenge had ruled his life for a very long time.

Despite her resolve, she reached out tentatively to Bastian's mind. A dark, stoic wall met her. An etheric knife stabbed into her head and she groaned. Even now, the spell told her to accept that Bastian was off limits. She would have to find a way to destroy all remnants of the spell's power, or reverse it.

Nestled between Dimitri and Duncan, and in Cirillo's care, she was protected. She was safe. Like a tiny snake slipping through her mind, Helmer's spell reminded her she wasn't supposed to be with Olympians. Helmer's repetitive persuasion fought for control in her mind, but an unnamed strength was beginning to weave its way, whispering that she herself had the power to control it, to compartmentalize it, to lock it away until she found the keys to release the magic and replace it with something else. Something wonderful. Something good.

"Is that snow?" asked Nathan in the front seat.

Aislinn raised her head from Dimitri's chest. Clouds of tiny, white flower-like debris were whirling around the car. Several pieces floated in front of Duncan, inside the car. One touched his cheek. He reached up a hand in wonder.

"Whoa, what is this?" he asked. "White and gold energy's around it."

*Anya.*

Aislinn sat up straight. What was Anya doing? Maybe she just wanted to make her feel better. That was probably it. Headlights flashed by, the vehicle heading in the opposite direction showed no signs of the snowfall that was surrounding their car. Cirillo exited onto Highway 485, headed toward his compound in King's Mountain.

A face materialized into Aislinn's mind. Like a ghost, the vacant, hopeless face of the brown-haired girl on the platform haunted her. Pain. Humiliation. Drugs. Despair.

Lost in her own pain for hours on end, she had forgotten the girl.

Dread hit the center of her stomach like a ball she had tried to catch but missed. The thought of ever setting foot on the grounds of the H3 made her want to vomit. But that face... how many more were there? Five? Ten? Hundreds? In and out, day after day, being auctioned off to their doom.

White light began to glow around Duncan like a cloud illuminated by the sun's rays. There was a shape forming in the light beside him.

"What's wrong, Aislinn?" he asked.

Aislinn could not speak, mesmerized by the double image. Then it moved. A figure radiating magnificence raised an arm. The arm seemed to extend until she realized part of a sword had formed. Aislinn stared, transfixed. This was it. The shimmering light she had seen in Cirillo's study had tried to warn her, to prepare her. With a mixture of wonder and dread, she understood.

"We have to go back."

"What?" every voice in the SUV chimed.

She looked up at Dimitri. "We have to go back. I can't leave that girl there. I don't know where she is, or, if she's already been... bought or something. But, I have to save her."

"What girl?" Dimitri asked.

"The one they were bidding on."

"Aislinn, you are in no shape to…."

"Dimitri, I got a small taste of what goes on there. I think girls are tortured and drugged until they give in and accept everything that's done to them, or whatever they're asked to do."

She turned to Duncan's brown face and stared into his golden eyes. "Duncan, I'm being told to go."

The light around him began to dissipate but still rippled beside him. She knew the precise moment Duncan discerned what she was inferring. His eyes were glancing at points around her head, seeing something she could not.

"Dimitri, she's right."

"Aislinn, what are you talking about?" asked Cirillo. "You saw trafficking going on?"

"Cirillo, it was the most humiliating thing I have ever seen. This is why all this happened to me. It wasn't about me. It was about those girls. We have to go back."

"Darlin,' you ain't goin' back. There is no force on Earth that could make me take you back to that pit. If anyone goes, it will be my warriors, but not you."

"But you don't understand. The light, angel, whatever, is telling me to go. I know where the…."

"Aislinn, you need medical attention," Cirillo insisted, his tone harsh. "Your going back there will be over my dead body. I won't risk you."

Her heart warmed at his dedication to her wellbeing, but it also made her angry. "Cirillo, I really appreciate that. But the message came to me."

"Then be the messenger."

She stared into his reflection in the rear view mirror. Perhaps he was right, but no one else knew all the secret tunnels and stairs like she did.

Something caught her eye and she turned toward Duncan. A flake of white wafted in front of Duncan's face and danced before floating in front of her and landing on Dimitri's forehead.

"Who is that?" Duncan asked softly, while Dimitri brushed the specter away.

"I think it's my sister, Anya," Aislinn answered. "And there's someone else. It's like a… a…."

"Angel," he finished for her.

"He's telling us to go," she said. "Well, me to go."

"Aislinn, tell me exactly what you saw at the H3." Cirillo was pulling out his phone.

"I saw a girl up on some kind of platform. Men were bidding on her. Maybe five or six of them. The girl looked drugged. The room had doors. All around. Metal doors, with locks. Electronic keypads. I was *in* one of those rooms. Eddie brought me out but we had to pass by the... bidding area, I guess you would call it. I think I heard voices behind the platform where the girl was. I think there were more girls in there, in rooms. Or waiting to be....” She swallowed. “Um, some guy offered ten thousand dollars for me.”

Cirillo’s eyes widened with a hard look of fury and disgust. He shook his head and gritted his teeth. “Horace has got himself a sex trafficking ring. Ken,” Cirillo spoke into his phone, pressing the speaker button, “did you see any signs of possible sex trafficking at H3? I’ve got Nathan, Dimitri, Duncan and Aislinn with me.”

“Sex trafficking?” Ken asked. “Not specifically, sir. In the few days that we’ve had them under surveillance, there have been several cars with totally blacked-out windows going in and out. Occasionally, one would disappear into an underground garage under the tower. Could have been anybody in those cars.”

“Well, I’m beginning to think we know how Horace Hawthorne made his millions. It wasn’t just the success of the H3. If he’s been engaging in human trafficking all this time... hmm, that explains why he is one of the biggest contributors to charities in North Carolina. And why he’s in with all the politicians. Gotta fool everybody, or bring them on board. If there’s any suspicion, no one will believe it. He may be providing for some of them.”

“What kind of proof have you got?” Ken asked.

“Aislinn says she saw a girl being auctioned. She looked drugged.”

Aislinn sat up. “And there were more in the basement. They called it the Dungeon.”

“Were they restrained, Aislinn?” Ken asked.

“Two girls were chained up. Their eyes were open but they looked doped up, and like they were too scared to speak.”

“I saw them, too, Cirillo,” added Dimitri. “I had to get Gabriella out of there as fast as possible, and we didn’t know anything about the two girls. I mean, some people are into that sort of thing, you know?”

“But I don’t think they were,” said Aislinn. “And....” Something occurred to her. “Cirillo, I had a spell *and* persuasion used on me. What if the girls there are told to believe that’s what they want? I mean, Helmer and Damian are Olympians. They could make them do anything, or believe anything.”

Cirillo gritted his teeth. “Olympians know the rules. Even rogues. That makes them the same as vampires. Ken, we’ve got to do something.”

“What if they’ve moved the girls already?” Nathan asked. “I mean, with us running around, surely they’ve moved them. If we go in there and can’t prove anything....”

"Duke said we took half of H3's security guards down," said Dimitri. "This explains why nobody called the police on us. Didn't want them poking around."

"What do you think, Ken?" asked Cirillo. "Would we be better off going in now while they're still putting their security back together? They know Aislinn and Gabriella were our targets, and we left after acquiring them. They'd never think we'd come back."

"It has to be tonight," Aislinn emphasized. "They can't have moved that girl already."

"Aislinn, honey, we have to have a plan," Cirillo stated. "We need intel on locations, security, and more people involved. This is a police issue as well as an Olympian issue. And we can't let any Olympians there use persuasion on police showing up. Every officer is going to need an Olympian beside them."

"Sir, no one's left the forest entrance since Horace took off in his limo," said Ken. "We've still got eyes on the place. If the tower is the main location where the illegal activity is taking place, then we've got to stop anyone from leaving there. It would be better if we had legit officials, and a warrant."

"Ken, we've got two witnesses as to at least three girls being held against their will. Can you get me a warrant?"

"I will make it happen, sir. Judge Railly hates trafficking. He won't care if I call him on Halloween."

"All right, let's plan this thing out. I want people back in position. I need eyes everywhere so the buyers can't escape either. I need people inside the tower searching every place where girls can be hidden. Ken, I'm going to need your persuasion. I'll also call in my brothers. Faces they haven't seen."

"Sir?" Ken sounded hesitant. "Do you really want this to go public?"

"I want to blow it wide open," Cirillo confirmed, anger radiating from his voice. "But, Horace is no fool. He'll have covered his tracks. If this has been going on for years, just think of where all the girls have gone, what's become of them. Probably boys, too. Oh, man, this makes me sick. Hey, Ken, remember the prophecy about Aislinn?"

"Yes. That she would change the family forever."

"Well, she's fixin' to do more than change that family forever. She's taking them down."

Aislinn quailed at the ominous words.

"Regardless, Aislinn," Dimitri whispered beside her. "*You* can't go back in there."

"I have to, Dimitri. I've been all over that place. All the hidden stairs… and the tunnels? No one knows where I was."

"I know. Remember, I was on the first floor when I saw Edward run off with you. I know where the hidden stairs are on that floor. And I followed them up to the third floor when Edward sic'd his guards on me. They took me down the elevator to that Dungeon."

"Ken," Dimitri leaned forward so Ken could hear him, "access to the Dungeon is through that underground garage. I busted the door open. Access to all floors is through two elevators, one is hidden beside the other. But you may need codes and thumbprint access, or just persuade whatever staff is on the elevator. Wait, they can also be controlled remotely. That's what happened to me. I need to know where the control room is."

"I did see the ramp where they temporarily park cars. I bet the girls are transported in that way so no one can see, and then put in the Dungeon before they're taken anywhere else. The place is full of torture devices. And believe it or not, it's shielded somehow from Olympian telepathy and other abilities. I'd love to know how they do that."

"All right, Ken," said Cirillo, "get me my warrant. I'm calling everyone back and getting them into position. We're going to need new faces and anyone with persuasion abilities. On your mark, we'll close in."

"All right, I'll call you back."

Aislinn swallowed. "Dimitri, I am terrified of going back there, but I think I'm supposed to go."

"Not gonna happen." Dimitri shook his head. "And this one's on Bastian's behalf."

"Leave him out of this."

"I care as much about my Uncle, as I do *you*. But half the people who work there saw you. We chased you all over the place. As soon as you're recognized, they'll know something's up. If they haven't moved the girls already, they'll have those girls outta there so fast...."

"But, there's no way you'll find the right hallways without me."

Dimitri stiffened and glared at her. *Then be my eyes.*

Aislinn sucked in a breath. She softened her expression lest anyone guess they possessed a telepathic link.

She focused hard and thought only of him. *Will it work?*

*You can guide me the whole way. Just keep sending me pictures. I can say I've been through most of the hallways. And, I actually have.*

Aislinn licked her lips. Her mind whirled. Could they keep such a ruse going, or would one of them mess up and inadvertently reveal to the others that they had formed a bond? Bastian would be furious. Marius would be incensed. They would both be in a world of trouble.

"Aislinn, I need to ask you something." Cirillo's brows were furrowed when their eyes met through the mirror. "If we are successful, this trial could go public, unless there is a huge agreement to keep it Olympian. Are you prepared to tell the world what happened to you?"

"Um...." She realized Cirillo did not know what all had been done to her, and was assuming the worst. "I didn't get sold or anything. And I wasn't... raped. I'm sure the others probably were. There was such terrible hopelessness in that room. Fear and pain was everywhere. And evil." She shivered. "But I can still testify to everything else. Being tied up. Being given foreign substances. Mental torture. And torturing Gabriella. And what Helmer said about... what he likes to do to girls to... to get them ready for buyers." She could tell by the averted eyes in the car that the men were uncomfortable with the subject. "I'm not afraid. He has to be stopped."

This time Cirillo's raised brows held a hint of pride. "At'a girl."

Aislinn swallowed and looked away. She didn't feel as brave as she sounded. The thought of stepping a single foot onto the H3 property had caused her limbs to start shaking again. Cirillo might keep her from being there physically, but now she would have to see it again, through Dimitri's eyes.

# CHAPTER 39

Dear Anya,

What am I going to do about him? I am so angry I want to just scream into his head. All this time I've wondered—no, feared—that what we had was *just* the blood bond.

But I miss him. I am less than whole without him. Every time the doorbell rings, my heart starts pounding. When he was around, I was so filled with his presence that I wasn't badgered by all the emotions of other people slapping me. He is a respite from all of that. Even now I can feel the emotions of every person in this house. I'd rather feel his.

They freed seven girls and two boys from the tower. So few. I just know there are more out there somewhere. Ken had to use persuasion to get the truth out of them. He's apparently really good at it. He had to do more of it in the presence of Cirillo, Marius, and two cops. Then he had to do it again in front of The Augustine, who arrived yesterday. Some rule of theirs for verification. I'm guessing it was Helmer that did a number on them.

Dimitri found my clothes at the H3. I want to burn them but they're holding them as evidence. Dimitri caught the scent and found a room with girls and boys clothes, and it was full of negligées and outfits they make them wear. I can't believe he could pick out my scent in all of that. Poor Dimitri. I think I know why.

My arm's still in a sling. Ma Beatie took me to a woman who just had a baby. She only worked for about twenty minutes, but it was enough so that I don't need surgery. Still hurt like hell the first night, but my body is healing really fast. At least that's one good thing about all this Olympian blood I've ingested. No one but Dimitri knows about his and Helmer's blood, and I'm keeping it that way.

The spell is gone, but I'm still having nightmares. Gabriella and Marius took me to see Father Davis yesterday. He said prayers and chanted things, read scripture, and anointed me. I had to say things too. Felt like an exorcism. Like they were pulling dirty energy out of my body. I swear I saw the dark shadows leave. Felt like I had taken a shower and was all clean again.

Plus, Gabriella's been teaching me all about affirmations. You say something over and over and focus on your will to make it true. It works pretty well, but I end up making it a prayer because it just feels like I should ask for it as well as being positive about it. Feels like more power is behind it, you know?

I'm at Gramma's now. Duncan and Dimitri are staying with us to guard the house. Marius consented to telling Gramma everything. I'm so relieved. Duncan and Dimitri got to do it. Well, me too. Gramma kept saying, "I just knew it! I knew there was something to all this!" She's always thought we were descended from psychic gypsies or something. Remember?

She keeps trying to get Duncan and Dimitri into secret conversations without Aunt Julia around, especially Duncan, since she trusts him. But Aunt Julia is so excited about handsome young men running around the house, she keeps giggling and wants in on every conversation. And she keeps baking and trying to feed them.

They're not minding that part.

Dimitri's smart and keeps asking for smoothies and puddings, saying he's got a toothache and can't chew anything. Ha! Too funny. Duncan keeps saying, "Hey, I'll try a smoothie, too." And Duncan got her to make chocolate, egg and lemon pudding pies. He eats the insides and puts half the crusts down the garbage disposal when she's not looking. They're a hoot. It's like having brothers around.

There was no way I was staying at Cirillo's with Eddie in the brig. It's a jail in the basement with thick bars. I think they have all kinds of things down there, but I haven't seen it yet. I don't want anywhere near Eddie.

The other tribal leader, The Plymouth, arrives at Cirillo's in a few days. I wondered if that was part of why Bastian hasn't come back.

It's only been two and a half days but it feels like forever. I can tell he's close by because the pull on my heart is not stressed. Sometimes I feel him just out in the woods. In the trees somewhere. He wanted to kill Eddie and he's mad at Marius for stopping him, and if he goes to Cirillo's, I think he's afraid he'll lose his mind knowing Eddie's just feet away in the basement. He knows he'll run down there and strangle him.

I talked to Gabriella about it. She says Marius can use the "blood vow" to force Bastian to come back, like what he did on top of the tower to get him to stop fighting. She says it's a psychic thing and a blood thing, and Marius has to concentrate hard to call the power into play. Something new with these people every day. I think I've just touched the tip of the iceberg. Anyway, Gabriella told Marius to give Bastian time. They didn't ask me what I thought.

I haven't called out to him. I feel his mind at times, like a window open and a breeze touching me. I can feel he has questions. After everything I've been through, I don't think I should have to explain anything. I guess I'll have to sooner or later. I'll have to testify at the trial in a few days. They are going to hold some kind of Olympian trial first. Don't know what the rules are yet.

I'm sure there'll be plenty of them. You know these people and their rules.

When Bastian does show up, I don't know what I'm going to say. Maybe you can help me. I called LaVanna. Didn't tell her about the Olympian angle of course, but told her Eddie tried to kill me, and my new boyfriend skipped out when he got mad because he wanted to attack Eddie. *Whoo!* You should have heard her. That girl knows how to give someone a piece of her mind. Now if I can just remember her words when I see him.

Love, Aisy

~~◊~~

Snow fell silent and cold around Bastian, nearly obscuring his view of the old house. Frozen flakes sparkled in the starlight and dissipated before they touched the ground. Nowhere else in the woods was it snowing.

He blew air out of the nostrils in his beak, wondering why Anya's spirit was hanging around him. Surely she knew his presence spelled disaster for Aislinn. He had accepted it, why couldn't she?

Everything in him wanted to spare Aislinn from pain, to keep her from harm, to let her go. And everything in him wanted to engulf her in his protective, loving arms, breathe her in, and never let go.

Aislinn's soft, musical laughter erupted from the house. Tilting his eagle head, his keen eyes caught hand movement in the living room beyond the kitchen bay windows. He burned with jealousy as Dimitri and Duncan threw pieces of popcorn at Aislinn, and she threw them back. She was happy. It looked like she would be happier without him.

A whirling cloud of fresh, fat snowflakes exploded into his eagle face and he shook them off, flapping his wings before settling back onto the thick oak branch.

*Stop it, Anya.*

He wanted to growl at her but his bird vocal chords wouldn't allow him.

She wasn't the one who had to feel the pain of loss every time someone tore Aislinn away from him, leaving him powerless. Powerless was not something he was used to feeling. He was still the Fearless Sebastian. Once he scented a vampire, there was no hiding from him. He would chase them to the ends of the Earth. And then he would lop off their head with glee, reveling in the satisfaction the bloody act gave him. Just like they had done to Cecilia.

It was that gruesome satisfaction that he was being punished for now, surely. He had taken his revenge too far. Now, each time he experienced profound joy with Aislinn, she was cut away from him, like another severed head hitting the dirt.

Maybe for every head he had detached, someone would be kidnapping Aislinn and putting her under a spell just so his heart would rip in two from the pain.

*Splat!* Another bucket load of snow catapulted into his face, nearly knocked him off the branch.

He shook his head and feathers violently, catching them in scraggly twigs and branches of the gnarled oak tree.

He squawked in every direction, turning on the branch, daring Anya to materialize so he could mentally yell at her.

The lamp in Aislinn's bedroom came on. His heart quickened as she changed into pajamas. He did not get to see much since she kept moving about the room. The lamp went out. The blue light of her electronic tablet came on.

Snowflakes whirled away from him like a soft tornado and regrouped outside Aislinn's window.

# CHAPTER 40

"What are you doing in here?" Bastian demanded.

Aislinn froze. Looming like a six-foot-five Viking in the doorway, the only thing that moved was Bastian's eyes as they skipped from Duncan, to Aislinn, to Dimitri, back and forth, gathered around Aislinn's bed.

Aislinn had only a second to wonder where he had materialized from since she had not heard footsteps, and he was wearing an unbuttoned, rumpled forest-green shirt and blue jeans, and his feet were absolutely bare.

Duncan stood, his movements fluid and graceful, but unhurried. He had been sitting at the bottom of Aislinn's bed gently coaxing her to tell him about her nightmare. Her screams had caused Duncan and Dimitri to rush to her aid in the middle of the night for the second night in a row, only to discover she had experienced another nightmare and the room was devoid of demons.

Well, corporeal ones.

Dimitri, who was standing on the other side of Aislinn, crossed his arms and faced Bastian. He and Duncan were wearing nothing but boxers. And they looked wonderful in them.

Dimitri spoke first, his eyes narrowing. "Taking care of Aislinn, since nobody else is."

Bastian's pale eyes blazed and sparkled like diamonds. "I'm here now."

"Oh, gee, let me get all excited." The sarcasm in Dimitri's voice unnerved Aislinn almost as much as the nightmare had.

It was clear that Aislinn *had* inadvertently created an unusual bond between her and Dimitri with the tiny bit of his blood she had ingested. Dimitri suggested privately to her that his consent to being her brother was the only thing keeping the blood heat from taking over. Still, any time Dimitri had stood too close to her, their bodies had felt the burning pull to be ever closer.

375

Thankfully, Duncan's presence had kept Dimitri steady. And distracted. They often sparred in the woods behind the house. "For practice," Duncan would say. If Duncan detected anything in Dimitri or Aislinn's auras that gave their fragile blood bond away, he had kept it to himself. He was smart enough to know Dimitri needed something to do to get rid of his pent up energy.

In the doorway of Aislinn's bedroom, Bastian stood with cheeks flushed and hands clenched tight. He took two steps toward Dimitri. Aislinn tossed her blankets aside and swung her legs over the edge of the bed, not caring who saw her pajamas, which consisted of a pink camisole and matching shorts.

She stood in Bastian's path, shielding Dimitri. "You are not going to take offense with him, Bastian."

Bastian squinted with suspicion. "So, you prefer him?"

"Oh, that would make it easy for you, wouldn't it? No. Dimitri is my brother. And Duncan's my cousin." She waited a few seconds before adding, "Besides, they stayed. You didn't."

Bastian's breathing deepened as he stared at her. Mixed emotions exploded from him in rapid succession. Aislinn threw up a wall in her mind as he tried to read her. He would have to work at knowing what she was feeling.

All the worry, soul searching and anger that brewed for the last two and a half days came back to her. Anger was taking the lead. If he had waited much longer to take action, her blood would be boiling. So would the blood heat, which was growing like an unfed monster. A monster now comprised of four Olympian men. It was a wonder Aislinn slept at all.

Bastian glanced at Duncan, then Dimitri. "This is between me and her."

Neither Duncan nor Dimitri moved. Aislinn realized they were waiting, gallantly, for some sign from her.

"Thank you Duncan," she spoke softly. "And thank you Dimitri. I appreciate you both for being here. I think Bastian and I need to talk."

As if she had flipped a switch, Duncan and Dimitri exited the room, both with a parting glare at Bastian as if to put him on notice that they were not far. Aislinn felt her eyes mist with gratitude for their protectiveness.

Dimitri's foot halted in the doorway, as if unable to completely withdraw from her room. She saw Duncan's brown arm reach in front of him, grab the doorknob, and close the door, forcing Dimitri to step back.

Bastian lifted his chin. Clearly he did not appreciate the challenge to his position as reigning male in her life. His jaw clenched several times as if working to control his anger. His expression changed from threatening to pensive to worried, as if weighed down by a sense of fate. Was he expecting her to dump him? It had not occurred to her he would think that.

"I haven't been far," he stated, as if in apology.

After seconds ticked by, Aislinn said, "Neither have I."

He stepped closer. Even that simple movement of his virile body made Aislinn's skin prickle and flood with desire. Her attention shifted to his chest, to his thighs, and then his groin. *Oh dear.* She raised her focus to his face and disciplined herself to remain there. If she allowed further examination of his incredible physique, she would be done for.

Every second they remained close caused the air to crackle with desire unfulfilled and needy. Aislinn was tempted to take a step back, but could not make her aching body obey.

*Oh, lord.* If she did not start talking soon, there would be no talking.

He was obviously having trouble as well. His darting eyes belied his attempt not to linger on her pink camisole and what its soft folds outlined. He swallowed as if it were painful.

His proximity was also dissolving some of her fury. She had allowed herself to think they were both healing these past few days, that they were just taking a hiatus from each other. She could have spoken to him telepathically at any time, especially after the excising of the spell. But she did not. And she most certainly was not going to grovel.

"Why did you leave that day?" Bastian blurted, surprising her.

Aislinn found that curious. She had told Gabriella, who surely informed Marius, who should have informed Bastian. Which meant Bastian must not have spoken to Marius. She could not imagine Marius letting him go that long. She suspected Marius was having trouble with his own desire to kill Helmer. Especially since Helmer had disappeared, giving him no satisfaction.

She crossed her arms. "Why do you *think* I left?"

He opened his lips to form words, but halted. "I asked you first."

"Fine. One, Eddie had my remaining family in a car and was going to crash it into a truck. My worst nightmare all over... *again*." Her voice cracked on the last word. "Two, the man I loved was busy healing someone, being obedient to his almighty leaders, while the sun was up, and while I needed him, and could not even *hear* me. Three, Eddie had a blood bond with me and said he could hear me if I contacted you, or the police. I didn't know how to block him out yet. And four...."

Bastian took a step toward her.

"Oh no you don't." She raised a hand, then her index finger. "You actually thought I went back to Eddie. Didn't you?"

His hesitation was an answer. "I... feared it."

"Then we don't exactly have a relationship built on anything solid, do we?"

"Sometimes spells have... residual effects." He licked his lips. "You might have been drawn...."

"But I wasn't. Well," she rolled her eyes, "I was put under a spell later. That was to save Gabriella. Which, if you really loved me…."

"What I feel for you is real, I assure you, my lady."

"What you feel for me was not strong enough to make you to stay and find out the real story, was it? Or help me through it? Or make me feel safe?"

He swallowed again. "I… was… feeling many things then." His eyes dropped to her silky pajamas and back to her face, though more with nervousness than desire. "One…" He raised his brows to show he was honoring her habit of counting reasons. "The love of my life was stolen away from me, for a *third* time in a week."

Aislinn felt her resolve begin to crumble at "love of my life." He had loved his first mate. That, she knew. Yet, he was referring to her as being even more special.

"Two," he continued, "another spell had been put on you, and you could not hear me, though I was searching desperately, and fighting anyone who got in my way."

He took a breath through clenched teeth. "Three, the man who has caused me so much pain, who took you from me, and was willing to kill you rather than let us be together—that man, I was prevented from killing. It was my right. Marius should not have stopped me. In the old days he would not have." His voice had become low and deep, his accent sharpening. His hands clenched and rose involuntarily as if remembering the moment. "My rage was so profound, Aislinn. I feared I would attack the other warriors for holding me back. I had to get away and clear my head."

It was her turn to swallow. She could not help sympathizing with him.

"And four," he added, "though I had saved you, even after all that, I still did not have you. God is punishing me. Surely. It is the only explanation."

Sorrow and pain filled his eyes, and made her chest hurt.

"Punishing you for what?" she asked.

"You know why. For enjoying the hunt. I could not wait to hear of another vampire. I could make him pay. I could make each one pay. I went after demons with equal vengeance. They saw my darkness. I saw it in their eyes. They would laugh. Then I would sever their heads."

"Seriously gross, Bastian."

"Sorry." He looked down at his hands as if seeing blood stains. "I have wondered how my sword functioned at all, or how the priest was able to bless it. I thought I had been given a reprieve. But no. You were a gift God taunted me with. My presence meant constant danger to you."

Aislinn took a moment to consider his heartfelt disclosure. Absorbing his emotions proved this was, in fact, the core belief that had kept him away. A belief so strong he might as well keep punching a hornet's nest, knowing the pain that would follow. "You think every time you get close to me, I will be in danger, and God's going to take me away?"

The wrinkles of pain forming around his eyes affirmed the answer.

"You know," she said, "considering the horrible and evil things people can do in this world, killing demons and vampires doesn't even make the top ten, in my book. Maybe not even the top twenty. Bastian, sometimes really bad things happen to really good people. We don't get to know why, and it wouldn't matter if we did. The reason would never be high enough. If people found out why things keep happening to them, some lofty end game of good, would they really be like, 'sure, no problem, keep making me miserable as long as something good happens in the end?'"

She raised her hands as if in entreaty, and then dropped them.

"I've had a lot of time to think these last two days," she continued. "My whole family died because of me. Because of Mr. Hawthorne's paranoia. When I discovered that it all happened because of a mage's prophecy about me, the entire world seemed to fall in on me."

She gave a self-deprecating huff. "If I did not exist, they would all be alive. One minute I feel responsible because I'm the reason, and the next minute I'm angry because there was no one to warn me. But what if they had? Seven girls and two boys were rescued from a life of slavery, Bastian. Cirillo's investigators are tracing the past and finding more. If the three commanders vote to allow persuasion to be used on the Hawthorne family, they'll be able to pull every memory and transaction out of them. Who knows how far it will go?

"But if I knew the death of my family would help rescue all those people, could I make the decision to let them die?" She shook her head. "I couldn't do it, Bastian. I'm not good enough. I'm not selfless enough. Such a decision would destroy me.

"But one thing is certain. Right now, I want to kill every member of the Hawthorne family."

Bastian's eyes widened in alarm.

"I want to take from them what they took from me. I've never thought anything like that before. In—my—life. Well, with the exception of Miss Spider-Legs. But now, I can actually think it for real. So… another Olympian change I didn't see coming. If I killed off his family, the prophecy would be complete, now wouldn't it? It would be over. I would be safe. Then again, no more people would be rescued because the family members wouldn't be around to interrogate. So I'm screwed. I am denied everything."

"Aislinn," Bastian took a step forward, "do not let yourself go down that path. You could lose yourself like I did. I know what you are feeling, and it hurts. I devoted my life to fighting demons, fighting on the side of good, rescuing people. And yet, my mate was killed. Brutally. It put me on a path to wipe out evil creatures who preyed on people, who sucked the life and will out of them. Yes, good happened. But where is the justice in that? For me?"

"I guess we have more in common than we thought." She raised both brows. "I never abandoned you, though. Did I? Yes, I left on a plane. My Gramma was sick, and could die. All I could think of was getting to her."

"You left with *him*."

"And you had told me very little, almost *nothing*. Nothing of the pain in my gut because of the blood bond, nothing of the insane blood heat, nothing of spells. Eddie orchestrated everything, and he played me. But nobody was dying in your world. Well, I guess I almost did. You saved me. And then you just left."

"You could not hear me." He sighed. "I was being punished while I had to wait for yet another of Edward's spells to be lifted. I did not know if I would be able to even hold you. It was... too many things."

"Yes. It was too many things." She nodded in agreement. "I told Dimitri it was too many things. But, he couldn't stop them from happening. I had to watch Gabriella get tortured. Did Marius tell you that?"

Bastian's face crinkled with remembered pain. "Marius was in anguish. As was I."

"I agreed to the spell, to save her. In case you're wondering. Seeing how you didn't ask. Would you have done any less?"

His jaw jutted slightly forward and he spoke through clenched teeth. "I would have killed him."

"Well, I didn't have that option, now did I? I'm a woman, and I was chained to a bed. *With* silver. One more thing you did not prepare me for."

Bastian took a deep, slow breath. "I did not know that was how you were put under a spell."

"Well. You didn't exactly stick around to ask how, now did you?"

"I truly am sorry."

"It wasn't enough that I feared for my family's life. It wasn't enough that I was kidnapped and had no choice but to agree to a horrible spell. It wasn't enough that I was thrown off a tower and almost died. You... just... took... off. And that made everything *way* worse."

"At least I caught you. I would have *died* trying."

After a moment of weighing several caustic replies, Aislinn opted for a stiff, "Thank you for that."

His silver-gray eyes examined the air around her, as if searching for the right thing to say.

"Do you still want me, Aislinn?"

~~◊~~

380

A swarm of electrified butterflies exploded in Aislinn's belly, crawling outward to every nerve, fluttering hopeful wings around female places. Apparently, for her body, this was an easy answer. Not so much her heart.

Without the blood bond exciting her body, what *did* she feel? Only in that moment did she realize everything about him *was* what she wanted, despite his recent transgression. A man who understood her abilities. A man who needed her and wasn't afraid to say it. A man whose mind could merge with hers so that their love, their desires, even their physical ecstasies, could be experienced together. A man willing to fight to protect her. And a man who was so good-looking it took all her strength not to adore him and forget why she was thinking this through.

But, he was also a man dedicated to a mission that would constantly tear him away from her. Endanger his life. Endanger hers. They would be dedicated to a tribe and a commander who had authority over them. She supposed it would be no different than if he were in the military. Plenty of women endured it. Could she?

His face began to show the strain of her hesitation to answer.

"Yes," she admitted. "I want you."

His shoulders visibly relaxed.

"But," she added as he took a final step closer, "I also want someone who trusts me. No matter what. Only a spell—a very powerful spell I understand, one that included my hair and blood—could have taken my connection from you like that. Both of Eddie's spells blocked our blood bond. That was a truly frightening experience, Bastian."

"As it was for me. I think it is only fair that you know you will always be a target if we are together." The agony on his face filled her with dread.

"Same to you, Bastian."

His brows raised in surprise.

"Think about it," she said. "I'm the face of doom for the Hawthorne family, which I understand includes lots of extended family not bound to any Olympian tribe. Horace Hawthorne still wants me dead. Is my heart any safer than yours?"

She could tell by the parting of his lips that he had not considered himself in danger because of her.

While he digested that fact, fingernails of fear clawed at her heart. Did she want this life? Threats against her family's life? Or Bastian's life? What would happen if she chose to have her mind erased? Would Marius honor such a request? Two and a half days was a long time, an eternity, to have no contact with Bastian. She could not imagine forever.

The wall that she had erected in her mind to block him out had softened, and she could tell he was becoming aware of her deliberations. Their future fighting demons for a living did not make for a calm, peaceful existence. Plus, the prophecy could not be undone. By now, all the families connected to the Hawthorne's, and all the Olympian families in the eastern U.S., probably knew of it. Was it over, or just beginning?

"I lost one mate," Bastian said, his face heavy with trepidation. "And… I lost my soul. Now, I finally have another. One who is perfect… and at every turn she is taken away from me. My soul is ripped out over and over again. Please Aislinn, let me keep you safe. Let me keep you near Marius and Gabriella's compound in Greece."

*Uh oh*, Aislinn thought, *the question of whose tribe is rearing its head.*

"I am so not ready to talk about tribes," she responded, shaking her head. "Yet. But there is something I do want to say." She stretched to her full height, thinking of her conversation with LaVanna, which now strengthened her resolve. "Know this, Mr. Olympian. If you ever leave me like that again, don't come back. Blood bond or no blood bond, I don't want a coward for a mate."

She saw his intake of breath, the tightening of his impressive arm muscles.

"No man has ever accused me of that, and lived," he said with a deadly calm voice.

"Well, I'm a woman, and I'm still standing." She pointed a finger at his face. "You hauled ass off that tower. Yes I know what you were feeling," she said to halt his mouth opening to explain. "And I get the whole fear of loss thing. The anger out of control. Even the fear of God punishing you. But you couldn't deal with me being under a spell so you waited until someone else took care of it. And don't tell me you didn't know when the priest exorcised that out of me because I felt your connection. You knew. And still you didn't come back.

"Not to mention that you were just plain pissed because they wouldn't let you kill Eddie. If you ever do anything so cowardly again, I will bombard your sorry ass with so much psychic energy, adding light and sound waves and whatever else I can call up—maybe I'll even play some rock and roll and project it straight into your brain—you will come crawling back to me on your hands and knees begging for relief. And then, so help me, I will kick your sorry ass out, all the way to China."

His pale face seemed frozen. He blinked twice. Then a slow smile began to widen across his cheeks.

"And you can wipe that smile off your face 'cause I'm fixin' to kick you out of this roo—"

Too late, he grabbed her in a blur and was swinging her in circles.

"Bastian, stop, you're making me sick!"

He kept kissing her face so that she finally gave in and giggled. "Okay, okay, just stop with the spinning!"

"My lady, I am so thrilled to have you in my arms again. I cannot find the words." He continued kissing her cheeks.

When he trailed kisses along her ear, continuing down until he was kissing her neck, she decided he didn't need words.

Sucking with his lips along a vein in her neck, he growled low and wicked, which sent shivers of excitement through her body. Anticipation of the glorious sensations he could elicit made her giddy.

As always with him, her body ached for every inch of his luscious strength. Before she could register where his hands were going, they had slid under her shirt, explored her soft waist, then moved up her ribs.

Helmer's leering smile in the clown mask flashed before her.

She gasped and slapped her hands onto Bastian's to stop them.

"What is it?" he asked. "What is wrong?"

"I... um... I just...."

He had already read the memory in her mind. "Oh no, what has he done to you?"

"I'm sorry, Bastian."

He removed his hand to brush back her hair and cup her face. "No, my love. Don't ever apologize for what someone else did to you."

She lowered her eyes. "I think it's going to take a while to get over that... being in that room. And... and...."

"Oh, if they would only let me hunt him down."

She felt the blast of rage billow out from Bastian's body like erupting volcanic steam. She could not blame him for the growing desire to hunt Helmer down and dismember him, which was what his mind was visualizing. For some reason, it was a balm to her soul.

"Aislinn," his voice was an urgent plea, "we cannot let what this disgusting man did come between us. Tell me what I can do."

"I don't know, Bastian. Maybe we just need to go slow." To her surprise, she saw the face of a man whose skin was the color of darkest chocolate flash across his mind.

"I have an idea," he said, responding to the memory. "Another warrior once told me of this."

"What do you mean? Who is he?"

"A warrior long ago told me what he had to do to help his mate overcome, well, abuse that she had suffered at the hands of another man."

"Really?" Her heart fluttered with hope.

"Come." With his arms still encircling her, Bastian lifted her and laid them both onto the bed, positioning their heads onto her pillow. Gently, he brushed back hair from her face.

"You put my hands where you want them," he suggested. "Tell me what you want, or just move my hands. And if you wish me to stop, I will honor your choice. Everything must be your choice from now until the fear is gone, and it has no power over you."

Aislinn's soul swelled with relief, though she felt a touch shaky at the prospect. Doing anything that might trigger memories from Helmer's machinations filled her with revulsion. But Bastian was offering a level of patience and understanding that she did not expect. Patience was not normally one of his virtues. This warrior from his past must have made quite an impression.

Bastian touched her cheek with his fingertips. Then his brows knitted with worry. "I hope he did not kiss you."

"No, he didn't."

"Then may I?"

"Yes." She smiled.

His lips covered hers in a gentle kiss. The simple, loving pressure ignited her body with tiny flashes all the way to her toes.

"My lady," he whispered in a husky voice, "can I kiss your neck?"

"Yes," she said through a smile.

His face nuzzled into the crook of her head and shoulder. Wet, succulent kisses pressed into her neck.

He stopped.

"What is it?" she asked.

"Edward's mark. I had forgotten that."

"I guess I'm not the only one that was abused." It had not occurred to her before that by abusing her, Eddie and Helmer had also abused him. In a way, her pain was his pain, just experienced differently. "How about you cover that mark with yours."

"Gladly. Now?"

"Um, in a minute. When I'm ready."

"That would be acceptable," he said. And she knew by the anticipation on his face that it was.

He watched her eyes intently as he rubbed a hand lovingly over her back. "Where would you like my hands to go, my love?"

*Anywhere. Everywhere.* She knew better than to suggest it out loud, but his hopeful expression showed he had read the unspoken desire anyway, and was relieved.

She reached for his broad hand and placed it on her stomach. To her shock, a blip of Helmer's face and hands materialized. She squeezed Bastian's hand and waited for the image to disappear. Memorizing Bastian's face and the patient, gentle love that shined from his eyes was what she needed.

She slid Bastian's palm over her hip and around to the smooth curve of her thigh. For a second, the clown mask appeared, with Helmer rubbing fingers up and down her thigh and partly under her red panties. She was surprised at the sudden look of restrained anger in Bastian's silver-gray gaze. She had not thought to block her mind from him, so he was seeing the flashes of what she experienced.

"Maybe I shouldn't let you see," she suggested.

"No, we do this together," he said. "I want to kill him, but I will try not to think about it."

She exhaled a soft chuckle. "That works for me. I hope… what if this takes a while?"

"However long it takes, my lady. Our time together is our time, not his. We will make so many good memories there will be no room for his."

"Now that's a plan, Mr. Olympian."

She could tell by the tiny movements in his fingers that his hands were itching to go farther than her thigh. She took a deep breath, grasped both of his hands, and slid them upward, over her stomach, under her camisole, and over her breasts.

His fingers straightened and rubbed across her hardened nipples, over and over, with precise pressure causing her to hum with delight. All the while, his tongue lapped her neck as he issued deep, throaty murmurs.

Then he whispered. "Does your heart yearn for me, my love?"

"Yes."

"Do you want me?"

"Yes."

"Do you need me?"

"Oh, yes." Aislinn could hardly speak. Thoughts of Helmer evaporated.

Bastian's caressing of her breasts was exquisite. A heady, sparkling sensation was racing through her head, making their aura of passion the only thing in existence in their own private universe. His desire surrounded her, filled her like sizzling electricity. She felt dizzy and intoxicated. The passion of the blood heat stoked the fire coursing through her. She would say yes to anything he asked her.

"Does your blood sing for me, my love?" His breath was hot in her ear. One of his hands had reached downward, stroking her stomach as they went, and found their way underneath her silken pajama shorts and into her swollen aching flesh. In exquisite circles, he caressed her.

"Yes," she answered breathlessly, forgetting the question.

"Let this claim mark now be mine."

She turned to expose her neck and Eddie's mark, then shivered with delectable anticipation. Bastian sucked on her skin over the throbbing veins, while another part of her body throbbed under his caressing fingers.

His mouth widened, and his sharp canines pierced her tender flesh. She gasped as tingles of ecstasy rose in intensity to the point of a glorious high that made her blood pound in her ears. It took only moments of the combined assault of his lips sucking at her neck, one hand massaging her nipple and the other hand caressing her wet folds to jolt her into spasms of mind-numbing delight.

He cupped his hand between her legs, slipping two fingers inside as if to feel her feminine muscles contract around them. He licked the wound on her neck, giving her additional sensations of pleasure. Sated and limp, she turned and buried her face lovingly under his chin. "I want to feel you inside me."

He groaned.

In a flash, his pants disappeared, leaving him deliciously naked. It was the first time she had witnessed his use of telekinesis, though it was so fast she only registered the material burning along her hip and a slight *thunk* as his blue jeans hit the floor.

She reached down and slid her pajama shorts off, and dropped them to the floor. Then she pushed him onto his back, and straddled him, enjoying his firm pectoral muscles under her hands.

Wide-eyed with delight, he grabbed her hips. A happy smile expanded across his face.

She rocked her wetness over him. He hummed low from the torment and closed his eyes.

Deciding to turn the tables, she leaned forward and whispered.

"Does your heart yearn for me, my love?"

"Oh yes, my lady." His voice rumbled deep and sensual.

"Do you want me?"

"Yes."

"Do you need me?"

"Always."

Something occurred to her. "Do you give yourself to me, Olympian?"

His broad hands encircled her waist, his thumbs rubbing her soft flesh. "Do you know what you are asking, woman?"

She smiled coyly, her voice teasing and throaty. "What am I asking you?"

"You are asking me to bind myself to you." He was poised, coiled as if to spring.

"Am I?" she teased.

"Do not ask lightly," he warned. The hopeful, almost frightened look in his pale eyes excited her.

She removed her camisole.

His mouth lunged for her breasts.

She threaded her fingers into his hair and inhaled the male scent of him, woodsy and wild.

As she opened her mouth to exclaim at the pleasures he elicited, pinpricks of pain shot through her gums. Rubbing her tongue along her teeth she realized there were sharp points on her canines that were never there before. She wondered if she could extend them as he did, if she could sink her teeth into him. The thought was liberating.

She forced his head to one side, reluctantly removing his talented mouth from her nipple. She leaned forward and scraped her teeth across his neck. He groaned with pleasure.

Still riding him, she pressed his body down into the pillows. Like a cat, she stretched out, rubbing her breasts across his chest, eliciting additional moans from him. She opened her mouth and aimed for his neck. He tilted his head to allow her access.

She closed her mouth over the curve of his skin and felt his fat veins pulse under her tongue. Life raced through them, sweet and promising. Pulling her lips back, she scraped over his skin and focused on her canines, willing them to descend. A ripping, burning sensation coursed through her gums. She grimaced through the pain and began to feel tiny muscles on her upper jaw working to extend her fangs.

With a triumphant smile, she bit down into his pulsing vein.

He roared with pleasure and surprise, and embraced her in his strong arms.

Coppery, savory blood erupted into her mouth. The elixir made her feel revitalized, intoxicated. Not expecting to taste the variant flavors in his blood, she sucked at his throat with renewed appreciation.

As he moaned with euphoria, she thrilled to the realization that she was able to create this for him. She raised her hips to allow his erect tip to rise and meet her slick opening. She lowered onto him, just an inch. His raging ecstasy rushed through her in waves. Their minds merged and expanded with the piercing elation wracking his body, which flowed into hers. Grabbing her hips, he pumped her luscious warmth over his shaft. She released his neck just as his torso shuddered with an intense orgasm, the strength of it bringing her body to climax with his, their minds so completely linked, they were one.

"Aislinn," he called out her name lovingly as their bodies rested. "You are my woman now, my mate."

"No, Mr. Olympian. You are mine."

## Epilog

Horace Hawthorne scanned the horizon of his extensive property, and seethed. All his life, he had been building a legacy that outdid his father, just as his father had outdone his grandfather. He was proud of that accomplishment. He even used his childhood mansion to create a Halloween party theme park that rivaled any other. Since it was indeed haunted by his grandfather, and not a place he wished to live, it made for a perfect setting. And it raked in millions.

Men were willing to pay exorbitant amounts for a pretty woman who would do anything they desired. Or a boy. Many of the young women and boys his nephew had taken off the street were already junkies, and many were prostitutes, or runaways. It wasn't like he had done anything *really* bad. The young men and women wanted drugs, food, and a roof over their head. He gave them what they wanted. In exchange, he got something in return. The business was, well, *business*.

The clever contracts signed by the buyers were written as service agreements, guaranteeing the "models" to be well paid. No records of cash exchanges were ever recorded. The models had all signed as well, *with* persuasion. Horace had learned to cover his tracks a long time ago.

Helmer's growing powers of persuasion made their "models" the best assets in the business. They showed a level of desire to please that was beyond belief, no matter what was asked of them. He was past the days when he had to look for buyers. They came to him. And they helped make his empire vast.

All of it was in jeopardy now.

He should have known. He should have acted. Like Olivia, his estranged wife, Edward had been a softie. The boy even had her green-gold eyes. They could not stomach the really tough decisions. Now, The Appalachian was in possession of Edward, and had the nerve to request Horace's presence at a hidden trial.

Helmer, Jerod, and Raven were all in hiding. Logan had disappeared. More than likely, the Olympians had killed the lusty vampire when he ran out into the woods. Which was a pity. The women were enthralled by his act at the parties when he bit them. It had been good for business.

Damian, whom he had trained well to keep his hands clean, was not in jeopardy. He had complied when the police and Olympians returned to the H3, and exclaimed that the safety and welfare of his employees was of utmost importance. None of the girls whom Helmer had programmed using persuasion remembered any involvement from Damian.

Still, Olympians were crawling over everything he had built like ants on a sugar mound. If they ultimately forced their combined persuasion on

Damian, he might reveal complicity, and that would put him in jeopardy as well.

All because of that stupid girl.

He should never have believed Edward killed her. True, she should have died in the car accident a year ago, which he and Edward had carefully arranged. But Edward's attempts to finish the job were shoddy at best.

Horace had called on demons he had not summoned in a long time. Even those demons had failed to kill the girl.

Demons had their limitations. If he called on more powerful ones, the kind that walked the Earth and commanded legions, they would be hard to control. Not that he wasn't still considering that option. But it was time to call on power that could get results.

There were plenty of Olympians who did not heed the uber-righteous patsies who devoted their lives to fighting demons and getting in the way of hard-working, sensible, albeit crafty, businessmen like him.

And like him, there were those who made deals with devils, and learned how to wield those deals in order to control their world.

He recognized Robert's familiar knock on his study door before it opened.

"Mr. Hawthorne, I have a Mr. Braxton here to see you."

"Send him in, Robert."

A tall man with shining black hair, captivating dark, ocean-blue eyes and a chiseled face a model agency would kill for, sauntered into the room. Dressed in an impeccable, expensive suit, his presence seemed to ooze sensuality and charm. His slight side smile flashed confidence in a wicked way as he approached Horace.

"Mr. Hawthorne," he said simply, extending his hand.

"Please, call me Horace." Horace steeled his expression so that no hesitation leaked when he shook the tall man's hand. He pulled his hand away from the firm grip and flexed it, disturbed by the residual tingles of power. Rumors claimed that Orion Braxton's magnetism tended to leave one nearly in love with the man, eager to meet his every demand. Horace needed to be alert and in charge.

And while Horace himself needed to stay sharp, Orion Braxton's distracting attributes were exactly what Horace needed to get the job done.

"Please, have a seat," Horace offered. "I have a deal to offer you."

Dear Reader,

*Olympian Blood* is the first novel in the series, *The Olympians*, which is a collection of paranormal romances linking unique characters and their challenges, triumphs and extraordinary relationships.

Your purchase of this book allows me to continue to write stories I love. And for that wonderful gift, I thank you. If you have enjoyed this novel, please take a moment to leave a review so more people can find and enjoy my books.

Warmest regards,

Crystal Reneau
www.authorcrystalreneau.com